SILVERSWORD

ALSO BY *CHARLES KNIEF*

Emerald Flash

Sand Dollars

Diamond Head

SILVERSWORD

CHARLES KNIEF

THOMAS DUNNE BOOKS/ST. MARTIN'S MINOTAUR
NEW YORK

Thomas Dunne Books.
An imprint of St. Martin's Press.

www.minotaurbooks.com

Library of Congress Cataloging-in-Publication Data

Knief, Charles.
    Silversword / Charles Knief.—1st ed.
        p. cm.
    ISBN 0-312-27302-9
    1. Caine, John (Fictitious character)—Fiction.
2. Antiquities—Collection and preservation—Fiction.
3. Private investigators—Hawaii—Fiction. 4. Teacher-student
relationships—Fiction. 5. Women archaeologists—Fiction.
6. Hawaii—Fiction. I. Title.

PS3561.N426 S5 2001
813'.54—dc21

                                        2001019175

First Edition: June 2001

10 9 8 7 6 5 4 3 2 1

As always, for Ildiko

ACKNOWLEDGMENTS

In the words of my great and good friend Alan Patricio, this book was a bear to birth. That it took twice as long to produce as any of the three previous John Caine novels is testimony to its level of difficulty. And once again, it was more than merely a matter of sitting alone in my writer's corner and slugging it out with my Compaq. While the task of the novelist always comes down to the mano a mano contest with the blank page, so much more is needed prior to that event to make whatever happens possible. *Silversword* is no exception.

For personal and medical reasons, and for pointing out when I have nearly made irredeemable errors in matters of sailing, I am obligated and delighted to thank J. E. Hartley Turpin, M.D., of Newport Beach, California. A true friend, a real family doctor, and one hell of a sailor, Hartley was also a valuable resource for the medical references in this story. Thank you, Hartley.

In matters of the Glock, Robert Gorgone, who carries one for the Portland Police Department, was without parallel in providing me with accurate information, and for correcting where I went wrong in *Emerald Flash*. Your timing helped us change the paperback. Thanks, Bob. I have always been a fair pistolero myself, but you're the pro.

For suggesting the Lua, and being the best bodyworker and Lomi Lomi teacher in the State of Hawaii, Penny Prior of Kauai will always have my undying gratitude and affection. Who else would I go searching for after a hurricane?

This book could not have been written without Robert Decker, formerly Scientist in Charge of the Hawaiian Volcano Observatory, for his guidance in all things volcanic, especially the Hawaiian kind.

As a founding member of the Ruthsters, which means I am an extremely fortunate writer, I owe my editor, Ruth Cavin, a great debt of gratitude. This is not supposed to be so much fun, is it? Since this is our fourth book together, having fun seems to be the St. Martin's Press standard operating procedure. With you, Ruth, it never seems like work.

Of course there's my wife, Ildiko, who has made my life so gratifying and abundant. It's as good as it gets when the love of your life is also your best friend. Every day is a new adventure. Every day is amazing. She has gentled and civilized me. I would not be the man I am without her.

Finally, as both an acknowledgment and a dedication, many veterans owe a debt to the men and women of the National Center for Post-Traumatic Stress Disorder, based at veterans hospitals around the country. As a fictional John Caine begins to rebuild his life using their good facilities, the NCPTSD helps real veterans of Vietnam and other armed conflicts of the last century. A statement of gratitude is in order for their assistance in helping veterans see that their nightmares, both sleeping and waking, are commonplace among those who have touched the tiger.

And there are no words sufficient for those whose lives were touched in the service of their nation. In no small sense, this novel is dedicated to all members, past and present, of all the armed services of the United States of America for your dedication, for your abilities, and for your steadfast faithfulness in time of need. The soldier, sailor, marine and airman of the United States military wears the only uniform in the history of the world that oppressed people are relieved to see coming. I am truly grateful that you have been there, and sleep well at night knowing you are there now. If prayers could be answered, I would pray that your might may never again be needed, that you would not experience the hell that is warfare, that your presence alone would impose a peace upon the world. As a realist, however, I know well that you will be needed because, in the inerrant words of Robert K. Brown, "the world never runs out of assholes."

As usual, Shakespeare says it best: "In faint slumbers I by thee have watch'd, and heard thee murmur tales of iron wars . . .

I ka 'olelo no ke ola a me ka make.
In the language is life and death.

—AN ANCIENT HAWAIIAN PROVERB

Chawlie picked his way through the sparse crowd, carefully treading a narrow path between the limousine and the place reserved for him at the corner of Green and Columbus. Daniel's men had cleared the space and no one on the street seemed to object. If they did, they didn't express it. One look at the serious young men tended to dissuade all but the most foolhardy. Their presence proclaimed power. Here was importance, it said. Here was hurt. If you didn't like it, the best thing to do was to hunch your shoulders and hit the cinders. Do not trespass. This part of the street belonged to someone with juice.

Despite a distant sun shining off the brass instruments of the band in the street, and notwithstanding that the month was May, I still shivered beneath my raw silk sports coat. A chill breeze blew in off the Pacific, reminding me of what Mark Twain had once remarked about the place, that the coldest winter he had ever spent had been a summer in San Francisco.

It sure wasn't Honolulu. In a way I was glad to be off the island for a few days. The Islands were changing again. A new type of violence had visited and I hoped it would not stay. Bomb threats had repeatedly closed Hanauma Bay, even before the summer season began. The main gate at Pearl Harbor had been the target of a drive-by shooting. A group of radicals had posted leaflets around Waikiki warning visitors that they had entered a tourist-free zone and could be killed with impunity according to the rules of warfare. Some group wanted the tourists and the military to leave and they weren't subtle about their wants and wishes. Honolulu is a small city, and it was becoming a war zone, if the zealots could be believed. California seemed somehow peaceful by comparison.

The sky was a pale robin's egg blue. The only trace of the famous fog was the curling gray blanket wrapped around distant peaks, poised like some invader ready to ride down into the lowlands to conquer us all.

Spicy fragrances of Chinatown surrounded us. Whenever the breeze shifted, a new spectrum of aromas drifted our way. My stomach rumbled. The morning had been too busy to include breakfast. Only the coffee perked in the hotel room during my hasty shower and a granola bar from the honor bar had sufficed.

Once this was over Chawlie would treat us to lunch. I hoped for Szechwan. He would probably insist on Italian.

The band, dressed in white-feathered shakos and red Eisenhower jackets with bright brass buttons, milled around the middle of Green Street while they fine-tuned their instruments and smoked one last cigarette before the procession. A few of the older band members glanced over their shoulders at the black Cadillac convertible and the hearse beyond. This group had been leading funerals in Chinatown for years. They knew their clientele. They'd seen their share of going away parties. But I'd bet large that they had never seen anything like this one. They had to be acutely aware of the violent potential that floated around them like autumn leaves.

I followed Chawlie closely through the crowd, lagging less than a step behind. If it disturbed his regular bodyguards that his haole friend had the primary responsibility for keeping the old man alive, they didn't show it. Maybe they thought I was doing penance. Certainly they knew of the stolen Colombian emeralds purloined by Chawlie's mistress, and my failed efforts on his behalf. They may have thought my presence here a punishment, a requirement of my continued friendship.

If they thought that they didn't know Chawlie and they didn't know me. I was here as a favor for an old friend. Nothing could wedge me from my island sanctuary unless I wanted to go.

I was here only because of my love for the old man.

Daniel and his men were certainly aware that I occupied the most dangerous position. If trouble happened, I would be glued to the target. It was my responsibility to protect Chawlie, regardless of the consequences, unmindful of the means or the methods.

As I said, they might have thought I was doing penance.

They might have known or guessed many things about the arrangement, but that one fact may have allowed them to actually enjoy their position of distance from the old man. We had invaded the realm of another Triad. That Chawlie had come on a peacekeeping mission, paying his respects to the family of a deceased rival, didn't matter. The Triad boss had reportedly died from a massive myocardial infarction in his office, alive one moment, dead the next, gone so quickly he collapsed without a sound. They said it was as if someone had turned off a switch.

Empty space now filled the top of the San Francisco Triads. Nature abhors a vacuum, and the young men had already proclaimed their intent to take out the remaining old ones who kept them from rising in the clan.

Chawlie had come to align himself with the sanctioned successor, another old, warm personal enemy. A lover of calm continuity, Chawlie thought a tong war bad for business. A simultaneous show of force and solidarity might cause those with ambitions to have second thoughts.

So it was that I kept my eyes on the crowd and my body close to Chawlie. The band began taking their places, tossing half-smoked butts, adjusting their hat straps, tugging on their jackets. The tuba player tried to retie his shoelace. I watched him briefly struggle with his instrument before giving it up as a bad idea.

Six stout young men carried the casket from the funeral home and solemnly placed it into the back of the silver hearse. They pushed it home and fanned out around the convertible, an honor guard or a bodyguard, their postures ramrod straight, their eyes on the crowd.

I scanned the rooftops, any of the high perches a gunman might favor. Nothing seemed out of place, but I could not see behind parapets and hoped either the local Triad or the cops would have the roofs covered. The sun was behind the buildings across the street. Anyone up there would have the advantage. I watched the crowd, attentive to a potential threat. I eyed the band, reminding myself that it was a funeral, and that the sole reason for Chawlie's attendance was to preserve the peace.

Yeah. Right.

I also remembered that Chawlie and I had bribed the funeral director the night before. All the man had to do was look the other way while we examined the deceased. A simple enough task, and one for which he had been well paid. Chawlie wanted to open the casket while nobody else was present. He wanted to make sure that his old rival was really dead. He wanted to stick pins in the forehead to see if the corpse flinched.

It didn't move.

I caught him sticking pins in the waxy flesh even after he was certain, a small, satisfied smile dancing on his lips.

I hustled him from the funeral parlor before rumors could start about my old friend.

A slim young woman with long, silky black hair stood up in the convertible and released a cloud of golden confetti. The bright paper squares scattered down the street, suddenly propelled by a brisk sea breeze. Some found refuge in the band, plastering their flimsy mass against white shako hats and black polyester-clad legs. It was the signal to begin the funeral march.

The bandleader nodded and they began to play a dirge, marching slowly in place.

A policeman blew his whistle and stopped traffic on Columbus. He raised his arm and signaled the band with a come-along motion. The funeral director closed the back of the hearse and hurried to the driver's side, glanced at the roof of his building, and got in. He seemed to be a worried man. From a hundred feet away

I could sense his tension and wondered if he had cause. If the man would take bribes from Chawlie, he would take payment from Chawlie's enemies. No poker player, the funeral director knew a disturbing secret and was having a difficult time hiding his knowledge of it.

I moved a step closer to Chawlie.

The day had a bad feeling about it. People who should have moved quickly slowed down. Those who should have moved carefully stumbled. It was as if we collectively acknowledged that something evil was about to happen and there was nothing any of us could do but consign ourselves to the inevitable.

The band marched to the corner, closely followed by the convertible.

Across the street a teenage boy in a black suit lighted a string of firecrackers and tossed them among the band members' feet. The tuba player hit a sour note as he leaped out of the way. He jumped sideways and crashed into the trombonist. They stopped directly in front of us, and the rows of musicians behind them stopped, too. It took them several seconds to get organized again, and by then the shooting had started.

Glass shattered in the coffee shop behind us.

I threw myself on Chawlie, pulling him down behind a young street sapling. The crowd shrank away, leaving Chawlie and me in the open, the slender trunk our only cover. My .45 was in my hand before I thought of taking it from its holster, and I scanned the street. The band scattered in all directions, the tuba player tripping over his shoelace, going down in a moment of bright brass and noise.

Another shot ricocheted off the concrete, striking a fleeing woman with a meaty slap. She fell beside us and lay still.

A third shot hit Daniel in the neck and he went down.

I could not find a target. I had Chawlie covered. Not very well, and only by my body, but covered. I searched for a way to hit back. The bullets struck only in our immediate vicinity. That told me that the gunman probably used a handgun, not a rifle, and that he was somewhere on one of the roofs across the street, the best location to bring fire down upon us. That also told me that Chawlie was the target. I needed to get him under better cover.

Bright cold sunlight covered the shooter, giving him all the advantage. From our position we had to look directly into the sun.

A silhouette of the gunman popped up and fired down at us, a specter only visible in the peripheral. His aim was high and the plate glass window behind us caved in completely. I fired back, a burst of three quick rounds, sending bits of shingles flying into the air next to his shoulder. He dropped back down, out of sight behind the structure.

Glancing back, I saw an opportunity.

I fired at the roofline below the spot where he had vanished, the big 230-grain bullets punching through the light structure. As I fired, I dragged Chawlie toward the coffee shop. A low wall, about two feet high and finished in rock-hard terrazzo, stood below the shattered opening. It might not protect us from high-velocity rifle rounds, but the polished stone surface should provide refuge from slugs fired from a handgun.

I saw movement again on that same roof, but held my fire. Daniel's men had finally pulled themselves together and were peppering the roof with their pistols. The security team by the hearse had disappeared, along with the passengers in the convertible.

"Are you hit?" I whispered to Chawlie, who lay silent and unmoving beneath me.

He mumbled. "Ask me if I am hurt."

"What?"

"Ask me if I am hurt."

"Are you hurt?"

"With big haole on top of me, shoved into broken glass on hard floor, you ask if I am hurt?"

"You're not hurt. Want to get up?"

Another bullet slammed into the sidewalk in front of us, ricocheted against the wall and screamed away into the distance.

"Chawlie stay here."

Sirens were approaching. I put my gun away, rolled off the

old man and pushed him as close to the low wall as I could. "Don't move."

He nodded.

With Chawlie under cover and the threat neutralized by Daniel's men, I leaped over the wall, keeping low. The woman was dead, sightless almond eyes staring into the beyond. An empty cloth shopping bag lay by her body. The bag was embroidered with a red dragon, the Chinese symbol for good luck. An innocent, she had been in the wrong place at the wrong time, and had paid the maximum price. Her luck had run out.

Leaving her, I crawled over to my young friend, his body sprawled in a growing pool of blood. Dark fluid welled from the vein in his neck. That was the good news. Had the bullet hit an artery he would have already been dead. The bad news was that the wound was through and through, the vein nearly severed. He was losing a lot of blood.

Grabbing Daniel's collar, I dragged him through the broken glass into the relative safety of the coffee shop. Bullets pocked the stainless steel cook line behind the counter. Blood flowed freely from his neck, leaving a long stain on the sidewalk. I reached into the open wound and pinched the vein together with my fingers, trying to keep the ends closed, trying to keep them from losing too much of his vital fluids.

"Daniel!" Chawlie had started to rise when he saw Daniel's wound.

"Stay down!"

"My son!"

"Call nine-one-one for an ambulance! Tell them where we are. Tell them we've got a man with a gun firing at a crowd from a rooftop. Several people hit. At least one dead. Tell them we've got one man with a severe neck injury. I'm holding him together, but we need help now!"

Chawlie opened his cell phone and stared hard at Daniel and me, then handed the phone to another young man who had materialized out of the chaos on the street. The kid punched in three numbers and spoke rapidly.

More shots came from another roof across the street, this time from a different angle. Most of them penetrated the wooden counter and plowed through the padded counter stools.

One hit me low in the back.

The shock of the bullet knocked the legs out from under me. The pain was instant and exquisite, an all-consuming, almost alive entity of white-hot energy that tore through my body and nearly took control of my existence. I fought the pain and the shock and the terror, focusing my total concentration on keeping my fingers in Daniel's wound, trying to prevent his bleeding to death. My fingers desperately wanted to desert their post and fly to my own wound. I forced them to remain where they were, my will stretching itself to its limits.

I focused on the hole in Daniel's neck, concentrating on holding those warm, rubbery, slippery tissues together. Nothing else mattered. Nothing else existed.

Except the pain.

The pain resided as an overwhelming element, a sharp violation. I refused to allow my thoughts to go to the place where they always went when I'd been shot before—"Oh my God, I've been holed!"—and to keep at bay the terror of what permanent damage might have been done.

Even as the final shots spattered against the pavement, I held on. Even as the sirens wound down in the street in front of the coffee shop, I held on. Even as one of Chawlie's men helped him to his feet, pausing to remove the .45 from my belt before disappearing into the crowd. Even as the paramedics found us stretched side by side on the tile floor like suicidal lovers, bathed in each other's blood, I held on, willing Daniel to live. They were bright boys and girls. They saw my fingers deep inside his neck, nodded to each other, and decided to leave well enough alone until we reached the hospital. We rode in the ambulance on the same stretcher.

Only until the Code Three toboggan ride ended at the hospital and we were rolled into the emergency room, and competent medical fingers took over for my own clumsy digits, did I release my charge of the young man's life and let go.

They wheeled Daniel from the emergency room on their way to surgery, a desperate carnival of noise and efficiency, leaving me alone in the corridor.

I rolled off the gurney, stretched briefly, felt dizzy for a moment, and then allowed the crushing pain to come. I bent over, steadied myself for an instant, one bloody hand on the stainless steel railing, and then watched with a kind of strange detachment as the blood-stained vinyl floor lazily rose up and hit me in the face.

The next time I opened my eyes I was alone, filled with pain and confusion. The world seemed dark outside my window, but I could only see a part of the sill and couldn't be sure. Only the light from the corridor spilled onto the tile near the door of my room, all I could see under the curtain that surrounded my bed.

A shadow shifted on the floor, an almost imperceptible motion. Someone occupied a chair outside my door.

I didn't know where I was, but I'd been here before. It wasn't déjà vu. It was mere experience. Another hospital, another injury, another long stretch of recovery and recuperation lay ahead.

But I was still alive, still breathing, still on the right side of the lawn. I wiggled my toes. Yeah, I could do that.

"Hello?" The word came out as a growling whisper. My throat was dry, my tongue stuck to the roof of my mouth, adhered by disuse.

The shadow elongated. A shape appeared, a smudge in the light, visible through the curtain.

"Yes, Mr. Caine?" My keeper was a young Asian male of medium height and muscular build. He seemed agile, a karate-ka, who looked as if he viewed his body as a temple and his abilities as a serious responsibility. He looked solid and dependable. His eyes were alert and intelligent. This was no mere meaty guard, sent to fill a place. His presence was not pro forma. I wondered from what dojo he had sprung, and why he felt it necessary to hang around outside my hospital room.

"Who're you?"

"Your bodyguard. Chawlie sent me. I am Felix."

"My bodyguard. Felix." I had never seen Felix before. "Are you happy, Felix?"

A look of confusion came over his face, replaced by a look of iron determination before he answered. "I'm gay, if that's what you mean."

"Your name. In Latin it means 'happy.' "

"Yeah," he said, collecting himself, visibly deciding that he had no reason to be defensive. "I knew that."

"Are you from San Francisco?"

"Yes."

"Are you still in San Francisco?"

"Yes. What do you need?"

"Water, please."

He filled a plastic cup and helped me drink, holding the back of my head. He was gentle, one of those natural caregivers. I wondered how effective he was at bodyguarding. Then I looked at his hands.

"Wing Chun?"

"Yes. And others."

"Firearms?"

"All kinds."

"You carrying now?"

"Of course."

I nodded, instantly regretting it.

"You need more painkillers? I'll ring the nurse. You have your own nurse. Several of them. You are their only patient."

"Please," I said, but he had already pushed the button.

"Whatever you need, Felix will provide."

"That's comforting," I said, as the nurse came into the room. A tiny Thai woman, she edged past Felix and looked as if she wanted to say something but thought better of it. She wasn't frightened. It was something else. Almost an awe of my companion.

"He is in pain," said my bodyguard.

She looked at me, as if requesting confirmation.

"I am in pain," I said, feeling helpless and overwhelmed by the almost total debility, so overwhelmed that I could not even hate the helplessness. Not yet. That, I knew, would come later.

She checked the chart, nodded, and left the room. When she returned she held a syringe filled with clear liquid. She injected the needle into the tube that fed my arm.

Darkness, blessed darkness, came again.

I spent more than a week in that hospital bed, Felix remaining outside my door like a faithful dog. Unlike a dog, however, I could not get him to remain in the room. He was polite but reserved. It was, I assumed, his way of keeping his distance. "I'll protect you," he seemed to be saying, "but only so far." A true professional, he would defend, but not to the death. Overwhelmed, he would cut his losses. I understood. My injuries were nothing if not an object lesson in going too far.

But Chawlie was a friend. So was Daniel. And I hadn't thought about the mortal consequences at the time. My actions had come from somewhere beyond thought, logic, or reason.

The way things worked out, Daniel's wounds were less serious than mine and he recovered before I did. He came to see me before he flew home, shuffling into my room, his neck covered with thick bandages, flanked by three mountainous young men, his human shields.

"I heard what you did. Thank you, Caine. You take care." His voice rasped. The bullet had damaged his vocal chords. The injury had not muted him, but scar tissue had given him an ominous whisper. He sounded dangerous. Almost as dangerous as he really was.

"You, too," I said.

"How you like Felix?"

"Not a bad guy."

"Mahu," he whispered, or tried to whisper, smiling a tight smile. "He likes boys."

"Good for him," I said, wondering why Daniel cared.

"He's the best in San Francisco. Maybe best in California. Little guy like that. Everybody scared of him."

So Chawlie had found the best bodyguard in the state to sit outside my door. Not only a bodyguard, but a fearsome warrior. And gay, as well. And Daniel had been uncomfortable to the point where he felt he had to explain it to me.

"So was Alexander the Great. Mahu," I said. "And he conquered the world."

"What?"

"Makes no difference."

Daniel shrugged. "It don't seem right," he said, offering his hand.

I took it.

"See you at home."

"Rest your voice."

"Rest yourself. Chawlie said he'd fly you home when you're ready."

"I'm ready."

"When they say you're ready. See you around, Caine."

I lay back and stared at the ceiling after he left, exhausted by the conversation. I craved agility. There was nothing I wanted more than the ability to leap from this bed and run out that door. But that wasn't possible. I barely had the energy to count the pinholes in the ceiling tile. It would be some weeks before I could do much more than totter around like an ancient on his last legs. I had no idea what they had done to me here, what permanent destruction the bullet's path had accomplished. I only knew that my lower body felt as if it had been plowed and planted with pain, and that they were having a bumper crop this year.

"Excuse me." Felix stuck his head in my room.

"Hi."

"Do you feel like speaking with a police officer?"

"Do I have a choice?"

He shook his head. "The time and the place may be changed, but the inevitable will happen."

"Sounds like a fortune cookie."

"Not so profound," he said. "You feel all right?"

"I feel like crap. Send him in. I've been expecting him."

Felix smiled. "Or not," he said, opening the door wide to admit a handsome, brisk woman in her thirties. She wore a charcoal gray business suit and a severe expression.

"Good afternoon, Mr. Caine," she said.

"Have a seat. And you may call me John. Pardon me for not getting up."

She didn't smile as she took a chair near the bed and unfolded a notebook. I started to speak, but she shushed me and showed me a star and identification with her photograph and handed me a business card imprinted with the Great Seal of the City of San Francisco. Her title was detective inspector, and her name was Shirley Henderson.

"What can I do for the City and County of San Francisco?"

"You were shot a week ago on Green Street. You and several other people. I am one of the investigators on the case."

"I don't know what to tell you."

"Just answer a few questions. Why were you at the scene?"

"Just visiting."

She looked at me, condescension written large across her features. "Oh, come on, Mr. Caine. You can do better than that. How did you get here? You are a resident of Hawaii."

"I flew in."

"We can't find you on any passenger manifest. How did you get here? Which airline did you fly?"

"Private jet."

"Are you here on business?"

"Just to visit old friends."

She bristled, unhappy with my answers. I wasn't sure where this was leading. I decided to be careful with this woman. I wouldn't lie, but I wouldn't babble everything I knew, mindful of my responsibilities and duties to Chawlie. "And you just happened to be standing at the corner of Green and Columbus when the shooting started."

"Yes."

"The fellow who just left, Daniel Choy. Do you know him?"

"Yes."

She nodded.

"Did you get a look at the person who shot you?"

"I was too busy ducking for cover."

She looked at me, her eyes telling me she believed nothing. "That isn't what I heard," she said.

I shrugged, and made a mental note not to do that again. Shrugging hurt as much as nodding. Maybe a little more.

"I spoke with the paramedics and some of the people in the ER. They said you kept Mr. Choy from bleeding to death. That you remained with him until he had medical attention, that you did not complain of your own injuries until you knew he was safe. He is just an acquaintance?"

When I said nothing she continued. "I spoke with people at Honolulu PD. There are all kinds of stories about you, Mr. Caine. I frankly don't know what's true."

"Reputations are difficult to build," I said, "easy to tear down."

"Do you own a .45 automatic?"

"Uh-huh."

"Is that a yes?"

"Uh-huh."

"May I examine it?"

"I don't know where it is."

"I could get a court order."

"I'll tell you the same thing under those circumstances."

"What happened in Kauai last year?"

"I don't know what you're talking about."

"Why did eight people die over there? Or was it nine? All foreign nationals. There is the strong suspicion that you killed them."

"You'd have to talk to whoever has those suspicions."

"I did. The legal consensus was self-defense. That's apparently why you weren't prosecuted. But all of them?"

She waited for an answer and I waited for her to stop waiting. This would be part of her pattern, a technique, something to distract me before she got to her main point. If I waited, she would eventually get around to it.

"And then I spoke with a detective in San Diego," she said after a while. "There was an incident on the Mexican border a few years ago. A shooting. Several shootings. You apparently have a tendency to get into these situations, don't you?"

I tried to shrug without moving my shoulders. I wasn't sure she noticed.

"I'm sure that was self-defense, too."

"It would always be self-defense."

"Self-defense?" she went on. "Is that what you were doing here? Defending yourself?"

"Some lunatic was shooting people in the street from a rooftop. I was looking for cover."

"Just minding your own business?"

"Yes."

"You have some interesting friends."

I looked her in the eye.

"I do know that you were in the company of the head of the most powerful Triad in the Pacific. HPD says that you're friends with him. Longtime friends. Old friends in the Asian sense. I know that the shooting took place at the funeral of a San Francisco Triad leader. I think you were here because of that funeral, although I don't know why."

"Is it important?"

"I don't know." She regarded me. "On the other hand, I heard stories about you that made me wonder. You have defenders, too."

"That's nice. I wonder who?"

"You had an empty holster on your belt when you came into the ER. It was custom made for a large automatic. A Colt 1911A

.45 automatic, to be exact. Expended .45 shells were found at the scene. No gun was found. Can you clarify that for me?"

"No."

"You know, a funny thing happened when the lab examined the shells. They found no fingerprints. Nothing. Not even a smudge. Now that's interesting. Normally we would expect to find a thumbprint where you would have pushed the cartridge into the magazine, but on these, nothing. As if you'd wiped them clean and wore gloves when you loaded the magazine. Did you plan to do some shooting that day?"

"I think the only one who planned to do any shooting was the man on the roof. He seemed to have a plan."

"I can't get over polishing the cartridges before you loaded the pistol. That's the mark of a professional. San Francisco has enough of its own problems without importing professional gunfighters."

I didn't like the way this was going. "Are you going to charge me with a crime? I don't believe you can prove that I did anything wrong. Or is getting shot against the law in California? I haven't read the codes lately."

"You're right. I can't prove anything. But I have doubts about you."

I just looked at her. She was not the only one here with doubts.

"Your friend. Chawlie Choy. He left town that night. Went back to Honolulu in his private jet. The uniforms who first arrived at the scene didn't know who he was, but they were Mandarin speakers. They spoke to him, but he complained in an obscure Chinese dialect that he was just passing by and saw nothing and knew nothing and they let him go. Unfortunate, but understandable. Apparently he complained like an old pensioner. By the time anybody discovered who he really was, he was gone."

"He apparently felt the weather here was bad for his health."

"By the way, Mr. Choy is paying your hospital bills."

"Nice of him."

She sighed. "The body of a young Asian male turned up several days after the shootings. Bad scene. Someone hung his naked body from the side of a building in Chinatown when they were done with him. Have you ever heard of 'Death by a Thousand Cuts?' "

"Chinese method of execution. They save it for special cases. Combines torture, mutilation and execution. I saw it once in Vietnam. They can make it drag out for days. Very nasty."

She regarded me for a moment. "You *saw* it once," she said slowly, as if that alone should convict me.

"I was just passing through. It wasn't my business."

"How could you stand by and let something like that happen?"

"There was one of me and five hundred of them. Nothing I could do but hele on. Had I interfered I'd likely have ended up there with the poor bastard getting my extremities sliced off one at a time."

"So you didn't get involved."

"It was that kind of a war."

She sighed. "My father said the same thing," she said softly, as if to herself. Then she returned, her eyes focusing, seeing me, but seeing someone else at the same time, someone she hated.

"So you know about 'Death by a Thousand Cuts.' This was horrible. What a way to die."

"Those things are always horrible."

"There was a gun. A 9mm. Hanging around his neck on a string. Ballistics matched it to the slug they pulled out of your kidney."

That she knew about my injury told me that she'd spoken with my doctor, and that she had gone to the trouble of getting a court order. Or maybe doctor-patient relationships were no longer protected in California. I didn't like the fact that she was spending so much energy investigating my actions. I had done nothing except try to survive. Now she tried to link me with the dead man, the one who presumably had shot me.

"He the shooter?" I asked.

"His fingerprints were the only ones found on the gun. They left one of his fingers so we'd know for sure. Left it in a bag."

"Case closed, then."

"That proves nothing. And now we have a new homicide."

"I don't know anything about it. I'm sure Daniel doesn't either. We were both in the hospital."

She nodded. "Of course. And Chawlie Choy was back in Honolulu."

"So how can I help you?"

"You could start by telling the truth."

"What can I tell you?"

"Why you were here. I know who you were with. I know you saved the lives of two criminal slugs that could have died, for all I care—"

"Harsh . . ."

"—their deaths would have made life a little easier."

". . . judgments."

She took a little breath. "So why were you here?"

I thought it over for a ten-count, deciding in the end that Chawlie could not be injured by my telling the events as I saw them. I'd stonewalled this woman enough. It only angered her and made her more determined. She had already compared me to a distant and hated father. Any further evasions would just make her more interested in Chawlie and Daniel.

And in me.

"Attending a funeral," I said, hoping I could be detached enough to reveal sufficient details to satisfy her, and yet not expose me to charges. For an instant I thought about asking for an attorney, but the urge passed. There was no reason to suspect that Ms. Henderson was anything other than what she said, and that her visit to my bedside was anything other than filling in the blanks.

"Your top man in the Triads died. Natural causes, but sudden. My friend came here to keep the peace. You know how things tend to get messy when the leader of any organization suddenly leaves the top spot vacant. My friend wanted to avoid a war."

"Your friend? Is that Mr. Choy?"

"I was supposed to keep him alive."

She nodded to herself. "This was a power play?"

"I don't know. Somebody seemed to think that with one down, they might as well go for the gold and get rid of all of them at once. All the old men. Leave it for the young ones."

"Oh, that would be swell."

"They'll have all the avarice of the old criminals, half the wisdom, and twice as much energy. Think what that would do to your crime statistics."

"So you—"

"I know nothing. That was speculation."

"But you know enough to speculate."

"Just what I read in the newspapers."

"Thank you, Mr. Caine. You've been absolutely no help."

"Anytime."

"I may want to come back and ask you a few more questions that you won't answer. Give you another chance to be evasive." She looked me in the eye. This was supposed to intimidate me. I'm not easily intimidated. I rather enjoyed it, proof that I was not as dead as I felt.

"I've told you all that I can. I was out of the action, trying to keep Chawlie from getting shot. When he was under cover I went to the first wounded man I could find. It just happened to be Daniel."

"You had to jump over the corpse of a woman to get to him."

"She was dead. I went for the living."

"You didn't even stop to look, did you?"

"I've seen enough dead bodies to know what they look like. She died when the bullet hit her in the head. I heard her die. You wanted two dead?"

"Her name was Jackie Chang. She was a grandmother who cared for five young granddaughters. Her daughter died last year in a traffic accident. The husband is off someplace. We cannot locate him. The girls are now homeless with nobody to care for them."

"Tough break."

"Oh, yeah, I'm sure you care a lot about that sort of thing."

"I'm sorry. But I didn't shoot her. And she died instantly. I was there, right next to her. I heard the sound of the bullet when it hit her."

"You saw the gunman?"

"Only a silhouette against the sky. Nothing else. He was busy trying to put bullets into my friend. I was busy trying to get Chawlie under cover. It was just too intense to make any observations that might help you now. I'm sorry."

"I can see that you and I don't see eye to eye," she said, her voice rising. "I can see that you will not make an ideal witness in this case."

"I told you all I know."

"I think you are lying!"

Felix and one of the nurses came in, their eyes on full alert. Our voices must have carried out into the hall.

"I think that you must go now," said the nurse. "He is a patient and—"

"I know what he is!" Henderson gathered her notebook and her purse and glared at me.

"Thank you for stopping by." I held out my hand.

"Save it," she said. She took one more look around the room and made a beeline for the corridor. The little Thai nurse followed her, as if she feared she would turn back and revisit her wrath on her only patient.

Felix shook his head. "She's pissed."

"Disappointed is all. Thought she'd solved the Patty Hearst kidnapping."

"Didn't they already do that?"

"Yeah. Judge Crater did it."

Felix stood there looking down at me, his face a mixture of relief and concern. I realized that I'd used up my store of energy and was thoroughly spent.

"You don't look so good," he said.

"I don't feel so good, Felix."

"I'll get the nurse."

4

A nother one."

Felix nearly smiled as he stuck his head into my room, announcing yet another visitor. Personal or official, he didn't say, but I could almost read his expression now and knew this was not an officer of the court, come to summon or depose me. Or another member of the medical profession, come to poke me full of holes.

Over the past four days my body had started to heal. I felt it grow a little stronger. My wounds began to close, a mixed blessing. They itched in places I could not reach. But I was able to sit up without the pain and they'd disconnected the plastic feedbag from the intravenous tube to my arm and let me eat real food. Not steak. A little mush, some Jell-O. Something to chew. I'd nearly forgotten the gratification of chewing and swallowing. It was a sensuous pleasure, the only one so far allowed.

Life is good.

"Hello, John." Barbara Klein walked in, a little hesitant, a little shy. I had wondered where she had been while I had been flat on my back, wherever I was, somewhere within the boundaries of her city.

She picked up the magazine I'd been reading. "*Glamour*?"

"It's all they've got here. I've asked Felix to run over to City Lights, but he's been too busy."

She studied the cover. "*Men's One Hundred Twenty-five Secret Sex Desires?*"

"I wanted to find out what the other one hundred twenty-four were."

She smiled at me, her eyes twinkling. I'd once loved those eyes, they way they looked at me. And then they didn't look at me with affection anymore, and we both were adult enough to admit that our fling was over. Somehow the friendship hadn't died along with the affair, a fact for which I was grateful, and for which I credited her wisdom.

"Hello, Babs."

She made a face. "You know I hate that name."

"Should have complained to your parents when you had the chance."

She gave me a lopsided smile. "Inevitable?"

I nodded. Nodding was fine. I could nod now. If I was careful and didn't get carried away with it.

"How are you feeling?"

"Better. Every day is better. They tell me I can go home next week. I can hardly wait."

"I'll bet. You know . . . I was here. When they first brought you in. Those first couple of days, they said you were going to live, that you'd been injured but it wasn't life threatening. They said you'd lost a lot of blood, and that you had internal injuries, and there was a risk of infection, but that you'd be okay. But one look at you and they couldn't convince me. You looked dead already."

"Only the good die young."

"You're no longer young. Even so, you're still indestructible, I see."

"Take me a few of months to leap tall buildings again. Even then, it might take a couple of bounds."

"I'll be watching."

She nearly looked at me the way she used to look at me. I saw her start to get that warm glow before she remembered and the warmth blinked out. "I heard what happened," she said, her voice husky.

"Whose version?"

"Chawlie told me. He said that you two were even again, whatever that means."

"He thought I was in his debt. He thought I was paying penance for a continuation of our friendship by being here."

"Why were you here?"

"It was a dangerous time for him. Someone had to watch his back."

"That's the only reason?"

"You were here. I was hoping to see you after he had performed his ceremonial duties."

She smiled again. This time it was a sad smile.

"He said you did your job."

"I'm happy to hear that. I haven't heard from him at all. Except through Daniel."

"Was Daniel the one who exchanged Claire's money?"

"Yep. One of Chawlie's sons. Or nephews. Or something. He called him his son, and I think I can see the resemblance."

"You were in his debt. Does that have something to do with your trip to nowhere with the mysterious Margo? That trip that took almost a year?"

"I was never in his debt, but that's how he sees it. I either failed him or I did exactly what he wanted me to do. I'm never sure which is true. He isn't either, I think."

She gripped my hand. Hers was warm and comfortable, and made me happy when she touched me. "I'm really glad to see you."

"Me too, Barbara. You're looking well. How's the student?" Barbara's son was a student at Berkeley, studying nuclear physics. He was the one who inadvertently caused us to come together in the first place. The day I met him now seemed a lifetime ago.

"David's fine. It's finals week, and he's ready to get out of the pressure cooker and cut loose for the summer. He wants to go back to Hawaii to dive again. David says there are some underwater caves of Maui and the Big Island."

"Incredible places. David will be fine."

"I'd be happier, knowing you're over there."

"Tell him to call me. I think I'll be taking some time off for awhile."

"From what? Do you ever do *anything* except lie around and work on your boat and fish and dive, or chase dolphins in your sleep, and then come out every once in awhile and get shot? Or take some woman you hardly know for a world cruise?"

"I'll just lay around and fish, and . . . that first part of what you said."

She smiled again, gently, her face softening. "I will always love you, you know." She almost said something else. I could see her tongue working. But she held it, and settled for retaining the gentle smile.

I knew what she wanted to say. I'd heard it before. And I knew that in her world, in her heart, she was right. So I made it easy for her.

"We'll always have Honolulu, sweetheart," I said out of the side of my mouth, the way Bogie would have said it. "You wore blue, the Hawaiians wore gray . . . and brown and red and green and pink and yellow and lavender—"

"Stop!" She laughed.

"—and fuscia." I watched her eyes. She was laughing, but her eyes were crying. "I told you before, kid. If you don't get on that plane, you'll regret it. No tonight, not tomorrow, but soon, and for the rest of your life."

"Now you stop that," she said, sniffing. "You did tell me that. At the Honolulu airport. And I did get on that plane. And I thought I'd put you behind me. And then you had to come here to my city and get shot. That's not my fault."

"It was not. And I'm grateful that you came to see me."

"I was here often. You were not here. Your body was in the bed, but John Caine wasn't here. Wherever you were, it wasn't here."

"I was dreaming of the lions."

"I was here, John. If you ever need me, I'll be here. I owe you my son's life, and that's something a mother never forgets, irrespective of the cruises you take with mysterious strangers."

She regarded me once more, started to say something, and then stopped. She went through the motions three times before she finally found the words she wanted to say. "It's really a shame about you and me, but we've been down that road so many times I can't go that way again. I don't think you can either. We can be friends. Not like people say to each other when they stop being lovers, but really friends, and that is something to cherish. I'll always love you. And I think I shall stay in love with you a little. But I cannot live with you, and you cannot live with me, and so we can be adult, and we can be friends."

"Yes."

"I'll tell David to call you when he gets to Hawaii."

"I'd like that. If I'm feeling better, maybe we'll take *Olympia* over to Maui or Molokai. Float around the chain for awhile, diving and listening to Jimmy Buffett. I'll introduce him to some nice girls."

"He'd love that. I'm glad that you're looking better. I'm glad that you survived. I want to say try to stay out of these kinds of situations, but I know that won't help, because you won't do it. You'll just do what you want to do when you want to do it. You always have and you always will. It defines you. Some people do what they want to do, they're just self-involved jerks, but I can't say that about you. You go out of your way to risk your life for other people. That's what you do. You went back into that wreck to rescue David, and he would have died that day if you hadn't, so I guess I can't criticize. But I can't stand here on the sidelines and cheer you on, either. Not when I have so much invested. So I had to back off."

"I understand, Barbara."

"I know. I repeat myself."

"I think you and I both want something different from life."

"What do you want?"

"I wish I knew."

She shook her head. "You are an adult, and you don't know what you want? So you're off here or off there, and you can't stay in one place long enough to put down roots. You live on a boat in the middle of the ocean because you're afraid that you'll take root on land. No commitments. No alignments. No responsibilities. You don't even have a pet, for God's sakes. That's a sad situation. You've been an adult for years and yet you won't grow up!"

I nodded. That was as accurate a description of my character as I'd ever heard.

"And that's the reason you're there and I'm here, isn't it?"

"I think we both made that clear, Barbara."

"I love you, God damn it!"

I smiled at her and she hugged me like I was made of broken glass. Then she withdrew and walked to the door, where she stopped and turned to face me. "You are a very difficult man, John Caine. I've never met another one like you. Loving you is both a blessing and a curse."

"Thank you for loving me, Barbara," I said quietly.

"It hasn't been easy," she said. "But I think it's been worth it, all the same." She smiled that lopsided smile again. "You're the e-ticket ride of men. You know that? It's thrilling, it's fun, and I wouldn't have missed it for the world, but eventually you have to get off and go back to the real world. Does that make any sense to you?"

"Yes."

"I'm on my way to Telluride. In Colorado. Ever been there?"

"No."

"The bank lent forty million dollars on a hotel project and the developer's way behind schedule. Like a year. The loan's running out and the deal's about to fall apart. I'm flying out in the morning to stick my nose in it and to see what's what. So you'll be gone when I get back. Watch my son if you can. Please? For me?"

"I'll do my best."

"Your best is usually pretty good. Even when you're all shot up, from what I hear. Good-bye, John." She clutched her purse, started to say something else, checked the impulse, and walked out the door.

Felix looked in on me. "That's a pretty woman."

"Very pretty, very smart, very strong. *Very* smart. Too smart to get mixed up with me for very long. She called me an e-ticket ride."

Felix looked confused. "Like the airplane?"

"From Disneyland," I explained.

He shook his head.

"Never mind. It's a generational thing, I guess."

"Doctor's here. He wants to examine you."

"Well send him in, Felix. Don't keep the man waiting."

The doctor was a slim young man, young for a specialist, proud of his work and impressed with himself. He had me lie down, which I did. Gingerly. When I got comfortable, he pulled up my gown and inspected his handiwork. He listened to my heart and my lungs, smiled, and scribbled in his chart.

"You seem to be healing beautifully," he said. "The incision is closing. It looks good. Surprisingly little infection. Your renal function is returning to normal. Should be one hundred percent in a few weeks. I think we can remove your catheter by tomorrow."

"I'd like that." Peeing in a bag was not something I wanted to get used to.

"When you came in I thought you were going to lose your kidney. The bullet damaged the midsection of the organ, so I had to do a partial nephrectomy."

"Is that bad?"

"Bad enough. You were shot in the back, but I had to go in through the front. You have a hole all the way through you, you know that?"

"Back to front."

"Both ways. I put in a stent from the upper chamber of your kidney to your bladder. It will have to be removed, too, but not just yet. I placed it there to keep scar tissue from blocking the chambers. You don't want that kind of pain, my friend." He scribbled in his chart, keeping his hands busy.

"I understand you live in Hawaii. I'll refer you to a urologist there who will remove it. There's no hurry, but within the next month or two."

"A month or two."

"Leave it in for six weeks, but no longer than two months. Any longer could be dangerous."

"Good to know."

"You'll have to refrain from strenuous physical activity until it is out. Of course, nothing for the next six to eight weeks. From the look of you—considering your age—you have continued to keep your body in shape. That's good. That's good. That has helped. But you'll have to take it easy for a few months."

"Considering my age," I said, thinking that a layoff of a few months at my age would put me way over into the soft side of life. It would be hell coming back. If I could. Maybe it was time to find something else to do.

"I didn't mean it the way it sounded," he said.

"Ageism."

"Whoa! I apologize."

"I know. It was a medical term."

He looked relieved, unaware that I was having some small fun at his expense. He was intense. Perhaps too intense. And then I remembered for whom he worked. Chawlie would have made my continued existence very important in this young man's scheme of things. He's like that. Chawlie can become very insistent when he wants something. Sometimes it makes people nervous.

"So when can I go home?"

"We're going to let you rest for another day or so. If you continue to improve at the same rate we'll let you go by Friday."

"That's great. What day is today?"

He laughed. "Tuesday. Don't you read the newspapers?"

"Too depressing. Too much politics. Too much violence."

"Considering what you've just been through, Mr. Caine, the newspapers should be restful. That police inspector talked to me, too. So did the ER crew. You were covered in blood, but we didn't know it was yours. You made no complaint. Nobody thought you were hurt until you fell."

"Haven't you ever had to hold on until something got done?"

"Often," he said, nodding. "During surgery you can't afford to let down. Not even a little bit."

"It was the same."

He nodded. "One thing I haven't had a chance to talk to you about, but it's important. The woman who just left made me think about it. Your body has received a great deal of trauma. Your whole system was shocked. Then I inflicted even more trauma to your reproductive system in my business of healing you. You may have some problems with lovemaking for some time. Don't worry. It'll come back. Just don't rush it."

"You're saying I'll be impotent?"

"For a short time. You should expect it. Everything will come back. Eventually."

"Eventually," I said. "Not a problem. That woman is a friend, and she's on her way to Colorado. I'll be heading back to Hawaii in a few days. Difficult to get together that way, you know?"

"Then it should be a restful time for you." He looked at me as if he didn't believe me. "Be best, you know. You need the rest. Six weeks, minimum, Mr. Caine. No strenuous exercise. Just relax." He patted my shoulder. "I don't want you to find out the hard way how bad it can be. I'll tell your doctor to arrange for an IVP before he removes that stent."

"Ivy pee?"

"Intravenous pyleogram. It's a noninvasive radiological test to watch how your kidneys are working."

"Write that down."

"It'll be on your orders when you leave. I'll call your doctor and discuss it with him."

"Or her?"

He laughed. "Or her," he said, walking from the room, a happy man, satisfied with himself, his hands busy with his charts and his pens.

T hey were coming through the wire.

After a vicious and thorough mortar and rocket pounding, deadly steel rain joining the monsoon already pouring on our unprotected positions, the barrage abruptly stops. Over the resonance of the rain, the shrill screeching of whistles, the clinking of equipment, the sound of a mass of armed men on the move.

Moving toward us.

"They're in the wire!"

A rash of gunshots, the rippling long stream of an M-16, the heavier, throatier bark of AK-47s.

Two ghostly figures approach the tangled razor wire, sappers come to blow a hole in our defenses. I shoot them both, my carbine on semi-automatic, carefully placing rounds only where the rounds have to go, conserving my ammunition, knowing there are more of them out there. Many more.

Too damn many.

Five or six more sappers follow, slithering up the muddy slope like lithe naked serpents. Covering fire from unseen infantry and a heavy automatic weapon keep my head down, bullets cleaving the air, a swarm of deadly bees. Streams of green tracers focus on my place of refuge, a lethal light show slicing through the darkness.

I lob a grenade over the edge of the trench. The sappers never see the baseball-size bomb as it tumbles toward them, lighting up the night, shredding their bodies.

The machine gun coughs a steady stream of fire, the gunner focusing on my muzzle flash. A flare rockets up from somewhere and hangs like a tiny white sun below the clouds, casting shadows in its weird pendulum light. I duck and move half a dozen meters away and catch five more men at the wire, freeze-framing them in the last moments of their lives. The machine gun finds me again, pulverizing the earth around my body at the edge of the trench, forcing me back down into the pit, making me crawl like a worm through a cold black ooze.

They keep coming. I can't kill them fast enough to make a difference. When one goes down, two more take his place.

I kill them and they fall away.

I kill them.

Still they come.

I turn to meet the man charging up the slope, now a huge target only a few feet away. He's carrying a long rifle with a fixed bayonet. I focus on the blade. It is aimed directly at my heart.

The blade keeps coming. It is a foot long, both sides sharp.

I see a hate-twisted face, deformed by emotion, exertion, fear, and determination, a man who wishes me dead, as frightened as I am, and as young. His bayonet reaches out for me. I shrink away and pull the trigger.

My gun clicks empty.

"Mr. Caine!"

"Wha?"

Felix took my hands in his and held them tightly, squeezing them gently to bring me awake. "You were crying out in your sleep. You were having a bad dream."

I nodded, the image still vivid, the fear leaving a bitter metallic taste in my mouth. I had had that dream before. An old acquaintance, but no friend, it visited me every few months, more or less, a souvenir of a living nightmare from many years ago. It was the first time I had come close to death. Really close.

Inches. Less. I suppose it's like sex. The first time is always memorable.

"Where are we now?"

"Almost home. Look out the window."

Honolulu sparkled from the air, a thin stretch of white high-rises wedged between lush green mountains and a topaz sea. I leaned forward in my seat to watch my island passing below.

"I was going to wake you, but you had that bad dream and started crying out before I could get there."

I must have looked strangely at him, because he went on explaining. "Not loud, but kind of a soft wailing. I know a nightmare when I see one."

"Have some of your own?"

He smiled. "Once or twice. You okay?"

"I'm okay. It's something that comes up from time to time. It's from a long, long time ago. Probably before you were born. You'd think it would be over by now. But it doesn't seem to want to let go of me."

"The moment of your death."

"You know, huh?"

"It causes the wailing. I have had it, too. Have you had it long?"

I nodded.

"You must have very nearly died once before. You must have been on the very threshold and defeated it. Part of you accepted your mortality when it happened. That part was willing to give up this body and fly to the next incarnation. The other part likes living here and now and rejected it. Those two parts battle each other in your dreams. You end up with nightmares, reliving the event."

I settled back and thought about the dream. Sometimes it wakes me with the sweats and the shakes. If it hits me in the wee hours of the morning I have to get up and walk around to get my heart rate back to normal, waiting for the adrenaline surge to wash from my system. Sometimes I don't get back to sleep at all, spending the rest of the night reading, waiting for the dawn, trying not to notice my hands shaking as I turn the pages.

"That sounds like it might be the case," I said, unwilling to acknowledge my fear to this stranger who had somehow become involved in my life. The dreams used to come only once every two years or so. Now it seemed that they came more often. I didn't know why.

"You've just had another trauma," said Felix, looking earnestly at me. "Your mind and your spirit are questioning why you keep putting yourself at odds with your own mortality. You go into harm's way. You're getting older. Maybe you should not do that any longer."

I looked at him through nearly closed eyes, ignoring his comment about my age. "Is that why you came along? I thought you were staying in San Francisco."

"Chawlie made me an offer I was unwilling to pass up. So I came. If I have to baby-sit you for a couple of months as part of the deal, that's okay, too. You're not too much trouble."

"Is that a compliment?"

"Not at all."

"The doctors told me to stay quiet for a couple of months. That's just what I intend to do. No excitement. I think I'll catch up on my reading."

"That policewoman. She didn't want you to leave."

There had been further conversations with Inspector Henderson, and they had become increasingly hostile. Felix had evidently informed Chawlie, because I was suddenly represented by counsel, a businesslike defense attorney named Andrew White who flew to my bedside the moment the detective walked through the door. I'm not sure, but I think I was almost arrested before I left California, Inspector Henderson not wanting to let me out of her jurisdiction. The attorney somehow mollified her, and promised that if my presence were warranted I would be there.

The woman who had been killed by the murderous young gunman was the focus of Inspector Henderson's investigation. In

Henderson's tidy mind the world was out of balance. Someone had to pay for that death to restore order to the universe. The gunman was dead. His targets had fled the state. I was the only connection to the killing that she could put her hands on. That I, too, was escaping was not, in her mind, acceptable.

There are a few times when lawyers do come in handy.

"But I left. I don't like California all that much. And this time I'm especially glad to leave."

"It will be fine. Don't worry."

I nodded, and tried to get comfortable while we made our final approach to the airport.

"You read much?" Felix asked.

I nodded.

"You don't look like a reader, Mr. Caine, if you don't mind me saying so."

"I don't own a television. Found it to be less than profound. Used to only watch the news, but I gave that up. It seems to be aimed at the trailer trash these days. Indecipherable crap. So I read. It passes the time."

"Novels?"

"Mostly histories and biographies. You?"

Since I had been released from the hospital and had left the area of immediate threat that San Francisco had become, Felix had suddenly opened up and began to try to get to know me. He probably didn't feel as if he would have to work very hard to keep me alive. I found that encouraging.

"I was an English major at San Francisco State," he said. "Read very many great novels. You ever read *The Old Man and the Sea*?"

"Yes. I like Hemingway."

"Me, too. That was his greatest novel. Probably one of the best ever. It said so much, and yet was very short."

"Clancy should have studied him."

He laughed.

"You ever read *Finnegan's Wake*? Or *Ulysses*?"

He smiled. "That's one of the reasons I quit school. The greatest novelist of the twentieth century? Somebody said so. Some poll of professors. I couldn't get through it. I tried. I really tried. I'm not stupid. But it was unfathomable. The experience made me question my commitment to literature. That, and other things."

"So how did you get into guarding bodies?"

"I was working my way through college as a martial arts instructor and club bouncer. Carrying a lot of units and working a lot of hours. Very tough schedule, but so was I, I thought. Many times people would ask me about bodyguarding and I suggested one of the better students. One day I thought, why not? And took the next offer that came in. It just so happened that the client was not paranoid but really was in danger from some bad people, and the first night I was on the payroll they tried to take him out. I got lucky and stopped them. Legally. The police, the client, the district attorney, everybody was very happy that it worked out the way it did."

"And word spread."

"Very quickly. The incident got a lot of publicity because of how it happened. Suddenly I had so many offers I could pick and choose, and I could charge outrageous fees. It brought me much more money than club bouncing or instructing, so I quit school. Now I do this full time."

"Just like Bill Gates," I said.

He nodded, a little proudly. "A little different, but the same idea. He quit Harvard."

"And one major difference," I said.

"What?"

"I'll bet you're not as tough as Bill Gates."

He flashed a grin. "We're landing," he said, noting the changing pitch of the Gulfstream's engines. "You'll soon be home, Mr. Caine. Back with your boat and your landlubbers and everything."

I looked out the window and saw the Waikiki beach party pass below, the venerable pink Royal Hawaiian and its white sand beach shimmering in the sunshine, the surf line dotted with bathers and surfers. "My landlubbers?" His use of the term finally cut through the fog, making me smile.

"Nautical term, isn't it? Raise the landlubber? Sheet the jib? Walk the plank, and all that?"

"I'll make you walk the plank if you raise any landlubbers around me, pal," I said. "You're going to live with me?"

"Don't look so alarmed. Chawlie hired me to make sure nothing happens to you while you heal. It should be easy duty here in Hawaii. I'm told you only have friends here."

"Sure," I said. "Nobody here but friends. You'll be safe."

"I'll just hang around and watch what happens. Don't worry about me. I can be very unobtrusive. I don't eat much. And I am being paid very well, so I plan to steal very little."

"Good to know," I said, settling back in my seat to wait for the touchdown, thankful once again to be back in the Islands. Thankful that Chawlie had felt grateful enough to help me while I recuperated from my wounds. Thankful, once more, all things considered, to be alive.

"By the way, Mr. Caine," said my watchdog, buckling into his leather seat across from mine. "Chawlie wants to see you as soon as we land."

6

"You look good, John Caine, for a man with a bullet in his back and a price on his head."

Chawlie rose to greet me, shuffling across his private reception room, arms raised, welcoming me home. I felt like some prodigal, returned after depleting my stolen inheritance.

"The bullet's gone to some evidence locker," I said, accepting his unexpected embrace, "but thanks all the same. What about the price on my head?" I didn't like the sound of that.

"Sit. You have had a long trip."

I sank down into a comfortable chair, lowering myself slowly and carefully, not wanting to dislodge what was inside of me, not comfortable with the thought of the stent, although I could not feel a thing other than the usual ache. Percodan and Tylenol had helped. But the pain was always there, lurking behind the chemicals like some caged animal, impatient to unsheathe its claws.

"You look tired, my friend," I said. Chawlie looked as if the weight of the world was on his shoulders. He was a serious man with few light moments. But this time he seemed to have more on his mind than usual.

"Wish you were healthy, old friend," he said. "Chawlie find himself fighting a battle he does not understand. Very few things make sense anymore."

"Is there anything I can do?"

"You can get healthy. Then we see what we can do."

"What's happened?"

"Fires, bombings. Somebody wants to put Chawlie out of business."

"Do you know who?"

He shook his head. "When I know who, I stop it. We are looking. We will find out, More worried about you right now, John Caine."

"Me?"

"According to my understanding, the San Francisco authorities are considering charging you with first-degree murder. Mrs. Chang, the woman who died because she was at the wrong place at the wrong time, she is the murder victim."

"I didn't shoot her."

"I know that. They know that. But the one who did shoot her is dead, and the authorities wish to punish someone for the crime. California law says that if you commit a felony, and as a result of your actions somebody dies, you are guilty of first-degree murder."

"That's insane."

"That's California. Land of crazy people. They make everything complicated. It has to do with balance, I think. Lotus Eaters' yin and yang. But do not worry. Charges are to go to the grand jury some time soon. Your lawyer says the facts are such that they might not indict you."

I had heard that grand juries would indict a fish for swimming in posted waters if the prosecutor asked them to, but Chawlie was there smiling at me, telling me not to worry, so quite possibly the fix was in. Even in California. The man had some reach from his little island perch here on River Street. But of course the Triads in California had similar power, and they now owed Chawlie a big favor for his presence, and for his support. I wondered if their power went all the way into a grand jury room, and decided that it probably did.

"Did you know that Mrs. Chang had grandchildren that she cared for? They had no mother or father, I guess."

The old man's eyes crinkled. "Yes. But they have an uncle, Uncle Chawlie. They are now provided for. Not to worry, John Caine. Chawlie does not forget his responsibilities."

"And the police will know that?"

"And who is responsible for the children's sudden wealth and security, yes."

"Money can buy just about anything, eh?"

"In this country, money can buy everything. But why should here be any different from the rest of the world?"

Why, indeed? "I am in your debt, Uncle."

"No. I am in yours. You saved me and you saved Daniel. There is no way I can repay you."

"I heard that the shooter was killed."

He nodded. "Young man, full of piss and vinegar, not thinking of consequences. Always consequences, no matter what you do."

Unless you had the money and the connections. That thought I left unsaid. We both knew its truth.

"So there is peace in San Francisco?"

Chawlie nodded again, smiling. "There would have been a terrible conflict had you not prevented my death, John Caine."

Remembering that old saw about the fate of those who perform good deeds, I kept my mouth shut.

"Your old friend Kimo has been around, asking about you. The good lieutenant was asked to make inquiries about your handgun, the one you lost before you traveled to San Francisco. He has also been aboard your boat to take samples of your .45 ammunition. He had a court order, issued by a judge in Honolulu, the result of a request from that detective in California. The judge is a good friend. I am happy to tell you that Kimo found no such ammunition. He could not find your firearm, either. You no longer have such a weapon."

"You've been busy." The way he explained it, Chawlie would have known about the warrant before the Honolulu police.

"Yes. California police not lucky. Your attorney tells me if they find nothing, they probably can charge you with nothing."

"Thank you, Uncle," I said, wondering about attorney-client

privilege, knowing that it didn't exist in this case. The lawyer reported to the one who paid him. That, too, was no surprise.

"Other problem. Because you were identified in the San Francisco newspaper, young rebels put a price on your head. They hired an assassin to kill you."

"And so, my bodyguard."

"Young Felix. Just so."

"You think he's necessary."

"Chawlie think that bodyguards are always necessary. Worked well for me in San Francisco."

I nodded. Carefully.

"How is Daniel?"

"He is well." Chawlie fingered the wattled flesh under his neck, lifting his chin. "He will wear the scar forever, but no matter. He still breathes."

"I am glad of it."

"It is best that you go now."

"You look tired, my brother," I said.

"It is difficult keeping everything together. I am an old man. And I am tired."

He looked tired. The bags below his eyes had bags. His face, which had always had a narrow, pinched look, was becoming skeletal. I wondered if he suffered from a fatal disease.

"Are you well?" I asked.

Chawlie smiled. "Thanks to you, yes. It is best now that you go." He rose and helped me to my feet. Chawlie was right. I was tired, exhausted from the flight, even though I had slept for most of it. But then, the dreams had not been restful.

"Chawlie understand that you lost your woman. If you need the warmth of a soft breast, Chawlie can send two or three little friends for you. They will help you relax."

"No thanks, Chawlie. It's a pleasant thought, but it might kill me."

He looked alarmed. "Everything all right?" He unconsciously grasped his own private parts through the rough cotton pants that he wore.

"I suppose. The doctor told me not to push it. Not right away."

His face brightened. "Oh, you are not shot there, but your doctor told you not to have sex! Stupid man! He does not know what you need."

"I need sleep. As you said, Uncle. Nothing more."

He nodded. "Chawlie understand."

"Thank you, Uncle," I said, hoping that he would forget the girls, thinking that at my age, even without my debility, their kind ministrations might cause me more pain than pleasure.

"Go now. Felix will go with you."

"Is Daniel around?" I wanted to confront him, to ask about his father's health.

"He is in California at the moment, but will return in a few days, and he will visit you."

So Daniel had come over on the jet that took me home. It made sense. If there were loose ends to tie up, Daniel was the guy to do it. Even injured, he was about the toughest guy I knew. Outside of Max. Or Kimo. Or me.

Chawlie leaned toward me, bringing me into his private space. "What can I do for you, old friend?" he asked. "You must rest. You must heal. You must have peace. And for that you must have privacy. I have opened my Royal Hawaiian suite for you. Nurses are there, good girls. They will help you heal."

"I want to go home. I want to go to my boat."

"How are you going to take care of yourself? Your wounds? You cannot live on your boat. Later, maybe. But not now. You live hard when you do not need to do so. That is your choice. But no need now. Now you need to let someone take care of you."

Chawlie was right and I knew it. For such an independent cuss, it was a difficult thing to admit. "Okay. For a few days."

"For a few weeks. Stay longer, sure, but a few weeks, at least. You must rest. Your doctor told me."

So the old man had been very busy on my behalf. I understood that it was a part of his gratitude. "Thank you, old friend. I shall stay there. For a few weeks."

Chawlie beamed at me, and I realized that I had almost

insulted him, something that I never wished to do again. The last time had had near fatal consequences. For both of us.

"You rest, John Caine," he said. "And do not worry about California laws. They cannot harm you now."

Chawlie ushered me to the door of his private quarters. Gilbert, his number one son, escorted me to the dining room of his restaurant where I found Felix waiting at the bar. He was drinking grapefruit juice. Through a straw. The things I knew about the young man made me doubt that it held anything other than grapefruit juice.

He smiled when he saw me. "Everything okay?"

"Fine. Is this your first time to Hawaii?

"Yeah." His admission had an almost guilty resonance to it.

"So you're happy to be here."

"I've heard a lot about this place."

"That's why you jumped at this assignment."

"Okay, you got me." He smiled shyly.

"Gilbert, Felix Chen here is a malihini, a newcomer."

Gilbert smiled his four-star smile, his teeth square and perfectly white. "Welcome to the islands, Mr. Chen." Always the consummate host, Gilbert seemed to ooze charm. Chawlie's oldest son, educated in only the best schools, he ran the legitimate businesses as the dutiful son and the restaurant as his personal fiefdom. Chawlie depended on Daniel for his operations. I wondered at the division of labor: Gilbert for the business enterprises, Daniel for the shadow empire. Somehow, Chawlie kept them in line. Only Chawlie could do that.

We said good-bye to Gilbert and went outside. "Don't worry, I'm not making fun of you," I said to Felix, patting him on the back. "Your age, I don't blame you. I'd probably do the same thing, I was you."

He smiled. "You know where we're going?"

"Royal Hawaiian."

"Where's that?"

"Waikiki. The heart of it. The Pink Lady's the grand dame of the beach. One of the best hotels in the world. She's the best place to be, if you have to be here."

"You make it sound rough. We're going to camp out there?"

"A suite."

He mulled that one over. "Chawlie's taking good care of you."

"He feels grateful."

"So how we going to get there?"

"Oh, I don't think you have to worry about that," I said, approaching Chawlie's silver limousine parked in the red zone in front of the restaurant, the same one that had brought us from the airport. "This is Chinatown. Chinatown is Chinatown, the same no matter where you are. But Waikiki is different from any-place else in the world.

"And I think, young man, that your first taste of Waikiki is going to be in style."

Instead of going directly to the Royal Hawaiian, I asked the driver to take us first to the Rainbow Marina at Pearl Harbor. I wanted to see my home. Just a glimpse. That was all I needed. I'd started to get the shakes from the trip and didn't think I could make it out of the car and down to the dock. So I took a long, long look from the marina parking lot, if only to satisfy myself that she still floated.

Olympia looked forlorn and neglected in her slip at the far end of the Rainbow's mauka dock, but she was still there, waiting like a faithful friend. For all the necessary work implied by her condition it was reassuring to see her. She needed work the way a wooden boat in the tropics needs work and she had not received any recent slave time. My condition precluded my performing the needed maintenance on her in the near future, either, so her predicament was unlikely to improve anytime soon.

She looked gray instead of her normally black shiny finish. A fine film of ash covered her decks and her sail covers, the result of a Hawaiian snowstorm. The sugar farmers out at Waipahu and West Loch had been burning cane again, the smoke and ash falling on Pearl Harbor when the winds shifted. I could not see them, but I knew that termites and wood-boring worms had probably taken up housekeeping in her hull, and barnacles, moss and weed were beginning to sprout their own colonies. I knew that the wooden laps would soon begin to move and leak if they were not constantly cared for. It was the curse of the wooden sailing vessel, this constant mandate for attention. Living abroad, with no obvious means of support, and therefore no obligation to be elsewhere, I'd always thought I would have the time to keep up with the required maintenance. But I hadn't planned to be away from her for this long. And I had never dreamed of this length of convalescence.

My body had suffered injury before. I had been close to death before. At my age this type of thing can really put the skids to you. Until you get over it. Until you master it.

I knew that it would be a long road back.

I also knew that I would have to find a way to get *Olympia* ship-shape again. Maybe I could con Felix into doing some of the work. Convince him it was a necessary part of his bodyguard duties.

Hell, I had the money, I could hire it done. Maybe this was a good time to have her hauled out and worked on. When I was honest with myself I knew I would not have the energy to live aboard for some time.

"Okay," I said to the driver, taking one last look. "Let's go."

In times like this I'd almost always done my wound licking alone.

Now, of course, I wouldn't be alone.

I knew that Felix's presence was both a kindness and a necessity. But part of me still resented the intrusion. I'd had all the intrusion I needed for awhile, every orifice trespassed during my hospital stay, including some new ones the doctors had made on their own. Felix was both a blessing and a curse, a typical Chinese conundrum.

Chawlie survived swimming with the sharks because he was brilliant and because he was careful. And also because he was ruthless. Trusting few people, his tentacles reached everywhere, farther than I had guessed. In his business information was everything. He just didn't wish that he knew what others were thinking, he *knew*. If he didn't possess a way, he would find a way. I thought Chawlie trusted me. He had every reason to do so. But that didn't mean he trusted me so far he would not keep an eye on me, providing me with a bodyguard and a protector who would also report back to him about my activities, my contacts, my likes and my dislikes. Even if nothing I did posed a threat at the moment, he might learn something about me that he could use one day, should the need arise.

I knew his intelligence operation was one of the best in the world, nearly as good as the Swiss. I had used information gleaned from Chawlie's sources before and probably would do so again. That knowledge made it difficult to resent this particular invasion of my privacy.

Still, I wanted to be alone.

I wanted to relax.

I wanted to sleep.

On my own turf.

The limousine turned off Kalakaua into the little lane between high-rise hotels and shopping centers and immediately lost nearly a century as it stopped under the porte cochere of the venerable pink stucco Royal Hawaiian Hotel. Built by Matson, the steamship company that had opened Hawaii to tourism so many years before, it had been the crème de la crème of accommodations for the cruising crowd. The passengers first stopped here on their way to the Orient, and later made it a destination in its own right. In the days before airliners, when Waikiki was a sleepy little section of Honolulu, the Royal Hawaiian and Moana Surfrider were the only hotels in town worth mentioning. Some still feel that way. I'm not sure I'm not in that crowd, but the Royal Hawaiian is one of the few places where the feeling of old Hawaii remains. As a bonus, it is where they invented the Mai Tai.

The doormen swarmed around the car as we stopped. Our bags were swiftly carried away. Chawlie's driver barked orders and the bellmen assumed a new attitude, switching instantly from attentive competence to a mixture of awe and fear. They knew for whom they worked. It put a little extra bounce in their step.

Someone produced a wheelchair and asked me to sit while they took me upstairs. My fatigue was so great I didn't argue. I allowed them to push me into the grand lobby and then into an ornate elevator, in which we sped to the top floor.

Felix stood beside me all the way, watching the surroundings, watching the bellmen, and watching the other guests in the hotel. I didn't think anyone would want to harm me here, but then I looked at him again and realized that he was drinking it all in. It appeared he had the same reaction to the Islands that I did when I first arrived. Felix seemed to be a Hawaiian at heart. He looked like a man whose soul had suddenly felt at home for the first time in his life.

His almond eyes became rounder and rounder as we reached the top floor and my minders pushed me down a corridor thick with the scent of fragrant island flowers.

"Welcome, Mr. John Caine," said a young woman, opening the door to Chawlie's suite. The driver rolled me into the living room of the suite, a spacious, well-lighted place with white wooden shutters on windows overlooking the beach, and with expensive Oriental carpets adorning the floors. French doors opposite the entry opened onto a sunny, tiled balcony. If all the interior doors opened on bedrooms, this was a four-bedroom suite.

Four nubile ladies welcomed me at the door, young Chinese women with fresh, beautiful faces. Nurses, Chawlie had told me. Nurses, he had said. Well, they were wearing nurse uniforms and white hose, and they each wore one of those silly hats that nurses wear that would tell you, if you were one of the initiated, what school they had attended. Nurses. They would dress my wounds, bathe me, and help make me feel better.

This was not what I had wanted, but it was what Chawlie had wanted for me, and it would have been churlish to register an objection. And besides, I was exhausted, wanting nothing more than to drop into a soft bed somewhere and fall into a deep and total sleep, a slumber with neither dreams nor fears. Chawlie's suite looked comfortable. And the view was terrific.

"You think you can make yourself busy for a while, Felix?" I asked.

"Sure. You, ah . . . ?"

"I'm going to sleep. By myself. For a long time. You're in Waikiki. It's fun out there. Go knock yourself out."

"You'll be all right?"

I gave him a Look. "I've got sunlight on the sand, I've got moonlight on the sea . . ."

"I'll take a walk on the beach."

"Go down to the Mai Tai Bar. It's right on the beach. Or head on over to Duke's. It's at the Outrigger, next door. They filmed that private eye television series over there."

"Really?"

"Really. The food is good and the drinks are generous."

He looked at me with a wounded look.

"I know. I noticed. You don't drink. But you can get an honest grapefruit juice over there, I'm sure."

Felix looked dubious.

"There's plenty of protection here. Chawlie didn't hire you as a nursemaid. Take some time off."

"Thanks."

"Have fun."

He turned and left the suite, apparently happy to have a destination, happy to explore. And happy, I thought, to be rid of the old man for a little while. He would not be a problem for me while he remained, and his company was intelligent and interesting. He could fade into the background when necessary and he might be helpful if ever he were needed. Chawlie had done well for me. But then, Chawlie always did. Chawlie always paid his debts.

I didn't know how long this enforced retirement would last. I didn't know how long I could stay down. After a life filled with travel and trouble I was not certain I could merely stay calm and quiet and safe and not go out of my mind.

But tired as I was, that prospect didn't seem so bad at the moment. And there would be the challenge of getting stronger every day, the challenge of rebuilding what the bullet had taken away.

I could do it.

It would just take time.

And time, it seemed, was the one thing I had in abundance.

"Mr. Caine?" One of the sweet young things asked. "Would you care for something to eat or drink? I'm sure you're thirsty and hungry from your trip."

"I just want to sleep." Food and drink were still strangers to me. I had memories of dining on great food and enjoying wonderful wine. But at the moment my stomach was a sour pit, able to tolerate little. Like my sex drive, my hunger for food and drink was flat.

"Of course."

She took my hand and helped me to the master bedroom, where the big king-sized bed had already been turned down over crisp, white linen. While I undressed, she pulled the shades and closed the windows. I was in bed before she turned around.

"I need to check your drains," she said.

When I protested, she smiled indulgently and did what she wanted, unimpressed by my feeble objections.

I lay quietly while she worked, watching her "tut-tutting" with her mouth while she checked my bandages and drains, lightly touching the unimpaired skin around the incisions, as if feeling for the heat of infection. Her fingers were cool, her touch not unpleasant.

"You sleep, Mr. Caine," she said quietly, apparently satisfied with her inspection. "You sleep as long as you like."

"What's your name?" Her lovely face paused over mine, the face of a tiny guardian angel, hovering over me.

"Angelica," she said.

"Of course it is," I murmured, thinking that even Chawlie's little playmates were more than playmates, and that Angelica's professional inspection gave me confidence that everything was going to work out just fine. The best I could do was to surrender myself to her care, and live each day as it came, and try not think too far ahead.

Just the way I'd always lived my life.

The pretty young nurses worked hard to help me heal. They tried almost everything. The way they cared for me I was confident that Chawlie's orders had been explicit.

But the only thing that would really make me heal was time and my body's own system. The doctors had done their job. I tried to be a good patient. I willingly did what the nurses told me to do. Up to a point. And then I did that, too. They were so sweet and earnest that I couldn't bark and I couldn't refuse them, even when I felt crabby and disjointed, even when I would rather have been left alone to rest and lick my wounds like an old bear. So I gritted my teeth and went along with every regimen they brought my way.

Chawlie had provided a large-screen television in the room. I tried to watch it, but nothing interested me and most of it repelled me. The news was scary. People were killing each other all over the planet, sometimes singularly, sometimes in organized groups. Europe and Asia, those continual hotbeds of organized mayhem for much of the past millennium, had decided to bring in the twenty-first with pogroms and ethnic cleansings, as if nobody in those places had learned a thing from the miseries of the past. I avoided the news.

In the daytime, the programming seemed to consist of victims and whiners or smiling plump ladies shaking their fingers at us from the other side of the screen, earnestly wanting us to see things *their* way. At night, the insipid comedies took over.

I left the TV off. The thing was too overpowering in the room, anyway.

For his part, Felix had little to do and was absent much of the time. Errands for Chawlie, he explained, as if that meant something. I had no need for a bodyguard; that was evident both to Felix and me, but the money must have been good, or he had found a friend, because he stuck around. As he once told me, it was an opportunity to work for the man who seemed to be a legend in the Chinese underworld.

It was good to see a young man striving to make his mark. Even in that kind of business.

Every day my nurses forced me to get out of the bed and walk across the room and down the corridor. And back.

All four of my nurses were there to support me. I returned from each excursion and fell exhausted into the deep feather cushions of the bed.

John Caine, action hero.

Every day they made me try again. From time to time, inertia took over and my body didn't want to leave the comfort and safety of the big old bed. When that happened, Angelica insisted, and so, in fact, would my conscience. Together the two of them guided me out of the bed and across the room and into the living room of the suite and down the hall again. I tottered around as if I were three hundred years old, and then wobbled back to bed, feeling as if I had accomplished something.

The doctor came to visit later that first day and fussed over my wounds and drains, telling me that he would take the drains out within a few days. He seemed pleased that the incisions were healing, as if he had anything to do with my improvement.

The bullet wound in the back and the incision in front gave me a hole that went all the way through me, in one side and out the other. The image both appalled and fascinated. It wasn't the first time my body had been holed. But this was one of the worst. And in one of the worst places.

But I was getting better, steadily improving in tiny increments. In a few days the nurses let me wander down to the lobby of the Royal Hawaiian and out to the lawn, a distance of maybe a couple hundred meters. A little farther than the Wright Brothers flew that first day at Kitty Hawk. My accomplishment was nowhere near as momentous, but seemed a true milestone.

Finally, the day came when I could venture outside and walk along the beach. I must have looked a sight, a big pale haole, skinny as a stork, his clothes too big for him, accompanied by a bevy of beautiful little nurses in their crisp white uniforms and odd little hats, every one of us barefoot.

With a nurse on either side I slowly meandered along the sand where the gentle waves lapped the shore. The warm water washed over my feet and caressed my ankles and then rushed back out to sea. I looked down and laughed because it felt good to be here, it felt good to be outside again, on the beach of my island, in the sunshine. It felt good to be alive.

My little nurses laughed, too, because they knew that I was healing. Their merry laughter reminding me of a mountain stream rippling over smooth stones.

That night, after Felix went out on his round of errands for Chawlie, we had a little celebration. Three bottles of Dom had been sent up from the hotel bar. We drained them before dinner and got a little giddy. Angelica looked at me as if I were some kind of conquering hero.

"You are a good patient, John," she said.

"The word is interesting," I said. "Patient. As in wait."

She giggled. "You must wait. Your body is healing. You will be well, soon."

I nodded. "Now tell me why they call what doctors do a 'practice'?"

She smiled a crooked smile. "You have lost a lot of weight."

"I'll gain it back."

"But a lot of it is muscle. It will be difficult for you. At your age."

"At my age?"

"You are not a young man. It will be difficult."

"You mean when I return to working out?"

"Yes. It will not be easy."

"Angelica, honey, if I shied away from things just because they were hard, I would have done something else with my life."

She shook her head. "Chawlie said that you are a good man, that you are like an ancient warrior. Chawlie said that you must once again prove to yourself that you are a man."

It took a moment before the subtext registered. "What are you saying?"

"Chawlie is worried about your manhood. He says it will be a problem for you if you cannot . . . do what a man has to do."

"Are you saying what I think you're saying?"

"Chawlie told me to make you happy. Tonight I think I will see what we can do."

"Wait a minute. That's not a part of your duties."

"It is if I want it to be," she said. "I am to make you well, and to make you well I am to make you happy."

"It's all right, Angelica. I'm old enough and tired enough I don't need you to do anything for me."

"I am not one of your American women who think sex is bad, or something merely to be bartered. I am a healing woman. Sex has much to do with healing."

"Thank you, but—"

"I notice when I wash you, your member doesn't even stir."

"Well, that's just . . ." I had no answer for that. I had noticed it, too, and it did bother me, but only a little. It had happened before, after major trauma. But she was a beautiful, healthy young woman, and when she touched me it should have caused some reaction. Even wounded, I wasn't dead.

"See, I can tell that it bothers you."

"But that doesn't mean you have to . . ."

"I don't *have* to. That's the point. I *want* to."

What do you say to that? The other nurses were watching and listening intently, keeping quiet, their warm, dark eyes following every nuance of the conversation. I had no idea what they were thinking. I wasn't sure I wanted to know. I felt like an object in a museum.

"I, ah . . ."

"We don't have to do anything right now, if it makes you uncomfortable, John. Drink your champagne. It will help you." She filled my glass again.

"Therapy, huh?"

"Chawlie wants to know that you're still a man."

"Tell Chawlie it's none of his business."

"He says that it is. If you cannot be a man in that sense, then he says you cannot be a man in the other."

"That's nonsense." Now I was getting angry. Chawlie had his ways and his culture, but he didn't have to impose them on me.

"I have to tell Chawlie what you do."

"That's even worse. You're a beautiful woman, but even if I were inclined to bed you on a moment's notice, I couldn't now because I'd know that Chawlie would be getting a blow-by-blow description."

She blushed. "I don't usually do that."

"That's not what I meant, Angelica."

"What shall I tell Chawlie?"

"Make something up. Tell him that I satisfied you eight times."

The other nurses laughed, hiding giggles behind their palms.

"Eight? Eight is a bad number."

"Okay, then. Tell him nine times."

They all laughed again.

"You mean that, John? Is that what you really want? We shall just talk about it, and then I'll report that to Chawlie, that you satisfied me nine times?"

"Yeah. It's not something I like to discuss with everybody in the room, and it's not something that I can do in cold blood. I'm sorry. I'm not turning you down because of anything you are, or because of anything you're doing, but this is not me."

She nodded, her face blank, and I couldn't tell if I had hurt her. I hoped not.

During dinner she stared at me as if I was some strange alien she had never seen before. It felt uncomfortable to be under such scrutiny. When dinner was over I excused myself, took a careful sponge bath, and crawled into bed.

I lay there staring at the ceiling, listening to the music from the Royal Hawaiian's luau on the lawn below, wondering what kind of fool I had become. Was I applying for sainthood sometime soon? If she wanted to do it, then who was I to play the blushing virgin? I'd been around the block a few times, and had nobody in my life at the moment. Why the heck not? The girl had her orders. Chawlie would know she was lying, and it might even be dangerous for her to lie to him, especially since I had said what I had said in front of the other nurses. One of them certainly would report what had actually happened.

Had I put her in an untenable position?

Would it be harmful to her if I refused?

Wow. That's a new one. Man refuses sex, thinking it is noble, and puts the woman in a difficult position.

Well, I did not want, under any circumstances, my sexual life reported to Chawlie. It was an intrusion I was not prepared to endure.

That was only part of it. I wasn't certain I could perform. In fact, I had my fears that I could not. There was no way to tell, but nothing had aroused me since the shooting. Little John just lay there like some disinterested Lotus Eater. I was male enough not to want to have that fact reported to my old friend. There's no telling what he would do, given *that* information.

The door opened and a small figure slipped into the darkened room.

"Angelica, I—"

She put her finger to her lips and shushed me. I watched as she removed that ridiculous hat and shook out her long, lustrous black hair. She placed the hat on the chair beside my bed and continued undressing all the way down to her fine, taut, golden skin.

"I grow old, I grow old," I murmured.

"What?" She unsnapped her bra and leaned forward to let it fall from her breasts.

"I was thinking of eating a peach." My voice became husky, my throat constricted.

She smiled and shook her head at my foolishness.

The band on the lawn below began playing one of those soft, sentimental hapa-haole tunes with plenty of sliding steel guitar in the melody line. It was sappy enough to be pretty, given the Hawaiian ambience, given the warm tropical night and the beautiful girl undressing in my bedroom. Angelica swayed with the music as she undressed.

I watched, wishing I could be aroused.

My psyche was aroused as was my spirit—I was acutely aware of the wonders and the pleasures that a young woman's body could provide—but my flesh was weak.

When she turned down the covers and climbed into the bed next to me, laying her soft warm breasts upon my chest, I wrapped her in my arms and held her close. She placed one smooth leg over mine, her knee nestled near my groin.

The music played on, but knee or no knee, nothing happened up here in the penthouse.

We lay quietly for a few moments, listening to the band. I could feel her sweet breath against my neck.

"Aren't you going to do anything?" she whispered in my ear.

"I don't think anything is going to happen."

She reached down and touched me, her fingertips lightly brushing me. It was a pleasant feeling, very erotic, but my body responded to no stimuli.

"I think I can make you interested."

"I don't know . . ."

"You don't have to try now. Maybe it's too soon."

"It was a good try, Angel. Damned pleasant, in fact."

"I will stay the night. Maybe I can make you happy."

"You have already made me happy, Angel. Not just in the way Chawlie means."

She hugged me.

"You are very gentle for a big man."

"I've learned to be gentle with angels."

She made a small sound in her throat that I thought sounded like contentment. I stroked her back, her velvety smooth skin wonderful to the touch.

"What are you going to tell Chawlie?"

"I will tell him you were a tiger, that you satisfied me ten times."

"Ten?"

"Okay. Seven. It's a lucky number. Eight is not a lucky number. It is two times four. I wouldn't want to give him the wrong impression."

"Then seven it is."

"Are you sure you can do nothing?" She raised up and moved against me, making both of very much aware of our nakedness.

"You would be able to tell."

"Would you like me to do something with my mouth?"

"No. Don't do anything. Just stay the night. If that's what you want to do."

"I think I'd better stay. The others will be watching."

"You take your job seriously." I mumbled my last reply, the fuzz from the champagne and the exhaustion of the walk on the beach catching up with me at last. Somewhere in the back of my mind I felt a stirring of something for the girl, a warm feeling, nothing more, and with that warm feeling a stirring in my loins. But it wasn't much, and it wasn't profound, and I was certain that she hadn't noticed.

She said something I didn't catch, and I fled this world for the one which we all share when we close our eyes and reach for those places in the corners of our minds that we keep hidden during our wakefulness.

And later I must have dreamed, but I remembered nothing of the dreams, and nothing of the rest of the night.

9

"You are really improving, Grasshopper!" Felix grinned at me as I stood panting, leaning against the sea wall in front of the Halekalani, one of the opulent, giant hotels along the sugar sand of Waikiki Beach. The concrete structure towered over our heads, providing shade in the middle of an early summer day. Its surface was cold and wet, and it felt good to lean against the smooth concrete after our long hike.

Felix stood immovable as a wave washed in around us, his feet planted in the sand like a statue rooted on steel rods. I braced myself as the little swell struck, allowing for the backwash. Despite my exhaustion it felt good to be in the sea again, even if was only my toes. The taste of salt in the air was pleasant, too. The sun and the sounds and the taste of the ocean combined to make me feel alive again.

"I walked. You ran," I grumbled. "And don't call me Grasshopper."

Felix had, indeed, run the whole way, from Diamond Head all the way to the Ala Wai boat harbor and back, sprinting ahead until nearly out of sight, then doubling back, ranging far afield and returning like a faithful dog.

We had covered a lot of ground, and Felix had covered it twice. It hurt me a little to see how effortlessly he stood there, letting the ocean burst against him.

"I'm pooped," I said.

"You're doing fine."

I nodded, hands on my hips, bracing for another wave.

Then I looked out to sea.

"A week ago you couldn't do this much."

"Yeah, right." I started moving toward the end of the sea wall, aiming at the wide sandy beach beyond.

"Not so fast. You've got to take it easy."

I walked a little faster. It wasn't a jog, and it wasn't quick, but it was the best I could manage.

"Hey, Caine! You're going to hurt yourself!"

I kept shuffling, waiting until I reached the corner of the sea wall and climbing up onto the stairs before I pointed out to sea, reaching the fourth step as a rogue six-footer crashed against the concrete, shooting white foaming spray high into the sky.

The surge covered me to my thighs, but I clung to the iron railing of the stairs and let the sea rush past, mindful of my incisions and the hysterical fit the doctors and the nurses would throw if I got them wet.

Water boiled in front of the concrete wall, a white raging maelstrom, and then washed back out to sea.

Felix had vanished.

I started to worry until I saw his form splayed like a starfish on the sloping sand, his eyes closed, his mouth open. I thought for a moment that he had been hurt until I heard his laughter rippling across the water. He laughed a belly laugh, a roar, a helpless release, a total abandonment to mirth.

He rolled over, swallowed water, choked, coughed, and rolled over again, so beset by his helplessness he couldn't get up.

Another wave washed over him and he disappeared beneath the froth.

Now I really worried.

He burst from the sea, a young Neptune with a happy, sloppy smile pasted across his face.

"You saw the wave!" He shouted.

I nodded, backing up the steps.

"You didn't tell me!" And he dissolved in laughter as another wave struck the sea wall.

I waited until he reappeared. "You seemed so sure of yourself!"

He pulled himself along the sea wall, suffering a continued battering, still laughing, but moving along in spite of the unexpected surge, the sea suddenly powerful.

He rounded the corner to the stairs and joined me on the sand where I had taken refuge. The sun baked my shoulders while I rested. It felt good sitting there, smelling the sea, hearing the sounds of the surf, feeling the tropical sun gently base me with its golden warmth.

It was good to be alive.

"You're improving," I said when he plopped down on the sand beside me. "Grasshopper."

He laughed silently, shaking his head.

"You always have to keep an eye on the ocean. She'll always do what you don't expect."

"She?"

"Like boats and old hurricanes. Figure of speech. From the old sailors."

He shook his head. "Were you trying to teach me a lesson?"

I nodded. "*Did* teach you a lesson. Don't get cocky around her."

Felix smiled, white even teeth in his bright brown face. "No," he said, "not cocky."

I stood up. It wasn't too difficult after all that exercise, or it wouldn't have been too difficult if I had had a crane and a bucket. Our long walk had winded me, and I didn't have much left.

"Time for my nap," I said.

"You really are getting better."

"It's a long road back."

"But you're on it."

"Stop with the platitudes, buster. I've done this enough to

know how tough it is. I'll make it. Your help makes it easier. But I still have to do it myself."

He slapped me on the back. "Sure you do, old man."

"Oh, shut up," I said, knowing I was being patronized, and knowing that I deserved it.

"It's only a little farther," he said.

"I know how far it is." I limped across the sand toward the Royal Hawaiian. We'd been gone for three hours, had covered nearly ten miles of ground, and I'd walked the entire way. I was tired, but otherwise felt loose and agile, the walk the stimulus I needed to get my blood going again. Too many days in too many hospital beds had clogged my fluids, plugged my head, and made me logy. It didn't feel natural not to be active. My body wasn't used to it.

What alarmed me was how easily I had adapted to the almost motionless state I'd been forced to accept.

Accept, hell.

I started to jog, an approximation of a jog, more of a shuffle, tossing one foot in front of another, making about twelve inches per stride. But I lifted my whole body off the ground, and it felt like a run. It felt good.

"Hey!" Felix shouted. "You're not supposed to do that!"

I could hear his feet pounding the sand behind me.

I ignored him.

"Hey! You're not supposed to run," he shouted, coming abreast of me.

"This isn't running. This is jogging." That's what I tried to say. What I actually said was, "This . . . *pant, pant, pant* . . . isn't . . . *pant, pant, pant* . . . running . . . *pant, pant, pant* . . ."

"Hey, man, what are you doing?"

I stepped up the pace and he stopped talking and started running in earnest, easily pacing me and then, after a moment's hesitation, and with a sly grin on his face, he really tore it open, leaving me in the dust, actually kicking sand in my face as he sprinted toward the Royal Hawaiian's wrought iron gate.

I caught up with him as he stood panting, his hands on his knees, staring at the sand.

"Damn you, Caine," he said.

"What?"

"You're going to kill me."

"Why? A little run like that?"

"No, you're going to get a heart attack, or your kidney thing is going to pop out, and then you'll be dead, and then Chawlie will send those goons of his after me because I'm supposed to protect you."

"Oh."

"Don't do that. The doctors all said you weren't to exercise."

I looked down the beach. "What were we doing?"

"That's different. You just walked."

"I'm still breathing."

"You okay?"

"I'm fine." Actually, I felt wonderful. Nothing came loose, nothing fell out, and no great pains ravaged my body. I actually felt terrific. For the first time in weeks I could hear my heart beating.

"Then we're both lucky. Please, Mr. Caine. Please try to hold it in for a little while. I don't want Mrs. Chen's little boy to go home to California in a piney wood box."

"Don't worry about it, Grasshopper," I said, slapping him on the back. "You're going to be fine."

"You want to get a grapefruit juice?"

"Or something," I said. "We can rest down here before we head on up to the room."

We trudged across the manicured lawns of the Royal Hawaiian, leaving a dripping trail behind. I was only wet from the thighs down, but Felix was soaked.

The Mai Tai Bar is one of my favorite watering holes in Honolulu. I've spent many afternoons and evenings there, sitting at the bar or taking possession of one of the white-painted iron tables, drinking and talking with friends, and watching the sun go down. We were too early for the sunset, and too early for the nightly show of song and hula. The bar was sparsely populated, the tourists almost equally divided between young Japanese honeymoon couples and seasoned citizen Midwestern American. I wondered about the relative demographics, but only until the waitress came and asked for our order.

"Two grapefruit juices," said Felix.

I frowned at him.

"Doctor's orders," he said to me.

"Where did I read that a glass of wine was good for you?"

"I have no idea," he said with an innocent expression. "Where would you hear such a thing?"

"What is it about you and alcohol?"

"My body is a temple. I take care of it. Stimulants are completely unnecessary. Even for you."

"Even?"

"You've got to get in touch with your body."

"Careful, pal."

"You know what I mean."

"I'll bet you don't eat meat, either." I hadn't seen him eat anything but fruit and vegetables since I'd met him. Of course, he could be sneaking a Big Mac when nobody was looking, but I tended to doubt it.

"Of course not. Nor eggs nor fish."

"Because it's good for you?"

"It's the worst thing you can do to your body."

"See these things?" I lifted my lip and showed him my upper teeth. "Those sharp pointy ones? They're canines. We humans are meat eaters. Omnivores, actually, but meat is an important part of our diet. It isn't a sin to shovel down a cheeseburger once in awhile, especially in paradise. It tastes good, too."

"All those calories? All that fat? Not to mention that before the cow was slaughtered it consumed huge quantities of Earth's precious resources. And it's bad for you. There's no upside to it at all."

"You wear shoes."

He grinned and pointed to a sodden pair of Eco-Sneaks. "Pure hemp."

"You swat mosquitoes? You step on cockroaches?"

He nodded. "They're pests."

"What's the difference? Pigs are cute, bugs aren't?"

"There's hierarchy. But I don't eat mosquitoes or cockroaches, either."

"You're what, twenty-five, twenty-six?"

"Twenty-six."

"I'm nearly twice your age. I've been doing this since before you were an impure thought. I've been stabbed, shot, blown up, survived a plane crash, a helicopter crash, had my boat sink from under me, I've been in more fights than I can remember, and I'm still standing. I'm the world champion at getting my health back after injuries."

Felix assumed a look of smug superiority. "You misunderstand."

"I understand that I don't need to be baby-sat by a kid who's still wet behind the ears."

"Now *there's* an expression! Was that original?"

"You know what I mean," I said, starting to get angry, but, interrupted by the waitress bringing our juices, I didn't have the pleasure of a full-blown tantrum. Felix signed the chit and she smiled and left us alone again. I decided to forget my temper. I didn't have the steam for it.

Felix took a sip from the tall glass, looked at it and set it down on the table. "We're just chemicals, you know."

"What?"

"You don't want to put the wrong chemicals in your body. Meat, especially red meat, is full of chemicals these days. They stuff hormones and drugs and all kinds of nasty stuff into those poor creatures before they slaughter them."

"Give me British beef and a Hong Kong chicken any day."

"That is beneath you," he said.

"So you're a vegetarian."

"A vegan. I eat no animal products whatsoever. Scientists are finding out that we're just chemicals. Our bodies, our minds, it's all just a chemical reaction. If you have the wrong kind of chemical reactions, you have problems. But if you have the right kinds of chemicals you can cure the problem."

"Excuse me, John?"

I looked up. David Klein stood next to my chair. I hadn't seen him approach. "David! It's good to see you! Pull up a chair."

When he sat down he looked at Felix and Felix looked at him, but didn't say anything. "David, this is Felix Chen. Felix, this is David Klein. He's an old friend and diving companion."

David smiled.

"Pleased to meet you," said Felix. His voice was soft, but he was guarded, as if he resented David's presence.

"Felix has been body surfing."

That earned me a nasty look.

"The front desk told me you weren't in your suite," said David. "They told me to check in the bar."

Felix smiled over the top of his grapefruit juice.

"You're here for R&R?"

"Yeah. Finals were a bitch, but they're over."

"David is a graduate student at Berkeley. When he gets his advanced degree in something or other, he gets to wear a neon sign on his forehead that says, 'BERKELEY' in red capital letters. Then people will think he's smart."

David laughed. Mom says hello."

Felix did not look happy. I wondered if he had taken an instant dislike to David, or if he felt as if he had to compete with him. The more I thought about it, the more that seemed likely.

"She still up in Telluride?" I asked.

"She flies up there every other week. The contractor finally understands that she means business."

"You met David's mother," I said to Felix.

Felix nodded. "She said you were a Disneyland ride."

David looked confused.

"She was expressing her deep disappointment with my inability to grow up," I said. When his confusion seemed to grow, I changed the subject. "You're here for how long?"

"A month or so. I decided to just hang out here for the summer."

"And you were hoping to stay on the boat?"

"I was hoping to. Mom said you offered."

"She was right. I'll give you the keys. I'm feeling better and we'll probably get out of here pretty soon. Then we can go diving."

Felix looked even more unhappy.

"Here you are!"

I looked up. My old friend, Lieutenant Kimo Kahanamoku of the Honolulu Police Department, stood at the table beaming down at me, Tutu Mae, his tiny grandmother, standing quietly off to the side. Kimo wore a pink Aloha shirt covered with startling green pineapples. He looked like a David Hockney painting, one of those larger-than-life, more-colorful-than-nature kind of canvases that he does. I made the introductions, while David and Felix stood to offer their seats.

"Sit! Felix, can you see about getting us a bigger table?"

"They told us you would be in the bar," said Kimo.

Felix smiled to himself as he hurried off to find the waitress.

"We must talk with you, Mr. Caine," said Tutu Mae, her voice a quiet rasp. "I have a student with a problem." For the first time I noticed an attractive young Chinese woman hovering at the edge of the group, a part of the group but detached, alone.

"Tell me," I said.

"I cannot say anything here in public," said Tutu Mae. "It is really very, very private."

"Then let's go upstairs." There wasn't anything I could do but listen politely. If Tutu Mae thought I could help the young lady, then it was possible that I could help her. Tutu Mae was a kupuna, one of Hawaii's greatest living assets, one of her culture's living legends. If she wanted help from me, then help was what I would offer.

Felix returned with our server. I held up my hand. "We're going to the suite. Anybody want anything? They can send it up."

"Coffee will be fine," said Tutu Mae. She didn't smile, but then, I rarely saw her smile. Kimo had once told me that she liked me, but I'd never seen any evidence of it.

"Yeah, coffee," Kimo nodded, taking the lead from his grandmother, even though I knew he wanted beer.

I looked at Tutu Mae, who smiled graciously. "Why don't we have a couple of pots sent up?"

The waitress nodded.

"Teetotalers," I said to the waitress.

"I'll have another grapefruit juice," Felix told her.

"If there's anything worse than teetotalers," I said, "it's vegans."

10

Who is the kid?" Kimo waited to whisper his question until we reached the suite.

"Son of an old friend. He's over for the summer."

"Get rid of him."

I raised my eyebrows.

"Your pet bulldog, too. Get rid of them both."

"Why?"

Kimo just stared.

"Okay." I called Felix over and he joined us, still dripping from his swim, dropping sand and salt water on an ancient silk carpet. "After you change you can drive David over to the boat. You remember where it is?"

"Yes."

"Here are the dock and boat keys. Tell him the bottom needs cleaning. You can help him. I'd be most appreciative."

"You want to get rid of us."

I pointed to Kimo. "Give David the keys to the Jeep, too. He'll take good care of it."

"Yo."

"Yo?"

"As in yo-ho, mi capitán." He pronounced each syllable with equal emphasis, giving it just a taste of Caribbean island spice mixed with the sarcasm.

"You know, Kimo," I said, "if I didn't know any better I'd swear I was being mocked. And in a really bad accent."

Kimo shrugged, uninterested. "Could be." He looked around the suite. "Where are your nursemaids? I hear they're something to see."

"Not my day to watch 'em," I said, annoyed by the questions. Since I had improved, the nurse force had been reduced to two, Angel and a night nurse. Angel had taken some personal time when I went walking with Felix, disappearing into the urban sprawl of Honolulu.

Kimo's eyes wandered around the suite. He must have felt alien here, a policeman in the den of the island's greatest criminals.

The two women settled in the parlor, sitting quietly, like poor relatives come to visit a rich uncle. Tutu Mae seemed to be lost somewhere in the huge overstuffed chair. The young woman I had guessed to be the student sat at the end of the couch next to Tutu Mae's big chair, as if protected from harm by proximity.

"It's nice to see you again," I said to Tutu Mae.

"I was told that you were ill," she said, inspecting my bare feet and damp shorts. She waited imperiously, expecting a defense.

"I'm pushing the envelope, ma'am," I finally replied. "Doctors said six weeks."

"You think you're smarter than your doctors?"

"It's not a matter of smarter. I just know my own body. It made demands on me for activity."

She nodded, her mouth a thin line. "Following your body's demands. That is the problem with too many men."

I didn't know if I was supposed to smile or not, but I couldn't help it.

"This is Miss Wong," she said, indicating the young woman, who smiled tentatively at me when I glanced her way. "She is a double doctoral candidate in archeology and anthropology at the university." She paused and stared at Felix, who had just entered the room pulling a clean white tee shirt down over his chest.

David, who had been standing quietly near the door, gazed at the young woman who had just been introduced. He looked stunned.

"Oh," said Felix, finding that everyone in the room had followed Tutu Mae's example. "We're just leaving. Come on, David."

He pushed David out the door and followed him.

When he had closed the door, Tutu Mae looked at me with her dark, autocratic eyes. "I have worked with Miss Wong for several years. She is intelligent. She is kama'aina, and she knows what is important and what is not. She is an honest person. She is a good person."

The young woman blushed at the compliment, apparently unfamiliar with receiving praise from Tutu Mae.

"Miss Wong's faculty adviser is not so honest." Tutu Mae looked at the door, as if expecting Felix and David to burst in on us. When they didn't, she continued.

"Do you know much about the history of our Hawai'i?" She pronounced it with the added glottal stop, in the way of the original inhabitants. When I hear it pronounced that way, I remember that it meant the place where we go when we die. Even then, to the ancient ones, Hawaii was heaven.

"I have read *The Shoal of Time, The Fatal Impact, The Kumulipo*. Other books."

She nodded. "A good start. Every Honolulu bookshop sells those. But there is much more." She looked at Kimo, studying his face in silent argument. After a moment she shook her head and looked at me. "You are a good man, John Caine. You know what is right and what is wrong, as does Miss Wong. What we are about to tell you must not leave this room. Do you understand?"

"I understand," I said.

"It is important that you believe what you just said."

"I can keep a secret."

She nodded. "Kimo tells me so."

Miss Wong stared through the thick lenses of her glasses, peering intently at me.

Tutu Mae reached over and touched the young student's

arm, flicking her fingers toward me. She had evidently made her decision.

Miss Wong continued studying my face for a long moment, as if trying to draw out vestiges of my character. Finally she seemed satisfied that I would not run out and shout everything I knew to everybody I met. "What do you know about the Spanish influence in Hawaii?" she asked.

"I didn't know there was any."

She nodded to herself and leaned forward, a posture of intimacy. "Officially, Spain never had contact with the Hawaiian Islands, although their treasure ships sailed back and forth across the Pacific for 223 years. For some reason they never found it, or if they did, they didn't think much of it. There are no records of any European reaching these shores until Captain Cook in 1778."

She paused as if deciding the direction of her next comment.

"You are a sailor, Mr. Caine?"

"Was. I live aboard my boat because I like the sense of it. If things don't work out here I can up anchor and drift off to another port."

She nodded to herself, taking my comment seriously. I reminded myself that her sense of humor was subordinated to her problem. Whatever it was involved sailors. I sympathized. A lot of young women over the centuries have had the same problem.

"Have you heard the treasure stories?"

"Not about Hawaii."

"Not one?"

"No. I didn't suppose treasure ships ever reached here, not like they did in the Caribbean."

"Written history says that the first European ships the Hawaiians ever saw were in Cook's fleet. The Hawaiians thought Cook was the god Lono when they saw him. Not only because he sailed into Kealakekua Bay at the height of the Makahiki celebration, but also because he was white, hairless, and sailed aboard a great ship with square sails, exactly like those of the god Lono-i-ka-makahiki. It was a tragic coincidence that this British explorer blundered into Hawaii at the exact time and place promised by

Lono, and sailing a square-rigged vessel so large it looked to the Hawaiians like a floating island, complete with trees and the thunder of cannon. Anyone with that much power just had to be a god."

I kept silent, knowing a running monologue when I heard one.

"The Hawaiian Islands changed from that day. Did you know that at the time before Cook this was the only true paradise left on earth? No trees or shrubs with thorns existed here. There was simply no reason why a plant should have them, and so, in the evolutionary process, those plants that found their way to Hawaii eventually lost them. The ne'ne geese lost their ability to fly because there were no predators and therefore no reason to use their wings. There were no mosquitoes, no cockroaches, no poisonous plants or animals at all. Infectious diseases were unknown because the population was self-contained. It was a soft and gentle place.

"In five short years after Cook arrived, the people began dying. Sexually transmitted diseases, air- and water-borne plagues, and the exotic insects brought by the whalers decimated them. It was the unfortunate price of contact."

She quietly stretched against the cushions, as if her back was tender from stress.

"Did you know that even today in Antarctica, the people who live and work down there dread the arrival of new people at the station? Always, without exception, the new people bring with them a load of new flu, colds and other maladies that make life miserable for the next few weeks. And Antarctica is isolated for only a few months at a time. At the time Cook landed here, the islands had been isolated for more than eight hundred years. Smallpox and syphilis killed eight out of ten Hawaiians, and that was even before American whalers introduced mosquitoes and the diseases they carried."

I nodded, having once visited the very creek in Lahaina where two ignorant seamen had dumped a cask of bad water loaded with the larvae.

Tutu Mae reached over and lightly touched Miss Wong's arm. She was going to tell me about the Spanish, and she took off into the ether and ended up lecturing about mosquitoes and syphilis.

I looked out the window. The day was perfect, one of those late tropical spring days that just break your heart with their beauty. Outside, palm fronds brushed gently against the windows. The horizon stretched to a stainless blue sky. This was all very interesting, but I didn't see what it had to do with me. Or what I could do about anything she told me. If it was background, and if I was smart enough to figure that out, she was going at it the long way around.

"I'm sorry, Mr. Caine. Tutu Mae reminded me that we have serious issues to discuss, and that I was wandering far afield. But you must understand the history to understand the present."

"Who said that?"

She looked blank. "I just did, Mr. Caine."

"Must be great minds and all that. And please call me John."

"Hawaii was a Stone Age culture before Contact. We had no metal. Everything used here was either stone or shell or wood or fiber, natural stock that grew or was found here.

"But there are strange things that are difficult to explain.

"Many years ago, Robert Langdon, a scholar from the Australian National University, wrote a paper about two alien artifacts found in the burial chamber of a Hawaiian ali'i named Lono-i-ka-makahiki, an evidently revered man who died at the end of the seventeenth century. Does that name sound familiar?"

"Cook."

"Exactly. The items are at the Bishop. I have examined them and find them extremely anomalous. One is a piece of iron embedded in a wooden handle, much like a knife or chisel, but badly degraded so that its original shape is in question. The other is a piece of heavy cotton cloth, eight feet long by one foot wide. Tests indicate that it has the characteristics of sailcloth.

"There were no cotton plants in Hawaii prior to Contact. The wood was determined to be oak, which never grew here prior to Contact. A piece of iron in a Stone Age society is alien and explainable in only one of two ways. The Hawaiians went there and brought it back, or someone came here and left it."

"How can you know which happened?"

"Hawaiian oral tradition speaks of the coming of the hairless, light-skinned people who were given wives and who became chiefs. And there is a map of the Pacific, also dating from the seventeenth century, that shows two islands, La Mesa and Los Mojas, at the approximate location of the Hawaiian Islands. Because of their isolation, these islands could represent no other land mass but Hawaii."

"So you're saying that the Spanish were here."

"It's possible. Many people have speculated about the shape of the feathered ali'i helmets and the cloaks that appear to be Spanish in origin, especially when no other Polynesian culture adopted similar helmets and cloaks. It gets even more interesting when you compare the Hawaiian royal colors of red and yellow with those of the Spanish monarchs, which were identical."

"All of which means nothing, I'm sure."

Miss Wong smiled. "Aside from your admitted ignorance of the subject, there have been long-standing rumors of a Spanish treasure ship that foundered off of Lanai in a hurricane, but no one has ever found the wreck site, or any trace of her cannon."

I noted that when Miss Wong got into her subject matter her shyness disappeared.

"I spoke earlier of treasure ships. It is historical fact that the Spanish made annual commercial voyages between Acapulco, Mexico and the Philippines from 1556 to 1778. They ferried treasure looted from Asian cities to Mexico, where it was trans-shipped overland, loaded into other ships, and sent across the Atlantic to Spain.

"It is historical fact that several of the treasure ships did not reach Mexico, victims of the great Pacific hurricanes. I spent time in Madrid earlier this year searching for the name of a certain ship, *La Reina de Plata*. It did not take me long. *La Reina de Plata* was one of the treasure ships that vanished on a return voyage from Asia, loaded with gold, silver and jewels. It left Manila in 1629 and never reached Mexico."

Her eyes burned with a kind of cold fire. Her forearms were covered with chicken skin. "Do you know why I looked for a certain ship? Why that name?"

I shook my head.

"Earlier this year I discovered the tomb of an ali'i in the most unexpected location. It was a combination of luck and circumstance that I found this tomb. It is difficult to get to, and has been hidden for hundreds of years. I have taken every precaution to ensure that nobody knows what I am doing and why."

She cleared her throat, sipped some coffee, and looked directly at me. Gone was the shy student. Miss Wong could not hide the pride and the awe in her voice.

"It is the tomb of a man I believe to be the greatest king of the Hawaiians, long believed to be lost, so well hidden that nobody would ever find it. With the tomb was treasure. Spanish treasure. On several of the artifacts was written the name of that vessel. All the gold and silver that could be crowded into the holds of a Spanish galleon is now in that Hawaiian tomb, resting with the remains that I believe are those of King Kamehameha.

"The Lonely One was buried with Spanish Treasure."

$\mathbb{T}$he Lonely One?"

I looked at Kimo, who shook his head. He was out of his depth here and admitted it. So was I. Spanish treasure? King Kamehameha the Great, first king of Hawaii? What could any of it have to do with me?

"Would you like some more coffee, Tutu Mae?" I asked.

"Would you happen to have a little rum? Could you add a small drop?"

"Certainly."

"Coffee isn't good for the body. But rum makes everything work," she said.

Kimo smiled and got to his feet. "I'll do it," he said. "I know how much a 'drop' is these days. I'm afraid that you wouldn't put enough in."

"Oh."

"Big drops," said Kimo, with a little grin.

I thought about it for a two-count. Felix wasn't around. "Give me some, too."

"Big drops?"

"I wouldn't want Tutu Mae to feel lonely. Anything for you, Miss Wong?"

"No, but thank you."

"You were saying?"

"Do you know about the bones?"

I noticed that Miss Wong lectured through questions. The technique usually irritated me. It's what people usually do when they know something in a narrow area and use it to demonstrate their superior knowledge. In that one area. In this case I felt that she was trying to gauge my level of understanding of the subject. It would save time, for example, if I knew something about the bones of the ancient Hawaiians.

"I know that the Hawaiians honor the bones of the people," I said. "They are sacred, if I remember correctly. The most important part of us, the part that lasts after our flesh is gone." I noticed that Tutu Mae rubbed her own elbow as I spoke, and I wondered if she might have been considering her own mortality.

"Good, Mr. Caine," said Miss Wong. "The bones of the common folk are honored. Bones of great men are revered. The bones of the greatest king these islands ever knew are valuable far beyond the mere scientific and historic. They have great cultural and religious significance, as well."

"So you think you found Kamehameha."

"I think I found his tomb. We're not sure. We're not even sure how to proceed with provenance. Because of where it is, and because of what is buried with it, I have a strong belief that what we found is the final resting place of Kamehameha I."

I glanced out the window, watching the tourists playing on the sand and the gentle surf of Waikiki. This was one of the old king's favorite beaches. I wondered how he would react to the giant hotels, the ABC Stores, and Crazy Shirts.

"Are you listening, Mr. Caine?"

"Yes."

"People have sought the bones of Kamehameha I for centuries," she continued. "Every so often someone claims to have found them. And then the claim is proven false and the poor soul is reinterred. There are plenty of bones in the mountains."

I nodded again, remembering the hundreds of skeletons

uncovered during the last hurricane. It took months to get them all back into their mountain burial caves.

"The search for Kamehameha has been described as the Hawaiian Holy Grail. It would be very good for the person who finds the actual site. If it were handled correctly."

Kimo brought the rum-laced coffee. I saw that he'd found a beer for himself.

"What do you mean?"

"If the site were plundered, if the material were removed from its location and brought to a museum or a university, there could be trouble."

"How?" It seemed odd, speaking of old bones as if they actually had power to cause trouble.

"The bones carry the mana, or spirit energy, of the family. We cannot move the bones because of the harm it would do to the descendents of the person in the tomb. I have been very careful to work around them. It has caused us a great deal of additional tasks, and it is not in the best of locations. But we have been extremely careful not to disturb the bones. You, of course, know about scattering the bones?"

"No."

"That is why Kamehameha's body was hidden in the first place. His people were afraid that if his bones fell into the wrong hands they could be used against his own. Or, worse, they would be scattered. There is a cursing chant, when you scatter the bones of your enemy. It destroys his spirit for all eternity."

I nodded, trying to go along. This wasn't my area. It was like listening to ghost stories. Interesting, but futile.

"Scattering his bones would be the worst thing that could happen to the Hawaiian people," she continued. If she had expected a reaction from me she had been disappointed. When I had nothing to say I contented myself with silence. "Because he was so powerful and important, the chief ali'i, the scattering of his bones could possibly lead to the destruction of the Hawaiian people's spirit energy."

I stared at her, wondering how this obviously bright woman could believe this kind of nonsense. She didn't see the disbelief in my eyes. If she did, it didn't bother her because she plunged ahead.

"In the hands of the Hawaiian separatists, the bones could become the catalyst for revolution. Those who had them would feel that they had been granted a power they would not otherwise have."

"You're not just talking about the Antiquities Repatriation Act?"

"You would know something of that?"

"I helped a friend rebury his auntie a few years ago. The female skeleton that had been in the University of California at Berkeley since 1928. I helped him retrieve it from the university. We brought it back and reburied it in the mountains of Kauai."

"I read about that. You were involved?"

"I just helped. But I learned about the Act." Some of the things that Ed Alapai had told me flooded back. The importance of the bones, the gravity of the Hawaiians' feelings about them. They were the only permanent things of the body. They would last. It was that permanence that granted them their importance. It had been extremely important to Ed. I had listened, and respected his wishes, and helped him return the bones, not questioning what it was he wanted, or why. This was the same thing. I listened to Donna Wong a little more carefully.

"So you know that we don't just plunder tombs for the educational value. There are more advanced techniques we can use these days. We need the information, but we do not have to scatter the bones. We survey. We videotape. We photograph. Everything. There are three-dimensional photographic techniques that virtually capture an object as if it were actually there. The only thing we cannot replicate is the weight. We make certain that everything we find is identified and catalogued, listed and captured electronically. If we have to take samples, we do so with a minimum of damage."

"You spoke of secrecy," I said, now really listening for the first time. "Yet you talk of 'we.' Who is 'we?' "

"My sisters and I are the only ones who have worked the site. We are the only ones who know exactly where it is."

"And it would be bad if the information got out?"

She nodded, her face a serious mask. "Very bad."

Tutu Mae said, "Think of the bones. The bones of Kamehameha should never be disturbed. It would be the same as disinterring those of Washington or Lincoln. But there are those who think they can take anything, as if it is their right. No one should have that right."

"If news of the treasure were to get out, there would be no stopping the media and the treasure hunters. They would tear the tomb apart plundering the gold and silver. They would destroy all of the other artifacts we found."

"What are you going to do with it?"

"When we're finished studying the remains and the artifacts we're going to seal the entrance so it cannot be found again."

"What makes you so sure nobody else can find it? You did."

"The old ones left clues. They thought they'd hidden it well, but they left enough clues for us to follow their trail. Still, they did a good job. It took two hundred years."

"If it's Kamehameha."

She smiled like the Cheshire Cat. "Yes," she said, as if she *knew*.

"Well, thank you for allowing me to hear this story," I said. "But what does it have to do with me?"

"Do you swear to secrecy, Mr. Caine? Do you swear that you will not reveal what I am about to tell you without my express permission?"

"You can count on it, Miss Wong," I said, wondering if I should hold up my right hand.

"You must know," said Tutu Mae, again surging out of the deep chair cushions, pointing a bony finger in my direction, "that this discovery belongs entirely to Miss Wong. No one else had the brains or the tenacity to make this find. It was not accidental. In fact, it was truly the work of genius."

Donna Wong blushed at the praise.

I finished my coffee and rum. There were worse ways of whiling away an afternoon. Even in Waikiki.

"There are only so many places the tomb could have been located," said Donna Wong. "Some scholars and even a few contemporary witnesses speculated that his bones had been thrown into the Kilauea caldera to avoid having them found and used by enemy sorcerers."

"Scattering the bones," I said.

"Yes. But tossing them into the volcano would have destroyed them, and that is not something you do with an ali'i's remains. Especially those of a Kamehameha.

"Since that made no sense culturally, and since the caves—do you know the Kona Coast, Mr. Caine?"

I nodded. It was a wasteland of lava, as barren of life as anyplace on earth, entirely inhospitable. Except for two or three luxury resorts that had been constructed there at great expense, nothing exists on the Kona Coast.

"Then you know that Kailua, where Kamehameha died, is close to the lava flows. There had been an eruption of Hualalai a dozen or so years before his death. He would have known about that. Most certainly he would have considered that. The most recent lava flows can still be seen today, running across older lava fields on into the sea."

"Isn't that one extinct? I thought only Kilauea was active."

"A volcano is defined as active if it has erupted during historic time. That means that any volcano whose eruption has been recorded in written accounts. Certainly Hualalai is still active, given those parameters. As is Mauna Loa, whose last eruption was in 1985, and certainly Kilauea, which continues erupting today. But Haleakala on Maui, which had a spectacular event in 1790, is also classified by the International Association of Volcanology and Chemistry as an active volcano."

"Oh."

"The problem the volcanologists have here is that written history in other places in the world dates back five to six thousand years. In Hawaii we have had writing for only a few hundred. Since Contact in 1778. Well, actually, now we know about a hundred years earlier, but those men did not return and aside from that map, which no one can account for, made no record of their visit. These may all be active volcanoes. They might awaken at any moment. It would not surprise me to see Diamond Head spewing lava someday."

I looked out the window at the peak of the old cone. It would sure drop the property values in Waikiki.

"In that lava desert we found ancient workers' camps. Large numbers of men had lived and worked along that coast at least a decade. But there was no other record or mention in contemporary sources as to the reason.

"I searched the stone records, the petroglyphs, and found something that fascinated me. A large lava boulder had been upended, turned over so that the flat side was face down. The exposed bottom had been turned over a few hundred years before, but still looked as if it had been exposed only yesterday. It was obvious what had occurred.

"At the edge of the flat surface I found etching in the rock, difficult to make out. It disappeared under the boulder so I knew that the rock had been purposely turned over, as if someone had attempted to hide the petroglyph. We brought in heavy equipment and turned it.

"At first it was disappointing. Someone had etched a detailed petroglyph of what appeared to be a maze on the flat side of the rock. The etching was faded, but not weathered by a thousand years in the elements, so we photographed it and brought it back with computer enhancement and studied it. Suddenly it hit me. It was a tomb. The petroglyph was a blueprint of a tomb that the workers were either constructing or repairing." She looked at me expectantly.

"Go on," I said.

"But where was it? We could see no natural structures that

resembled the blueprint, as we came to call it. We hired aerial photographs in black-and-white that showed us nothing. Then we had some done in color.

"The color photograph also showed the reef and the underwater rock formations in the shallow waters off the coast. Something about the blueprint matched the formations about half a kilometer from the campsite.

"The tomb was in the water!"

"It was underwater?"

"The island is dynamic. This part of the coast was above water six or seven hundred years ago. The island of Hawaii is so heavy that it sinks into the earth's mantle as the volcano grows higher. It's the largest mountain on earth, and it can't get any bigger. It has reached critical mass for equilibrium. As it grows, it also sinks. Someone had built a tomb in the rocks along the coast back when the old lava tube, a cave formed by flowing lava, had been above the surface, or possibly in the shallow surfline. Two hundred years ago it would have been in even shallower water but would have been at least partially submerged. That's why I think repairing. I think this was a forgotten tomb or hiding place in the early nineteenth century, when Kamehameha died. That he knew about it was almost certain. He knew most of this coastline. This was his home as a young man.

"We began diving the next day, using SCUBA and lights. It took us a month of searching, but we found it.

"We found a lava tube predating the 1802 Hualalai event, with its shallow side almost completely obscured by lava and coral. The deeper side, however, was open. We swam into the tube and found a chamber cut from the rock. Inside the chamber was a stone maze. At the end of the maze was the burial chamber. That was where we found the remains of the large man and the Spanish treasure."

"That's impossible."

She smiled tiredly. "It would seem that it was possible. And that is why no one has found it until now. Nobody had considered the fact that the island is constantly sinking. What was possible two hundred years ago would not be possible now, given their technology. We had to slip out of our paradigm."

"When did he do this?"

"I can only speculate, but I feel that the Hualalai eruption gave him the idea. There's no record of it, so this is strictly guess-work, but I think that he chose the site, thinking that he would eventually be buried by the lava. Of course, it never erupted again. If it had, we would never have found him."

"You know Pele, the goddess of fire," said Tutu Mae, speaking softly from the deep cushions in the chair."

"Of course," I said.

"Kamehameha and Pele had a close relationship. When he fought King Keoua for control of the Big Island in 1790, a large force of Keoua's warriors were marching from Hilo to Ka'u to attack Kamehameha. Madam Pele lives in Kilauea, you know. She protects those whom she loves and destroys those she dis-likes. Keoua's men were destroyed. The volcano erupted, throw-ing red-hot lava boulders high into the air. The explosions brought down Pele's fire onto the warriors and their women and children, wiping them out entirely."

Donna Wong nodded. "It is known that Pele loved Kame-hameha, and that he returned her love. So we think that the eruption of Hualalai provided him with the location of his tomb."

"He would rest with Pele."

"Yes."

"And the eruption of, when did you say it was?"

"Eighteen-oh-two."

"And the eruption of 1802 gave him the place."

"Yes. He saw it happen almost exactly between the place where he was born and where he had decided to die. He must have thought it would be a place where he could be laid to rest."

"So he prepared his tomb well in advance of its need."

Donna Wong nodded. "Just like the Egyptian Pharaohs."

Now I sat back in my chair, fascinated by the story. "So how do I come in? You've got your career ahead of you right there. You've made a discovery that will make you rich and famous."

"That's the point. I am not getting credit for it."

"There have been some threats," said Tutu Mae.

"There is a problem," said Kimo.

12

You don't have to shout," said Tutu Mae. "We can hear you, Kimo."

"I wasn't shouting."

"It sounded like it to me," said Tutu Mae.

"We have a problem," said Kimo, after taking three of four deep breaths. "Miss Wong . . . Donna . . . her adviser at the university is taking the credit for her work. In effect, it is theft, but I can't do anything about it because the act is a purely civil matter. That doesn't change the fact that it is theft. Theft of intellectual property is still theft. Her discovery is her property, and it is theft of her hard work and reputation."

"Does she have an attorney?"

"Yes. Woman named Tala Sufai. You might have heard about her. She won that case against the newspaper last year. She's handling the civil matter. There will be papers to serve, that kind of thing."

"Oh boy," I said.

"There's more."

"You said something about a threat?"

"The other problem is related, we think. And it may involve something criminal, which is where I come in."

"Is this the treasure? All that wealth suddenly coming to the surface?"

"Yes. And no. Remember that Donna does not plan to bring any of it to the surface. She plans to leave it there, honoring Kamehameha's last wishes. And honoring the bones. She is in the process of extensively photographing and cataloguing the contents. The number of artifacts is numerous. It would take years to do it right on dry land, and she doesn't have that luxury. She is taking great pains to avoid contact with the bones. She has studied what is near the bones, but not the bones themselves."

"If it is the king," I said.

Tutu Mae looked at me with that sharp glance of hers and for an instant I thought I was going to be chastised again, but then her features softened, and she nodded. "If it is the king."

"Do you know for sure or not?"

She looked at Donna Wong, and then back at me. "No," she said. "We do not know for sure."

Kimo said, "Wait a minute. That's a point, but it's not something you should worry about." He looked at Miss Wong. "Donna, why don't you tell Mr. Caine what has put you at odds with your adviser?"

"I will not reveal the location of the find," she said quietly. "I wish to keep it exactly as I found it. I do not wish for the find to be disturbed any more than I already have."

Now I understood the problem. Leaving the Hawaiian Holy Grail along with a king's ransom in treasure at the bottom of the sea was an act of self-denial that a few people could understand, let alone actualize. The archeological find and the Spanish treasure, along with their historical and sociological implications, would make her a rich woman, and a famous one. So she had principles. Strong ones. Something that was rare and precious these days. No wonder Tutu Mae had taken her on as a special case.

"What about the threats?"

"Her adviser disagrees with everything she wants to do," said Tutu Mae. "He wants to haul it all up, bring it to the university, hold a news conference, and tell the world what he found."

I looked at Donna. "Did he have anything to do with it?"

She shook her head. "He doesn't even know where it is. Otherwise he would have done it already."

"Does he know what you guess?"

"About Kamehameha?"

I nodded.

"I haven't told him this is a tomb."

My head swam. "You haven't told your faculty adviser? How can he advise you if you don't tell him what you're doing?"

"I never did trust him. He tried to get too close to me early on, and so I kept my distance. I have been working directly with Tutu Mae for help and advice, only telling him what was necessary to get a little funding from the university. It isn't much, and I've had to find a private investor who has given me some funds, enough to proceed."

"Does your private investor know?"

"No." She answered a little too fast for me to believe her.

"I recently learned about my adviser's plans to publish a paper about the treasure," she continued. "I gave him the early photographs and findings when I thought I needed university backing. Then I tried to publish an early paper on just the treasure this week and coincidentally sent my paper to the same publication where my adviser had sent his. The editor returned it with a scathing note."

"I thought he didn't know the location."

"He doesn't."

"Then how can he claim he found it if he doesn't know where it is?"

"He'll claim it is a work in progress on a secret site. The French did that with the Cosquer Cave. They published photographs and articles on the Neolithic cave paintings and engravings without revealing exactly where they had been discovered. They still guard its location as if it were a national secret." She reached into her folder and laid out photographs of a huge assortment of silver and golden artifacts, jumbled together in what looked like a cave. Overlying the artifacts were red and white striped cables laid out in a grid, each object numbered with a white tag.

"Wow," I said.

"He sent his article in more than three months ago. It's set for publication. Since he is senior, and I am so late with the initial paper, my authorship is suspect."

"Let me get this straight," I said, mulling the implications. "This guy wants to drag it all up and put it in some museum. But he can't because you won't tell him where it is. And so he's publishing a paper, using your work, so he alone can claim the credit for the discovery. You could easily disprove his claims but you won't because you would have to reveal the location of the tomb, and you don't want to do that because you haven't told anyone that it's a tomb. And you haven't told anyone about the bones because you think it is Kamehameha. Do I have that right?"

She nodded.

"And what about the threats?"

Kimo stirred again. "Have you ever heard of Aha Kuka O Na Kanaka?"

"Hawaiian rights group. A little on the militant side. They have a grand scheme, if I remember it right. They went to give Hawaii back to the Hawaiians?"

Kimo said, "We suspect the group has a striking arm called 'Silversword.' We've had some bombs recently, some terrorist incidents."

"Somebody did a drive-by on the main gate at Pearl."

He nodded. "Same people, we believe. So far they haven't killed anybody, but it's only a matter of time."

"So arrest them."

"Arrest who?" He held up his hands. "I'd love to. Just point me in the right direction."

"Silversword. That's a plant."

Tutu Mae said, "Hina hina. It only grew here in Hawaii, and used to cover the slopes of Haleakala. It grew so thickly that the mountain looked as if it were sheathed in silver in the early morning light."

"It grew?"

"There are still some surviving specimens high up near the rim, but the plant is nearly extinct, the victim of an alien ant."

I raised my eyebrows.

"The flower depends upon a native bee for pollination. The bee has almost been wiped out because it lives underground. It had no natural enemy, so it lived where it pleased. When the ant was introduced to Hawaii at the end of the nineteenth century, it began invading and killing the queen in its ground nest, carrying off the larvae. The bee could not adapt quickly enough. With the bee gone, the plant soon followed. Now it only grows where the ant has yet to travel. In a few more years both the hina hina and the bee will be gone forever."

Kimo nodded. "The group calls itself Silversword because they see themselves as threatened with extinction, just like the plant."

"So they're a bunch of dreamers," I said. "Who's going to give this place back to the monarchy?"

I saw Tutu Mae's face when I said that and had one of those oh-no moments when I wished I could have called my words back. Her expression went from hurt to rage and back to hurt, and finally settled on resignation, all in the space of an instant.

"You truly do not understand, John Caine," she said softly, the words striking like a hammer covered in velvet. "Maybe you are not mature enough for this task. Maybe you should go back to live on the mainland where you came from and leave us here."

"I am truly sorry, I—"

"You do not know the pain that your words have caused me." She looked at Kimo. "I would like to leave this person now. I must go home for my afternoon nap."

Kimo looked sadly at her. "Now Tutu Mae, why don't you let him apologize? He just said what he said without thinking."

"He said it without thinking. That's right. He has no feeling for what we have suffered."

Kimo turned to me, his brown eyes as warm and gentle as I'd ever seen them. And filled with hurt. "John," he said, his voice tender. "You don't seem to recall that Hawaii belonged to the

Hawaiians for over a thousand years. Some say two thousand. Some do not know how far back we go. We do know that a thousand years ago the great canoes stopped sailing between Tahiti and Hawai'i, and we were isolated until the Europeans came. Everyone seems to have forgotten that we managed to do just fine here without England, without the United States, without Russia, or France, or any of those other nations who lusted after Hawai'i. Because of Sanford Dole and his cronies we lost our queen, we lost our sovereignty, and we became an unwilling colony of the United States, even though we are the thousands of miles away."

Kimo paused and looked at me, as if expecting some sort of a response. I nodded.

"We are a colony, John. We know it. Washington knows it. We exist for one thing, and it isn't tourism. We exist here because of Pearl Harbor. We're an outpost, protecting the western coast of the United States's mainland."

"But I thought you upheld the laws."

"I do uphold the law, John. But don't take it for granted that I'm just another one of your haole friends who can make fun of the mokes and the kanakas and then push on with the day."

"I am truly sorry," I said. "I understand what you are all saying. Please forgive me for making such a reckless statement."

"I accept your apology, Mr. Caine," said Tutu Mae, her eyes still blazing. "But I would like to conclude this interview while the day is still young." She smiled from behind her thick glasses. It wasn't a warm smile. It was just her way of letting me know that I got away with my impolitic statement this one time, and that I would have to watch myself from this point forward.

"You said there were threats?" I said, trying to get back to the point.

Kimo nodded. "Silversword somehow knows something about Donna's discovery. They have claimed the treasure under the Antiquities Repatriation Act. They demand exclusive access to the artifacts."

"They don't know anything about the remains?"

"Aside from Donna's sisters, who have been the only ones to

dive with her on the site, and those of us in this room, no one knows anything about the bones."

"So they're after the treasure."

"One appraisal, a rough one, exceeded one hundred eighty million dollars in gold, silver, and jewels. It could be more."

"And you want to leave it on the bottom of the ocean."

"It was his final wish," said Miss Wong.

"How do they know about it?"

"We believe that Silversword is based at the university. My adviser may have had them as his students."

"So you might even know them?"

She nodded. "But I wouldn't know them as members of any group. I keep to myself. I don't pay attention to other students."

"How have they threatened you?"

"They will take action if they are not given access to the site."

I looked at Kimo. "Do you believe them?"

"It seems difficult. They are mere children."

"Who shot up Pearl Harbor's main gate and bombed a couple of tourist sites."

He shrugged. "We don't know that they did that."

"Yes you do."

He shrugged again. "They left leaflets."

I nodded. "So was Miss Wong threatened personally?"

"Only by extension. This genius put himself into the spotlight with his article. They do not know that she exists. She is not in danger. Not yet."

"He have a name, this talkative, lying thief? Something besides stupid and greedy?"

"Howard Hayes. With an *e*," said Kimo.

"Haole?"

"Like yourself, Mr. Caine."

"So what do you want me to do? Exactly?"

"We want you to look into Professor Hayes's past and find out the identity of the other students he has wrongfully cheated. If he will do it once, he will do it many times. If you look into his past you will find a pattern. A thief will continue to steal as long as he can get away with it. We are looking at getting him removed. It is difficult with tenure. But it is not impossible. This time the stakes are too important, and we know the student in question. We know that she did the work on her own because Tutu Mae was the one she confided in, the one who confirmed her suspicions, who talked over the clues with her as she carefully proceeded."

"Only her sisters know about this?"

"They're the ones who helped her in the field."

Keep it in the family. Very Chinese. Trust only family.

"And in the meantime?"

"You can serve the papers on him. There will be an injunction against publication some time within the next ten days."

"Why me?"

Tutu Mae looked around the suite, the crystal chandeliers catching rays from the bright sun pouring in through open windows, the sound of the Waikiki surf a mellow background. "We heard you were sick," she said. "We didn't want you to get depressed."

Kimo smiled. "You had some time on your hands. This looked like a project that you could do without straining yourself." He looked at my sandy feet, dry now, but evidence of my inability to stay in the sick bed. "And it won't get in the way of your beach walking."

"All right," I said. "The guy's a college professor? I'll look into his background. If he's anything like you described him I'm sure there are people out there who will be happy to talk about him."

"What will you charge for your time?"

Suddenly the entry door opened and Felix walked in.

Donna Wong leaned forward and covered the photographs, gathering them into a stack and shoving them back into her briefcase.

"Sorry," said Felix. "I didn't mean to interrupt."

"We're done here," I said to him, knowing he was harmless to Donna Wong and her precious treasure. "I'll charge dinner. A big dinner. At your place, Kimo, complete with the pig." Kimo and Neolani gave a luau that was difficult to forget.

He nodded. "Can do. Whenever you say."

"I'm moving back onto the boat in a few days. I should have what you need by then. It will be good to get out of here."

Kimo smiled, looking around the suite. "Yeah. It's kind of depressing. This isn't your style, Caine."

"What is my style?"

He shrugged off the answer, but I knew it as well as he did.

"I know this isn't your kind of case, either, but it's a start."

"Hey, the guy's a university professor. He shouldn't be any threat. And I've been injured. I've got to start on the easy ones and work up from there."

The telephone rang while I was taking the sun on the lanai. I lay there dozing, my eyes half-closed against a tropical sun. I was content on my perch overlooking the deep green lawn and the white sandy beach with Diamond Head off to my left, looking exactly as it had looked for a hundred thousand years. The Pacific was there, too, not so much a part of the background as it was the dominant feature of existence. The silvery blue surface stretched all the way to the ends of the earth in one vast plain, meeting the distant horizon in a sharply defined, but slightly curved line, one blue blending into another, the sky a pale reflection of the sea.

I heard one of the girls inside running across the hardwood floor, flying to the phone to answer it.

"Wei?" She answered in the Hong Kong fashion. She listened intently, and then began screaming something in Mandarin to the other girls. Whatever she said was very loud and very fast and very Chinese.

"Angelica!"

I understood that part.

"Angelica!"

My head nurse answered from the other room, and now I could hear her short, choppy footsteps as her shoes rang against the oak. The one who had answered said something earnestly and quietly to Angelica, and she spoke into the telephone, her voice and manner bespeaking great respect. She spoke for a short time, and then replaced the handset.

"Chawlie called," I told her when she stepped out onto the lanai.

"How you know?"

"I'm a detective."

"He is coming. He wants to see you. Now."

"Where is he?"

"In the car. He will be here soon."

Girls were running all over the suite, speaking in a high-pitched, nervous chatter, picking up imaginary debris and straightening furniture and pillows that were, by my reckoning, pristine.

"Should I dress?"

"You look fine." She regarded me for a moment. "Put on a shirt."

"I can do that," I said, sitting up in the lounge chair and reaching for my tee shirt. "He say what he wanted?"

"He wants to see you. Something has happened."

That didn't sound good, but I could wait for bad news. I shaded my eyes and gazed across the sand to the perfect waves of Waikiki. Only a few people were riding them, probably because they were so small. When the weather is fine this side of the island doesn't get much surf. Today the Pacific Ocean was almost a lake.

"Where's Felix?"

"In his room."

Angel's eyes widened. "I thought he was gone. He told me he didn't want him here." She put her hand to her mouth and ran to Felix's room.

I sat back and waited. I was getting good at waiting. It could easily become my new occupation.

Someone knocked on the door. One of the girls went to answer it, and Daniel came through and looked through the French doors at my lounge chair. I smiled and waved. He nodded and disappeared.

Felix's voice, sounding apologetic, said something I couldn't quite catch. Daniel answered him. I heard a door open and close, and Daniel said something harsh and vicious. Angel apologized. The door opened and closed again, and then I heard nothing more. I waited, doing what I was good at.

Ten minutes later Daniel reappeared and beckoned me into the cool interior of the living room.

Chawlie sat in an armchair, his hands in his lap. Daniel and another Chinese man I recognized, but whose name escaped me, flanked him, sitting in straight-backed chairs. The old man smiled when he saw me.

"John Caine. You're looking better."

"Feel a little better, too. Your nurses are doing wonders for me."

"That is good. Have some bad news for you. Better sit down."

I did, taking a seat in the big silk sofa across from him.

"I talk with haole lawyer in San Francisco. Police there are not going to leave this alone. They want to charge you with murder."

I felt hollow inside. We had been almost expecting this, but it shocked me to actually hear the words. I struggled to keep calm and to listen. What Chawlie had to say would be important.

"The grand jury is looking at it right now. May be some time before they do it, but it looks as if they will indict you."

"And what do we do?"

"What do you want?"

"What I want doesn't have any meaning in this," I said. What I wanted was for all this to go away. I wanted to be left alone. I didn't want some group of faceless, nameless people who had never heard of me to be presented with a body of evidence that demonstrated that I was criminally responsible for the death of one Jackie Chang, an innocent bystander in a gangland shooting on the streets of San Francisco.

"Are you feeling better?"

"I'm getting there. Tomorrow they're removing the drains."

"You going to the hospital?"

"Yes."

He sat still and looked at me.

"Chawlie, I'd like to go home."

"Of course."

"This has been wonderful, but I think I need to be alone."

"Nurses not doing good things for you?"

"They're terrific, but without the drains I think I'll be fine without them."

"Tomorrow, after the hospital, you come back here, spend the night. If you are feeling well after a night here, you go home the next day. How's that?"

"That's fair," I said.

"I can get nurses to come visit you after you move back onto the boat."

"That won't be necessary."

"But they will be available, if you need nursing," he said, deadpan. "If you go to prison you won't see a woman for a long time."

"Thank you, Chawlie. I hadn't thought of that."

"But do not worry, John Caine. Chawlie will take care of everything."

"Even then?"

He looked at me and shook his head. "Especially then."

"So tomorrow?"

"Day after. You stay two more nights. You will not feel like going anyplace after operation."

He had a point.

"Okay," I said. "Day after tomorrow."

Chawlie smiled warmly, and I knew that I'd pleased him. He was a very odd old duck, and his attentiveness to my needs was touching, but what I needed now was time alone, on my boat, in my own bolt-hole, where I could be with my thoughts and where I could figure what I would do with the time remaining.

If Chawlie's information was correct, the next several months would be more than challenging.

"How is Felix?" asked Chawlie.

"Bored. He'd like to go home." I noticed that Daniel didn't want Felix around when Chawlie came by.

Chawlie nodded. "We need him for special project. Daniel will contact him."

"I'll tell him."

Chawlie raised his hand. "No need. Daniel can do it."

I understood. This was another level of Chawlie's schemes. I was tired of the gaming, but then I rarely tolerated it.

Olympia called to me from her mooring at Pearl Harbor. I had the urge to go to her, to loosen her lines, and sail to some other country. Get all my cash from Chawlie's vault and sail to whatever port would take me. I had the urge to flee the country, to become a fugitive. I knew I would never do it, but underneath the urge was the terror of enforced confinement and the horrors of prison. It wasn't right that they would do that to me. Why was this woman pursuing me? Why did she make it her business to see that someone paid for the death of that poor old Chinese grand-mother?

There were no answers. There would be no answers. I knew that I would stand and face the charges when they came, and that Chawlie would stand by me the whole way, using his power and his wealth to whatever advantage it would lend me.

I would remain here, with my happy little nurses, and I would go home in two more days, after the doctors had removed my surgical drains.

A couple more nights in this mink-lined prison and I'd be home.

14

H ow does it feel to be home?"

I sat propped against cushions at *Olympia's* aft deck railing, relaxing in the gentle warmth of the afternoon sun. As plush as the Royal Hawaiian had been it felt damned good to be home at last.

"I assume the question's rhetorical?"

"Oh, yeah," Felix said.

"Then you already know the answer." I stretched and turned my face so the sun could baste me. Doctors tell us we can get too much sunshine for our own good, that sunburn gives us basal cell carcinoma, melanoma and other horrors. But at the same time they're forced to admit that people commit suicide in countries where the sun goes dark for months at a time. But with my sun-lined old rugged hide, I don't worry about too much sun. And right now it felt good to feel the rays gently touching my face.

"How's the house guest?"

"David? He's fine. What a bundle of energy."

"That's something, coming from you."

"He loves this place. He's diving the *Mahi* tomorrow."

I smiled, remembering that's where I had met the young man in the first place. "He's been there before. He wants to meet Bowser?"

Felix nodded. "He likes that eel." Bowser is a twelve-foot

moray that lives in a hole in the bow of the old wreck, about a hundred feet down off the Waianae Coast of Oahu. He's different from most sea monsters you'd ever meet. This one eats out of your hand and loves to be petted vigorously behind the ears, or what passes for ears on an eel, just the way you would pet a faithful retriever. That's why he's called Bowser. He reminds you of a big old dog. Except he's green and slimy and he has huge orange eyes and nightmare fangs.

"You going along?"

Felix nodded. "I'd like to see this thing."

"Be careful."

"He told me about how you saved his butt."

"I don't think he'll do that again."

Felix shook his head. "I'll guarantee it. He said he had never been so scared in his life. And then you came and got him when he had all but given up hope."

"I just did that to meet his mother."

"She's one nice-looking lady."

"I didn't think you'd notice."

"Beauty is truth and truth is beauty."

"Keats?"

"I forget."

"I thought you were a literature student."

"Was. Forgot it all now." He shifted his haunches and peered across bright water toward Ford Island. "I'd like to go out there to see the *Missouri* and the *Arizona*. And the one on the other side, the *Utah*? All that happened here so many years ago. It's like, it's so peaceful here it just seems impossible."

"Yeah. I've had those same thoughts. Why don't you and David go out there?"

"He, ah, doesn't want to spend too much time with me."

"Oh. I thought you guys were getting along." That wasn't true. I don't know why I said it. From the beginning they had entered into some kind of cosmic competition. I'd seen the beginning of something even more serious.

"I didn't do anything to make him shy. Somebody told him

that I was gay and now he acts like he's uncomfortable around me."

"I thought all you kids were nonjudgmental these days."

"Nonjudgmental is different from uncomfortable. I respect him for it. David's a nice kid. For a kid. He's very smart, and he's very keen on Hawaii, and he thinks the world of you. I try not to violate his space much. You know what I mean?"

"I don't know much about you, Felix. You got a steady, a friend?"

"A friend?"

"A boyfriend."

"Someone sensitive would call such a being a lover."

"Okay, you got a lover?"

"See? Even you get squeamish about it. No. Not at the moment. I used to, but he's gone."

"It happens." From the way he said it I wasn't sure if gone meant "gone," or "dead." I decided that if he were dead, Felix would have said so. I decided that I'd play it light. I was enjoying my time at home and didn't want to do or say anything that would drag it down.

"Nothing lasts forever, is that what you're trying to say?"

"Nothing does."

"I'll go along with that. We were very happy until he died."

"I'm sorry. I thought . . . never mind. Was it AIDS?"

He shook his head. "Funny, but that's the first thing you'd think of, isn't it? A young man in the prime of his life? Why else would he die? Of course you'd think it was AIDS because he was gay. No, it was an accident."

"Terrible."

Felix nodded, his eyes fixed on a place far away from the Rainbow Marina.

"I'm sorry. I feel as if I intruded."

"No, you didn't. I'm a little sensitive about it. But I'll get over it eventually. I'll grow cold and calloused, and I can forget him, given enough time."

"Wow."

"Sorry, John. I get carried away."

"Can you hand over my pack?"

He reached behind him and handed over my new North Face climber's pack where I kept my cellular telephone. Kimo and Tutu Mae had given me an assignment to track down former students of Professor Hayes. I had to talk to some of them by then. Talking to them I didn't mind, but finding them was the challenge.

Fortunately I knew a young man who knew everything there was to know about computers and the Internet. I knew about finding people. If he could locate the names of the students I'd do the digging and plowing. The best thing about the set-up was that I could complete my investigation without ever leaving the deck of the *Olympia*.

I punched in the numbers for Petersoft, gave my name to the receptionist, and was put right through to the office of the president.

"Adrian here."

"John Caine calling."

"How are you doing? Are you here in town?"

"I'm sitting on the aft deck of *Olympia*, floating here in Pearl Harbor, catching some rays. There's a rainbow over the Ko'olaus, but not a cloud in the sky over my head."

"Break some more eggs, will you? Why'd you have to tell me that? I haven't seen the sun in three weeks."

"Busy?"

"Like you wouldn't believe."

"How's my stock?"

"Solid, man. What can I do for you?"

"Can you run a search for graduate students who have had a certain professor? You'll have to go back to every school this man taught, and then run a cross-check on—"

"I know how to do it. Do you have the schools? Or do I have to check every institution in the country?"

"I've got the schools." Tala had supplied the professor's bio and résumé. It covered every institution where the man taught.

"That's easy. When do you want it?"

"How soon can you run it?"

"This evening soon enough? I've got a meeting in a few minutes. A new product line. Too bad you're not here. The geniuses in R&D have really come up with something."

"Will my stock go up?"

"Like a skyrocket."

"Keep up the good work, Adrian."

"So this evening is okay?"

"This evening is terrific." I could start my phone calls this afternoon.

"Give me the name of the schools and the professor. If you have the years it would make it simpler, but I really don't need it."

"I've got everything." I read him the list of schools and the years in question and spelled the professor's name slowly, making Adrian repeat it twice. No sense running the search more than once.

"I'll tell Claire you called. Are you going to her wedding?"

"I wasn't invited."

"Do you want me to tell Claire that you called?"

"It's okay with me. Who is she marrying?"

"You don't know him. I don't think. He's her new lawyer. This one's a good one. I think."

If I knew Claire, he would have to be a guy who would obediently march to her tune. She would keep him on a short leash. But I didn't say any of that to Adrian. He knew it better than I did.

"She ever come in anymore?"

"Hardly ever. No reason to. I'm running the store."

"Don't be so modest."

"Yeah, well." There was a moment of silence, an uncomfortable lapse when we both ran out of things to say. "Can I e-mail that to you?" he asked, finally.

"Sure. You've got my address?"

"I set up the account."

"Oh." I had forgotten that. Adrian had also given me my first lesson in computers. I used my laptop for many things now, searching for obscure information that could never have been found without the Net. I would not have had the time. "I appreciate this, Adrian."

"My pleasure, John. If you'll excuse me."

"Sure. Take care."

"Call me anytime."

We both hung up.

"He'll have that list by this evening," I told Felix.

"What?" He leaned against his forearms, watching a pale sun slowly descend over Ford Island. The vog, or volcanic smog, was thick with the sulfur from Kileaua, the young volcano going through a particularly active phase. Spectacular sunsets were the result of all that natural pollution. But could it be pollution if it was natural?

"Nothing. Why don't you take some time off and go to Waikiki tonight? I'll be all right. Busy, in fact. I'm not going anywhere."

"You noticed?"

"Noticed what?"

"That I'm restless?"

"Oh, yeah."

"Only if you're sure you're okay."

"I'm fine."

"I'm supposed to be your shadow."

"Just don't get in trouble."

"No trouble. Not me. Not Felix." He smiled a grim little smile and got up and climbed down the ladder to the lounge, a young man living his life a day at a time, without roots, without a partner, and without a feeling of where his life should be going. In many ways he reminded me of me.

He reminded me of me except he was much, much younger. A man my age should have grown out of this by now, should have settled down decades ago, should have had children, should be concerned for their college education, all of it. Somehow I had missed all that, the American dream. Now I was incapable of it. It would be laughable to try. While I had been otherwise occupied the chances had flown by.

I couldn't be happier.

I waited in the cockpit until Felix returned, dressed for the city. He said nothing, but held up the Jeep's keys. I nodded as he leaped over the side and jogged up to the parking lot of the Marina Restaurant, happy once again to be on his own.

When he was gone I felt a heaviness pass. I no longer needed a companion or a bodyguard, or whatever the hell he was. Chawlie's gift now weighed on me. I would tell him the next time I saw him. I would thank him profusely, and I would tell him that I was feeling fairly good. I could even jog a little. I could not swim until all the wounds and the incisions completely healed, but I generally felt okay. And I would then ask Chawlie to send the boy home. Have him join the little nurses as a pleasant part of my life that was no more.

More than ever I was now a solitary man.

I headed down the ladder to the lounge to fire up my new computer and see if I had any e-mail.

I had an assignment. It wasn't much of one, but it was something. It would keep my mind busy for a few days.

Just what I needed.

15

True to his word, Adrian e-mailed me the list by three o'clock Hawaii time, early evening California time. When I downloaded and printed the document I found a stack of thirty-two single-spaced pages in the Deskjet and another search on my plate. When I had asked Adrian to run a search I had neglected to ask him to update the former students' current addresses. I attacked the list and had updated phone numbers for half of the first page by dinnertime. I brewed myself a pot of Blue Mountain, made a tall sandwich of fresh turkey, pepper cheese and jalapeños, and perfected my search techniques. By the time Felix came wandering in at two in the morning I had covered five pages.

"Still up? You waiting for me?" Felix yawned and covered his mouth with the back of his sleeve. His clothes smelled of smoke.

"I can make you some hot cocoa."

Felix put his crossed fingers in front of him and made a face. "No. Thank. You."

"You have fun?"

"Danced. Danced again. Danced some more."

"Your legs must be tired."

"You really want to know the details?"

"Not really."

"I drank grapefruit juice all night."

"Better eat some yogurt. Balance out all that acid."

"Thanks, Mom." He looked over my shoulder at the screen. "What are you doing?"

"Detecting."

"The easy way."

"Doesn't seem so easy." I explained what I was doing. He listened intently, then had some suggestions. I tried his ideas and found that he had cut my search time by a factor of five.

"Leave it to you Xers," I said, logging off and shutting down.

"This help?"

"A lot. Thanks."

"No problem," he said, yawning. "Where's David?"

"Asleep. Long time. He went to the movies, then came home and crashed."

"He no help?"

"I didn't think to ask."

"He's a scholar. And a propeller-head Xer. Why not?"

I shrugged. "Got a brain freeze, I guess." Truthfully, I had hardly noticed the young man when he returned, so absorbed was I in my task.

"You're tired. Go to bed." Felix shook a finger at me.

I smiled, "Thanks, Mom."

I went to my stateroom, undressed, showered carefully, mindful of keeping water away from my wounds, and crawled under the percale. I lay on my back, staring at the bulkhead above, my mind energized by its efforts, refusing to shut down.

It was a daunting task I had started. I could see hundreds of hours expended just to find the single lead. And I didn't know what I looked for. I only had an idea that this Hayes who would steal one student's work would have done it before. He would have been successful. So I looked for a bitter or angry scholar, one who would remember the professor.

There was an unspecified time in which to accomplish the task, too. Kimo said he would call when Tutu Mae secured the appointment, but he didn't know when.

I hoped I had a month. But then I didn't. The thought of spending a month in the communications cabin, on the phone in front of a computer screen did not thrill me.

But it was the job I had agreed to do, and it kept me busy. On my *okole*, and indoors, wasting the beautiful summer weather, but busy.

I turned over and buried my face in the pillow, trying to sleep, trying not to think, reaching for oblivion.

"They're coming!"

"They're in the wire!"

"In the wire!"

"The wire!"

"We're overrun!"

The dream again. All the horror again, the shots, the blood, the killing.

A man carrying a long rifle with a sword-like bayonet comes running at me. I turn to face him.

Only a few feet away, the sharp steel point lunges at my chest.

I pull the trigger.

It snaps on an empty chamber.

I look up into the man's face.

He stares back at me, his almond eyes round with hatred.

I sat up in the darkness, my chest heaving, my heart pounding. Somewhere off in the distance I heard the sound of a car radio playing rap, the angry bass sounds dwindling until they no longer intruded.

"Shit," I muttered, unsure if I had actually screamed the scream I had remembered in the dream. When nothing stirred I lay back and concentrated on finding my center.

A memory of a particularly bad day, the dream marked the moment when my terror went past the stage where it meant anything to me anymore. I was never again frightened of death. It had come to visit and had gone away, but it had left its imprint on my psyche.

Weak as I was, I found no fear in me. Wounds heal. Bodies mend. There were few predators who walked the earth that could make me bend. I would not allow myself to be frightened by what lay before me. Nothing the state could do, and nothing the denizens of any prison could do, could break me.

Nice try. Good pep talk.

Now all I had to do was believe it.

I turned over and allowed the gentle rocking of the hull to lull me back to sleep, a stranger in an even stranger land.

Howard Hayes was a big man with a wheatshock of thick white hair that stood straight up from the top of his head and then fled in every direction. Costumed in dark brown tweeds and a red bow tie in his harshly air-conditioned office, he looked the part of the university professor so well I knew it had to be calculated. Nobody ever wore tweed in Hawaii. Not even the missionaries.

He also wore a superior, knowing smile as he ushered us into his office, a comfortable dark cave at the top floor of the faculty building, an office with heavy oak furniture that might have fit at Cambridge. There weren't enough chairs, so Kimo and I stood against the back wall, leaving the seats for Donna and Tutu Mae and Tala Sufai, Donna's attorney. Tala was a big Samoan woman, almost as big as Kimo, and nearly as strong. And maybe smarter than anybody in the room except Tutu Mae.

"Would you care for coffee?" asked Hayes pleasantly, as if he had no idea why we had suddenly descended upon him.

"No." Tutu Mae's answer was abrupt.

"How about the others?"

"Sit down," she said. "We're here to talk, not make house."

Hayes raised his eyebrows and looked at Kimo and me, as if expecting a rational explanation from the males in the group. Kimo and I stared back. Hayes's eyebrows, so bushy and so clearly intellectual I wondered if he'd had implants, worked up and down his forehead as if he thought great thoughts, then he sadly stared down at his desk for a moment and sat down heavily behind it.

His chair creaked under the weight of all that ponderous consideration.

"We are here because of the situation that has developed between you and Ms. Wong." Tala Sufai spoke first, her demeanor crisp, letting him know we were here on serious business, as if Donna Wong and her entourage had not already telegraphed the intent.

Hayes picked up a pair of reading glasses and fixed them to the bridge of his nose. "A situation? Miss Wong is my student."

"You are the adviser for her doctoral, excuse me, her *double* doctoral degree."

"That is correct."

"She has made a discovery, an important discovery, that you seem to have taken as your own."

He looked at Donna, those eyebrows raised nearly to his hairline. "Miss Wong, what have you told these people?"

"Do you know who I am?" Tutu Mae said.

"Of course." Hayes became cautious. He knew how much Tutu Mae meant to the university. And how much power she actually wielded. Living legends have a way of getting what they wanted. Hayes must have known that because he became instantly wary.

"Ms. Wong has been working with me since before the beginning. I have been helpful to her in many ways. She confided in me before she told you about the find."

Hayes smiled thinly.

"Now you seem to have forgotten about her contributions. We understand that you intend to publish a paper about the discovery."

"Now wait a minute—"

"Let me finish. You did not discover the site, Donna did. You did not do the primary research, Donna did. You merely advised her, although, if one were to look into it one would find that you did not advise her as much as I did. You did agree, however, to keep this discovery secret. And now, from what we hear, you intend to publish Donna's findings without regard to that promise, and without proper attribution to the actual discoverer."

"I assure you—"

"I'm not done. Rumors are circulating among Hawaiian rights groups that you have found a tremendous amount of Spanish treasure here in the Islands. That alone would prove contact prior to Cook and would make the discoverer famous. Donna has not told anyone. Her sisters, who are the only other people in the world who know the facts, have not said anything. That leaves you. And we understand that you intend to publish the findings. And that you would be the sole recipient of the honors. Is that correct?"

"Madam, I am not accustomed to having people barge in on me in my office and make accusations—"

"We didn't barge, we had an appointment. And we're not making accusations that you haven't heard before." She looked at me.

I pulled out my notebook and quickly reviewed the notes I had taken over the past week, the results of interviews I had pulled up from the database that Adrian had run for me. With his help I had no trouble locating a number of previous victims of the professor's duplicity. "Do you know the name Jim Maurer?" I asked.

"No."

"You should remember him. Nice fellow. Quite bright. Some people say brilliant. One of your students about five years ago. He teaches now at the University of Virginia. He remembers you. Very well, in fact. He claims that you took one of his papers and published it as your own."

Hayes shook his head. "That's ridiculous!"

"How about Alan Patricio?"

"Never heard the name!"

"Funny, he made a stink here at the university some years back. Same charge. Something about Polynesian migration traced through DNA. Mr. Patricio's work made some huge gains in the theory, from what I've heard. And you published the paper as your own. There was a hearing."

"I was exonerated."

"So you do remember?"

"There was nothing to the charges. They were baseless!"

"But you recall his being your student. You once called him the best student you ever had?"

"Yes. He was brilliant, but he didn't know—"

"How about Barbara Perez? That name ring a bell?"

"Barbara who?"

"Another student of yours. She made the same claim when you taught at Washington State, working with Native Americans. You were her adviser at the time when she dug into ancient mud-flows along riverbed locations looking for evidence of tribal civilizations that were wiped out by volcanic eruptions. She made a wonderful discovery, an entire river village in situ. You published her work as your own. The resulting attention and publicity got you your place here in Hawaii at this university. You don't remember Barbara Perez?"

"I don't see how all this applies . . ." His voice trailed off and he placed his hands on his temples and squeezed his eyes shut, his eyebrows bunching up into one continuous line behind the narrow lenses of his reading glasses. We watched him in silence while he pulled himself together.

"Professor Hayes?" Donna Wong spoke, her voice quiet. When he did not respond she repeated his name.

He raised his head and looked at her. "Yes, Miss Wong?"

"We had an agreement."

He continued staring at her but said nothing.

"I don't care that much about my doctorate. Oh, that's not true. I do care, it's been a lot of work, but it's nothing compared to the importance of what is out there. You, yourself, said that this was the most important archeological find in the history of these islands. Tutu Mae agrees, and speaking as kupuna, she agreed to let me study it as long as it was not disturbed, and as long as the location is never revealed. If you publish the Spanish connection, people will not look beyond the existence of the treasure. They will not understand how important it is that the Spanish had been here before the British, or their possible influence on the Hawaiian culture. They will only seek the treasure. Nothing else will matter."

"You think I would do that?"

"That is what I have heard. Is it true? You know there is more work to be done at the site before we're finished. We have to go back. If you publish now, the site will be exposed. It will be a secret no longer. And we will not be able to finish our work."

Hayes leaned over and peered at her above his reading glasses. "Miss Wong," he said, his voice heavy with the pedantic tone of a man used to lecturing, "I told you we do not own the work. It does not belong to us any more than the earth belongs to us. This is science. We *must* publish. It is our duty to let the world know what we have found. We—"

"Professor Hayes."

He looked away from Donna, startled by Tala's interruption.

"We are prepared to file a lawsuit and get an injunction against whoever agrees to distribute your paper. We are prepared to take the case to the chancellor if you will not stop publication immediately. We will use Tutu Mae as Ms. Wong's expert witness, and use field notes against you. I believe that when we prove our case you will lose your tenure and your job."

The man smiled a nasty smile. "Threats," he said.

"I can assure you that these are not idle, Mr. Hayes. I have the papers ready to file. It all depends on your cooperation."

"Miss Wong, I demand that you remove yourself from this office at once. And take Miss whatever-her-name-is with you. I do not have to listen to this."

"You are making a grave mistake," said Tutu Mae.

"I think not. There will always be detractors from great discoveries, but it rightfully belongs to me and to me alone. I pointed the way for Miss Wong here. I did all of the primary research to enable her to make the final discovery. She built her case on what I had done years before she was even born."

"That's ridiculous—"

"The world only remembers the one who publishes, not the one who sues."

"Is that your final word?" Tala leaned forward across the desk toward the man. As big as she was, it looked like a threat. Hayes ignored her and looked directly at Donna.

"Now get out of here, Miss Wong, and take your attack dogs with you. I am not intimidated, and I shall do as my conscience dictates." He stood up.

"You have no right—"

"You are becoming tiresome, Miss," he said to Tala. "File whatever papers you wish to file. The dogs bark and the caravan moves on."

Tutu Mae used her cane to raise herself from the chair. The cane was a stout koa wood stick with a thick brass head. I hadn't ever noticed her having it before, but now, as she rose to a standing position, it looked like a weapon. When she was fully erect she grasped it in front of her, her gnarled fingers white around the smooth grain.

She stood rooted in place and stared at the professor for a long moment and then turned and marched from the office. Everyone but Donna followed Tutu Mae. I stood near the door where I could watch.

"You will keep the discovery of the treasure a secret," she asked. "That's earth-shaking, but we need a little more time."

"We may have our differences, Miss Wong, but I have no desire to allow thieves and plunderers to raid the site." Hayes' voice was gentle, as if he were speaking to a child. "You know that I could not reveal the location of the site. If you call off your dogs I shall mention you as a part of the team."

"If you would only wait a few months."

"It's out of my hands, Miss Wong. The paper has already gone to the printer, from what I understand."

She stared at him. "You don't know what you're doing."

"I know very well what I am doing."

"Then you don't know what kind of damage you're going to cause."

"It's a Pandora's box? Is that what you're saying?"

She nodded dumbly.

"Great discoveries always cause great upheavals. This island needs an upheaval."

"Revolution?"

"Thomas Jefferson would have been proud of you, dear. According to the great democrat we're way overdue for a revolution."

I couldn't stand this pedagogue any longer. "You think we need a war, Hayes?"

He looked up at me and raised one thick eyebrow in a manly sort of way. "They're always exhilarating, and they tend to clean out the cobwebs of a society. It's a purifying experience."

Kimo put a meaty hand on my shoulder. "Leave it, John."

Donna stood. "I'm going back to the site and I'm going to finish my work regardless of what you do, Professor Hayes."

"That's the spirit," he said, almost proudly. It seemed strange to me, her treating him with such respect, him still playing the doting pedant.

"I wish you wouldn't do this."

He smiled and looked as if he were about to pat the top of her head. "I wish I didn't have to. You've all got my motives wrong, Miss Wong. I'm not doing this for myself. There are larger issues afoot here."

She nodded, as if she understood.

Maybe she did.

"I wish you well, Miss Wong," he said, putting out his hand.

This time I was proud of her. She turned and walked out of the room, leaving him standing there with his hand out.

Standing by the door, I looked around his office, at the framed certificates on the wall, at the awards, the citations, the flotsam and jetsam of a lengthy and active academic career.

"You speak of war as an abstract," I told him. "You're about the right age. Did you serve in Vietnam?"

"It was an immoral war. And I, ah, was deferred because of my student status."

"So the only thing you know of war is what you read. It's all theoretical to you, people killing people. Is that it?"

"Do you have a point here, or is this just some macho posturing?"

"Someone once told me that the true test of an intellect is knowing when it is beyond its ability to understand the situation," I said. "I think you're right about there."

"Oh, please, Mr. Corn, or whatever your name is. That is very tired stuff. Some of my first-semester students can insult me better than that."

"You write it down when they do? Copy it and use it next semester?"

"Get the hell out of here!"

"Catch ya later, Hayes," I said, shooting him with my forefinger and following Donna Wong from the room.

17

I could just kill him!"

Donna Wong balled her fists and held them close to her chest, leaning against the elevator wall, her sudden explosion of passion surprising. In the professor's office she had been controlled and subdued. I thought that was how she handled it. Wrong again. I was glad I hadn't studied psychology.

"Somebody will, he keeps that up," I told her.

"I don't think that's necessary, Caine," said Kimo.

"Why can't he just leave it alone? Why does he have to spoil this?" She turned anguished eyes on me, but I had no answers for her. I had learned that people are what they are, and there's no explaining them or their behavior. It's as if we all have demons that drive us. God knows I had demons of my own.

Tutu Mae hugged Donna to her frail body as the young woman broke down and sobbed. "There, there," she said. "There, there. It will be all right."

"This is the greatest moment of my life. And he's stealing it."

Tala Sufai leaned in and hugged Tutu Mae and Donna, gathering up both of the tiny women in her huge arms. They stood united until the elevator reached the ground floor and the doors opened. A young man in tattered jeans and a bright red Aloha shirt tried to enter, but backed away when he saw the three women locked in an embrace inside the cab.

"I'll just find another one," he mumbled, disappearing down the corridor.

"Are you feeling better?" asked Tala.

"I'm okay."

"Then we'd better go to my office. I've got papers for you to sign."

I assisted Tutu Mae from the building into the sun-blasted Honolulu afternoon and helped her into the car. Kimo walked by my side, saying nothing until we reached the parking lot.

"Thank you, Caine," he said when we stood next to his Cherokee. "Your finding those students helped our case."

"I was happy to do it."

"You want to collect your fee tomorrow night? Come over about five."

I nodded.

"Julia and Karen will be delighted to see you."

I smiled. "She's getting bigger every day, isn't she?"

"Going to school now. Quite the scholar."

"I'll be there. Thanks, Kimo."

"John Caine!"

"Yes, Tutu Mae?"

"You did fine. Thank you."

"You're welcome."

"Are you fit?"

"Not quite, but getting there." The truth was that I had paid mightily for my beach run, and spent the next few days worrying about the interior appliances that I might have unnecessarily stressed, and wondering if I would have to make a trip to Tripler Hospital to have them replaced. Every wince, every twinge communicated the shadow of a greater pain that I finally concluded existed only inside of my imagination. I don't have much of an imagination, but pain is a great teacher, and I learned to enjoy my restfulness, thankful that I had to do the detective grunt work in front of my computers.

"When can you dive again?"

"Three, four weeks, maybe. Whenever all my incisions heal. And that other stuff."

"Could you take Donna to the site on your boat?"

"Of course."

"She lacks funding. Keeping this secret is daunting, but the university will have its demands to go with its funds."

"Golden rule," I said. "He who has It, makes Them."

She looked as if I had lost my mind. "She will need protection. She will need guidance, and she will need a larger dive platform than she had before. I think she will need your help."

"I've got two young men living aboard. Do you trust them?"

"Do you?"

I thought about it. Felix would be close-mouthed if it was in his interest. David seemed to think that Donna was the most interesting thing the Hawaiian Islands had to offer. I doubted either of them would cause a problem, and I knew that both young men would be intellectually curious about such an opportunity. "Yes."

"Then bring them. They can help."

"When will we go?"

"How soon can you be ready?"

"A few days."

"Then that's when you will go." She sat back in the back seat of Neolani's Cherokee and closed her eyes. I thought she had fallen asleep until she said, "I would love to dive there, too. Do you think I can?"

"You want to see the site?"

"Do you think an old lady can dive to the site?"

"I don't see why not."

"Then I want to do it before you seal it."

"Seal it?"

Donna looked over her shoulder from the front seat. "If Professor Hayes didn't agree to our request we knew we had to do something to protect the bones. We've decided to seal the entrance after we're done with our work. With explosives. That way nobody can enter it again."

Kimo shook his head. "No way I wanted to hear that."

"It's the only way, Kimo," said Tutu Mae. "Otherwise treasure seekers will find it. This is the only way to leave the bones in peace."

Donna reached across the seat and took Tutu Mae's hand. "You will see the king before we close up the cave."

"Thank you, child. John Caine, please bring your young friends to dinner tomorrow night. They could probably use a home-cooked meal. From what I've heard, you bachelors are out all night eating greasy restaurant food."

"I'll bring them. From what I remember of Kimo's barbecue we'll be eating greasy home-cooked food."

She laughed and closed the door.

I watched them drive away feeling more confused than before. Now I had agreed to turn *Olympia* into base support for the final dives on the tomb. What if it was the old king's final resting place? And I couldn't dive? I would love to see the tomb, the treasure, and the bones of Kamehameha.

I'd find a way. Buy a dry suit or just take the chance at infection, either way I'd see the king's tomb.

Felix waited at my Jeep, enjoying the sun, chomping a yellow apple and reading *The Lexus and the Olive Tree*. He had showed no interest in the meeting. There were too many people in that small office, anyway.

He nodded to me. "Gilbert called," he said between bites. "Chawlie wants to see you. I'm to drop you off and circle the block until you come out."

"Tough duty."

"I've seen worse. I've seen something that paid worse, at any rate."

"So you don't want the boy anymore. Is he a problem?" Chawlie and I occupied a corner window booth in his restaurant, overlooking Nu'uanu Street and the bronze statue of Sun Yat-sen. Someone kept the old Chinese leader's statue covered with fresh flower leis. I wondered if Chawlie had anything to do with that.

We were alone in the corner. The other tables were vacant, his waiters skillfully guiding new guests to other locations in the dining room.

Gilbert had met me at the door and taken me directly to the old man's table the moment I walked in. Chawlie's face was grim when I saw him, almost, but not quite, displaying rare emotion. He had been reading a book, which he quickly closed and put his arm over the cover to hide the title. Whatever he had to say to me was not good news. Maybe it was the air. Every person I knew of Chinese descent was having an emotional day today.

I began the conversation by observing that Felix had been terrific, but that I probably didn't need him any longer.

Chawlie countered with his question.

"It isn't that, Chawlie," I said. "He's fine. And he's been very helpful. I just don't think I need a bodyguard."

"So send him home."

"I will as soon as I'm back from the Big Island."

He raised his eyebrows.

"I'm going on a sail to the other islands. Just to get away. I'll take Felix with me and then send him home after that."

"Have him come see Daniel before he goes," said Chawlie. "I may have other work for him."

I nodded. "Thank you for all that you did for me, old friend."

"You saved Daniel. You saved Chawlie. How can we repay you?"

"You have."

"No. Not yet."

I waited, knowing there was more. He wouldn't send for me, saying it was important, unless it really was important. "What are you reading?"

Chawlie almost blushed. He pushed the little hardcover across the table.

"*Meditations*? I didn't know you read Marcus Aurelius."

"The man had it right. I am considering death. Can it be that there is nothing after this?"

"I think he was a doubter, but he covered his bases."

"You remember incorrectly, John Caine. He said that if there is no governor for this tempest, then just be content that you, yourself, have a ruling intelligence."

"Are you looking for peace, old friend?"

"It's not important. When will you leave for Hawaii?"

"Two days at the most."

"Leave tomorrow. Tell no one where you go."

"Why?"

"You have problems coming your way. San Francisco is sending your arrest warrant to Honolulu police. Your friend, Kimo, will be the one."

"I just spent an hour with him. He didn't mention anything."

"He doesn't know yet."

I nodded. Chawlie would have been informed long before anybody in the police hierarchy here.

"Is this the murder charge?"

He nodded. "California police crazy. They are angry because old woman was killed. You are the only one they can charge. Like some vacancy in the universe if nobody is charged with crime. So they charge you."

"When will the warrant arrive?"

"Two days. It's being held up in processing in San Francisco."

Had Chawlie arranged for that, as well? I was afraid to ask. "Can it be held up a week?"

"Impossible. Maybe another two or three days, that's all."

"That should be sufficient."

"You think Kimo will deny knowing where you are?"

"I don't think so."

"You think he would come after you?"

"Probably. If he thought it would do any good."

"Or he could pretend to search for you."

"I'll speak with him."

Chawlie's eyes widened at the thought of dealing with a policeman not of the clan, but he nodded. "You know the man. You deal with him. But if you are here in Honolulu in two or three days he won't be able to help you."

"I understand."

"I have a lawyer here who will represent you when the time comes."

I nodded. "Thank you. I know one I'd rather have."

He flitted away my thanks with a wave of his hand. "As you wish. That was a bad day, wasn't it?"

"For a lot of people."

"We can't put it behind us."

"No."

"Maybe they will let us, after this."

"I'd like to think so."

He looked sadly at me. "You hope, you mean. Hope is a childish emotion. You never grow up, do you?"

I shook my head. "Not if I can help it."

"You will in the coming months, I think. If you survive."

"What do you mean?"

"They want to imprison you for the killing of that woman, Mrs. Chang. Maybe even execute you. They wish to make an example. You are a warrior. This they do not understand. You have been through much in your life and you will go through much more in the next few months. Chawlie will be there, helping you with whatever you need. But you will be alone many times, and for a long time you will be in prison, whether you are found guilty or not. Chawlie has been told that prison is not a good place to be. Even an American prison."

I shuddered. Prison would not be easy if I were young and healthy.

"Chawlie is making a defense for you. It is not easy, the way that Henderson police person put the charges together. But Chawlie hired good California lawyers, and they will do a good job. It is best now if you go quickly. Find a cove where you will not be found for a few days. Rest and heal and wait until they come for you.

"When they come Chawlie will be ready with your lawyer to do whatever it will take to bring you home."

I sat mute, my head racing with emotions and questions. I

wasn't ready to be in jail. I was weak. I still had healing incisions in my back and my side. There were monsters in those places that would eat me alive in my current condition.

"I will do as you say," I said, after a few moments.

Chawlie nodded. "It will be a hard time."

"Yes."

"Chawlie is grateful, and remembers why you are in trouble."

"Thank you."

"While in jail you will be protected."

"Here or in San Francisco?"

"Wherever you go Chawlie will have people watch over you. You will not know who they are, but they will be there. Do not worry."

"I will not worry."

"Whatever you need, you just say to Daniel. He will be in San Francisco and will see you every day, if he can. Otherwise, as much as they will allow him. He is a lawyer and will work with your legal team."

"That will help."

"Also, he is a witness, so he cannot be your attorney."

"I didn't know he was an attorney."

"Now it is best if you go. Chawlie has much to do. And so do you."

I got up and left him sitting in the sunny corner of his restaurant, looking off into the distance at nothing in particular, his hand on *Meditations*. Perhaps he had read my future and didn't like what he saw. Perhaps he was contemplating his own mortality. Perhaps he knew more than he was willing to tell me, and that burden dragged on him.

I didn't worry what Chawlie thought. I had troubles enough of my own.

They say there's no rest for the wicked.

No wonder I felt so tired.

I wore a pale tan Aloha shirt with a muted pattern of white cranes, light tan gabardine trousers and a new pair of dress leather sandals to Kimo's party. I brought two bottles of wine, a La Crema Pinot Noir and a Kendall-Jackson Reserve Chardonnay. For Kimo I brought six bottles of Edelweiss Dunkel. And I brought Felix and David. Felix came because he had to. David came because he knew Donna Wong would be there.

They buried the pig at dawn and the beast had baked underground all day. We arrived just as the crew finished shoveling out the last of the sand from the carcass. The tart aroma of cooked pork carried across the yard by the gentle onshore breeze made my mouth water.

"Welcome!" Kimo called to us. He wore a brilliant green Aloha shirt graced with orange parrots. A smudged white apron almost wrapped around his girth. A tall white chef's hat perched on top of his head. He looked about eight and a half feet tall.

"Here," I handed him an Edelweiss. "You look naked."

Kimo beamed. "Thanks."

"You don't seem surprised."

"You didn't bring it, you would have had to go home to get it."

"Make house! Make house!" Tutu Mae embraced each of us, individually and warmly. "Welcome, John Caine, and your friends, too." She took David by the hand. "Come! Come! Donna is in the kitchen—let's bring her outside."

She dragged David into the house. He went unreluctantly.

Felix grabbed the wine and wandered off to open the bottles.

"Hello, Mr. Caine." Karen Graham kissed me on the check and held me at arm's length. "It's nice to see you." Karen was a former client. And a good friend.

"You look terrific," I said. And she did. Slender and bronzed from the sun, her blue eyes accenting her marvelous tan, she wore a red sarong wrapped tightly around her body. She was a woman who had only recently discovered the power of her sexuality.

"I know," she said, her eyes smiling. "I'd like you to meet Kirk." She presented a chubby-soft young man, who self-consciously shook my hand.

"Please to meet you, Mr. Caine," he said.

"As am I, Kirk," I said, feeling parental. Somewhere in the back of my mind I understood that this was a serious meeting, that Karen had orchestrated it, and wanted my approval. "Do you live here?"

"No. Yes. I mean, I live in Kailua."

"He is the assistant manager of the Parkside in Waikiki," offered Karen.

"Across the street from the Ala Wai?"

"You know it?"

"I do," I said, having once followed a subject to the place.

"Kirk was a customer, and then he asked me out."

"How's the flower ranch?"

"It a *farm*. And it's wonderful. Those additional acres we added have just started producing, and sales are really up."

"Have you seen her farm, Mr. Caine?"

"I have," I said. "Impressive." From where I stood, the riotous colors banked up the shallow hills behind Kimo's compound like a grounded rainbow.

"She's done well for herself," said young Kirk. "For a woman alone." He explained her operation to me in painful detail, telling me facts I had known for years. Then he launched into a long history of his short life, ignoring Karen, ignoring me.

"How do you like Julia?" I asked when he took a breath. It bothered me more that Karen just stood there, accepting it. But then Karen always was an accepting soul.

"Sweet kid." He said it so fast it sounded rehearsed.

"Kirk just loves her," said Karen, hugging him, her face glowing.

I would have felt better had Kirk said it.

"Go get me another drink," he told her. It was less a request than an order.

"I'm glad you've apparently found happiness, Karen," I said, using only the one qualifier. She would have disappointments in love, but I'd like to see her meet at least one good young man on her way through life. At the very least I hoped that Kirk wasn't as bad as her former husband. Having Kimo toss one husband into Pearl Harbor was enough for one lifetime. But it seemed like Kirk was heading in that direction. This time it would be my turn.

"Hey, John!" Charles Kahanamoku, Kimo's youngest son, waved to me from the fire pit.

"Excuse me." I leaned over and kissed Karen's cheek and escaped to the company of the young men cutting up the pig.

"Got the duty again, I see," I said, observing the young man down in the pit, grease up to his elbows, ashes and soot smeared all over him.

"I get it every year," he said, grinning. "It's either because I'm the youngest or I do it the best."

"In whose opinion?"

"Everybody thinks I'm the youngest," he said innocently.

"Keep up the good work, kid."

"Hey, Mr. Caine, I heard you were sailing to the Big Island. It's summer. I'm not going to summer school. Need a crew member?"

Charles had crewed almost eleven hundred miles of North Pacific with me a few years before, and he knew *Olympia* as well as anyone alive.

"Did you ask your mother?"

"Dad said—"

"Did you ask your *mother*?"

"No, but—"

"Ask your mother. If she says it's okay, then I'd love to have you along."

"You mean it?"

I nodded. "You're a good crewman. They're hard to find."

"Just a *good* crewman?"

"You're young yet. Still wet behind the ears."

He grinned. "I'll go ask her." He started to climb out of the pit.

I pointed to the pig. "Hungry."

"What?"

"Everybody's hungry. You, who claim to be the best at carving this beast, must first complete your job. Then, when everyone's been fed, you may go ask your mother."

"Yeah, yeah, yeah, yeah," he said, and bent to the task.

I saw Kimo standing next to his wife, one huge arm around her waist. They stood apart from the festivities, just observing, content, it seemed, to be near one another. They were in every sense of the word a couple. Each was only a part of the whole. When I saw them together, as they were now, the big beefy kanaka and his tall, elegant wife, it made me envious. Kimo had many things I never would. He had a home, surrounded by family; soon he would have grandchildren. Most important, he had his Neolani.

"They sure are a handsome couple, eh?"

Tutu Mae stood beside me, an Edelweiss in her hand. It seemed that she had materialized out of nowhere.

"You reading minds these days, Auntie?"

"I'm reading faces. Yours. I see what you think. Your thoughts are almost hanging off your face."

"Oh."

"Sometime you come here, bring plenty money, and we'll play poker. Howzat?"

"I'd never play poker with you, Tutu Mae."

"Not with a face like you got. You lose your shirt."

"Only if we're playing strip poker."

She laughed and slapped my shoulder. "You wanna play strip poker with an old lady?"

Donna Wong and David Klein walked up just as Tutu Mae slapped me. Donna laughed, putting her hand in front of her mouth. David's color rose a few notches.

"Hi!" I said. "Tutu Mae and I were just planning this evening's entertainment."

Tutu Mae hit me again.

David blushed furiously and Donna giggled. I noticed that they held hands.

"I think Auntie changed her mind."

"John Caine, you are a wicked, wicked man."

I looked wide-eyed and innocent at David. "What'd I say?"

"I don't want to know."

"Mr. Caine—" Donna said.

"Call me John."

"I know, but you're too old for me to call you by your first name. It's too familiar."

"Monica called him Bill."

"And also the Big Creep. Would you prefer that?"

"Now you speak of that old scandal?" Tutu Mae looked shocked, perhaps a little tipsy. "Do you have a diseased mind?"

"I think we've established that," said David.

"I was just standing here, minding my own business . . ."

"Planning strip poker."

"No, but—"

"And presidential scandals. Didn't you get enough already?"

"But—"

"Stay away from the young children, John," said David. "You're a bad, bad influence."

"Mr. Caine, can you be serious for just one moment?"

"Of course, Donna."

"We need to leave tomorrow. Can you do that? I'm worried that there won't be enough time, and every day that goes by is another opportunity lost. I can have all my gear down at your dock by six. Would that be all right?"

"The earlier the better."

"Six is fine. David's going. And your Felix?"

"He's a bodyguard."

"Can he dive?"

"He dived the *Mahi*."

"We may not need him, but it would be good to have him along."

"Just in case, you mean."

She nodded.

"He'll be a good addition, anyway. He can help sail. How about your sisters?"

"Anything on water. Or in."

"My kind of people."

"So six?"

"Six it is."

David and Donna walked off, hand in hand, speaking only to each other.

"Another happy couple," said Tutu Mae.

"Seems to be contagious."

"I wish all the couples here were happy."

"Karen and Kirk?"

She peered up at me through her thick lenses. "Sometimes you're less stupid than usual," said Tutu Mae.

"That was a compliment?"

"Only an observation."

"But a correct one."

"That little girl just can't seem to find a decent man."

"Are there any decent men?"

She looked at me again, giving me the slow once-over. "Yeah," she said, "but they're either too old for her or too young for me."

"Caine, got a minute?"

Kimo took my arm and led me away from the group. From

where we stood I could see a corner of Karen's flower fields, and the sugarcane and the ocean beyond. A gentle onshore breeze brought the fresh sweet scent of the cane.

"Good party," I said.

"Yeah. It's your fee. That was good work, finding those former students of his."

"It wasn't much." The truth was that it probably cost me five hundred dollars in telephone charges, and took me over a hundred hours of pure grueling spadework. Even with the Internet. But I'd never tell that to Kimo. Let him think that I was smarter than I really was.

"We will win with that information."

"Win?"

"Tenure committee. We filed the suit and the complaint on the same day. This afternoon. Tala thinks she can get the injunction very quickly, and that we can prevent him from publishing."

"Does anybody ever win these things?"

"Remember Petrocelli and OJ?"

"Touché."

"Read this." Kimo handed me a baby blue flyer, one of those computer-generated things with crude graphics and punctuation to match.

"It's a proclamation of independence," I said. "Who is this Hina Hina Kanaka Maoli?"

"Another activist group. This one hates all haoles, white or black. Hates the Chinese, the Japanese, the Filipinos, Portagee. Want the island for themselves."

"Turn the clock back to the Stone Age?"

"Something like that."

"So from now on this place belongs to the Kanaka Maoli?"

"So they say. I think there are some people who feel fairly strongly in the other direction."

"Maybe I'd better start calling you *Mister* Tonto, just in case."

Kimo grinned. "Don't say something like that in the wrong circles, Caine. These guys seem like they're serious."

"This proclamation of sovereignty wouldn't have anything to do with rumors of the treasure, would it?"

"I think you can count on it," Kimo said. "Look at this one." He handed me another flyer, this one printed on a pale green sheet.

"Oh, ho!" I said. "And this one is their demand that the treasure be immediately turned over to this Kanaka group. 'Bloodshed is threatened.' That's a nice touch. Isn't that coercion?"

"Look who signed this one."

"Silversword," I said. "The same group that's been threatening tourists."

"Hina hina is Hawaiian for silversword. The same group we talked about earlier. They are nameless and faceless. I'm a Hawaiian and I don't know who they are."

"But you're a cop, and therefore outside the pale."

"Not the way I see it."

"But the way the revolutionaries are going to see it you're as bad, if not worse, as us haoles. You're a traitor. They're patriots. You've sold out. They're holding on to the true path. You cannot be trusted."

Kimo nodded.

"Lots of groups. It's hard keeping them straight."

"That's the best part of this. While they argue about which is treading the true path, we get to find out who they are."

"Silversword and Hina Hina are the same?"

He shrugged. "It makes no difference. They're all cockroaches."

"So what do you want me to do with this?"

"The university received a bomb threat today. The male, who spoke in a falsetto, said that Donna Wong would be killed unless the site is turned over to the exclusive use of the Hina Hina Kanaka Maoli."

"Was Hayes mentioned?"

"Nope."

"And they apparently know nothing of the tomb."

"They would be shouting that from the rooftops. There would be people in the streets."

"You're serious."

Kimo nodded.

"So you want me to be her bodyguard? Is that it?"

Kimo nodded again.

"I'm not exactly at my best. Or hadn't you noticed?"

Kimo grinned. "Then put your bodyguard to work. Donna's been here at the house since we received the threat. I hear you're going out tomorrow at six. We'll have a couple of cars around, just so you won't be worried."

"The way I feel I'd have to tell them to hold still while I hobble off and find a cop."

"So use your Mr. Chen."

I looked at Kimo, trying to find something in his expression that would tell me what he really thought. "You don't like him much, do you?"

"Just stuff I've heard. I don't like your other friend, either."

"Chawlie?"

"He's not my cup of green tea."

"But you're willing to use any of us if it suits your purpose."

"It saves the taxpayers' money."

"We'll keep an eye on things for her." I handed him back the flyers. "And these are just the rantings of a couple of overeager students. They threatened the university? You know and I know that they see that as their primary focus, so they'll threaten it as they would fight with their parents. But I don't think they're serious."

"We've already covered that. This paper comes from the computer lab. Both colors. Some stock of each color is missing."

"So they're just students."

Kimo nodded. "Could be. They tend to get a little passionate, politically. Remember the sixties?"

"Oh, yeah."

"Got one of my sons all hot and bothered, too. He'd listen to these guys, probably already has." He held up the flyers. "Some of this stuff sounds like one of our dinner-table conversations."

"Not Charles?"

"No, another one. James."

"Another Kimo."

"He won't use that name, says it's a missionary name and not from the islands. He wants to be called Keola."

"So you call him . . . ?"

"James."

"Tell Charles to come down to the boat at five. We're leaving as soon as Donna loads her gear aboard."

"His mother say it's okay?"

"I'm assuming."

"You know what that makes out of you and me."

I nodded.

"Yeah, you're right. I better talk to Neolani."

"Yep."

19

Charles came knocking at the gate at twenty minutes to five, catching all of us asleep. I climbed out on deck, stretched, yawned, and wandered down the dock to open the gate and let the boy in. A tiger-stripe sun hung just above the horizon, thin dark bands of clouds partially obscuring its orange face.

Kimo waved his coffee mug at me as he drove off, leaving the young man in my custody for the next several days. He must not have though me such a desperate criminal, to leave his youngest child in my care. That told me that the warrant had not yet hit Honolulu.

I wondered just how long I could string out this dose of freedom. Between the hospital and the threat of jail, my life seemed limited. Chawlie advised me to tell no one of my destination. And then I agreed to take the son of the police officer who would come for me when the warrant was delivered.

It made no sense, but there was nothing I could do about it now.

Charles brought a cardboard box of hot manapua Neolani had made for the trip, and I munched on one as we tramped down to my boat. The white doughy exterior hid a delicious apricot filling, and I got some of it on my beard, which is exactly what you're supposed to do with these things.

Felix and David dragged themselves out of their bunks, splashed water on their faces, and pitched in to help prepare *Olympia* for sea while I percolated a pot of strong Kona.

Donna's sisters arrived promptly at six, dragging diving gear along the dock, still rubbing sleep from their eyes.

By six-thirty we were ready to go but there was no sign of Donna Wong. That didn't sit well with me. This was her party and she hadn't made it. I looked for David and found him below lashing the air bottles so they wouldn't roll around in rough seas.

"Did you keep the lovely Miss Wong up all last night?"

He shook his head. "No, sir. I took her home. We just, ah, we just . . . I didn't stay more than ten or fifteen minutes." He blushed while lying, something I found refreshing. Lying is an art, I suppose, that gets easier the more you practice it.

"And during the ten or fifteen minutes you were there she, ah, didn't say she would be late, did she?"

"No, sir. The last thing she told me was that she'd see me here at six or a little before." He looked at his watch. "She's late, isn't she?"

"Yep."

"Do you want me to call her?"

"I think that would be a good idea. I'll finish lashing the tanks."

He nodded, wiped his hands on his shorts, and headed for the communications cabin where I keep the telephones.

He had done a fairly good job of securing the dive tanks to the bulkhead. We didn't want these high-pressure bottles rolling around loose in a rough sea. If something were to happen, if one of the valves became dislodged, the tank could explode. At 2,200 pounds to the square inch, the compressed air would detonate like a stick of dynamite. That would make me very unhappy, seeing a hole in my hull caused by simple carelessness.

I had just finished securing the last tank when he returned.

"No joy," he said. "All I got was her answering machine. I left a message. Ditto on her cell phone."

"Probably means she's on her way. I'm sure she has a good explanation. Maybe a piece of her equipment broke down and she had to work on it."

"She was the one who wanted to get going early."

"Well . . . that's one thing you're going to have to learn about close relationships with women. Sometimes you have to wait for them. Sometimes they'll have to wait for you. It works out."

"I'm worried about her."

"Now *that* I can't help you with."

"What do you mean?"

"When you love somebody you can't help but worry about them. It goes with the territory."

"Who said I loved her?"

"I just made the leap. I watched you two together. It shows."

"We're deeply in like. She doesn't want me to tell anybody."

"So who did you tell?"

He nodded, understanding coming into his face.

"Why don't you wait at the parking lot. When she gets here she'll want to unload her equipment as quickly as possible. And she'll be embarrassed by her tardiness. Don't say anything about it, and when she says something, just be understanding. Not patronizing, understanding. Patronizing is worse than giving her a hard time. Believe me."

"Okay."

"They don't teach you these things at Berkeley, but it's good for a man to know."

David looked at me as if I had said something profound. I had been trying to make him smile, but he just didn't have it in him this morning. Either he was worried for Donna or he needed a couple more mugs of Kona before he got his brains going.

And I guessed that I needed more coffee before I got my own brains going. Didn't Kimo say she had received a death threat yesterday?

"Was there a patrol car parked near her house last night?"

"Yes. Parked right at her door. Two guys in it. They waved at us when we went in."

"Were they there when you left?"

"Yes. They smiled at me when I walked by."

"Did you talk to them?"

"No, sir."

"Did they look like they would be there all night?"

"They had a big thermos with them, and I think they looked pretty comfortable."

So they would be there in the morning, was his conclusion. One that I shared. No use worrying the kid about the threat. If Kimo hung a couple of his people on her, then she would be safe.

"I'll fire up the engine and let it idle and you take Felix and Charles with you. That way you all can probably make just one trip."

He nodded.

"And don't give her a hard time. It's ungentlemanly."

Nodding again, he scurried off.

I double-checked all of the tanks and climbed up to the galley and poured myself a second mug of coffee. *Olympia* was deserted, all the young people apparently having decided to wait in the parking lot together. It felt good to be alone again, not to have to mind another person around.

The thought of spending time locked behind concrete and steel wasn't something I wanted to contemplate on this fine and sunny morning. When the authorities decided to bring down fire and brimstone upon me, I would do what I could to resist. But I was not going to waste this priceless Hawaiian day, and the days afloat ahead of me, worrying about it. What would be, would be. And I would take each day, good or bad, as it came, and treat it as the gift that it was, rare and precious, until they ran out and they didn't give me any more.

I looked out the porthole and saw Donna's truck arrive.

David and Charles and her sisters immediately went to the rear of the pick-up and began unloading Donna's equipment. David went to the window. I couldn't tell what he was saying to her, but I hoped he remembered my little speech. *Olympia* is a small vessel. Much too small for a lovers' quarrel. There was nowhere to go when one of them had to get away from the other.

I looked at my watch.

Eight-seventeen.

More than two hours late.

When the procession trooped up the gangplank I saw her face and recognized both fear and rage in equal parts and wondered if David had done everything backwards. But then I saw that he held her hand, and was physically supporting her, and I wondered what had happened that had made her so late, and so angry, and so scared.

S he ran out of gas." David reported the source of Donna's trouble as I was trying to negotiate *Olympia*'s passage through the narrow mouth of Pearl Harbor. It was an inopportune time to talk.

"Hmmm?" I was concentrating on keeping all of *Olympia*'s bow paint intact, slipping between a buoy on my port side and a stationary marker on my starboard.

"She ran out of gas. That's what made her so mad. She was furious with herself."

"Uh-huh." It didn't sound believable. The girl had too much on the ball. Furious with herself or not, she wouldn't have run out of gas on one of the most important days of her investigation. It wasn't in character.

"She got onto the Kam Highway and sputtered to a halt over by the Aloha Stadium. Took her over an hour to get to the gas station and back."

The Aloha Stadium was just around the corner, less than a mile from the Rainbow Marina. She could have easily walked here and one of us would have driven her back. She was a brilliant woman. She carried a cell phone. She didn't have to walk anywhere. She could have called Triple A, or me, or any number of people to come help her. But she didn't. That meant something else had happened. And she didn't want us to know.

I didn't share my conclusion with David. He had enough on

his mind, being newly in love, or lust, or like, or whatever malady he currently suffered from. I didn't want him to think his new lady friend was feeding him falsehoods.

"Let's get those sails up," I said to him instead. We had cleared the harbor and were now ready to become a sailboat. "Charles!"

"Yo," he called from the foredeck. White spray was already splashing high across the bow.

"I'm going to raise the mainsail."

"Yo."

"Yo? Where'd you learn that?"

"From Felix. It's sailor talk."

"Sure it is. Where's your parrot?" I turned to David. "Take the wheel." I carefully crept forward to raise the mainsail, mindful of the need of keeping dry. "Keep her on the same course. Right toward Diamond Head." I pointed to make sure he understood. He was a college student, working on fuzzy logic, or something. I wanted to make certain that he knew this was not just theory.

It didn't take Charles and me long to get all the canvas out there and filled with air. Actually, it wasn't canvas, it was Kevlar, but canvas is what they've called sails for more than a few centuries and I was always one of those traditionalists. It goes with my analog watch.

Kevlar is expensive, but it doesn't rip until it gets old, and then it just disintegrates. When I had to replace all the sails just after my first trip across the Pacific, the salesman sold me on the virtues of Kevlar. It sounded terrific, and costing as much as it did it just had to be the best thing I could buy, right? Well, yeah, but only for a short time. These sails were on their last voyage. And when I replaced them this time it would be with canvas. Traditionalists should know better.

Assuming, of course, that I was free to spend my money and travel where I chose.

I swore that I would not let the threat of jail hang like a cloud over me.

I wouldn't even think about it.

Uh-huh.

"Thanks, David," I said, taking back the wheel.

"I didn't run her aground."

"That's a bare minimum," I said, noting that he was having trouble keeping it on course. The winds were tricky, and we would have to tack until we passed Diamond Head. We could have set course directly for Hawaii as soon as we hit blue water, but I wanted to hug the shore along Waikiki, sailing just off the reefs. I just liked being offshore for awhile, letting our spirits gradually disengage from the island.

Sailing offshore on a bright and cheery day always lifted my spirits. With a compatible group of youngsters on a treasure hunt it should have been a merry event. But Donna's unexplained tardiness and the hurry-up attitude that went with it, plus my own personal troubles, made it a little less festive than it should have been. Sure, there were some serious scientific issues to be settled, but these were young people, and I never knew young people who didn't look for any excuse to party.

When we had established course with the Honolulu shoreline on our port side, I got an idea.

"Charles."

"Yo?"

"Take the wheel," I said. "And stop saying 'yo.' "

I went below and rummaged around in my communications cabin. When I returned with my ukulele they greeted me with laughter and disbelief.

"Hey, what's this?" Felix pointed and smirked.

"My guitar shrunk," I said.

"Floor show time?"

"Where's the grass skirt?"

"Do we have to sing along?"

Donna, who had been sitting alone in the lounge, came topside to see what the commotion was about. She shaded her eyes and watched the big clown with the tiny uke.

"I have never explained our motto here at camp," I said seriously, trying to get their attention. "Clean mind . . ."

"Oh, no."

"Clean body . . ."

"Jeesh!"

"Take your pick."

That broke the ice.

"Somebody get me another cup of coffee."

Donna took my empty mug and disappeared back into the gloom of the cabin, her mouth a straight line.

So she was not buying my corny routine. She had enough on her mind to keep her sober and level. But she was also a warm-blooded woman—at least that was what I presumed from the hints dropped in David's conversation—and she knew how to relax. I was just trying to get her to feel a part of the group. It was her party, after all.

By the time she returned with my Kona, I had launched into my hapa-haole rendition of "I'm Going To Maui Tomorrow," and I had the kids singing the chorus.

It was just silly enough to appeal to them. Felix, who had stayed on the edge of the group, joined in, and Donna remained on deck, warming either to the sunshine or the song. She didn't sing, but she clapped her hands when it was over.

"Do you know another one?" Susan, one of her sisters, asked.

"No."

"That's it?"

"That's all I know."

"You're kidding!"

"I practiced for hours to learn that song. Couldn't stand listening to myself enough to learn another one."

"May I try?"

I handed her the ukulele and she immediately began strumming so expertly I knew I'd been set up.

"You've done this before."

She smiled and winked at me and continued playing and singing a beautiful little tune about cutting cane and the evil luna who ran the plantation. I wondered if she knew that the ukulele had come from the Portuguese luna, who had been brought to Hawaii to supervise the cane growing and harvesting. And then I guessed that she probably did, coming from such a scholarly family.

We reached Diamond Head and I told Charles to set a course for the Big Island, one that would take us close to the western coasts of Molokai, Lanai and Kahoolawe. This was as much a sightseeing tour as a scientific expedition. And the winds were favorable. We would be on a broad reach all the way until we reached the Alenuihaha Channel.

When she finished I asked her if she knew "Aloha 'oe."

She answered with her fingers and her lovely young voice.

"Ahola 'oe, aloha, 'oe,

"E Ke onaona no ho i ka lipo,

"One fond embrace, a ho'i a'e au

"A hui hou aku."

"Farewell to you, farewell to you,

"Fragrance in the blue depths,

"One fond embrace and I leave,

"Until we meet again."

When she finished no one made a sound. There was only the simpatico white noise of *Olympia*'s hull as she rushed through the sea, and the snapping and groaning of her sails and her rigging. Susan had sung it so clearly and sweetly that it affected us all.

"The Queen wrote that," said Susan, clearing her throat. "Liliuokalani wrote it for her brother the king when he left for an official visit to England. He came down with a disease there and he returned home in a coffin. It was the end of Hawaii as a free nation."

"The Bayonet Constitution," I said.

"You know the history."

"I remember the hundredth anniversary. The papers wrote a lot about it at the time."

"The Queen—the only reigning queen Hawaii ever had—was arrested and placed under house arrest for years afterward. And the islands became a part of the United States."

It wasn't that simple, but she got the salient points of the story.

"It was a sad time."

"Are we resurrecting the bad times? Is what we are about to do going to destroy the peace of Hawaii?"

"I don't know how we can."

Donna finally spoke. She had been listening intently, leaning against the cabin structure, but now she came into the group and sat down among us.

"What we do is no secret," she said. "Everyone knows where we are going. We are being followed. And these people will plunder the treasure and desecrate the king's remains."

She pointed.

Two hundred yards astern of us a white motorsailer plowed through the rough seas, keeping a course identical to the one *Olympia* sailed, I had noticed them earlier, as we changed course at Diamond Head, but had thought nothing about it. Now they plugged along, keeping pace with us.

"Is this going to be a problem?" I asked.

"Yes. If they find Kamehameha's tomb."

"But they're not dangerous."

"Not these people. There are others."

"Felix!"

He had fallen asleep in the sun. Now he roused himself. "Wha?"

"Get the glasses in the com shack. Keep an eye on those guys. I want to know the registration number and the name of the boat."

He turned and looked, nodded to himself, and went below. When he came back he carried the big 50 × 300's and a pad of paper.

"Mr. Caine?" Donna touched my arm lightly.

I turned and saw that she was crying.

"Can I speak with you? Privately?" She looked at David, as if she were afraid that he would want to comfort her.

I gave him a look that warned him away.

"Come below," I said, taking her hand and leading her down into the cool, friendly shadows of the lounge.

Have some coffee." I poured her a mug of the bitter dark brew. She accepted it and sat at the lounge table with her hands around the warm mug as if she were cold, but did not drink it. She had stopped crying and seemed calm, almost serene, now that she had made up her mind to speak of what had disturbed her.

I sat across from her and waited. Sometimes people need only a sympathetic ear. They do not expect you to solve their problems for them. Just talking it out with someone you trust will give you the tools to work out your problems.

Donna needed someone who could listen. She already knew that I had the talent. David, most likely, did not have it. Not yet. He was young, and smart, and could learn it, but he had not yet mastered the skill.

She shuddered, took a sip of the Kona, and looked at me. Behind the calm surface of her eyes, a storm of emotion was raging. "I wanted to kill him," she said.

"Hayes?"

She nodded. "I went to his house this morning. Before the sun came up. His lights were on. I don't believe I would have had the courage to wake him up, otherwise, but they were on and since he was already awake, I pounded on his door. I wished . . . I wanted to give him one more chance to stop publication before it is too late. He laughed at me."

She took another sip of coffee and shook her head, as if trying to rid her thoughts of the confrontation. When it didn't work, she continued. "He said that this was much bigger than I could understand. He said . . . that I was a girl, a student, who could not understand the larger issues. I needed . . . I needed more years before I could appreciate the opportunity . . . that lay before me.

"I lost it then. I just lost it. That never happens. I always keep myself under control. It's my family's way."

She shook her head, as if not believing what she had done. "I started screaming at him, right at his front door. I said things I have never said to another person. Not ever. Unthinkable things."

She looked at me. "I threatened to kill him if he published the article. I said it loudly enough that half of St. Louis Heights must have heard me." She shuddered again. "He grabbed me and pulled me inside the house and shut the door. He is an old man, but big, and I am a small woman. I felt trapped. I did not know what he was going to do to me."

She closed her eyes. "I did something else I've never done before. There was a vase on a table, a big ceramic thing with flowers in it. When he shut the door he just kept dragging me back to the rear of his house. I grabbed the vase and I hit him with it. It broke and . . . he let me go. Water went everywhere. I ran to the door and escaped. I got into my truck and drove away.

"I never hit anybody in my life. Not once. Not even as a child. I hit this man because he frightened me." She sighed, her lip trembling, as if she was going to cry again.

I waited, knowing there was more.

"He didn't fall down when I hit him, but he cried out and he released me. I'm sure I didn't hurt him very badly. But can they arrest me for hitting him?"

"That's battery. I'm sure you could say that you feared for your life. That would make it self-defense."

"But I could be arrested?"

"I suppose so. You'd have to ask Kimo. He'd know." I took my cellular phone from its charging cradle and offered it. "You want to call him?"

She shook her head. "I don't want to call attention to my crime. Hayes will file a complaint and have me arrested. He's that kind of man."

"Can anyone prove you were there?"

She nodded.

"The neighbors? They couldn't know who you were, unless they took down your license plate. I don't know if you'd notice this or not, but there's probably a zillion attractive Asian women on this island about your age."

She shook her head again. "There was a witness. Actually, two."

"In the house?"

"Yes. A big man. Polynesian—I'm not sure from where, but he was big and he wore a yellow tee shirt and red shorts. He was sitting in the living room when Hayes pulled me in. He saw it all, but he didn't move to stop Hayes from dragging me, or to stop me from hitting Hayes. He just sat there and watched the whole thing."

"You said two."

"There was another man. In the kitchen. I caught a glimpse for an instant but I didn't see his face. Just a shadow, a slender figure."

"Happened that quick?"

"Yes, but the one on the couch had time to stop me. I had to run by him to get out the door."

"It wasn't his fight. Some people are like that."

She nodded. "I was one of those. But not now."

"Did you see the men before you hit Hayes?"

She shook her head. "I was too afraid."

"No. You saw the other men. That's when you hit Hayes."

"What do you mean?"

"Just remember that you saw two other men in Hayes's living room before you hit him. That way, the truth is there, up front. A small woman, being dragged into a house with three large men inside. What you did is self-defense. Nobody can blame you for anything."

"I understand."

"This is your freedom you're talking about. Once it gets into the courts, the truth means nothing. It's how you present your story. That's all that counts."

I gently pushed the telephone across the table. "You had better call Kimo and tell him what happened. From what you told me, it was a foiled kidnapping. You were in fear for your life. You defended yourself and got away. It's that simple."

"But I'm going to be arrested?"

"Not necessarily. Not if you file the police report first. Maybe Hayes will be arrested."

She nodded, thinking it over. I could tell that she liked that possibility.

"What did you do afterward? Why did it take you so long to get to the boat?"

"Oh . . . I drove around. Up to the north shore. To that park near Chinaman's Hat where I knew I could think. I wanted to come to the boat, but I was afraid that they would find me there. I didn't know where to go. I'd never faced anything like this before."

"Why didn't you call us? We could have helped you right then."

"I was too ashamed of what I had done."

"Did you notice anybody following you?"

"I didn't see anyone."

I pointed out the porthole. She couldn't see the other boat, but she knew what I meant.

"If news of the treasure gets out, and you're linked to it, you would be a pretty popular person. That Hawaiian group, Silversword, is demanding to know the location of your find. Lots of people want to know where you might be going."

"Yes. That's the truth, isn't it?"

"You had a police escort. Why didn't you take advantage of that?"

"I didn't think they would have allowed me to go to Hayes's house."

"You planned on going there?"

"I wanted to give him one more chance. He was my adviser. He was my teacher. I once trusted him. I wanted it to be like it once was."

Didn't we all wish it were so? "And now you're afraid you'll be arrested."

"That would ruin everything. I would be humiliated. And I could not dive on the site until it is cleared up, and every day is precious. We have so much more work to do there, and I cannot miss a day."

"What's the rush? You might be delayed a couple of days, but in the end you would be released and could go right back."

"Don't you listen to the news?"

"I try not to."

"There are earthquake swarms on the Big Island. They are saying that there might be a new eruption."

"Moana Loa?" It had last erupted in the eighties and nearly inundated Hilo before the lava flow stopped, literally, at the suburbs. Kilauea continuously erupted, but that was on the other side of the island, more than a hundred miles away.

"Hualalai."

"Where's that?"

"Right on the Kona Coast. It's a shield volcano. Directly above the site."

"I didn't even know there was an active volcano there."

"I told you that first day I met you. It is a small vent, but powerful. It last erupted in 1802. During the reign of Kamehameha the Great."

"This is the one?"

"No one is certain, but the Volcano Observatory issued a warning yesterday. It could erupt at any moment."

"And this lava flow—the site is right in its path?"

"Historically, the flow covered the shallow entrance of the ancient lava tube where the tomb was hidden."

"And that's where you want to dive?"

"Yes. We have to finish our work."

"Okay." That's what I said. Calm on the outside, nerves of steel. What I wanted to say was, "Holy Cow! A volcano!" But I managed to control myself.

"Our lava here doesn't flow very fast. Hawaiian volcanoes are not like other ones in the world. There are no pyroclastic flows that run down the mountainside at hundreds of miles per hour, the kind of killer flow that destroyed Herculaneum and Pompeii. Unless enough ground water mixes with the buried magma plume under pressure, our lava here is slow and gentle."

"What happens if the water does mix?"

"Then we have a violent detonation. Hanauma Bay is an example. It blew the side of the crater out to sea. Kilauea exploded twice in historic times, once in 1790 and again in 1924. It nearly destroyed Hilo."

"Encouraging." I was having trouble keeping my cool. Hilo was more than thirty miles away from Kilauea. And this young lady wanted to park my boat directly in the path of a rumbling caldera. I smiled, hoping I didn't look like a jack-o'-lantern.

"But we would have many days' warning."

"That's comforting."

She smiled for the first time all morning.

"You make me laugh, Mr. Caine."

"You frighten me, young lady."

"You cannot dive, anyway. You still have your stitches in."

"That's true."

"Then why are you worried?"

"Force of habit," I said, nudging the cell phone. "You need to make a phone call. Tell Kimo what happened. File a police report. Get it official before Hayes does. Then let me talk to him." I looked out the porthole, wondering if our friend was still back there. "I want to see if he can get these guys off our tail so we can put you to work."

22

I returned from the lounge and took the wheel from Charles.
"Watch your heads, everybody," I said. "We're going to come about."

Four pair of eyes swiveled in my direction, faces with blank looks stared back at me.

"I don't want you finding out the hard way why these things are called booms."

Comprehension blossomed. My passengers ducked and we turned abruptly, swinging the long heavy boom of the mast around with the wind and momentum, and then cut across the path of the following craft.

"Where are we going?" asked Charles.

"Back to port."

"We forgot something?"

"We're going to lose something."

The motorsailer continued on its course, but I saw a lot of activity in the cockpit behind the superstructure.

Charles pointed, and asked almost laconically, "We going to ram them?"

"Just give them a little something to think about. Felix!"

He had been watching through the field glasses. "It's the *Iola* out of Honolulu." He read the registration number he had written on a pad.

"Keep them in sight. I want to know what they're doing."

"You're on a collision course."

"I know."

Donna came up from the lounge, the telephone still in her hand. She saw the other boat and that we were closing in on them and looked at me for information.

"Tell the Coast Guard it's the *Iola*. Out of Honolulu," I told her.

She repeated the name of the boat into the telephone, listened to the reply, then hit the END button. She sat on a cushion near the cabin wall and waited.

Someone in the cockpit of the motorsailer started waving as it became clear we were not going to change course. *Olympia* sailed on, serene and majestic, and headed directly toward where their amidships would be if one of us didn't change course. I was confident that they would change course. *Olympia* was larger than the *Iola* and might sink the smaller craft if we really did collide. But in order for them to avoid us they would have to change course, and they would lose the wind in their sails. What I was doing was against the rules, but then following us wasn't nice, either. I could not prove that they were following us, but we were not in a position to take the chance. If they were just a bunch of nice people out for a sail I could get in trouble for this. That thought made me smile. How much more trouble could I be in?

Kimo had called the Coast Guard. Whether they had nefarious intent or not, the only thing the Coasties could do was conduct a safety inspection. Having the blue jackets board would slow them down until we were well on our way and out of sight.

Which brought something to mind.

"Charles, you know where the life jackets are?"

He looked at me as if I'd lost my mind. Then he nodded.

"Break them out. This part of the ocean is about to be visited by the United States Coast Guard. I don't want them to think we're not following their rules, either."

He nodded, understanding brightening his face, along with a broad smile.

"What's the plan?" Felix asked, his eyes still glued to the big night glasses.

"You see any life jackets on those guys?"

"Not a one."

"I called Kimo to get these guys off our backs. He couldn't do anything, but together we thought of calling the Coast Guard. The motorsailer isn't doing anything wrong. It's a big ocean out here and people can sail anywhere they damn well please. But the Coast Guard can stop and search any vessel for safety violations. They do it all the time."

"Safety inspection?"

"Why not? You think these guys are sailors?"

He looked again. Two of the men aboard were running forward to wrestle with the foresail. There was a lot of loud, profane discussion going on, parts of which echoed across the water. "It doesn't look like it."

"The Coasties love to board marginal sailors. They always find the most interesting stuff aboard. I'll bet you that's a rental, but even so they're overloaded. Too many people for the life-saving equipment. And I'll bet on recreational drugs."

"So we're going to wear those bright orange things while they're around?"

"You think it clashes with your outfit?"

His look told me that my remark was beneath contempt.

"We'll wear them until the Coasties leave. And then we can break out the skull and crossbones and the cutlasses again."

"If they stop them, why won't they stop us?"

"The fix, as they say, is in."

He smiled. "You have a devious mind, Mr. Caine."

"Yes. I do. Don't ever forget that."

"What if we hit him?"

"We won't."

The motorsailer backed off from its course, its sails luffing, and we passed in front of them by less than twenty feet. One of the beefy young men at the bow gave us the finger as we sailed by. I smiled and waved back.

The sweet smell of marijuana drifted across the water toward us.

"Bingo on the recreational drugs."

"You can be the biggest asshole when you want to be, can't you?"

"Just showing them who the big dog is, that's all."

"I think I shall always cherish the original misconceptions I had about you."

Iola turned in a wide circle, trying to follow us. I calculated our relative positions, and then turned the wheel.

"We're coming about again," I said to my passengers.

This time I didn't have to explain myself. We swung around and sailed by the motorsailer as it had completed its turn. This time Charles and Felix tossed bright yellow water balloons as we closed on them. One missed, hitting the water beyond, the other splashing harmlessly against the cabin.

"It's war!"

"Where did you get those?"

Charles grinned. "Filled them up when I saw those guys following us. Thought we might have some fun."

"You have more?"

"Sure." He handed me a red balloon.

I gauged our positions and shouted, "Coming about!"

While we turned everybody started scrambling for balloons. Charles was down in the galley filling them as fast as he could and tossing them up to the cockpit.

This time it took nearly twenty minutes to run them down because they tried to evade us. But we were bigger and faster, and we eventually caught them from behind, coming alongside, momentarily matching their speed while everyone aboard *Olympia* unloaded water balloons onto the hapless crew.

We soaked the men at the wheel.

One of the big men went below and came back with a shot-gun.

"Oh, my, he doesn't want to play any more," said Felix.

"Fuck you, haole!" said the man with the shotgun. He carried it at port arms, not threatening, but the potential was there.

"I don't know what your problem is, but I'll bet it's hard to pronounce!" shouted Felix.

"Coming about!" I heeled *Olympia* hard to starboard as soon as I saw the gun, catching the breeze, taking us away from them as fast as the wind could carry us.

"They're following," said Charles.

"Go fill up some more balloons."

"All out."

"Then we'll just have to outrun them. Can't fight without ammunition."

He laughed. Then he pointed. "Here comes the cavalry," he said.

A white and orange forty-one-foot patrol boat was steaming toward us. I adjusted course and began turning again.

"Coming about!"

The boom swung again.

Olympia turned and we resumed our original course toward the west coast of Molokai.

The motorsailer turned, too, trying to follow us.

Behind us, I heard the *whoop, whoop, whoop* of the Coasties' siren. I looked back. The patrol boat was closing in on the motor-sailer. Two seamen dressed in blue denim stood at the bow; one had a loudhailer to his mouth, ordering the *Iola* to heave to.

"Victory is sweet," I said. "It's time to break out the cocktails."

Felix looked at his watch. "It isn't even eleven o'clock in the morning."

"Then break out the grapefruit juice. I just want to celebrate our little victory."

He glanced back at the patrol boat, now alongside the smaller motorsailer.

"How long will they delay them?"

"An hour, minimum. But they're going to give it a thorough inspection. When they discover that the young men on board are carrying illegal substances, the boat could be confiscated."

"Is *that* what we smelled?"

"Oh, yeah. They got plenty *pakalolo*, you bet."

"You play rough," he said.

I nodded. "We wanted them off our tail."

"Jesus."

"Forget about them."

Donna stared at the patrol boat and the motorsailer, blue-clad Coasties swarming over the smaller craft, the tableau slowly vanishing in the distance. Then she looked at me.

"Safety inspection?"

I nodded.

"Just like that?"

I smiled. "What did you want me to do, shoot them?"

She shook her head. "I do not want any violence."

"Me, either."

"Grapefruit juice?"

"Charles, show her where the cold locker is, will you?"

He got up and climbed down the ladder to the lounge. As he passed me he said, "I know now why you wanted me to come along."

"Always need a gopher, kid."

"Thanks."

"But the thing is, you're such a *good* gopher."

He nodded, and disappeared, and I couldn't help but see the smile on his face before he was lost from sight.

23

The remainder of the voyage was nothing to write home about, unless you counted the spectacular views of Haleakala from twenty miles off Maui's western shore and the magnificent views of a cardinal red, volcano-adorned sunset. With no visitors, no lurkers, nobody following us, we had a peaceful and comfortable journey.

Skimming by the islands of Lanai and Maui, watching the tip of Molokai in the near distance, I always wondered at the abilities of the old Hawaiians who sailed these waters in open canoes. While this gentle day was an example of how pacific the sea could be, these waters could be as rough and as unpredictable as any in the world. And yet they did it, living out their lives in isolation. Until Cook came and changed the place forever.

I felt lucky to be here. On trips like this I always thanked whatever gods may have dropped me here, a convenient port to escape the power of a hurricane. I had been literally blown to Hawaii by the Pacific devil winds. I liked what I saw and decided to stay. I've remained here ever since. This trip I had more than one reason to be grateful, but I wondered if it would be the last I would undertake of my own volition.

Arriving off the Kona Coast of Hawaii, we dropped our sails and motored among gentle swells, the massive bulk of first Moana Kea and then her big sister Moana Loa soaring up into the heavens off our port side. South from the lush green hills of the northern tip of the island, the Kona Coast seemed a wasteland of ancient volcanic upheavals. The black lava landscape was utterly devoid of vegetation.

Aside from two sturdy resorts clinging to the coast, only the Queen Kaahumanu Highway snaked across the shore, a ribbon of smooth black asphalt between the rough field of boulders. Nothing else existed. Between the jagged edge of the lava coastline and the green jungles of Moana Loa far inland, the sharp a'a lava boulders owned this side of the island.

And above the jungles, midway up the western flank of Moana Loa, a small but steady stream of white steam slowly meandered into the sky. Some of it hung in a horizontal line, a solitary cloud shading the coastline.

"That would be Hualalai?" I asked Donna, who was guiding me toward her secret diving location. She had planted neither floating buoys nor electronic signals to mark the spot, relying instead on recorded GPS coordinates and monuments, probably a good idea, given the curiosity factor of any given stray diver.

"The white smoke is good news," she said. "It's active, but not nasty. When it turns gray, we'd better get out of here."

"Good to know," I said, watching the young volcano.

"Pele was always Kamehameha's guardian. But he seemed to resist her up to the last."

"I've had some relationships like that," I said.

"She has come to life to guard him once again."

"You think?"

"It is what the ancients would have said."

"Maybe they would be right."

I steered *Olympia* far enough offshore to keep me happy, and to keep her bottom intact. There were coral reefs and submerged volcanic rock piles left over from the last eruption, and we drew a lot of water to the bottom of our keel. Donna seemed content keeping our pace slow and steady. It gave her the opportunity to watch for those who would watch for us.

"Over there," she said quietly, pointing to a spot on the surface where the water boiled in the current, indication of a coral head not far below.

"Not there."

"That's the reef, the entrance to the lava tube. It's a wall, going about sixty feet straight down to a sandy bottom. Anchor just to the *makai* of it."

"Charles!"

He came aft, his face a question mark.

"Grab Felix and the anchors and get ready to toss the iron on my command."

"Yo."

"We're going to put two anchors aft and one forward," I said to Donna, "so we don't swing if the weather turns nasty."

She nodded her understanding.

I turned *Olympia* into the wind to give us a little more drag with our freeboard. It made the engine work a little harder and we slowed even more. I came about so we were motoring through the deep water along the reef's outer edge. When we approached the place where the water boiled over the submerged rock I pointed to get her attention.

"This close enough for a diving platform?"

"It's perfect. I think we were just about here before."

"Then this is where we anchor. Okay . . . now!"

I ran the engine in reverse while Felix and Charles tossed the anchors far out from *Olympia*'s stern and then ran to the bow, ready to throw the bow anchor when I signaled. I eased the boat forward after we caught the drag. One of the boys would dive to firmly set the anchors among the rocks, but for now we were secure. When I was sure we had our footing I cut the engine and listened to the gentle breeze rushing across the surface of the sea and the lazy surf as it broke against the distant rocks.

The Kona sun already started to bear down. You could really feel the Tropic of Cancer. The breeze would not be enough to keep us from broiling in the tropical sun. Felix leaned against the railing, looking down into the clear cool water. "Can you and Charles rig the awning?"

"Charles is checking the anchors, but I'll help him as soon as he's back."

"He's diving alone?"

"David's going now. They couldn't wait to get wet."

"Can't blame them." When I was their age I spent most of my time in, on, and under the water.

"They're bringing spearguns."

"Then we'll have some fresh fish for dinner. Can you cook?"

"Depends."

"Depends on what?"

"What the instructions say. These fish come with microwave instructions?"

"I'll barbecue."

Donna's sisters emerged from the cabin wearing wetsuits and carrying diving gear. They moved in a businesslike manner with an economy of motion, assembling gear and pulling cables.

I watched them and found myself wishing I could go with them.

"Going to get crowded down there."

"They're going to set temporary lines to the cave. They'll find the entrance and then mark it for us." Donna smiled as David jumped in, falling backwards into the clear water, one hand over his mask, waving at her with the other, a big sloppy smile below the silicone.

"He seems smitten," I said.

"He's a nice young man," she said.

"But . . . ?"

"But? There was no but. I said he's a nice young man."

"But what?"

She sighed. "There is more to it," she said curtly. "Much more."

"Such as things a young man cannot know?"

She looked at me, her head slightly tilted, her eyes squinting in the bright summer sun. "Are you fishing, Mr. Caine?"

"Yeah. I'm fishing. You've got a lot on your mind and you can't turn it off. This whole thing has you all in knots. You've had death threats. You're about to lose your discovery to some dumb son of a bitch who stole your research. You could reveal the location of the tomb to prove him wrong, but you won't because you have some kind of code of ethics that won't allow you to reveal it. So you're in trouble with your peers, and you're in trouble with the Hawaiian rights activists, who also want to know where it is, and you're in trouble with the guy who stole your stuff in the first place. So what does a Berkeley physics major, a guy who thinks about fuzzy whatzits, know about life? Is that where you're going with this?"

"That's part of it. But not all."

"What is the rest? Can you tell me?"

She shook her head.

"Okay. So think about it. If you ever think I can help you, just holler. I'll do what I can."

"Like with those guys on the motorsailer?"

"Yeah. Like that."

"I don't have those kinds of problems now, Mr. Caine. My needs are more complicated. You're a good man for direct action—I'd heard about it and now I've seen it for myself—but I doubt that you'd have the capacity for nuance necessary to face what it is I am facing."

"Gee, thanks."

"I mean you no disrespect, Mr. Caine, and I am extremely grateful for your time and the use of your boat. For what you do I'm sure you have no parallel. But this is more complex and convoluted than you are probably used to dealing with."

And with that she disappeared below to change. Well, it wasn't the first time I had been shown the door by an intelligent woman, but this was a first from one about half my age. And what was that she said about a capacity for nuance? I couldn't quite grasp that concept so I supposed she was probably right. I obviously lacked it if I didn't know what it was.

Charles popped up beside the stern, holding a spear with a fat mahi mahi wriggling on it. The fish was almost as long as his speargun.

"Hold on there, pardner," I said, stretching down to grab the fish and the speargun. "Looks like dinner."

"There was a whole school of them under the boat. I dived down and found myself right in the middle of them."

"Did you set the anchors?"

"Not yet."

"Get to it. Those rocks look pretty sharp."

He rolled gracefully into a vertical dive and disappeared below the surface like a humpback whale. The last thing I saw of him were his black fins descending vertically.

I envied him. This place looked lovely. And he would get to see the royal tomb. He would have one heck of a story to tell his grandchildren, of the time when he swam down into the depths and witnessed something that nobody would ever see again.

And nobody ever would, if Madams Wong and Pele had their way.

I looked up the mountain and watched the white steam as it drifted across the face of Moana Loa. Maybe the old ones were right.

Maybe we had no business doing what we were doing.

Maybe we should just leave well enough alone and let Madam Pele do what she would do. It would happen anyway. There was nothing we could do to stop her.

And maybe Donna Wong was right. Maybe I did indeed lack a capacity for nuance. Whatever that meant.

It didn't matter. I had something to do that even I could understand. Something that needed direct action, for which I had been told I have ample talents.

I had something I knew how to handle.

I had a fish to clean.

24

Three days of focused work passed aboard *Olympia*. Donna and her sisters went into a frenzy of hard labor at the tomb site, photographing and cataloging the contents, making dive after dive into the dark, narrow lava tube. Charles and David did what they could, acting mainly as mules, lifting, dragging, and moving heavy equipment, refilling air tanks, hosing down the gear, patching hoses—doing all the tedious maintenance chores required by any seagoing operation. Felix acted as divemaster, watching the girls' bottom time, making sure that they didn't exceed the collective maximum time at depth and get into trouble.

We all kept a weather eye on the volcano. Pele cooperated, showing no sign of life other than the pale wisps of smoke and steam that drifted across the flank of the great mountain. I watched the smoke, willing it to remain white as long as we anchored downstream of a potential lava flow.

The weather could not have been more ideal. Kona boasts of 357 days of guaranteed sunshine every year and we got our share. The ocean remained glassy, the Pacific living up to its name, resembling a huge placid pond.

My injured tissues continued to heal. The stitches in my stomach itched like crazy, the lips of the surgical wound beginning to grow together. My old stomach had turned soft from lack of exercise, and now it sported both a bulge and a zipper. Oddly enough, the entry wound had completely closed, leaving only a bright shiny pink button in the small of my back, my souvenir of San Francisco.

"Why don't we head over to Kailua this weekend?" I asked Donna while we dined on our third evening at the site. The sun was beginning to set in the western sea, a ruby red sky gracing the curve of the horizon. We ate casually after a long day's labors, balancing paper plates on our laps while we lounged topside on cushions. It was too hot to eat inside, even this far offshore. Even at night. Half of the crew slept on deck.

"We've got a week's work and then we're finished. Why don't we do what we have to do here and then celebrate?"

"No interim celebrations?"

"We are so close. We've almost catalogued every item on top of the pile, and we're working on the next layer. But they're big items, and we can move through them pretty fast."

"A few more days?"

"There is something beyond. Some sort of chamber. To get there we'll have to remove our tanks. The entrance is tight."

"Another chamber?"

"It looks natural. But we don't know."

"Seven days?"

"Five to seven? Depends."

"Look!" Felix pointed toward the black mass of the mountain above us. High up the slope, the mountain glowed a dull red, a pulsating pinpoint of fire about the size of a star in the night sky. It grew while we watched.

"It's starting."

"What's starting?" The glowing point of light shrank, then grew again. The mountain rumbled a low moan with a vibration that could be felt through the deck of *Olympia*.

"I don't like this."

"Hualalai. It's erupting." Donna put down her plate, went below and came back with the big night glasses.

"Should we leave?"

She shook her head, watching the mountain. "No. But we

have to watch it. It's about ten or twelve miles from the coast. That's not much, but the lava won't flow fast. Not here."

"You hope? Or you know?"

"It's not that kind of volcano."

"You hope."

"We should post a watch. All night."

"Pour me another cup of coffee. I'll stay up until midnight."

"We'll all stay up until midnight tonight. Can't miss this show. A new Hawaiian volcano? Are you kidding?"

"You may not have your week, Donna," I said.

"We should dive tonight."

"Can you do that?"

She looked at me as if I were hopelessly dense. "It's dark in the cave."

"Oh. Yes. Right."

"I think we should make another dive tonight." She looked to her sisters and they nodded agreement. All three women looked exhausted, but their eyes shone with the excitement of the challenge.

"Charles, David. You guys up for this?"

Both young men nodded. The mountain rumbled again and the tiny red glow brightened. A thin ribbon of light separated itself from the glow, slowly spilling down the mountain's flank, a lava flow trickling from the caldera.

"It's major," Donna said to herself.

"How long do we have?"

"A day or two. Maybe a week. Who knows? It could stop. They do that."

"But not tonight?"

"No. We'll be okay tonight."

"You hope."

"Stop saying that! Of course I *hope*! I'm an archaeologist, not a volcanologist. I am *hoping* because I want to complete my work. God knows there hasn't been anything but obstacles in my way. I don't know how I'm going to do it, but I'm going to finish it if it's the last thing I do."

I glanced up at the mountain again. The lava trickle had widened to a river. Fires burned along the edges of the flow as the foliage caught fire.

"Might be, if you get caught in the tomb."

"You won't let that happen, will you?"

"No."

She handed me the night glasses. "Keep a sharp eye on that thing, Mr. Caine." And she went below.

The fire slowly crept down the mountain. It sure didn't look like it was in a hurry. I'd always thought of volcanoes as dangerous, explosive things, like Mount St. Helens or Mount Pinatubo, but I was learning that there were different types. Some were even gentle. And of course those would be the Hawaiian kind.

But even the gentle ones could kill you. So Donna and her sisters, and David and Charles went back into the water to get as much information as they could before the tomb disappeared forever. Maybe Donna was right. Maybe it was Madam Pele who wished for the tomb of the great king to disappear beneath molten rock, so that when Donna was done with her work the tomb would be ultimately sealed by Kamehameha's eternal ally. And maybe I'd had too many grapefruit juices.

I watched the little party disappear beneath the surface, and followed their lights through crystal clear water to the edge of the coral reef. Once again, I envied them.

A sound separated itself from the background noise and I realized that I had been hearing it for some time without identifying it for what it was. I scanned the horizon for the boat and saw it, a large motor launch, lights blazing, looking somehow official and important. It traveled on a course that would take it straight to our anchorage. Watching it, I had a premonition that the world had finally caught up with me.

"Felix?"

"Yo."

"Can you and David run the boat?"

"What?"

"Can you and—"

"I heard what you said. Why?"

I pointed out to sea. "Remember what Chawlie told me?"

He nodded. "They're coming for you?"

"I have that feeling."

"Charles can run it."

"Then he's captain if I get dragged off of here."

"He's a kid."

"So were you once. And so," I said, "was I."

The police launch came alongside and we caught their lines, hauled them in and secured the boat to *Olympia*. Two slim young men leaped aboard, followed by Charles's father. Kimo looked at me, a sad expression on his moon face, and I knew that what he had to do really hurt him this time.

"Caine," he said, nodding.

"Hello, Kimo."

"I've got the sad duty to arrest you on a warrant from California. The grand jury returned a bill of indictment against you for that woman in San Francisco. It's murder. First degree." He shifted his feet, looking uncomfortable. "They were going to send the extradition team from Honolulu, but I said that I'd take you in. It's better, yah?"

"I suppose I'm grateful."

"Do I have to cuff you?"

"No."

"Okay. Now I got one more piece of bad news. Where's Donna Wong?"

"Underwater at the moment."

He looked as if he didn't understand. I pointed up toward the mountain. "She's got some work to finish, and she thinks time is about to run out."

"How long she been down there?"

"Half hour, forty-five minutes."

He nodded.

"Got some coffee? Gonna be a long night."

Together we waited for the divers to return. Kimo said little. His two local escorts said nothing. They seemed content to sit on the railing of my boat and give me intimidating looks. To them I was a murder suspect, one of the bad guys.

I watched the two cops, a kaleidoscope of images spinning through my head. Arrested. Charged. Indicted. For the murder of a woman that everyone knew I did not kill. Not even the prosecution claimed that I killed her. Most knew that I would have protected her if I had had the chance. Jail, prison, other horrors loomed. But for some strangely articulated California law and the tenacious determination of one San Francisco detective who wanted to charge somebody with something, I would not be in this situation. It had been tough before. But now it would be painful.

And it might be a long, long time before I would again see a night as lovely as this one.

Charles was the first diver to reach the surface. He smiled broadly when he saw his father. As soon as he crawled out of his fins and tanks he ran to the man and gave him a wet bear hug. When he realized that Kimo had come here to arrest me he backed away and stood mute.

Donna and David returned next. She stopped still when she saw Kimo, her fear a cold blanket.

"Donna, would you like to dress in something warm?" he said to her, a friend asking a friend something innocuous, yet the question sounded threatening when it came from someone in authority.

"What? I don't understand?"

"You've got to come with me, girl. Your professor's gone and got himself killed."

"What . . . does that have to do with me?"

"You were there. Or close enough. People saw you. And you told me so, yourself. So we need to speak with you back in Honolulu about what happened that morning."

She stared at him, rooted to the deck by her fear.

"Do you understand me, Donna?"

She gave an almost imperceptible nod.

"You are under arrest for the murder of Howard Murdock Hayes. You have the right to . . . to . . ." He mumbled the required Miranda warnings. "You have the right to remain silent. You have the right to an attorney, but don't worry about it because I already called her before I left. And don't tell me nothing. I don't want to hear it."

She nearly smiled. "Am I under arrest now?"

"You and Mr. Caine. Both of you. I'm bringing back two murder suspects, and both of them friends." He sighed. "Get dressed, girl. We'll wait."

"But . . ." She pointed toward the mountain.

"Get dressed, Donna," he said gently. "Don't make this any worse than it already is. Tutu Mae and Neolani both won't speak to me. I don't like it, either. But better it's me than somebody else. Believe it."

She blinked rapidly and went below, her eyes filling with tears.

"Go put on some shoes, Caine, and lose the watch and your knife and all that other stuff you carry. Just bring some cash money. You'll be all right."

"My attorney—"

"I already called Chawlie. He'll have somebody meet us at the jail on Beretania. They'll be there when we arrive."

"You called Chawlie?"

Kimo nodded. "Figured he already knew about it, but it didn't hurt to call. Gave him a schedule."

"Charles?" I asked.

The boy looked at me, not quite registering the significance of the events swirling around him. "You're in charge of the boat. Stay as long as you can. Donna's sisters will do the diving now. And David. You're not to go into the water. I need your experience handling *Olympia* so you can take them home."

"Are you sure?"

"You're not just a gopher any more. Now you're the captain."

"Dad?" Charles looked at his father.

"It's okay, son," said Kimo.

"Are you sure?"

"Mr. Caine needs your help now. He's depending on you."

"What about Donna?"

"She's only a suspect. But I've got to take her in."

"It's not right."

Kimo nodded. "I know, son. But it's what I got to do."

25

"We will fight extradition, of course," said Tala Sufai, sitting across the stainless steel counter. We were separated by a heavy gauge steel mesh covering the opening between us, and by her freedom to get up and walk away from this place. I would remain, my desires no longer important. Now they were more basic. Like living and breathing, and making it through each single day, one at a time.

I had been underground for four days. I'd had regular visits from Daniel and Tala. Even Gilbert had come once, bringing small white cardboard boxes of dim sum, most of which I shared with the jailers. Chawlie had sent doctors and nurses to give me regular checkups. And Tala was only one of the attorneys assigned to my case. If it hadn't been for the circumstances, I would have been honored by all of the attention.

"You still have some rights, you know," she continued. "They just can't ship you off to another state without a hearing. And we can make it cost them."

"But I'm still in jail," I said, thinking about the low concrete bed, the stainless steel toilet, and the steel door with the tiny window opening into the underground passageway. My temporary living quarters were in the basement jail of the Honolulu police station. I hadn't seen the sun since Kimo had driven me into the underground garage and locked me in.

"Bail will be set and your friend will meet it. Normally they would keep you here—or at Halawa Prison—until your hearing, but in this case the judge will allow bail." She looked at me, a smile gracing her handsome face.

"You sound sure of yourself."

"It's been arranged." Tala smiled at me and put one large palm onto the screen, as if she wanted to pet me. "This is a serious case, John, but we will fight it here. If they get you to California, well . . . it's a first-degree murder charge. The district attorney alleges special circumstances. Your life is in jeopardy. It's not that you killed anybody. From what I understand you actually saved lives. But the law does not distinguish. A woman died. An innocent. You participated, they claim, in a gun battle that was the proximate cause of her death. The State alleges that you committed a felony that either directly or indirectly led to her death. Therefore under the law, you should pay for her death."

"What did I do?"

"You shot back. With intent. The formal charge is felony assault with intent to kill. In California, there is the modifier, 'With the use of a firearm,' that makes it worse and qualifies you for the additional penalties. The police officer on the street there—not even a real cop, but a reserve officer, out on parade duty—he is their star witness. He claims he saw you with a gun in your hand and that he saw you fire that gun at the sniper."

"That's self-defense."

"That's one way to look at it. That may be the way we're going to present it. The trick is to get a judge over here to look at it that way."

"And so I'm the bad guy?"

"According to the law in California. Fortunately, since Hawaii does not have capital punishment, California will not ask for the death penalty. Only life without parole."

I shook my head, feeling drained. "They don't have a weapon."

"Part circumstantial evidence, part eyewitness. You wore a holster on your belt when you were brought into the emergency room. That implies that you had a gun in your possession, even though they can't produce the gun. It also argues premeditation. The prosecution has the holster, bloodstained and ugly. The fact that it's your blood is unimportant. It's a grisly piece of evidence. How a jury will react to it is another consideration. Since it is your blood, the prosecution might not want to offer it as evidence. If they do I'll make them sorry that they did. I almost hope that they will.

"And there is an eyewitness who will swear that you had a gun in your hand. All of which they will have to bring over here to satisfy a judge in Hawaii before they can try you in California. Hawaii does not have such a law, and I'm going to work hard on that part of our case. Judges don't like to challenge the efficacy of other states' statutes or regulations. There is a chance that the judge might see things my way. You never know.

"But don't get your hopes up.

"Not every extradition request is honored. Sometimes a local judge may feel that the prosecution from the other state may be a little overzealous. Let's hope this is one of those times."

She mopped her forehead with a white handkerchief. I thought it chilly down here in the bowels of the police station, but Tala apparently felt more heat than I did, as if all of the pressure was on her.

"In the meantime, we'll know what they have through discovery. That's our best and first line of defense at this stage. We will know what they know, and then we'll find how to beat them."

"What about Donna?"

"According to the prosecution you are a potential witness in her case. I have no idea what they have as yet because they haven't released any of their information to me. But they'll have to do so soon. I think they're still pawing through the traces right now, and they'll find out that she could not have killed Professor Hayes."

"I worry for her. The timing could not have been worse."

"You've got problems enough without worrying about her."

"She's my client, too. I have to worry about her."

"What do you want me to do?"

"How soon can you get me out of here?"

"I made no guarantees, but I might know where I can find a judge who agrees with my position that you are Mr. Upstanding Citizen, despite all evidence to the contrary, and I'll get you released on bail by tomorrow. Maybe the day after. You'll have to surrender your passport and sign some papers, but you should be free."

"Even in a capital case?"

"There is no precedent for this in Hawaii. Normally murder is murder. Except the D.A. in San Francisco wants to put the guy in prison who saved two people. Sorry, I didn't mean that."

"Thanks."

"I did not mean to be impolitic. The point is that there is no law in Hawaii like the one in California. Here it is not a crime. Here it would have been self-defense. So you never know how the judge will rule.

"Hopefully, we'll get one that hates California."

"Easy to do."

"You have reason to feel that way."

"You'll need an investigator on the Wong case. I'm already working for her."

"You want to investigate her case while you're out on bond?"

I nodded.

"Terrific." Tala closed her eyes. "Just terrific. But okay. You got it. It's crazy enough to appeal to me. I like it." She got up, leaving me sitting there, handcuffed to the other side of the screen. "Sit tight, Caine. Don't go anywhere. I'll have you out of here in a day or so."

"I'll stay here. Promise." I raised my right hand, rattling the chain.

She smiled. "You do that, John. And quit worrying."

"I've got nothing else to do."

Tala nodded her understanding.

"Do some push-ups," she said.

26

I nmates call it "Hang Time." I'd never thought of it before, but that's exactly what it was: not living, but hanging. In suspended animation.

Hanging in a hole in the ground, in a concrete room three paces each direction, ten feet square, with a concrete bench that doubled as a bed, a stainless steel toilet and a drain in the floor, was like being shelved. There was a lot of waiting, watching the television camera in the ceiling, the one that watched dispassionately as I slept, or paced, or used the toilet. An accused murderer, I had no privacy. As a guest of the City and County of Honolulu, my movements were monitored, restricted, and chaperoned on the rare excursion from my cell. I was a prisoner, a commodity to be housed.

Daniel came every day. Tala was busy, he reported when she didn't make the visit. Trying to get me out. Working the system.

She was preparing for my hearing.

Daniel's voice would probably never heal. The bullet that grazed his vocal chords had given him a permanent whisper, along with a red wandering scar across his neck from the bullet wound and the tear that I had inadvertently caused. To some people that would have been a tragedy, an occasion for scarves and plastic surgeries. But with Daniel I could tell that he liked it. He was young, and it provided additional menace to his already threatening countenance. He wore an open silk shirt, the top buttons exposed to better show off his trophy, a reminder of the day when he and Chawlie had almost joined their ancestors.

As Chawlie's top lieutenant, Daniel sat outside the jail while I remained inside, something that I was sure the local cops found amusing.

"Howzit?" he asked, the question a quiet growl.

"No problems," I responded, keeping it simple. Daniel may very well be Chawlie's most brilliant son, or nephew, or whatever he is to the old outlaw, but he prefers to keep his verbal intercourse within narrow limits. In that way he is very much the young Chawlie, the one I had first met years ago.

"How's that lady attorney working out?"

"She's fine."

"We had that other one for you. Big-time defense guy. You want this broad?"

"I've seen her in action. I trust her."

He nodded, his eyes shinning pebbles regarding me through the wire mesh.

"People say you're gonna have to go to California."

"I suppose it's true." I knew that Daniel meant Chawlie when he referred solely to the generic.

"People say you should be all right, though. Not to worry."

"What have I got to worry about?"

That made him smile, although it could have been gas. The corners of his mouth rose and fell in a fraction of a second, returning his face to its normal condition, empty of expression.

"You made the papers." He handed copies of the *Star Bulletin* and the *Honolulu Advertiser* to the guard, who searched them and slipped the papers under the mesh.

"I'll read them later," I told him.

"There's a television reporter who wants to interview you."

"Oh?"

"Tell him no."

I nodded. Too much coverage could be detrimental to my

friendship with Chawlie. Daniel's mission was to convey Chawlie's displeasure, should the reporter actually put my face on television.

Not that they would. I have a face, as they say, for radio.

"You need anything?"

"I'm fine."

"Okay." He stood up, the interview over. Daniel's mission was over. He got the information he had sought, and he delivered the message he had been sent to deliver. Daniel never asked questions out of sentimentality or concern. I had no idea if he liked me or not and it didn't matter. I had no idea if I liked him, either. But I had saved his life, and the life of his patron, and that did matter to both of them.

I watched him walk away, a big man, not tall, but broad, carrying himself in such a manner as to convey a greater height and weight than he possessed. It was a practiced walk. Some would call it macho or pretentious. But there was nothing macho about him, if you look at the original intent of the word. Daniel was merely tough and deadly, and he literally was the prince of the kingdom. Like the princes of old, who stayed that way because they were the toughest in the land, not merely because of their birthright, he would have to fight for the throne once the king had passed. Every day he had to prove himself anew, rewarding friends and allies, punishing or eliminating enemies and rivals.

"Let's go," said the guard.

We walked down the long, harshly lit concrete corridor to my cell. Cameras buried in the ceiling followed me everywhere. The place smelled of disinfectant that almost blocked the odor of urine. Somewhere in the block someone pounded on a steel door and screamed a continuous unintelligible wail, a protest, I was sure, to the forces that had conspired to confine him here. My door was a solid steel affair set in an iron frame poured into the concrete wall of my cell. Only a tough plastic window, nearly opaque from prior guests' ravaging attentions, provided me with an impaired view of the corridor. It was my only view of the world outside of my four walls.

I hadn't seen the sun since I'd come here. Tomorrow or the next day I would be in court. Hopefully, the courtroom would have windows. This was my ultimate punishment. More than the deprivation of my liberties, tossing me into a hole in the ground away from a gentle sun and my rainbows was a slow death.

So I lay down on the thin green pad that I used as a mattress and read the *Advertiser* and the *Bulletin* and tried to avoid any mention of my name.

"They're in the wire!"

I look at the man as he push me into the wall, holding me there, pinning me with the long bayonet, I never before seen such hatred on anyone's face.

I awoke quietly and lay still, my body bathed in sweat, disoriented and unsure of my whereabouts, unaware of the line between dream and reality. I consciously controlled my breathing, panting quietly and shallowly, not daring to make more noise than was necessary. I did not remember if I had screamed. The cell had an eerie light at all hours of the day and night, so the time didn't matter. Down here there was no dawn and no sunset, no day and no night. The place was always in dim light, like a barely remembered dream.

My nightmare began to feel like an old friend compared to my current reality. At least back then I could run away. Maybe not far, but I could move beyond this three-pace room. Here I had no choices to make. Here all the reality I could find was in four cold walls, a low concrete ceiling and a hard, sterile floor. Nothing else exited. Not here. Outside, people were walking the beaches, celebrating life, making love, fighting with their spouses, taking exams, earning their daily wage.

My breath no longer came in shallow pants, and I found I

could take a deep breath and feel the calming influence of that simple action. As long as I could breathe I still held some hope that there must be a way out of this. I had Chawlie on my side, and Tala Sufai, and Kimo. There were cracks in the prosecution's case that Tala would turn into chasms. I scolded myself because I knew there had been warning signs, demanding introspection. I might get out of here, and I might have another chance to discover what was important in life, and what was not.

God knew I had the time to think about it.

The door opened and I sat up.

A guard motioned for me to come with him.

"You're a popular guy today, Caine," said the jailer with a wry grin. He was not a bad sort. Aside from the fact that he would prevent me from leaving, I found I could not dislike him. "Your attorney's here."

I stood up, stretched my back—that concrete mattress was about as firm as they had, I supposed—and followed the guard. If Tala was here it was because she had news.

Introspection could wait.

27

"You've read the newspapers?" Tala carried the same edition of the local paper I had back in my cell. She was clearly unhappy, the implication that whatever she had read had been responsible for her current disposition.

"I haven't had the time."

"Well, maybe between your hair appointment and aerobics class, you might squeeze in a minute or two to take a look. I need to know if they printed the truth."

"Now I'm curious."

"I took you at face value, Caine. Referred by Kimo's grandmother, I thought you were just some retired Navy stiff who augmented his pension with odds and ends. If half of what the *Advertiser* wrote is true my job is going to be twice as difficult. Now I'm beginning to understand why the DA filed on you. With your background . . ." She hesitated, staring at me through the mesh. Looking at those angry eyes I was almost glad I was behind the screen.

"With your background," she continued, "I began to understand why law enforcement has a hard-on for you. District attorneys seldom bring charges for cases they don't think they can win. It's as much a political decision as a legal one. Normally—for *normal* people—a case like this would have been an automatic non-filer." She shook her head, as if trying to deny the reality.

"But when I read that you killed eight people last year on Kauai—"

"It was self-defense."

"Don't interrupt me. It's rude. You killed eight people last year. And before that you were somehow involved in a dozen murders in California and Mexico, and—" She held up her hand before I could speak. "And you killed that snuff film producer before that. Some say you executed him and dumped his body at sea. You did all that and got away with it. You literally walked away from more killings than Charles Manson. You were a free man. You got a free ride for all of it. And then you flew to San Francisco, carrying a concealed weapon, and shot it out on the street like it was the OK Corral. You didn't ask permission. You just assumed that you could get away with it again."

"It was self-defense, Tala."

"All of them? That's a stretch."

"It's all true. I was outnumbered, my life was in danger."

"Wyatt Earp was a deputy marshal when he shot it out with the Clantons in Tombstone. And he was indicted for murder. He had to leave the Arizona Territory. He never went back."

"I believe there were political implications."

"You're going to have to explain many of your actions, Caine."

"You weren't there."

"You going to say that to the judge? The jury? You weren't there? That's your defense?"

"It will take some time to explain."

"The *Advertiser* is calling you a hired killer, an assassin with a lot of blood on your hands. Is that what you are?"

I raised my hands in surrender.

"Where were you when Howard Hayes died?"

"Is that your defense for Donna? Blame me?"

"Professional ethics forbid it, seeing as you're also my client. But it's a fascinating concept."

"What are you saying?"

"You are a liability to your own survival. I am now convinced that the California DA might have a decent case. Your background will hang you if they can get it in, and they'll find a way to get it in, regardless of what the rules of evidence and the United States Supreme Court have to say about it. Any good attorney could sneak this in, get it in front of the jury."

She sat there looking at the newspaper in front of her, slowly shaking her head. "I can claim that you were the victim. The bullet that killed Jackie Chang came from the same gun that shot you. We can argue that you were a hero, saving Daniel Choy and Chawlie Choy from certain death at the risk of your own life. I mean, my God, you got shot yourself. But once they put your past on trial, parading one law enforcement officer after another in front of the jury, and all of them loving to see you burn, you're sunk."

She folded her hands in front of her and held my eyes with her own. "You ever see some old actor get an Oscar for a lukewarm performance, and you know that he got it for his entire career and not for just that one movie? Remember John Wayne in *True Grit*? That's one example. Well, you're up for a citation, boy, and it's no honor. You have to remember that if you are convicted it won't be for this one act in San Francisco, but because of your entire life of violence."

She put on a pair of half-glasses and studied the newspaper. "The jury will not be sequestered, you know. If the DA is smart this will be in the San Francisco papers. Your jury pool will already be poisoned before you ever get to court. And judges read the paper, too. Some of them even like seeing their names in print." Tala opened the newspaper and went to the second page, running her finger down the left part of the page until she came to what she was looking for.

"Do you recall an officer on our neighboring island of Kauai? Guy named Tyler?"

"Yes."

"Officer Tyler told the *Advertiser* that you killed eight people last year and then fled the country. Is that true?"

"It was less than eight."

"How many?"

"Seven."

"Jesus Christ, Caine! Do you want me to debate the definition of 'is'? Did you really kill seven people?"

"Six," I said, recalling Margo's last-second recovery, saving me by putting three bullets into Danny Fenn's heart just before he put one through my head. I never knew if I had killed the captain of that boat that followed us. His body never turned up, but then again, neither did he. It would be better if I didn't mention it.

"Six. Not eight. Six. *Only* six people? You're sure?"

"Six."

"What were they? Women and children? Cripples? Sick old people begging for euthanasia? Or did you bother to ask? Just got up one morning on the wrong side of the bed and said to yourself, 'It seems like a good day to kill six people?' If I'm going to represent you, I need to know these little details."

"Where is this headed?"

"I'm trying to make up my mind whether or not to withdraw from this case. You're not helping."

"They were armed professional assassins. Ex-soldiers. They had been hired by the brother of Thompson, the serial killer I supposedly executed a few years ago. I was protecting a client in Kauai and these guys just started raining grenades on us from out of the blue. It was a miracle we both survived, but the only way we could survive was to kill every one of them. They had been promised a million dollars to bring back my head."

That sobered her. She looked at me, her eyes wide. Then something changed behind her eyes. She transformed from a professional listener to a judicious thinker again. "Were these soldiers from Australia?"

"Ex-soldiers."

She considered that.

"May I ask if you have personal knowledge of what happened to the man who hired these assassins?"

I shook my head.

"No, I may not ask? Or no, you have no knowledge?"

"Let's not get into details."

"God damn you, Caine, you might as well just plead guilty and get over with! And I'm not the one with the hard job. I've got to represent you at your extradition hearing. Your California attorney will have to explain all this to a jury. But I've got to get a judge to agree that California law does not apply here in Hawaii. We have no law equal to it, and so if I strictly argue the technical points we might have a chance. But only if the judge doesn't read the papers."

"Fat chance, huh?"

"Yeah. And the two cases are linked in the press, your San Francisco gunfight and the murder of Professor Hayes. Just like the press to get them both confused. Even the *Wall Street Journal* ran an article. Not about you, but about the Honolulu case. It's got everything that sells: a scholastic scandal, murder, the implication of Spanish treasure, political and historical possibilities, and even a hint of sex, just dropped in by the reporters to keep the hoi polloi interested."

"Nothing I can do about that."

"Existentialist, aren't we today? There's nothing you can do about anything right now except help me try to save your neck. Kimo's got his hands full running down the source of the story. Some of Donna's files were posted on the Internet. Whoever's doing it is using the same server in Sweden that puts out child pornography. They won't reveal their clients to anyone; they're very proud to be serving scumbags.

"We're presuming that the reports on the Internet had been in Professor Hayes's possession when he was murdered because they don't cover the location of the site. Their publication has caused a minor uproar within the local Hawaiian community. There's people hopping mad out there. Some of them don't even know why they're angry, they just know that they're plain pissed off."

"How's Donna?"

"How's Donna? Your neck is on the line and it's 'How's Donna'? She's fine, is how our Donna is. She wants to get back to the site. That volcano stopped erupting the morning you were brought here, so her sisters are working that new area she uncovered just before you both were arrested. There's even more stuff back there, so it's going to take more time."

"So how is she?"

"She reads all day and works on her paper. In jail, out of jail, she works."

"Tell her I hope she's fine."

"I'll give her the message." She leaned back and looked at me through the wire mesh, staring at me as if I were some wild animal that deserved to be caged. "I'm not mad at you, Caine. Not really. I just don't like to be surprised by what I read in the papers. I try to run a professional shop. I like to know my clients. I didn't know that you were a mass murderer when I took you on."

"Will this affect the possibility of bail?"

"Not really. You were never charged in any of those deaths, so previous adjudication will prove helpful. They were arguably self-defense. You have some community leaders who will stand up for you. You have an impressive military record, and you have the history of standing up and taking whatever the state throws at you after one of these episodes. I can even understand that time after Kauai. From what Kimo tells me, you didn't run just for yourself, you were protecting your client. That's a plus in my book, not a negative."

"You're still my attorney?"

"Oh, yeah. You do this well on the stand tomorrow and we'll be fine."

My brain stumbled, tripping over the multiple implications. "You want to go over that one more time?"

"This was a test, Caine. You didn't get angry, you didn't collapse, you answered my questions under pressure. And with some grace. I wanted to see how you acted when the heat was on. I think you'll do fine for your hearing tomorrow."

"Tomorrow?"

"A bail hearing. I'm trying to get you out on bail so I can string your extradition hearing along. With luck, we might delay it for weeks."

"Is that good news?"

"You like living in this hole?"

I shook my head.

"I'll bring you a suit. You do own a suit?"

"Aboard *Olympia*, off Hawaii."

She nodded to herself, considering the implications. "Okay, what size?"

"Forty-six long. Pants thirty-four, thirty-four."

"You're sure?"

"Haven't changed for decades."

"I think you'll look good in gray. It'll go with your jailhouse pallor."

"Thanks."

She smiled at me, her eyes warm and expressive, a far cry from how she had looked at me earlier. "I'll try to get you out of here, John. I can't completely protect you from California, but I'll make them bleed a little when they get here, and I can lay the groundwork for your defense over there. Just do what you did today and don't worry. I'm a damned good lawyer and I'm smarter than the average bear, and we'll make those suede-shoe California boys think twice about trying to drag one of our kama'ainas back to California just because he was trying to protect himself and his friends from getting gunned down in the street. *Their* street."

"Sounds good to me."

"It may be only a bail hearing, but our focus is to get you out of here as quickly as possible."

She gathered her papers and stood up, her arms full. "Oh by the way, Wyatt Earp came to California and was busted for carrying a concealed weapon. In Alameda, in fact, just south of where you had your troubles. They fined him fifty dollars, which back in those days was a lot of money. He left the Bay Area after that. Never went back. I don't think the place agreed with him."

She paused on her way out, looking back at me and smiling in a maternal kind of way.

"If you get out of this, and I hope that you will, you had better think of old Wyatt the next time you return to the Bay Area. It apparently didn't agree with you any more than it agreed with him."

28

The hearing seemed pro forma. Tala had done her spadework prior to stepping into the courtroom. The prosecution was local and listless, as if this were a favor for a distant and demanding cousin. California was not directly represented. The hearing had been set so fast they could not react, and so they had reluctantly agreed to let a local prosecutor stand in for them.

The judge was a tiny blond haole woman with a no-nonsense attitude and the air of a harried schoolteacher. We were on the docket with two dozen other cases. When the bailiff announced "People of California versus John Caine," we assembled before the judge. I felt no particular terror at this stage of the proceedings. The experience so far, aside from my time spent in durance vile, had merely made me feel like a kid sent to the principal's office.

Tala explained why bail was in the best interests of the State of Hawaii, the prosecution had no objection to my immediate release if I handed over my pistol permit and passport, and everyone rested, waiting for the judge's decision.

I could see the fine and invisible hand of Chawlie somewhere in the proceedings. But only the bailiff was Chinese. Everyone else was something else.

It apparently didn't matter.

The judge levied a fifty-thousand-dollar bail, which Tala

immediately put up in cash. She also handed over my pistol permit and my passport; the realization that Kimo had been in charge of the documents while I was in jail explained how Tala had so instantly acquired them. I was told that I could not leave Oahu without written permission from the court, but that was my only restriction. Before I could thank the judge we were hustled out of the courtroom, the bailiff called for another criminal to stand before the bar of justice, and I was a free man.

Relatively speaking.

Tala, Felix and I walked from the courthouse into a brilliant Honolulu afternoon. The day was so pretty and the sky so blue it seemed punishment enough just to have been inside.

"You still have a hearing on the extradition matter, and it won't be as easy as this one," said Tala, as we strolled along a jacaranda-shaded boulevard. We ambled toward the Sunset Grill, one of those clean, dependable restaurants within walking distance of the courthouse that did a quiet but steady business on a weekday afternoon. "The judge had been inundated by requests for bail from members of the Honolulu Police Department. Your cooperation on another case was cited as the reason, along with your public spiritedness, and your sterling character."

"So they lied."

"So they lied," she said. "Under oath. And you owe me for the suit."

She fingered the lapels. "Nice, huh? Olive green looks good on you. And double-breasted is the only way to go for your build. Nice tie. Very classy."

"How much?"

"I'll put it on the bill," she said. "Along with these drinks."

We took a table at the window of the bar, which overlooked Ala Moana and part of the industrial section of the port. We couldn't see the water from our table, and it was doubtful whether you could see a sunset from the restaurant, but it was comfortable inside, quiet and peaceful, and the drinks were generous.

Kimo joined us, another surprise. He smiled and clapped me on the back when he suddenly appeared at our table.

"Good to see you out of jail, man," he said, loud enough for everyone in the restaurant to turn their collective heads in our direction. He looked at Felix, who nodded curtly, clearly uncomfortable to be in proximity to the big cop.

The waitress came to our table and asked if we'd like something to drink, as if we had come to a bar for any other reason. She was a young blonde dressed in a starched white shirt and black skirt.

"I'd say a bottle," said Tala, her eyes challenging me.

"A bottle it is."

"Champagne."

"Fine."

"Dom?"

"Of course."

"That will cost a fortune."

"Chawlie can afford it," said Kimo, deadpan, glancing at Felix.

Tala nodded, and the waitress went away.

"Chawlie make the bail?"

I pointed toward Tala. "My attorney had the money in her purse. You'll have to ask her."

"Attorney-client privilege, Lieutenant," she said, smiling sweetly.

"Don't matter much to me," he said.

"So what about Donna?" I asked.

Kimo looked again at Felix. "Don't you have anywhere to go?"

"I'm fine," said Felix.

"You don't get it. I don't want to talk in front of you."

Kimo stared at the young man, who stared back, one immovable object in direct opposition to another. A challenge had been thrown down and answered.

"Felix," I said gently. "Why don't you take a walk?"

He looked at me, nodded silently, got up and carefully pushed his chair back into the table. I watched him walk out of the restaurant. He didn't look back.

"That didn't hurt, did it?" asked Kimo.

"You don't like the kid, that's your business," I said, "but you don't have to be rude to him."

Kimo shrugged. "He's a cockroach, Caine. Just because he's *your* cockroach doesn't hold much water with me."

Tala leaned forward and put her hand on the big man's arm. "He's gone, Kimo. You were going to tell us about dropping the charges."

He glanced at the door before answering. "The ME feels that the blows to the professor's head could not have been made by a slight, short person such as Donna. And they didn't get ceramic bits and pieces out of the wound as they originally thought. It seems they found broken bits and pieces of tiger shark teeth in the man's head."

The waitress came and showed us the bottle. We smiled. She smiled back, hers a little strained, having heard the last part of Kimo's account.

She popped the cork and poured each of us half a glass.

"Tiger shark?" I asked after she had gone.

Kimo lifted his glass and toasted Tala. "To the best attorney on Oahu."

I joined the toast and sipped the bubbly, the first alcohol in my system in some time, aware that it would quickly go to my head, and not caring even a little. I looked out the window to the bright Honolulu sunshine and felt vast gratitude for my Samoan champion and my Chinese patron.

"Hear, hear," I said, with a little more feeling than I'd intended.

"Thanks, guys. It's not every day that the arresting officer attends a bail party."

Kimo smiled.

"You were talking about shark teeth," I said, already feeling the bubbly rush.

"You ever go to the Bishop Museum?"

"Of course."

"You ever see that old war club that Cook brought back to London after his first voyage here? It had been a gift of Kamehameha I. It had been kept in Buckingham Palace for a couple of hundred years. The Brits sent it back about fifteen years ago."

"I know the one."

"Somebody stole it while you were floating around off the Big Island. Big flap around the museum. It's priceless, and they didn't have adequate security on it."

"Who would want to steal it?"

He took a sip of the Dom and smiled. "Guy could get used to this," he said. "*Who* stole it is a stupid question. I don't care who stole it. They got other detectives to investigate that. The point is that somebody *did* steal it. The question is, how does it relate to Professor Hayes's killing?"

"And?"

"The professor died from blunt force trauma. Not easy to kill a big guy like that—crush his skull—if you're just a little girl."

Tala sniffed, and Kimo smiled at her, showing the edges of his straight white teeth. It reminded me of a shark opening its mouth, ready to gather in an evening meal. "Young woman," he said. "That make you happy?"

Tala said nothing.

"Hard thing to do for a small-framed young female-type human person," he said finally.

"So how do the two crimes relate?"

"Tiger shark teeth. It's the bridge to both cases. Somebody wanted to have the mana that Kamehameha's war club would give them. Did you know that somebody stole his pipe from a museum in Kailua? Happened about the same time."

"Somebody is collecting Kamehameha memorabilia."

"Amassing his mana, is what's happening."

"So how does this relate?"

"The ME said that he found koa wood splinters in the wounds on Hayes's head in addition to the teeth. Fresh wood. Don't ask me how he can tell the difference, but he says he can. Koa wood splinters and tiger shark teeth bits and pieces equals a newly minted war club."

"So he was killed with a replica?"

"They wouldn't have wasted the original."

"You're going to use this to get the DA to drop the charges against Donna?"

"Going to try. Going in Monday to lay out the new evidence. I think he will once he sees what I see."

"Anything else?"

"Lots. Found other stuff in the professor's apartment that made it appear that he had been killed by someone else."

"Like?"

"Forget it. You don't need to know."

"He's my investigator on the case, Kimo," said Tala quietly.

"Then he can get the information through discovery. If it ever gets that far."

"So you think she can really get out of jail?"

"We'll see. I got another lead that I can't talk about. Not yet." He took another sip of the champagne, closed his eyes as it fell down his throat and appeared to be enjoying the charge. But when he opened his eyes he didn't look happy. "Uncovered something that might be a direct line to the doer or doers."

"Which you think will clear Donna?"

He nodded and sipped the champagne again, finishing off the glass. His silence seemed to be reluctant, as if he really wanted to talk to us about it, but couldn't. Something profoundly bothered him.

"Did that Internet stuff have anything to do with it?"

He nodded.

"So you think Silversword did it."

He poured himself another glass, drank it down in one gulp, and looked at us. "Do you guys know the real meaning of mahalo?"

"What?"

"Mahalo. You know, every time you walk into a tourist shop and buy something, or if you go to a tourist bar or restaurant, or when you get off the airplane at the airport, the flight attendant always smiles and says, 'mahalo.' "

"Yes."

"Do you know what it means?"

"It means thank you." It was a fun word to say. I liked the way my mouth moved when I said it.

He shook his head. I could tell that the fizzed alcohol had gone to his head a little, not easy to get a buzz on two glasses of champagne if you're close to three hundred pounds. But then, this was Dom. "That's what they want you to think," Kimo said. "That's not it.

"When the first Europeans came here, when the whalers brought syphilis, gonorrhea, typhoid, tuberculosis and measles, diseases that killed us by the thousands, when they introduced the flea, the mosquito, the cockroach, and the Norwegian rat, the old Hawaiians told them, 'mahalo.' When the missionaries came and forced us to wear heavy wool clothing to hide our nakedness and their shame, clothing that made us itch and sweat and gave us rashes, and when they introduced the kiave trees with their thorns to make us wear shoes, we smiled and said, 'mahalo.'

"When the missionaries decided that we needed a written language so they could steal our island legally through written contracts, and they assembled the first Hawaiian dictionary, the word mahalo became the word for 'thank you.' The missionary who wrote the dictionary wasn't a bad man and the people couldn't bring themselves to tell him what they had really been saying to him, so the definition passed into writing.

"When Dole and his band of haole businessmen assumed the kingdom for themselves we really started saying 'mahalo.' Every chance we got, we'd say 'mahalo.'

"And so now, when the waitress brings the check and says, 'mahalo,' to you with a smile, she really isn't saying thank you. Even if she doesn't know it."

"Okay," I said. "Now I'm curious."

"Whenever a Hawaiian says mahalo to a haole, it doesn't mean thank you."

"I get it," said Tala, covering a smile.

"What?"

"It means 'fuck you.' "

"And this has something to do with Silversword?"

"Mahalo. Fuck you, Caine. Just . . . fucking . . . mahalo. I can't tell you and I won't."

Tala looked at me, her black eyes huge with concern.

Two tracks of tears ran down Kimo's cheeks.

29

Kimo shoved his chair back and started to get up, his face contorted, as if he were trying to flee. Then something changed in the man, as if a mechanism had broken inside of him. He just sat there, his great shoulders slumped, his hands in his lap, studying the floor as if searching for something down there.

"Kimo—"

"Hush, Caine," said Tala. "Let him alone."

She gave me a look that told me I had blundered. At the same time, the look told me that I was not alone in my social incompetence, that almost all men should be lumped into the same group. We just don't know what to do when one of us crumbles.

She might have been right.

But how did she get all that into just one look?

We waited for him to pull himself together again. Life in the restaurant swirled around us with conversation and noise. We remained under a cone of silence, a frozen tableau. The waitress didn't approach. The busboy left us alone. People avoided our table, sensing that something was happening here that had nothing to do with them. It's the herd instinct, I suppose. Let one of us stumble, the others will avoid the scene, hoping that by keeping away from the one in trouble they will not be so infected.

I sipped the champagne while I waited. It was too good to waste.

"I'm all right," said Kimo after a long silent consultation with the floor.

"Want some coffee?" asked Tala.

"Naw. I'll just get on home." He raised his eyes to mine, smiling a sad, lopsided smile. "Glad you're out of jail, Caine."

I nodded.

"Try to stay that way. It was kind of lonely out here without you." Kimo rose to his feet, supported by the chair. Tears still tracked his cheeks, but he refrained from wiping them away, letting them flow.

I wished I could have helped, but I wished more that he could have shared his grief, because grief was what I was witnessing. But he had his reasons for keeping the source of his wounds private, and there was nothing I could do about it until he saw fit to tell me.

I could have guessed, given what I knew, but guessing is bad sport, nothing more than building paper tigers and tearing them down. Not satisfied with wasted efforts, I would wait until he told me what it was that hurt him.

I watched my friend lumber from the bar, a huge and unhappy man, battling his demons.

"So what's bothering him?" I asked Tala.

"The Hayes case. He knows what's happening. He knows who's responsible. He doesn't like to learn the things he's learning."

"Silversword?"

She nodded.

"What'd I miss?"

"One of the newspapers received a letter signed by Silversword threatening to bomb one of the Waikiki beach hotels. Kimo reasons that the threat is similar to one received by the professor just before his death. Both are written. Both contain similar grammatical and spelling errors."

"Hayes received a threat from an illiterate? So why arrest Donna?"

"Kimo told me he couldn't rule her out. At the time all of the evidence pointed to her."

"The note could have been faked."

"Exactly. And when the second note came we both thought it would clear her. It looks like the same paper, the same computer font, the same grammatical errors, too. The spelling is abysmal. The paper is the same as that used at U of H. The font is a Microsoft Word font. Taken together they mean nothing. HPD uses the same paper. Kinko's uses it, too. But too many things point toward the university. That's where Kimo thinks Silversword is based. There's always a radical element at the university. It's part of its history. It's natural for new and old ideas to be taken to the extreme in that kind of an environment."

"Terrorists at Manoa?"

"Someone who works there, maybe. Or is a student with access to the storage closet or computer lab. But who knows? It's not necessarily there, but evidence is starting to build."

"So it may not be significant?"

"Just a small piece of the puzzle. But it will help our case. That's really all I care about."

"Point taken."

"Kimo told me that the strange thing about these native Hawaiian groups is that they're just no Hawaiians left anymore. Look at me. I'm Samoan, not Hawaiian, although a tourist walking in the door would naturally assume that I'm from this island. There are two dominant Hawaiian rights groups, and they can't work together because of a basic disagreement as to what a Hawaiian really is. What's the definition? They began arguing that a Hawaiian is a person with at least 50% Hawaiian blood, but nobody in either group was 50% Hawaiian, so they dropped it to 25% and argued passionately. Few of either group could boast 25%. The best any of the groups could muster was 12.5%, and they argued about that because that wasn't a clear majority, either. It's like the old south. You were a slave even if you were only 1/64 part African. You may have had blond hair and blue eyes, but according to the old laws you could still be a slave because of that 1/64. It's the money. It's always been the money."

"What do you mean?"

"The federal government owes the Hawaiian people—not the state, the people—hundreds of millions of dollars in rent and reparations. The President of the United States made a big apology back in 1996, and then nothing happened while the Hawaiian groups tried getting their collective gear together. They couldn't. So they can't get their money. It remains in trust, gathering interest. More millions get dumped in every month.

"The State of Hawaii is holding even more money—more hundreds of millions. Those accounts are frozen, too, until some responsible and recognized group comes forward."

"But isn't Kimo Hawaiian?"

"Neolani is 100%, but Kimo is 75%, so their children—their natural children—are 87.5%. But nobody's asked them to join one of these groups and it's unlikely they would ask to join. This whole thing is not about what's right, it's about recognition. And about money.

"I honestly think someone would have asked Tutu Mae to head up one of these organizations if they were legitimate. She's the ranking expert on all things cultural and historical, she works closely with the U of H and the Bishop, and she is 100% Hawaiian. That tells me everything I need to know about the groups seeking recognition."

"*Cui bono?*"

"Who benefits? You bet it's *cui bono*. That's all it is. It's always the case. As with the professor's murder."

"Does Kimo have a suspect?"

"He doesn't say, or he won't say, but something's eating him. Whatever's happening is starting to accelerate. I think Kimo feels it's about to spin out of control."

"Because?"

"Because that's what I think. Because while you were in jail somebody set fire to one of the beach hotels. Nobody was hurt and property damage was minimal, but add arson to murder. Then two tourists got mugged in Ala Moana Park. They weren't seriously hurt, but their attackers, described as big, young and Polynesian, thank you very much, shouted 'Hawaii for Hawaiians' before they ran off."

"Kimo loves this place—"

"Of course he does. But so do I. So do you. Neither of us is Hawaiian, according to those neoteric ethnic cleansers." Tala took a last swallow of the champagne. "And therefore our opinions do not count. I think Kimo feels responsible for these guys. That would explain a lot."

It would not explain the depth of feeling that my old friend demonstrated in that now empty chair, but I didn't say anything. I drained my glass. The bubbly had gone flat. So had my celebration. Neither of us had anything left to say.

"I was going to tell you to go home, John Caine, but I'm afraid you can't."

"I'll bunk at the Royal."

"Don't make it sound like camping. You've got the presidential suite."

"I'd rather be aboard *Olympia*."

"Yeah, I know. There's no place like home. The judge will let you go to Kona if you want. I'll put the letter in front of her first thing in the morning. You can fly over as soon as she gives her blessing."

"I'd like that."

She looked at me. "Enjoy your freedom while you can, John. Today was easy. But the next round won't be."

"What are you saying?"

"To toss in some baseball metaphors, I'm saying that this was the warm-up, the preseason game. I'm saying that you were the home team today, and we used the home-team advantage. But you're going to be out on the road in San Francisco, with a different pitcher, and in an alien ballpark. You won't have a friendly umpire like you did today. And you won't have me."

She regarded me over the top of her glass, her huge dark eyes solemn and serious.

"I'm saying it ain't over till the fat lady sings," she said "And truth to tell, this one may go into extra innings."

A ringing telephone woke me, sending waves of adrenaline tremors through my body. Or it could have been the dream, something malevolent, something I could not quite remember in detail now that I found myself startled back into consciousness. The room was bathed in soft morning light. Reality could be a peaceful place. But the dream had contained something evil, something that stole my normal morning cheerfulness from me like a thief.

Something that left me with the shakes.

I reached for the receiver. Angelica had already picked it up.

"It's for you," she said, handing me the telephone before she gracefully rolled from the bed and strolled into the bathroom. I admired her golden skin from her shoulders to her perfect, tiny feet before answering.

"Caine."

"That one of your little nursemaids?" Kimo's gravely voice greeted me cheerfully, not something I would have expected after last night's events.

When I hesitated, he pushed on. "How you feeling this morning? You able to leap tall buildings with a single bound?"

"I might need two or three until I get some coffee."

"Got some coffee downstairs. Pure Kona, if the menu can be believed."

Kimo had seemingly thrown off his funk. I wondered how he had managed.

"What's up?"

"You're the defense investigator of record for Donna Wong. Her attorney called this morning to remind me of that fact. Counsel was fairly persuasive. So I'm extending an unofficial invitation to you—in your official capacity—to accompany me on a search for The Truth, capital T, capital T. It's rare, I know, for the prosecution and the defense to cooperate so thoroughly, so openly, so—"

"I know. You're wonderful. What do you want?"

"Come with me. I need another pair of eyes and ears. I don't trust my own . . . anymore."

I wondered if Kimo had meant "my own" as his own people or his own eyes and ears, but I didn't ask. If it were the former, he would tell me.

"When and where?"

Angelica came back into the room and lay down upon the crisp white linen, stretching her lithe body next to mine. I could feel her soft, moist skin where we touched. I made the mistake of looking into one of her deep brown eyes, so dark it was nearly black. Inside the pupil, a spark of mischief lived. I knew where that was going and felt myself drawn into the dark pool. Looking into the whirlpool, I had missed part of the conversation. Kimo was saying something to me on the telephone.

"What?"

"I said I'm downstairs, having coffee. Can't afford anything else here. I'll be waiting. Come down as soon as you can pry yourself loose from your, er, little nurse."

"Have breakfast. Put it on my tab."

"Sounds good to me."

"I'll be down in ten minutes. I've got to shower and brush my teeth."

"Floss. Take fifteen. And leave your watchdog. I don't want him around."

"Do you have to go?"

"Kimo wants me to back him up. I'm not sure why, but he wants me with him."

"And you will go? Just like that?" She rolled over on her back, raised her arms over her head and stretched like a tawny cat.

"Yes," I said, watching her smooth, supple skin in the morning light.

"You seem to be better than when I first came to your bed."

"Better?"

"More able."

"And you report this to Chawlie?"

"Someone does."

"Not in detail, I trust."

She smiled. "Not in accurate detail, anyway." She rolled back over. "Are you sure you must go now?"

"I gave my word."

"But you will be back?"

"Tonight."

"Don't get too tired, John Caine."

I rolled out of bed and patted her bare bottom, enjoying the tactile sensation on my palm. To me she represented the return of pleasure. She taught me secrets of lovemaking that I, an old war dog, had never even heard whispered before. Chawlie did indeed know what he was doing. Angelica was an expert in the ways of the Tantra, and she was teaching me about the chakras and the kundalini. Suddenly I didn't feel so old.

"I'm going to shower. Rest. I'll be back tonight."

She watched me as I crossed the room, as still as a golden statue.

I watched her in the mirror, watched her watching me until I closed the door and got ready to meet the big policeman who had summoned me.

"This guy Hawaiian?" I asked as we approached the suspect Kimo had chosen. The kid sat on one of the wizard rocks at Waikiki beach, the Diamond Head side of the police substation.

"Chinese-Portuguese-Japanese-Filipino. Not Hawaiian, but who's counting? He's in solidarity with the Hawaiians, you know?" Kimo smirked. "This guy has no clue we're here, does he?"

As Kimo had explained it to me over his plate of rice and eggs and a double order of Scottish bangers, he had narrowed down the suspect to one of three people, all part of an unofficial group at the U of H, each having some affiliation with Hawaiian-rights groups, each having access to the computer lab. Kimo wanted me more as a witness, I supposed, than as an investigator. But with Kimo, as with Chawlie, his motives were more likely to be discovered after the plan was already in play.

The young man sunned his lard on the wizard rock, headphones in his ears, oblivious to everything but the Jawaiian reggae rap blasting his senses. The gain was maxed on the set. I could hear the angry bleating ten meters away.

Kimo slapped the kid on the sole of his bare foot.

He sat up, startled.

"Need to talk to you," said Kimo.

The kid shook his head.

Kimo ripped off the headset. "I NEED TO TALK WITH YOU!"

"I think he heard that," I said.

"What?"

Kimo picked the kid up by his belt buckle, bringing him more or less to a standing position, not an easy feat. The kid weighed close to three hundred pounds. "I SAID—"

"I heard you, man," said the kid. "Put me down."

"Got any Maui Wowie?"

"What?"

"How about some Aloha Gold?"

"Huh?"

"You dig elephant?"

"What?"

"What's your permanent address?"

"What?"

"Does your mother know you play with yourself?"

"Hey!"

Kimo put the kid down. "Your name Francis Quionnes?"

"Yeah. You gonna arrest me?"

"You got a guilty conscience?"

"I want a lawyer."

"Just asking a couple of questions."

"Didn't feel like you were asking questions. Felt like you were hassling me. And I want a lawyer."

"Hey, Francis, we only want to talk."

"Fucking pig," said the kid. "Why you hassling me? I didn't do nothing."

"He's probably right," I said, "considering the double negative."

"You a college student?"

"Was. Not no more."

"English major?" I asked.

The kid ignored me.

Kimo gave me a sour look.

"Could you prove your whereabouts if I gave you a date and a time?"

"Since when do I have to prove that in the land of the free and the home of the brave? You ever read the Constitution?"

"Can you spell that?"

"Keep your mouth shut, Caine." Kimo braced the kid. "Got a little education, do you? Been spending your nights at the U of H computer lab? Oh, I forgot. You were tossed out, right? For stealing supplies. Abusing the system. Why don't you get a job?"

"Why don't you get a *real* job, man? When we Hawaiians take back our islands from the—"

"You Hawaiian?"

"What?"

"Can you recite the *Kumulipo*?"

The kid looked blank.

"Can you count your ancestors back to Havaki'i?"

"I—"

"Which island does your family call home? And what does that mean?"

"You fucking pig. You think you're Hawaiian, but you work for the haoles. If you cared, you'd join us."

"Who is us?"

The kid looked at us in silence, knowing he'd opened his mouth and put his foot in it. All the way to his shinbone.

"Come on," said Kimo. "You said 'join us.' I want to know what that means. Who is 'us,' exactly?"

"I said too much."

"Maybe. Who is 'us'?"

The young man shook his head.

"Is it Silversword?"

"I want a lawyer."

"Why? I'm just asking questions. What's a lawyer going to do for you? You got a guilty conscience?"

The young man wouldn't budge. He closed his mouth and shook his head, as if the words would slip out otherwise. He reminded me of a huge mutant toddler, caught in the act of some wanton disruption, refusing to acknowledge his guilt.

"Thanks," said Kimo, after a few long moments of staring at the kid. "You've been very helpful."

Kimo turned his back on the kid and walked away from the wizard rocks. He looked like a mountain, moving toward Mohammed.

"Mahalo," I said to the kid.

Kimo snickered.

"You won't be laughing when you arrest your own son!"

Kimo turned and charged the kid, slamming him down into the sand. Standing over him, he pointed a finger the size of a sausage at the kid's face. "You have something to back that up with?"

The young man smiled, shook his head, and said, "Got a little education, do you? Everybody knows you're not supposed to use a preposition to end a sentence with."

Ready for the response, I stepped in to intercept the coconut of a fist that arced toward the kid's head. "That's enough, Kimo! Drop it!" His eyes were wild, and I knew his secret. "Just drop it."

He looked at me, flexed his muscles to loosen the adrenaline charge, relaxed, and stepped away.

"Yeah," he said. "It's not worth it."

I noticed that he was still breathing hard. Kimo was trying, and not successfully, to hide the powerful emotions that were streaming through his body and his soul.

"I'll take it from here, Kimo," I said.

He nodded, looked down at the kid on the ground, shook his head, and walked away.

I waited until he was gone, lost in the crowd near the police substation. Then I helped the kid to his feet.

"You know what you're talking about?"

"Fuck you, haole. You gonna beat me, too?"

I shook my head. "Not worth the effort."

His blank look was rewarding.

"Do you know what you're talking about?"

"About what?"

"About Kimo."

He gave me a knowing look and raised the middle finger of his left hand.

"Then mahalo to your mother, too," I said, meaning it.

31

He's in there, Caine." The desk sergeant pointed over his shoulder toward the tiny cubicle of an office behind the counter. I could see a pair of size fourteen sandals on the desk behind the door, wiggling just enough to let me know their owner was in an animated telephone conversation.

The sergeant made no offer to open the gate so I waited outside, lingering next to the standing rack of long boards belonging to the Waikiki Surfing Association. It was the oldest surfing club in the world. Kimo told me once that his grandfather had been a charter member. Or was it his great-uncle? All I could recall was that they had the same last name. They used to call him Duke.

"Caine!"

Kimo stood at the glass door of the substation.

"You coming in or not?"

"Don't you think it would be better if we talked outside?" The tiny station had many pairs of ears, and Kimo had things to say that didn't need to be repeated. Especially among his colleagues.

"Yeah," he said thoughtfully. "Let's go for a walk."

I trudged through the soft sugar sand to the water's edge, looked behind me to make sure he was there, shucked off my sandals and waded in until the warm Pacific covered my thighs. Kimo followed, and we waded along in the clear, shallow water, following the shore, heading toward the Royal Hawaiian. Wading in the surfline, pushing the warm water past our legs, forced us to use our thigh muscles. For some strange reason it had a calming effect. I'd always found that this particular exercise, striding through the sea on a bright, beautiful morning, provided enough of a lift to get me out of any particular funk I might find myself in.

"You ever have kids?"

"Me? No. Never married. Never settled down."

"You don't need a piece of paper to get children, Caine."

"Then 'I don't know' is the absolutely correct answer. Or 'probably not.' Or 'not that I'm aware of.' Take your pick."

"Children. You bring them into the world, or into your home, and you devote your life to them. You love them, you feed them, you raise them, and then they break your heart."

I didn't answer, having no experience in the matter.

"You heard what he said." Kimo didn't look at me when he talked, and he waited until we were beyond earshot of the nearest tourist.

"I heard."

"I lost it."

"I remember." My hand still felt numb from catching the blow.

"I'm sorry."

"It's okay."

This time Kimo looked at me, peering at me from under the shade of his huge hand covering his forehead, squinting in the bright morning sun reflecting off the water. "You really think so?"

I shrugged.

"You heard what he said. It's something I heard before. From someone close to me. I refused to believe it then."

"You do now."

He shook his head, like a horse trying to discourage a fly that kept buzzing around his ears.

"You know which son?"

He nodded. "It all fits."

I waited, knowing there was more.

"He's really been pushing this Hawaiian thing. At home, during the dinner hour, he keeps beating on us—me—to work for his group. You know, I forgot which group he got involved in at the college, but it's one of those with more Chinese than Hawaiians, one of those with the 'We're all brothers of color, united against the white man' crap."

"The evil white overseer."

"That's you, Caine."

"Have to practice twisting my moustache while I tie the maiden to the railroad track."

"Don't joke about it. That's the way they see it. And I'm not sure they're that far wrong. The Portagee, when he came here, was the luna."

"They were vicious bastards, carried a whip like Indiana Jones and they treated the plantation workers like shit. I know the story."

Kimo snorted. "Yeah, but the workers weren't Hawaiian. We'd already been mostly killed off by then."

"And above the Portagee was the white man."

"Portagee's white. He's just not as white as the ones with the money."

"It's my burden, I suppose."

"I don't need your asshole routine right now, Caine. I need some sound thinking out of you."

"As a friend? Or as Donna Wong's investigator?"

Kimo nodded. "Fair question." He suddenly kicked the water ahead of him, sending silver showers high into the air. "Okay," he said, kicking the water a second time. "As a friend. And a friend of my son."

"You going to tell me which one?"

"No."

"So what do you need?"

"You've got your extradition hearing tomorrow. You knew that, didn't you?"

"No." That sent a flood of adrenaline down my spine. Chicken skin erupted on my forearms. My back felt a sudden chill.

"I thought Tala said she'd call you about it. Nine in the morning. Tomorrow."

"You pulled me out of my hotel room before she had the chance. Unlike some people, she probably didn't want to wake me." Kimo nodded, but said nothing. "So I've got one more day of freedom left? Is that what you're telling me? I just got out of jail, and now they're going to send me to California?"

"Probably."

"Then why am I spending my last day with you?"

"You've got today and tonight to help me put the capper on the Hayes case so I can get the judge to drop the charges against Donna. She won't have you around after you're extradited, and frankly this case is just a little too close for me to be impartial. I don't want this to get around the department until I make the arrest, and I need you to keep me from killing the suspect. I can't afford to lose my job. My family needs the money."

"You're really asking me to spend the day with you, knowing that I'm going to go to jail?"

"Keep you out of trouble," he said.

"I am a felony suspect."

"You're always a felony about to happen. But I need you today."

"Okay," I said, my thoughts not on the day ahead, but the day after. And the day after that. "What about Tutu Mae?"

"What about her?"

"She's the expert in Hawaiian culture."

"I'm bringing her in as a consultant on the case. She knows everything about this kind of stuff, man. She will know how to deal with it."

The way he said it I wasn't sure if Kimo meant "criminal" stuff, or "Hawaiian" stuff, or "family" stuff. I decided it didn't really matter. She had enough wisdom to go around for all three.

"Look, Caine," he said, staring at the sand through the shallow, clear water in front of him. "It's accelerating. A Japanese honeymoon couple was carjacked on the north shore last night. The husband is the hero of the hour, engineering an escape before he or his wife was seriously hurt. But the kidnappers got away, even though one of our off-duty guys happened to be there and chased them into the jungle. The only thing the witnesses can agree on, and that includes our officer, is that the suspects were young, Polynesian, and that they shouted political slogans as they tried to hijack the convertible."

"You think it was Silversword?" I wanted to ask if the son was home, but I left it alone. If what Francis had told us was accurate, Kimo's son may have been involved in a murder. Or a series of murders. Carjacking was short time, compared to that.

"Maybe. If they're trying to make a name for themselves."

"Carjacking? Kidnapping? They're branching out."

"Keeping the crimes local, is what they're doing. They haven't attacked government buildings, although that's who they say they have their beef with. They don't want the FBI on their tail, I guess."

"Who shot up Pearl Harbor?"

"You mean recently? There's more than one loony on this island."

We reached the beach in front of the Royal. The attendants were raking the white sand patch in front of the old pink hotel, setting out pink lounge chairs for the guests in exactly the same way they had set them out for over fifty years. Over my shoulder Diamond Head rose above the Waikiki skyline like a familiar friend.

"I want to follow up what Francis told me," said Kimo. "I want to prove that he was talking out of school. I want to prove that Donna didn't kill Hayes, that somebody else did."

"Who did it?"

He shook his head. "That's why I need you today, Caine. I need a friend with me. I really don't think I'm gonna like what I'm gonna find out."

32

We found Little Ricky Lee holding court at Duke's Gym, impressing the boys with his prowess on the speed bag. I vaguely knew of Little Ricky, as he was called when he was out of earshot, and had seen him at the gym for years. I knew him as a braggart and a bully, a guy to avoid.

I never knew what he did for a living, but the man gave the impression that whatever it was didn't take much of his time while it paid large rewards.

Kimo told me that from what he understood, Little Ricky drove a bright red Corvette, which he habitually parked in the rear of the topless bar across the street from the gym. When he wasn't ringside at the topless bar he was at the gym. He never seemed to be anywhere else. It limited his life experience, according to Kimo, but made him easier to find.

"Why this guy? He's Chinese," I asked Kimo on the way to the gym. Kimo drove his Jeep Cherokee, not his Mustang with the blue police light on top. I found that odd.

"Oh yeah?" smirked Kimo. "I heard he's pure Hawaiian."

"Is he?"

"Pure bullshit is what he is. He's been hanging with that porker we talked to at the wizard rocks, and sometimes he works for your friend as an enforcer."

"My friend?"

"That Chinese criminal."

"Chawlie?"

"Only sometimes. Just low-level stuff that I know about. He's not connected. I doubt that Chawlie ever heard of him."

"Chawlie doesn't hire enforcers, does he?" I had trouble keeping my face straight.

Kimo raised one eyebrow and looked at me. "I don't know if you're putting me on with that wide-eyed innocence, but I hope you're not that stupid."

"So how did this guy's name pop up in this investigation?"

"Ricky knows things, and he hangs with people, but he's strictly free-lance. That topless bar's his office. People come and go. Sometimes he sits with his clients, makes a deal, and goes out and does whatever it was he agreed to do. He's such a small-time crook that only the young cops are interested in him."

"So why are you interested?"

"Ricky's been hanging with Francis, and with . . . other people that know Francis, guys down from the university."

"No names."

"No names, thank you. Like I said, he's a free-lance kind of guy. I figure that if he works enforcement for one group, he'll work enforcement for another."

"Silversword?"

"Yeah."

"It's pretty thin."

"Yeah."

"But we're going to brace him, aren't we?"

"Uh-huh."

And then I understood. Ricky was a hard case, or he thought he was a hard case. In either event, he would not speak willingly with the police. So that's why Kimo had brought me along. He was not going to talk to Ricky Lee under the cover of his badge. He was going to talk to Ricky Lee as the father of a boy who might be in deep trouble. A badge came with responsibilities and limitations of authority. And Kimo was not going to worry about the restraints that also came with the badge.

"Here we are, and Little Ricky is at home." Kimo pointed to the red convertible snugged up against the back of the concrete block building on Kalakaua Avenue, the car surrounded by plastic trash cans to protect it from an accidental collision. The cans looked like boat bumpers.

"He takes good care of his car."

Kimo parked next to the Corvette. He walked all the way around it, examining the tags and the safety stickers. From what I could see everything was legal. Kimo must have thought so, too, because he did nothing to the car. I was sure that he would have radioed for a tow if he'd found any excuse.

"A man has to take pride in something," said Kimo. "This guy can't really point to anything else in his life."

Kimo was wrong. When we found Ricky Lee we found a tiny warrior, stripped to the waist, with superb muscle definition and lightning reflexes. He was dancing with the speed bag, tapping the leather with such a brilliantly coordinated effort that it looked easy. Tapping was probably the wrong word, but that's the way it looked. Except that Ricky's tap sent the speed bag flying, rebounding off the board, only to be met with another fist. He never missed. His rhythm was flawless. He was fast as a snake. Ricky could be proud of his hand-eye coordination, as well as his Corvette.

We watched among a crowd, both of us at least a head taller than the other gym rats, until he stopped. Ricky didn't just taper off, or abandon the bag in full flight, letting it take its course. It just stopped. One touch and the bag came to an instant arrest. Ricky was fast. And he was proud of it. Turning around, pulling off his gloves as if he expected applause, Ricky smiled until he saw the two of us. Then his smile faded and became a scowl.

"What chew want?"

"He knows you?" I asked Kimo.

"I don't think so."

"What chew want?" The little warrior was suddenly in front of us, hostility and sweat pouring off him in equal portions. The gym rats disappeared, leaving us alone in the boxing room.

"I want to talk to you, Ricky." Kimo smiled, and I noticed that Ricky had managed to become cornered by the bigger man. Kimo had skillfully maneuvered him. He had nowhere to go if Kimo didn't want to him leave.

"Not to me. Talk to my lawyer."

Kimo looked at me, his eyes pleading. "Nobody wants to talk to me today. Why is that?"

"You eat Thai food last night?"

Ricky made a move toward Kimo, his body moving so fast he was a blur.

"Nope," said Kimo, and hit Ricky Lee in the jaw with his left, his forearm coming up to meet the smaller man's assault.

Lee fell to the mat and lay still.

"You kill him?"

Kimo rolled Ricky over until he was face up. "Probably not." He patted his face. "Get me some water."

I went to the cooler, filled a cup with ice-cold water, and brought it back.

"Thank you," said Kimo, drinking half of it. He stood there, considering the still form at his feet, and then poured the remaining half on Ricky Lee's head.

"Hey!" Ricky instantly reacted, leaping up from the mat in one smooth motion. Kimo pushed him back to a sitting position.

"Guess I didn't kill him," he said, his voice a mixture of innocence and disappointment.

The smaller man sputtered, shaking his head, wiping the back of his hand across his face. "I'll have your badge for this." Even on the floor, even looking up at a man half the size of Godzilla, the little guy was on the offensive. I almost liked him, if for nothing else but his spirit.

"Sure you will, Ricky," said Kimo. "Did I say I was a cop?"

"You focking broke my jaw."

"No I didn't. I could have, but I didn't."

"I'm going to sue you."

"For what?"

"Assault!"

"Assault? Did I hit him?" Kimo turned to me.

"I didn't see anything."

"You got any other witnesses?"

"Fock you, man. I know who you are, and I've seen *you* before," he turned on me. "You work out here once in a while. I've seen you."

"I didn't hit you either."

Ricky snorted, almost a laugh. "What do you two turds want with me?"

"How long has it been since you were up to St. Louis Heights?"

"I wanna see some ID."

"You said you knew who I was. You don't need ID."

"Gotta get your badge number."

"I heard you hang with a group from the University of Hawaii. Talk about revolution, reestablishment of the monarchy, that kind of stuff."

"I never been to no university."

"How about grammar school?" I asked.

Ricky snarled at me. "Hey, you ever say anything that's not smart ass?"

Kimo gave me the hard stare. "Pay attention to *me*," he said to Ricky. "You know people who do?"

"Do what?"

Kimo sighed. I thought he was going to hit the man again. "Do you know who I am?" he asked instead, his voice gentle. "Come on, Ricky. You said you know me. What's my name?"

Ricky looked at him out of the side of his eyes, his head turned toward the floor, studying the giant in front of him as if what he saw was just too bright—or too ugly—to gaze at directly. A small smile came to him after a moment.

"Yeah, I do," he said. "You're the Jolly Green Giant."

Kimo shook his head, tiring of the game.

"You got your beanstalk parked outside?"

"You don't know—"

"I know you got a badge, and I know you're in deep shit trouble. I'm going to file a complaint against you this afternoon. And so is my friend. We'll both press charges."

"What friend?"

"You know the one. You knocked him on his ass in Waikiki this morning, Lieutenant Kahanamoku."

Kimo looked at me and winked. "You know, I think you might be right," he said. I wasn't sure if he directed the remark to Ricky Lee or to me; he was looking at the ceiling when he spoke.

"You going to report me?" he said to Ricky.

"Assault. That's a felony."

"You ought to know. How many times you been busted for felony assault?"

Lee shook his head. "You're not going to go there, you big moke. Just go away and leave me alone."

"Ricky . . . Ricky . . . Ricky."

"What?"

"I want to get this right. I don't want to misunderstand what you said. You said my name and my rank, and told me that you are going to go to the police station and report me for felony assault. Is that correct?"

Lee knew something was up but he was already too deep into the conflict and incapable of backing out the way he'd come. I watched his muscles flex along the tops of his shoulders. He was poised, those snakelike reflexes on full alert.

"Yeah, cop. What you going to do about it?"

"I hit you once. That's all."

"See? You admit it!"

"I only hit you once and you're going to report me for assault." Kimo looked at me, a theatrical frown on his face. "Does that seem right to you, Caine?"

Lee snaked a look at me when Kimo said my name.

"Does it?" demanded Kimo.

"No," I said. "Once is not enough. Not if he's going to report you."

Ricky's head swiveled back and forth between the Kimo and me, trying to follow the path, almost getting it but not quite quick enough to follow where this was headed. The one concept I was certain he understood was that he was in trouble.

"You're right," said Kimo, but only after his sandal had stomped down on the leading foot of the little warrior. Ricky tried to jerk away but found himself pinned to the mat. Kimo popped him in the jaw before Lee could get his hands up and he went down like one of those weighted punching dolls. I almost expected him to rise, but he was unconscious before he hit the mat.

"You have a real technique, Detective," I said as Kimo checked Lee for vital signs for the second time.

"He's got a code. He wouldn't tell us anything anyway." Satisfied that Ricky was not seriously hurt, he got up and wiped his hands on his pants. Lee's body was still covered in sweat.

"You knew that before you came here."

"Yeah."

"Then why, may I ask, did we go through this?"

"It felt good."

"Punching Ricky Lee because it felt good is not good police procedure."

"You're lecturing me about police procedure, Caine?"

"Just pointing out some possible holes in your technique, is all."

"Come on. We'll talk about it in the car."

"Aren't you worried about the report?"

He grinned and shook his head. "A Ricky Lee does not go to the authorities to settle his disputes; he won't go anywhere near the station unless he's in handcuffs. He will not try to get me fired. It's not his style."

"I didn't think beating suspects was your style."

Kimo put his hand on my chest. "You got an attack of morals all of a sudden, Caine?"

"Call it wisdom."

"Call it whatever you want, but I need to know what Ricky Lee knows, and I don't have time to ask him twice."

He waved and smiled as we passed the reception desk on our

way out the door. People were craning their heads toward the boxing room like a prairie dog colony, trying to see what had happened.

"You got his attention. I'm not certain it did you any good."

"I got what I wanted," he said. We were on the sidewalk in the bright morning sunshine. Traffic was heavy and we waited for a light down the street to clear before we could jaywalk safely. "And now I've got his attention. He'll try to find a way to get back at me. When he does, he'll make a mistake. I'll own him then."

I nodded. It made sense.

"And what would you have done, given the circumstances?"

"Given the circumstances? You mean if I knew that he was part of a group that was drawing my son into a dangerous situation?"

Kimo started to speak but changed his mind. It registered that he almost hit me for answering the question the way I had. There were boundaries here that I was not supposed to cross.

"Yeah," he said, after a moment.

"You mean, would I have hit him?"

He nodded.

"Harder. And more often."

We walked by the red Corvette. I knocked over a trash can.

"I would have kicked him, too."

Kimo drove the Cherokee from the narrow confines of the tall buildings of Honolulu up toward the great expanse of tract homes and cane fields of Mililani. Planted smack in the middle of the island on the great alluvial fields between Oahu's two shield volcanoes, Mililani was a bedroom community serving both Honolulu and the military bases that bordered it. Formerly agricultural, Mililani had sprung from cane fields, and now was surrounded by sugar cane, the dry whispering stalks hard against the chain link fences of the cookie-cutter backyards.

We rode in silence, each in his thoughts.

As we passed Halawa Prison I turned away from the mountains and gazed toward Pearl Harbor, even though I caught a glimpse of a rainbow high up the emerald slopes above the prison. I always stared at rainbows.

"Can I ask you a question?"

"Sure," said Kimo.

"I may not be the guy to ask this, being on trial for murder and all, but did you attend some seminar? Or is this just something you thought up all by yourself?"

Kimo almost smiled. "What, you don't think I'm being nice to these lolos?"

"I'm just wondering about the level of the violence. That's not like you. I'm no cop, but this doesn't look like the smartest way to ask questions. Unless your real name is Torquemada."

He nodded. "I'm trying to see if they'll tell me something under stress."

"You're stressing them. I'm just not sure if you're doing yourself any good. Or your son."

"There's things . . ." He shut his mouth after a moment.

"You don't want to tell me. I understand. But you brought me along for a reason."

Kimo was silent. I let him be, watching the landscape. We had reached the end of the highway, just outside Schofield Barracks, and found the narrow two-lane road. The road ran through pineapple fields that seemed to stretch unbroken from the Waianae Mountains on the west to the foothills of the Ko'olaus in the east. Beyond the green hump of the pineapple fields ahead was the pale blue Pacific Ocean graced with columns of billowy white clouds. Up this high it was easy to tell we were on an island.

"That's why you're along," Kimo said after a moment. "You're supposed to keep me out of trouble."

"You're already in trouble. Both of those guys have reason to report you."

"They won't. They know I'm here because I'm a father. Not because I'm a cop."

"You think one of your sons is informing them?"

"How do you think Ricky Lee knows me? Do you think he knows every cop on the island by name?"

"Probably not."

"So why would he know me? I've never crossed his path before. Not officially. But he knew me as soon as I walked into the gym. How come?"

"Point taken."

"And he knew you, too, Caine. He reacted when I mentioned your name."

"I noticed that."

"So you're the detective. Deduce something."

"These guys are connected to one another just the way you thought they were, and Francis, who also knew you, called Ricky to tell him of our encounter, so Ricky expected us to pay him a visit, too."

"How does that explain their knowing our names? I can see him describing us, but our names?"

"Yeah."

"Come on, you're better than that."

I knew the answer. I just didn't want to say it out loud. Not to Kimo. Not in his current mood.

"Come on, Caine. I want to know if you figured it out, or if your brains are down, too."

"They know you because of what Francis said. He identified you, he mentioned your son, so he knows you through your son."

Kimo nodded. "So how do they know you?"

"I've been to your house."

"And you've met my son. It's okay, you can say it."

"And I've met your son."

"Who identified you as the detective for Donna Wong . . ."

"Who must have known what I was doing—"

"Who identified you as the detective for Donna Wong."

I nodded, sensing that if I did not agree with him, he would continue to press the issue. "And where does that leave us?"

"That, Caine, leaves me with the possibility that I've got a murderer living under my roof."

The road descended through cane and pineapple fields until it came to the Waialua turnoff and we followed the road down toward the beach. Kimo had his thoughts and he had his problems. I wasn't certain I wanted to trade, even though my own were bad enough.

He parked the Jeep in a dirt lot fronting an old stucco and corrugated metal-sided bar within rock-throwing distance from the Waialua sugar mill. I recognized it for what it was, a workers' bar, a place where laborers gathered after a shift. It was not a place for haoles. It was not a place for cops.

"We're going in here?"

"One of the guys I know told me about this place."

It took me a moment. Kimo seemed to be reluctant to speak the kid's name. "Your son?"

He nodded, staring at the covered entrance to the bar. Two big men sat on the railing in front of the bar and drank beer from brown bottles and stared at the Cherokee. It wouldn't be long before we would be the focus of attention.

"This where they meet?"

"Sometimes. There's a guy here named Bumpy Kealoha, one of the leaders of the Aha Kuka O Na Kanaka. He tends bar. Runs a Hawaiian commune on the north shore. The place is supposed to be a hotbed of radical political thought."

I couldn't tell if he mocked himself, so I let it alone. "Your son used to come here?"

"A few months ago, a couple of uniforms stopped him just down the road and he failed the Breathalyzer. They called me instead of taking him in. Professional courtesy. Like a fool I came to get him. Probably should have ordered them to arrest him."

"So you talked on the way home?"

"*He* talked. I couldn't get him to shut up. You know drunks. He told me all about his new friends, how they were going to change the world. I thought it just a bunch of college-boy stupidity."

"So this bartender, you gonna beat him up?"

"Don't know."

"You know I'm not supposed to fight. I'll go in there with you, but if it starts to get nasty . . ."

Kimo looked over at me. "You don't have to. This isn't your fight."

"Is it yours?"

"My son is involved in something. These guys know things that I need to know."

"You think they care?"

"Not yet. But they're gonna."

I stared at the two big guys sitting on the railing, each bigger than an NFL lineman. They continued staring at the Cherokee, drinking slow draughts of beer, aware of us watching them.

"You can't beat all of them up. Even if you could it wouldn't do any good. What's the purpose?"

"My purpose?"

"What do you hope to accomplish? Get information? You expect them to tell you, a cop, and me, a haole, all about their fantasy plot to overthrow the government? You already know enough to get it out of your son. You've got enough to sit down with him, and with Tutu Mae and Neolani, and learn everything he's into. He'll tell you now. I'm sure of it."

Kimo settled in his seat. "Well, in the first place I don't think James would be willing to talk to me. We had a hell of a fight about this whole thing last night when I got home."

"Oh."

"And in the second place he packed his gear and left afterward. I don't know where he is."

Kimo gripped the steering wheel in both of his huge hands, his knuckles white.

"You asked my purpose? My purpose is simple. My purpose is to find my son and bring him home."

I nodded toward the two giants sitting on the porch railing. "We going to march in there like a couple of Old West gunslingers and make them talk? You think that's going to happen?"

Kimo nodded to himself, his mouth a tight line. Something was going on in his head, but whatever it was he wasn't ready to share.

"You know, five years ago I'd have gone in there and cleaned the place out with you. I'd have done it because you needed the back-up, and I'd have understood how you needed to take out some of your frustration on these people." I pointed toward the bigger of the two laborers. "Five years ago I would have happily walked into that bar and grabbed the information for you, no matter how many heads I had to break. But not now."

He looked at me, still silent. Then he said, "How far can I trust you, Caine?"

I shrugged. It was a useless question.

"You know about the *lua*?"

"Hawaiian martial arts. I've heard it's effective, but you don't share it with us haoles. You teach it only in secret societies."

Kimo snorted. "You make it sound like the Chinese Triads."

"Warrior societies are the same. It's the same as the Knights Templar. They can be a force for good."

"But not necessarily," Kimo said. "Lua dates back to Kamehameha's time. The Alapai Guard practiced lua, perfecting it when they were the king's personal bodyguard. Now it forms a basis for father and son traditions. I was about to bring James into my lua brotherhood. He had resisted earlier, but a combination of what he was hearing at the university and his level of maturation made him change his mind."

"He changed his mind?"

"Then he changed it again. He refused to come with me, although joining my lua brotherhood would have previously satisfied him. It was all he wanted since he was very young."

"He'd already joined another group."

"That's exactly what happened. He broke from the family and joined a rogue group."

"How did you find out?"

"I caught him practicing defensive moves he would not have known. Do you understand? He *could* not have known what he knew without personal instruction."

Two more men had joined the giants sitting on the porch railing while we talked. Another appeared in the doorway, a shadowy figure, standing out of the light.

"That's him," said Kimo.

"That's him who?"

"Bumpy. In the doorway. He's been to the house. With James." He reached for the door handle. I gently put my hand on his shoulder.

"So you've seen him before. He'll keep. If he's connected to those other two he'll know why you're here. Give it some time. Once you've got something on him you can come back and do it legally."

"This place is where they meet."

I looked at the giants watching us, seeing them now in a different light.

"Just think about what you're doing before you do it," I said. "If you still want to go in there I'll go with you. Not happily, but I'll go."

Kimo looked at me for the long moment, staring me in the eye as if he were considering what I'd said. I'd have given anything to know exactly what was going on inside his head.

I knew what he'd decided when he opened the Jeep's door.

"Lock your side," he said.

The four giants parted as we walked up the steps, and closed ranks behind us. I'd been in some dingy little bars before, but this one might have been a contender for the top spot. Gray linoleum, sticky from beer and whatever else, partially covered a termite-infested plank subfloor that deflected under our weight. Roaches ran marathons back and forth across the floor. The back bar was an ancient, hand-carved mahogany affair that didn't belong with the tin roof and the dirty stucco walls. A lone high window painted over with aluminum paint, inexpert brush strokes creating a mad pattern, provided the only light except for the harsh glare of a low fluorescent hanging over a tattered green pool table. The joint didn't even have a beer sign. A five-bladed fan turned lazily overhead, barely disturbing the heat inside. Flies buzzed above our heads, dodging the fan blades for sport.

I didn't turn around, knowing that it would cause one of our escorts to say something. I did not want to give anyone an excuse to start a fight. If Kimo started one, it was his option and his business. I was here to watch his back. Watching the look of hatred on the face of the four giants surrounding us, I wished my back was in better shape. If this was a warrior society, there could be more than just a little trouble.

"Lieutenant Kahanamoku," said the bartender, his courtesy exaggerated. "What may I do for you this afternoon?" The man smiled when he addressed Kimo, amusement crinkling around his eyes. At least one of us in the bar thought this was going to be fun.

"Where's James?"

"James?"

"My son."

"Oh, you must mean Keola."

Kimo nodded, as if he could not speak.

"I don't know, Lieutenant. I didn't think it was my day to watch him."

"Kimo," I said sotto voce, when I saw his hands flex. Then I regretted saying anything.

"Yeah, *Kimo*," said the bartender, speaking in the carefully syncopated patois of a wised-up, but oppressed, minority. "Your *haole* friend here is talking to you. All your *haole* friends call you by your missionary name? You ever call your son by his missionary name?"

"Where's James?"

"I don't really know. Haven't seen Keola for a couple of weeks. Not since the pigs busted him for DUI. Of course *you* got involved. Once the pua'a realized who his daddy was they would have called you, huh? So he didn't exactly get arrested and lose his license or anything like anyone else's kid, huh? You protected him, didn't you?"

Kimo stared stonily at the bartender, his hands flexing and unflexing. I was beginning to lose the hope that we might get out of here without getting banged around.

"I am looking for my son," he said, his voice even and controlled. "I am not looking for trouble. I—"

"Trouble? In here? We have a respectable place, Lieutenant. We don't mean to cause you or your haole friend any trouble."

"—I'm just looking for my son."

"Then I suggest you file a missing person's report."

Kimo nodded, and I knew that violence was close.

"Did you know Howard Hayes?" said Kimo.

"That professor who got himself killed? That guy? I heard

about it, but I didn't know him. He never came in here, anyway, and I never been to college. Why? You think I did it?"

"Could be, Bumpy."

"That why you're here? Or you looking for your little boy? Which is it? I'm confused."

"You ever heard of a group called Silversword?"

"Yeah. I heard of it."

"I heard you're the leader."

"Me?" The bartender raised his eyebrows in mock surprise. "I'm just a bartender. I don't lead nobody, except the occasional drunk to the shitter."

"I'd like a beer," I said, interrupting the ebb and flow of the conversation, trying to keep it from moving toward the inevitable.

The bartender just looked at me.

"What kind do you have?"

"You mean it?"

"I'm thirsty. This is a bar. I'd like a beer." I knew I was pushing the envelope, but there was nothing to lose at this point. If I didn't do something, Kimo was going to get into his third fight of the day. And lose this one.

"Sorry," said Bumpy, shaking his head. "Fresh out."

The four giants behind me laughed. Two of them leaned against the bar, one on either side of me. I felt an elbow in the ribs.

"Excuse me," said the guy on my right.

"Sure," I said, grinning. "You sure you don't have any beer? These guys have beer."

"They got the last ones."

I felt Kimo move quietly, not really seeing it, but sensing his position changing.

Violence floated in the air like an albatross.

"Hey, what's that?" I pointed to the fly-blown refrigerator in the back bar.

"Reefer."

"Open it."

He gave a slight shake of his head, then grinned and opened

the chipped white door. Beer filled the interior from top to bottom.

"Well, what do you know?" he said. "Forgot about these."

"I'll take one of those," I said.

"Sure. Sure." The bartender pulled a long-necked bottle from the refrigerator, popped the cap and set it on the stained mahogany top in front of me. "To your health."

"Thanks," I said, reaching for the bottle. Before I could grab it, the bottle was snatched from its place in front of me. I turned and watched the man on my right drink half the bottle in a long, single gulp. He watched me as he drank my beer, looking for a reaction.

He got nothing.

He finished and set the bottle back down in front of me, never taking his eyes off mine. He wore a small, satisfied smile after he put the bottle down. Then he belched a long rumbling growl.

I stood my ground, giving no sign that I was annoyed, or happy, or unhappy, or that I cared where I was or what I was doing. I gave no sign that I even knew the potential in the air. You could almost smell the musk.

"I just drank your beer, haole," he said. "What're you gonna do about it?"

I looked at him. I looked at the man who suddenly appeared behind him, who was bigger than him. A third giant stood behind him, bigger and meaner-looking than a grizzly bear.

Kimo stood behind that man; he looked ready for anything, fight or flight.

"Any man," I said, careful to enunciate each of my words properly, not wanting to allow a misinterpretation of anything I said, "who's man enough to drink my beer while he's looking me right in the eye . . . I have to buy that man a drink of his own."

Tension fled the room like a warm breeze.

"You not going to fight me?"

"Why should I?"

He shook his head, having no answer.

"Bartender, bring this man a beer. Another beer. He likes . . ."

I examined the label of the bottle in front of me. "Since he drank half of it I'm guessing he likes Bud."

The big fellow grinned at me. "Yeah. Dat's true."

"I could tell by the way you chugged it down. You think I was going to snatch it out of your hand and you wouldn't have a chance to finish it?"

He laughed. "Yeah, man. I thought you was gonna hit me."

"Just because you drank my beer?"

"Sure!"

"You must have a low opinion of us haoles," I said.

He laughed again, joined by his friends. "Yeah, man. I do." He slapped me on the back, just above the kidney. I rolled with the blow, winced inside, but kept smiling.

The door opened. Out of the corner of my eye I saw Ricky Lee enter the bar. He didn't see Kimo and me until his eyes adjusted to the dim light inside the bar. By the time he recognized us it was too late to back out gracefully. Kimo leaned against the bar, watching the small man, his face utterly devoid of expression.

"Hey there, Ricky," Kimo said. "We keep running into each other."

To his credit, Ricky stood his ground. He'd already tangled once with the big cop and it didn't look like he wanted to repeat the experience. His eyes shifted from Kimo to me, then back to Kimo. It must have confused him to see us getting along there so well.

"Call your office, Lieutenant," said Ricky. "Your boss wants to talk to you. He don't like you beating on people."

"I'll do that," said Kimo, smiling. "Maybe tomorrow."

"I think you should call him now."

"I'm busy. Want a drink?"

"You buying?"

"Can't afford it. Caine here's buying."

"Pour Mr. Lee a beer," I said to the bartender.

"Mr. Lee doesn't drink," said Bumpy, a little stiffly, a little fearful. "He says it is bad for the temple that he calls his body."

Where had I heard those words before? Then I remembered that Felix had said almost the same thing to me not long ago. Well, they were of a kind, if I thought about it. Two sides of the same coin. They shared the same generation, the same cultural background; they had the same interests. Hell, they even held the same attitudes. The two young men might have been friends had circumstances allowed it.

"I don't think I will drink with you," said Ricky Lee, turning to leave the bar.

"Hey, come on, I only hit you a little bit."

"Yeah, I know," said Lee. "My mother used to hit me harder than you did. All the same, I'll skip it. Gotta go."

"What's your rush?" Kimo moved toward the smaller man, but cautiously, the way a lion would approach a cobra.

Ricky backed away from the large cop, keeping the door within easy distance.

Kimo advanced, moving to cut off the entry as a means of escape. "You really should have a drink with me," he said. "Let bygones be bygones. I'm not your enemy. I'm your friend."

"Yeah, you're my friend. Don't come any closer!" Ricky reached under his shirt and pulled a pair of long black sai from his waistband.

Kimo stopped, watching the foot-long Chinese fighting irons, deadly in the hands of an expert. The two weapons would more than make up for Ricky's smaller size. The only way Kimo could take him would be to shoot him.

"Whoa," said Kimo, putting his hands up.

"Leave me alone," said Lee, his voice low and steady. "Leave me alone and I will not have to protect myself. You've got a gun. I don't carry. It's not illegal to protect myself. Even from a cop."

Kimo nodded, unwilling to debate a pair of sai. He stepped back a few steps. "You just bought yourself some real trouble, Ricky."

"Like I didn't have it already. Why're you following me?"

"Wasn't. Caine and I were following a trail. You showed up here after us. You hunting, too?"

"Let me go."

"There's the door," Kimo pointed.

Ricky did not take his eyes off Kimo, the tension between them holding them together, yet apart, like the simultaneously opposing and attracting poles of two magnets, wanting to separate, yet unable to do so.

Another shadow eased into the bar, aware of the tension, yet unaware of the participants.

"Felix." I said the word aloud.

Ricky turned.

Kimo lunged.

Ricky turned back but it was too late. Kimo had pinned him to the grimy linoleum. Felix saw me and tip-toed around the combatants. "You need help, Kemosabe?"

"Kimo might," I said, but was wrong. Kimo had already disarmed the smaller man and turned him onto his face, cuffing his hands behind his back. He moved automatically, with precision and grace, not a motion out of place.

He hauled the little man to his feet, the twin black sai in his left fist looking like toys.

Felix turned to face the others in the bar. They stood quietly, but alert, watching Kimo and Ricky, showing no appetite to become involved. "Looks like I got here just in time," he said.

"How did you find me?"

"LoJack."

"Come again?"

"LoJack. Kimo's Cherokee has the tracking system. I asked Tala to make the call and they gave her the location. Saw the bar and knew you had to be in here."

"Having grapefruit juice."

He nodded. "Sure you are."

"Am I under arrest?" asked Ricky.

"You wanna go to jail?"

"No."

"Then behave yourself," said Kimo, hauling him outside into the harsh afternoon light.

"Let's go," said Felix. "You finish your grapefruit juice?"

I nodded. We followed Kimo and Ricky out into the dusty parking lot. Felix faced the wall, his hands cuffed behind his back overshadowed by the big cop. Kimo unlocked the cuffs and stepped away from the little warrior, as if expecting a counter-attack.

Ricky rubbed his wrists and stood still. He didn't even turn around.

"This is a warning to you, Ricky Lee," said Kimo. "Don't try me. You pull a weapon on me again and I'll hurt you. You behave yourself and we'll get along. You understand me?"

Still facing the wall, Lee nodded slowly.

"Okay then," said Kimo, turning around and pocketing his handcuffs. "That was a wasted effort," he said, watching Ricky disappear.

"Whole day was," I said.

"Learned some things."

"Yeah?"

"Didn't find my boy."

"He might be back home. You call?"

He shook his head. "You got your ride home, I see. I think I'll just head for the barn. See if he came back. Tutu Mae will know what to do. I'm sorry I dragged you out all day with me. I'm sure you would have rather done something else with your time."

"And miss all this excitement?"

I turned to Felix, who stood off from the group, as if afraid of what Kimo might do next.

"Take me back to the Royal Hawaiian," I said to him. "There's just enough time left to take Angel to a nice dinner and a walk on the beach. Tomorrow will come soon enough and I think this is one of those nights when it will pay for a man like me to stay up all night."

At my request, Felix dropped me off at the curb at Kalakaua Avenue and Seaside. He let me go alone. I was sure that he wasn't happy about it, having spent some creative effort to find me, only to lose me again, but I gave him leave. I wanted to be alone.

I strolled through the rows of shops to the green lawn in front of the old pink monarch of Waikiki. It's a form of time travel to enter the Royal Hawaiian from the street. You leave one millennium and you suddenly return to the last one, where the pace is slower, the architecture more refined, and the world seems to have stopped spinning. At least while you remain.

I wished I could have made the world stop spinning. Ancient Hawaii had places of refuge where criminals could seek absolution for their crimes. As long as they remained behind the walls they would be safe from prosecution and punishment. Even capital crimes were forgiven if the priests granted it. I wished it were the case with the Royal Hawaiian.

"Good evening, Mr. Caine."

The woman behind the front desk smiled at me expectantly.

"Good evening," I said, aware of the beer stench and stale cigarette smoke that I wore like a bad suit.

"You have some messages here," she said, handing me a pile of pale pink stationery.

"Thank you," I said, unable to recall the young woman's name.

"Enjoy your stay with us," she said, turning to her companion behind the desk, whispering, I was certain, about the friends that I had in high places.

I skimmed through the messages while I rode the elevator to my suite. Tala had called, informing me that my hearing was in the morning. "Wear your suit," her message said. She had called three more times; the last time the message was marked "Urgent." That had been at three o'clock, some six hours before. Daniel had called twice; his last message said he would try my cellular, something I had forgotten to bring with me. Felix had left a message.

Missed communications. Errors in judgment. People trying to help, whether paid, or paying off a debt. On what might have been my last day in paradise I had been in limbo, almost as if I had already moved on and taken a room in purgatory.

I opened the door to the suite to find it deserted. Angelica was gone, flown to whatever coop she flew to when she wasn't at my side. The rooms smelled of her, a lingering flowery scent that made me think of lilac and smooth tan skin. The bathroom was vacant of her toiletries, the closet empty of her clothing. She had left no note. She had fulfilled her duties and would not be coming back.

One more sign that life was changing. Tomorrow would be the determining event. Tomorrow we would see what kind of stuff John Caine was made of.

On the counter of the wet bar I found a note in Daniel's block printing. "See Chawlie," was all it said. "See Chawlie" was all it needed to say.

I took off my stinky hunting clothes and carefully washed myself from head to toe, mindful that I would be doing that myself now that my nurses were gone. Satisfied that I no longer smelled like a sodden barfly, I dressed in light wool trousers, a silk Hawaiian shirt of muted pattern, and my best pair of sandals. Chawlie would expect me. And he would know when I arrived at the hotel.

I called downstairs for a taxi to take me to Chinatown.

36

Chawlie stood when he saw me, an uncharacteristic event. He took my arm and led me into his private chamber behind the round red door, sat me down and personally served me from his own teapot. That, too, was atypical. He said nothing of substance until the room was vacant but for the two of us.

I sat against the pillows, leaving the green tea untouched on the table, and waited, knowing that this was what Chawlie expected. He took his time, stirring a little brandy into each of our cups. I could sense the expectation in him. He knew something, and he wanted to tell me what it was. Whether he would tell me or not would be up to him. I doubted at the moment that he knew what he was going to say.

Finally he raised his head and looked at me. His eyes, normally unreadable black pebbles, were alive with sadness.

"Have you considered life and death?"

"As life and afterlife?"

"As life and no-life. Skip the children's tales. Here we have light. There we have only darkness. We have nothing."

"Yes. I have considered it."

"What do you think?"

"I think that no one really knows."

Chawlie smiled a knowing smile. "You hedge your bets, John

Caine. You want to believe, but you cannot be honest with yourself?"

"That's possible, old friend."

"*Old* friend. That is the problem, isn't it?"

"Is this part of your efforts toward enlightenment? Or is it because you see the approach of death?"

Chawlie started when I said that. "You are reading minds these days?"

"No, but don't bluff an old bluffer when you're feeling like this. You're holding more aces than most people. You've had it better than most kings who ever lived. And now you seek enlightenment. You want to live forever. Of course you would, the life you've lived. I would, too, if I were you, *old* friend."

"Chawlie is getting along in years. Things that interest me now never interested me before. And things that used to stir my passions no longer hold my interest."

I nodded. That explained the recent lack of young female attendants.

"Do you think Daniel can handle the enterprise? Or is he too harsh?"

"He's a brick," I said. "Daniel can handle anything."

"He's ruthless and smart. He would kill and he would not be caught if it were required. And he would not kill unless necessary. He would do anything to protect me. And the enterprises."

"He reminds me of you many years ago."

Chawlie nodded. "I have had that same observation. He is right to take over."

"What about Gilbert? I thought he was your number one son."

"I'm not Charlie Chan, I'm Chawlie Choy. Gilbert is a nice boy, but he does not have what it takes to lead. It pained me, but I have reached that conclusion. It is only Daniel."

"And what will you do?"

"I have my bonsai trees, and I have my concerns and hobbies. It is not too much to ask for me to spend my remaining days in contemplation and peace."

The old man had found his bolt-hole, and he was contemplating passing the scepter. That he would discuss it with me was fascinating. That he would actually go through with it was another thing entirely. But I knew he had been contemplating the move.

I had seen it start when Daniel had been shot. That event had caused the thought processes to follow.

"Daniel would be the perfect one to take over."

"Would you help him, John Caine? He will need your guidance."

"You would be here."

"I will not, whether I am in light or in darkness. Once I leave this place I will not return."

"You are going to China?"

He gasped, his mouth open. "Why would you say that?"

"If you were here, on this island, watching, you could not help yourself. The only way you could turn over the reins to Daniel would be to leave. Go to China, buy your peace and retire."

"That's exactly what I was thinking," said Chawlie. "If I go I will miss you."

"Are you going soon?"

He sighed. "It is more complicated than that. Chawlie got you in trouble, John Caine. Chawlie did everything he could to help you. It is not enough."

He expected an answer but I didn't know what to say. I nodded gently, to let him know I was listening.

"Chawlie find out that lady detective from San Francisco wants to convict you. It is all her doing. She is ambitious person. She is also a dangerous person. I sent Daniel to find out about her. She is not married. She is without children. She only has one passion. That is to convict, convict, convict. She is the one who put you in jail. Without her, you would not be in trouble. Daniel knows where she lives, what is her schedule. And she is now in Honolulu, here for your hearing tomorrow. Chawlie and Daniel both ask your permission to kill her. Tonight."

That was a surprise until I thought about it. I let the thought float effortlessly in my consciousness, considering it. But I knew the answer I was going to give. "No," I said.

"She will kill you with her authority!"

"It's not right, Chawlie. I appreciate the offer, and I understand that she is doing what she is doing for reasons other than justice. But killing Shirley Henderson cannot get me what I seek, either."

Chawlie closed his eyes. "Daniel can do it, make it look like she had a bad meal."

"No, Chawlie," I said, hoping he would understand the threat. "She may have set the wheels in motion, but they cannot be called back. Killing her would solve nothing. It would create more problems for all of us."

"John Caine, I try to stop this case. Chawlie knows many people, here and there. He pay much money. Nothing he does can stop it. Only this *woman*," he emphasized her sex, much as he would use the word as a curse, "this woman is your worst enemy."

"No, Chawlie. There will be no killing police officers on my account."

"Then you are a fool, John Caine."

"I may be a fool, but you are not killing that woman."

"Then what are you going to do?"

"I know that you support me. I know that I will be protected, in jail and out. I know that my lawyer here and my lawyers in California will do the best job that they can. I don't like the system any better than you do, but I will face whatever comes."

"You cannot trust in the system. Only family."

I nodded. "Sometimes it seems that we cannot. But sometimes we do not have any other choice but to trust."

"You mean that?"

"Yes."

"Then Detective Henderson will be protected, as well."

"Thank you, old friend. You would do me a disservice to kill her."

He nodded. "Daniel told me that you would say that."

I wondered about the power that I had held in my hand. Anyone has the power to destroy. Even the weakest among us can destroy the lives of those around them. But the power to save is one that only the truly powerful can claim.

"Is that all?"

"Good luck tomorrow. Daniel will be there with you. He will testify that you saved his life."

"Do you think it will help?"

"Nothing will help you now. Your life is in the hands of the judge here in Honolulu, and in the hands of twelve strangers in San Francisco."

"That's not true."

"What?"

"My life is in *my* hands. It's always been in my hands. Whatever happens from this point forward, I caused it to happen. Not Shirley Henderson, not you, not the district attorney, not that crazy gunman who shot Daniel and me. This is the path that I went down a long time ago. And this is the result. It should not have been a surprise. My kind went out of fashion a long time ago. The world is a soft place now. I'm not even sure that my kind are needed anymore."

"Don't feel sorry for yourself, John Caine," said Chawlie. "The world is still a hard place. Those who say that warriors are out of place in this world are foolish. They are sheep, trying to ignore the wolves. They dare not look into the shadows for fear that they might see those who wait."

"That won't do me any good now."

"Maybe. Maybe not. Your trial will tell. Whatever happens, do not, for one instant, lose faith in yourself, in what you are. And do not lose faith in Chawlie."

"Do not worry, old friend. I will never forget."

"Perhaps you are the wiser man. Daniel also argued against killing the woman. Only Chawlie thought it a good idea."

"It isn't a good idea."

Chawlie bowed. "She will owe you her life and not know it.

She will always hate you and will never know that she lives because of your generosity."

"It wasn't generosity."

"Wisdom, then."

"You don't kill people who don't threaten you. It is the state that threatens me, not the detective. And you can't kill the state. As bad as it is, you have to trust, sometimes."

Chawlie nodded. "Chawlie hope for a good outcome in the hearing tomorrow, and Chawlie hope for a good outcome in the trial in San Francisco. And Chawlie hope you come back so you can help Donna Wong with the gold she found in the king's tomb."

"How did you know about that?"

"Donna Wong is family. Daughter of distant cousin. Chawlie know about gold before Detective Kahanamoku's grandmother know about the gold."

"Are you interested in the gold?"

"Only that it is protected. Chawlie doesn't need gold or silver. Sunken Spanish treasure always cause problems for those who find it. If not from treasure hunters, then from the state. And you, yourself, told me that the state cannot be killed when it threatens you."

"She means to bury it."

"Volcano bury it, I think. There's not much time."

"Then there's not much I can do about that."

Chawlie nodded. "As you said, you just have to trust sometimes."

"Are you mocking me?"

"Yes," he said. "Chawlie never want John Caine to take himself seriously. All these thoughts, all these proclamations. You need a woman, my friend. Someone to take your mind off of tomorrow."

"Angelica's gone."

"You go now. You'll find her when you return to the Royal Hawaiian. Chawlie asked her to move out this afternoon, but told her to return after I had spoken with her. And with you. She will make this night one you can remember for a long time."

I nodded. It might have to suffice. I was not too proud to feel grateful that Angelica would be there to comfort me with her sleek, warm body and the talents that made me smile. She was the pleasant diversion to keep me from dwelling in the dark regions I might be tempted to visit if I spent the night alone.

"Thank you, Chawlie."

"Hurry, John Caine," he said, smiling.

37

"You feel okay?" Tala leaned across the table and straightened my tie. I didn't think it needed it. It just seemed an easy way for her to show concern.

"Fine," I said.

"You sleep well last night?"

"Yep." The truth was that I hadn't slept until early this morning, and then my old friend the nightmare had awakened me, this time with a surprise visit from Ricky Lee. Between Angelica and the Vietnamese warrior with Ricky Lee's face, I had managed to get in an hour's sleep. Maybe less.

"We're scheduled fourth," she said, ignoring my curt reply. "That means we're up around ten o'clock. We'll have to be there when they call the cases, but then we'll just have to cool our heels until the other hearings are done. It'll be a breeze. You've done it before."

I nodded and took another sip of Starbucks's best, wishing I didn't have to claim experience for such things. Felix sat on a banquette across the room, watching people come in and out. He'd been castigated by Daniel for shirking his duties, so he watched me now, even though my biggest threat came from the criminal justice system.

"The heart of the prosecution's case is that someone died while you were in the commission of a felony," she said. "Self-defense is not only a right in this country, it is a duty. And self-defense against a shooter of unarmed people in a public place is becoming less of a crime than it is something to admire. Unfortunately, they're not so progressive in California.

"And they can't really get you for self-defense, either. Their whole case is based on your holster. There's no gun. Your prints aren't on the shells. They can only *presume* that they were your cartridges. They can only *presume* that you had a gun, or that you fired it—there were no paraffin tests taken of your hands so they cannot prove that you even fired a gun. Did you know that? Your doctors would not let the cops have access to you until it was too late—for them.

"Anyway, that's not good enough. They can *presume* all they want, but only on their own time. The prosecution can't just *presume* away a man's liberty. They have to prove it. I think I can make those mainland suede-shoe snake oil salesmen eat their words. At worst you committed a misdemeanor by discharging a firearm within the city limits. But we're not going to argue that. We don't have to. At best, you saved two people's lives at the risk of your own. Witness the hole in your back. They don't have a case. They'll fold."

It was pleasant listening to her passionate speech. I knew she was partially trying to make me feel better and partially practicing her presentation before the judge. We both knew she was logically and maybe even legally flawless. And we both knew she was fighting a losing battle. The state of California wanted me in prison, and they would not rest until they got me into their jurisdiction. Fortunately, the only way they could get me was to use the system, their system, and fortunately their system was geared toward protecting my rights.

I'd had some second thoughts about the liberal court system since being charged with murder. Depending on how this whole thing shook out, I might be inclined to change my mind about the laxity of judges. So far they'd been kind to me.

So far.

"Kimo will testify on your behalf once we get to the character phase of the hearing. Daniel will testify what you did for him. He's going to show off his scar. An emergency room physician will testify as to your condition and to the condition of Daniel when you both came into the hospital. Those are your witnesses. They'll take about an hour. The prosecution will present the police officer who will swear that he saw you fire *a* weapon, and a lab technician who dug out .45-caliber shells from the parapet of the roof from across the street." She smiled a huge, toothy smile. "I read the report. Do you know how many bullets they recovered from the shooting scene?"

"Not a clue."

"Sixty-seven. Do you know how many of them were .45 caliber?"

"Eight."

"How did you know that?"

"Do you want me to answer that?"

She glanced around the coffee shop. "Remind me not to ask you that question on the stand, okay? You're right. Eight. All the others were 9mm, fired from six different guns. All eight .45-caliber slugs were found in a small circle in the parapet wall, lodged in the framing. Eight .45-caliber shell casings were found near where the police officer saw you fire a pistol. But you don't have to explain anything. You didn't fire a pistol. Nobody can prove that you had one. All they can do is guess that you had one based on the presence of an empty holster on your belt."

"Isn't that bad enough?"

"I hope they use the holster. It's covered with blood. Your blood and Daniel's blood. That will put the prosecution on the defensive, trying to explain your blood on the holster, along with Daniel's blood, when they cannot produce your supposed firearm."

"Sounds okay."

"The best part is that the police officer who saw you fire your gun is not a good witness. I took his deposition and he flunked, as far as I was concerned. And Daniel will testify that he saw the cop cowering facedown in the gutter, looking for cover, not looking at the shooting."

"But Daniel wasn't conscious all the time."

"Let the prosecution prove that."

I nodded. She had it covered. It wasn't airtight, but it was better than I'd hoped.

"Am I to testify?"

"Oh, yes. You're up for it, aren't you?"

"I'll do anything."

"Then you testify last. I want you to tell your story. All of it, except for your firing a weapon. You don't, by the way, own a .45-caliber firearm, do you?"

I thought for a moment, then said, "Not now."

"That's not good enough."

"No."

"That's better. You're still hesitating. That question will come up and you'd better get it right."

"So what did I do?"

"You covered Chawlie and you dragged Daniel into cover. You did what you did with his neck wound, saving his life, and you got shot in the back for your efforts. That's your story. That's all you say."

"You're the boss."

"I like the way you say that." She squeezed my hands. "You're going to be fine. I know you've been up against worse stuff than this. And don't worry. I've got a feeling that California is outclassed in this one."

"I hope you're right."

Tala smiled. "I hope so, too." She looked at her watch. "Are you ready? Are you up for this?"

"Yep."

"Then let's go over there and watch the other cases. I want to get a feel for the judge and see what makes her tick, what ticks her off, and what pushes her buttons. That woman is the most important person in your life right now. You'll only spend a few hours with her, but they will be the most important hours you've ever spent with a stranger. Don't you think it's a good idea to get to know something about her?"

"Whatever you say," I said.

"Come on," she said, and then pointed to a large leather brief-case parked on the terrazzo next to her. "And your friend over there gets to carry the paperwork."

It was as Tala said it would be. The judge heard the arguments and the witnesses on both sides and then said that she would render her judgment in writing in due course. Tala approached the bench for clarification and was told that Her Honor felt that she had to study the applicable case law, and she wished to consult with an expert in California criminal law. Tala seemed very pleased with herself, and nearly called it a victory. I was to remain free under the terms and conditions of my existing bond.

"It could have been worse," said Tala, "but I think I know why Her Honor chose to draw this out. I devastated that cop on the stand. Did you see him sputter? He couldn't testify if you fired a gun or played the ukulele. I'd love to have him on the stand in front of a jury."

"You might get that chance," I said.

"Not here, and I'm not licensed to practice in California. Someone else will have the pleasure."

"If the judge rules that I'll go to trial."

She quit smiling. "She'll rule. And you'll go. There's no question that California's wishes will not be honored. The judge knows that politics are more important than the law. If she doesn't, she'll never get another criminal back from the mainland. She has to send you back, regardless of what Hawaiian law says. But she wanted to beard them a little, and so she'll draw it out as long as she can."

"That mean we've got a good case?"

"In Hawaii we've got an excellent case. In San Francisco, I'm not so sure. I *am* sure Chawlie will provide you with excellent counsel there."

"Did you get me permission to leave the island?"

Tala produced the judge's letter with a flourish. "I got it yesterday, while you were playing cops and robbers with Kimo."

"So you knew the outcome already?"

She nodded. "The judge and I had a long, long talk."

"So why did you make me sit there for two hours and watch the other cases."

"I wanted you to understand that everybody in Hawaii is doing everything they can to keep you free. But it's not going to be good enough. In the end you'll have to go. I was hoping you would learn something in there that might help you when you actually go to trial in California. And I wanted you to see what you were up against, so it wouldn't be so scary when you're actually on trial."

"I guess I thank you for that."

"You'd better."

"So I can fly to Hawaii?"

"Donna Wong is in town, along with David. They've come back for supplies. You can fly back with them tonight."

"I can really go?"

"You're a free man. Enjoy it. At least for the moment."

So by one o'clock on a picture-perfect Hawaiian afternoon I was a relatively free man, relatively free to go where I pleased, within the usual limitations. The only cloud on my personal horizon was the certain knowledge that the state of California could recall my freedom at any given moment.

But that was somewhere in the future. My very able attorney had secured for me a few more days of freedom. I would not mope around my suite at the Royal Hawaiian and waste them.

Not knowing where anybody was, I went walking on the beach, Caine's solution. Everything seemed to be getting better at once. Angelica had helped me over a problem that would have become a big one in my own mind (unless they sent me to prison for the rest of my life). My wounds were healing. My strength and endurance, which had fled, seemed to be hovering just beyond reach. Once they took that stent out of me I was sure I could resurrect the old body within six months.

I sat on the crown of a sandy beach and watched the tourists play in the gentle surf. The sea and sky were nearly an identical shade of pale blue. Out beyond the reef, a catamaran with shocking pink sails slid effortlessly across the surface of the ocean.

I realized that I had come to a major life decision point and had sailed across it as effortlessly as the catamaran skimmed the surface of the sea.

Where had all that new-found wisdom gone?

I grinned, shading my eyes against the afternoon sun. I would continue to grow older. I'd just never grow up.

My cellular telephone rang. I unclipped it and pushed the SEND button, recognizing Donna Wong's cellular number.

"Hello!"

"Mr. Caine," said David Klein's voice. "It's Donna! She's been kidnapped!"

"Where are you?" I found myself standing, having no memory of rising from my sandy perch.

"We had just stopped at the bank in Pearl City to get some money from the ATM when three guys swarmed us. They took her."

"Call the police."

"They're already here. I didn't know what else to do but call you after that."

"You okay?"

He hesitated, then said, "Yeah."

"Which bank, and where?"

He told me. I knew it, just on the perimeter of the Pearl City Shopping Center.

"I'll catch a cab. I can be there in twenty minutes. Maybe less."

"I'm not going anywhere," he said.

"Call Kimo." I was already moving inland, toward Kalakaua where I would find a taxi stand.

"He's here. I called him first."

I nodded, realizing that I had been third in the equation. At least he had called me before he sent his Christmas cards.

"I'll be there, David. We'll find her. Don't worry."

And with those platitudes uttered, I had done all I could. I hit the END button and began shuffling toward Waikiki's main drag, looking for transportation.

39

It took almost the whole twenty minutes to reach Aiea. When I reached the bank the place was ablaze with flashing lights. When I saw two City ambulances I started to worry. One wagon screamed past as we drove in. Somebody had been damaged, and seriously.

I paid the cabby and started toward the scene. A motorcycle officer stopped me; I pointed toward Kimo, who motioned for me to come, and the motor cop let me through the tape barrier.

Kimo stood with a rugged-looking haole detective whom I recognized from the Greek drug case several years before. Jim Husing had been working undercover then, mining the lucrative drug trade between Asia and California and Hawaii, getting more than his share of good cases. He had been a manhunter, and a damned good one. And when I had found myself in over my head he had backed me up, saving my life. I had already managed to get myself shot in the leg. Jim and his partner kept me alive.

"Jim," I said, acknowledging his presence.

He nodded, probably wondering how I got myself involved in a kidnapping.

"What happened?" I asked.

Husing looked to Kimo, and then to me.

"It's okay," said Kimo. "He's family."

Husing looked doubtful but he said, "Do you know Donna Wong?"

"She's my client."

"She's been kidnapped."

I didn't like the way Husing said it. Matter-of-fact, as if he were describing a computer part. "What happened?"

"Her boyfriend, David Fein—"

"Klein. David Klein."

"David *Klein*, her boyfriend, gave us a description of three attackers. Probably another one driving the car. He got the car, too, the license and everything. Two broken arms, broken teeth, a possible concussion, and he gets the license and a pretty fair description. Must be some kind of rocket scientist."

"He is."

Husing looked at me as if I'd lost my mind. "That kid?"

"He's at Berkeley, studying physics. Smarter than all of us put together."

Husing looked dubious.

"So how is he? Broken *arms*. As in two? Possible concussion. That doesn't sound good."

"He'll be okay. He'll be in a lot of pain for a couple of weeks. But he'll be fine. Nothing permanent."

"He tried to defend Donna?"

"Yeah, but there were two big guys and one little guy. The little guy had a pair of sai, Chinese fighting irons. Very good with them, too, from what I hear. He's the one who did the damage. The others were mere muscle. Big, dumb and slow."

I glanced at Kimo. He nodded his understanding. David Klein had either run into Ricky Lee or he'd found his doppelganger.

"And he saw the license plates?"

"Not that they'll do any good. They were false plates. Hawaiian Homelands. Sometimes the firebrands put them on their car, refuse to pay homage to the state of Hawaii. Call it illegal. We've always got a beef going with those types, one way or the other. They put their own license plates on their cars. They carry their own insurance, although I've never heard of anybody collecting when they hit one—"

"You're saying this car had Hawaiian plates?"

"That's what he described."

"Hawaiian Homelands," said Kimo softly.

"And the car?"

"White Toyota, Klein didn't know the model or the year, but it he said it was an old one. Early eighties. It had a light blue interior. And it was ratty."

"Ratty?"

"Like they never cleaned it inside. Full of fast-food wrappers and stale potato chips."

"Kimo," I said. "One of the guys Donna saw at Hayes's house the day he was murdered was a slender Chinese male. That mystery man matches Ricky Lee's description."

Kimo almost smiled. "And he matches the fellow here. And then there's the sai."

Husing had led David through the scenario several times before the ambulance took him away. David and Donna had withdrawn two hundred dollars from the ATM and were walking across the parking lot toward her truck when the Toyota pulled in front of them and three men got out. Two were young and Polynesian, and the third man was a slender Chinese male David swore he had not seen before. One of the Polynesians struck David with his fist, knocking him to the ground. The other one pulled Donna into the back seat. David got up and attacked them. The little Chinese male pulled the fighting irons from his waistband and broke both of David's arms near the wrist. He clobbered him on the head for insurance and David fell to the pavement. When it seemed certain that David wouldn't get up again, they all jumped into the Toyota and drove off.

We had Ricky Lee down pat, but the other two were a little more difficult: young, Polynesian, and heavy. There were probably three hundred thousand people on the island who fit that description.

"This your warrior society?" I asked Kimo.

"I hope not. What do you think, Caine?"

"What was she doing without protection? Did you guys forget about the death threat?"

"She just flew in this morning. Didn't tell anybody. I was busy. At your hearing."

"Tala knew she was here."

"Tala is her attorney."

"Excuse me, guys, did you ask David if he noticed anyone else using the ATM? Was there a line of people waiting to use the machine?"

"I didn't ask," said Husing, "but it's always possible. This is a busy branch."

"You want photographs of the kidnappers?" I asked.

"What?"

I pointed at the ATM. "Those things take photographs all the time. Or video. Whatever. About once every ten seconds they record what's right in front of them along with the background. Do you suppose the timing was right?"

Kimo studied the position of the ATM, the alignment of its face to the place where David said Donna had been forced into the Toyota. He squared it off, looking from one locus to another.

"It's possible," he said. "Let's go take a look." He stopped and put his hand on my chest. "I almost forgot, Caine," he said. "*You* stay here. You're a felony suspect, not a peace officer. Stick around, though, because I still want to talk to you."

I found a concrete bench in the sunshine and sat down and enjoyed the warmth while they went inside. It was a good place to think.

On the surface it looked as if someone had taken Donna for what she knew. That appeared to be the only reason. It wasn't what she had, or what she had done, so it had to be for what she knew. That being a logical assumption I started working on the other part of the question. Who benefits? With one hundred eighty million dollars in gold and silver and jewels at stake, just about anyone could benefit. But there was something else. As much money as one hundred eighty million dollars was these days, this whole thing had a different feel about it. Something I could not put my finger on. Something just out of reach of my faculties. It was about the money, or was not.

The problem was that I had no idea which direction to go.

If they wanted the treasure why kidnap Donna so publicly? If they wanted access, and they knew where she was here on Oahu, they could have quietly followed her to the treasure site. Why kidnap her in broad daylight? Why do something that would bring in the FBI, CID, and the other alphabet agencies? Why not keep it close and personal? What was going on here?

I wished I could have spoken to David before they took him away. That must have been him in the ambulance. By now he would be in the emergency room, under the care of medical professionals who would not appreciate my questions, would not even allow me inside. I knew that questions had to be asked. I hoped the right ones would be asked.

Donna had been kidnapped, taken by Ricky Lee and his compadres in broad daylight, leaving clues all over the place, pushing the envelope about as hard as it could be pushed. Why not take out an ad in the paper?

It couldn't be just to stop Donna, or to get the location from her. The secret of the site would not be secret long. According to what I understood, Donna and her sisters would not be there much longer.

I rubbed my eyes and let the images flow. The morning *Advertiser* claimed that the volcano had been erupting continuously. Hualalai's lava flow almost reached Queen Kaahumanu Highway yesterday, and then it stopped. According to one of the experts quoted in the paper, if it went off again and breached the road the lava would roll into the sea. Once it reached the sea her sisters would have to abandon the site completely.

But first things first. Before I returned to the site we would have to find Donna. Alive, I hoped, and in one piece.

Kimo and Husing came out of the bank, each man carrying a small white cardboard box. Neither man looked happy. Kimo was talking on his cellular telephone.

"You were right, Caine," he said, holding the cell phone away from his ear. "The ATM picked up the whole thing. Those tapes are used over and over again, so the quality is terrible. We're taking the tape to the lab to look at it again. I think they can enhance it to where we might get some good evidence out of it."

"You're welcome."

"Didn't say thank you, you know what I mean?"

I nodded. I knew what he meant.

"Just got the call from the courthouse, too." He held up his cellular phone. "That lady judge issued her ruling. She didn't wait long. Probably got a lot of pressure from the governor's office. You bond is revoked. That lady detective is coming to take you back to California. They got you booked on the midnight flight out."

"She ruled already?"

"Probably didn't want you to fly over to the Big Island and then have to pay me to come get you. She had no choice. You understand that?"

"I know." I knew I had to go. I wasn't so sure about my fortunes in a California courtroom. I felt flimflammed by the courts here, telling me I could go and then yanking away my freedom all in the same afternoon.

"You better come with me."

"You call Chawlie?"

"I called him. Waste of time. He already knew."

"So what are you going to do about Donna?"

Kimo didn't answer my question. He didn't take me to jail, either. After he put me in his Mustang, Kimo took the Kamehameha Highway west toward the Hawaiian Homelands. When he turned west instead of east, putting Honolulu in his rearview mirror, I knew something was up but I said nothing. Sometimes it's better to wait.

When we turned off the Farrington Highway, just a little way past the Kalaukauila Stream, I knew he was taking me to his home. I watched the parched landscape fly by my window and waited for Kimo to open up.

It didn't take long.

"I need your help, Caine," said Kimo after a long, pregnant period of silence. Ahead I could see bright colorful patches on the yellow hillsides. Karen Graham's flower fields.

"I'm supposed to be in jail. How can I help?"

"James was on the video. He and one of his friends I recognized. And Ricky Lee."

"James is with Ricky Lee?"

"He's in big trouble. We find him, we send in SWAT. This is a federal case now. They'll send in the Hostage Rescue Team. They'll kill everybody in sight and say they're sorry afterward."

"You can't mean that."

He nodded. "That was my fear talking. They're professionals.

But to them James is a kidnapper. He might have shot up the main gate at Pearl. He's got one chance."

"So when the court called and told you to bring me in, you balked."

"That Henderson woman is at Beretania, waiting for us. When we don't turn up she's going to get angry."

"So what's she going to do?"

"She can protest, and I'll tell them that I gave you some compassionate time. Chief will chew my ass, but I'll survive. I will get in trouble doing this, but I want you to talk with Tutu Mae," said Kimo, as he pulled onto the grassy lawn of his family compound. Three high-roofed wooden structures stood on a small knoll above the Kamehameha Highway. Behind the homes, a colorful blanket of flowers covered the hill. Two acres of tropical flowers bloomed in wild array, blessing the senses with their presence.

"Talk to Tutu Mae?"

"She thinks you know things that you don't understand."

"That's a given."

"She thinks that if she tells you what she knows, and what I know, and . . ." He took a deep breath. "If we pool our resources we might figure out what is going on. There's much more to this than what we see on the surface."

I nodded. The thought had occurred to me. Chawlie had mentioned the same thing the other night, alluding to events that I would have thought were unrelated.

Kimo pulled himself from the Mustang and trudged inside, the weight of his children's troubles and the events of the day very heavy on his shoulders, leaving me, a wanted man, alone in the car with his keys.

I climbed out and followed, mindful of the trust.

"Make house, John Caine," said Tutu Mae, embracing me. "I made some iced tea for all of us." She handed me a tall, moist glass, filled with tea and sweetened with a wedge of pineapple, and waved me toward a seat at a round oak table.

"Thank you, Tutu Mae," I said, sitting where I was told.

"And how are you, John Caine?" she asked, sitting primly in a straight-backed chair.

"I'm fine, so far," I said, not knowing how much Kimo had told her about my legal predicament.

"You no longer argue with your doctors?"

"No, ma'am," I said.

"You look gaunt, as if you need to eat. Would you like something?"

"No thank you. I am not hungry." The truth was that I could not remember when I had been hungry last, the injury and the worries robbing me of my appetites.

Neolani came in and I stood and shook her hand. She kissed Kimo and they had a whispered conversation and she left. She looked sad, the only time I had ever remembered her being so.

"Mr. Caine," said Tutu Mae, "I understand that Kimo told you about the lua."

"Yes."

"And he told you that he is a member of a lua society."

"Yes."

"And you have sworn to secrecy."

"I have."

She looked at Kimo, who nodded.

"You must not tell anyone what he told you. Under no circumstances."

"I understand."

She looked at me through magnified lenses for a long time before she nodded to herself. "You should have been born Hawaiian," she said.

"What does it matter how we are born?" I asked. "When it is only the content of our character that's important."

"Sometimes I cannot tell if you mock me. That was a quote from Martin Luther King. Is nothing sacred to you?"

"It makes sense."

"It makes more sense than anything they talk about today. Any of them."

I didn't have to ask who "them" was. I knew what she meant. It was any of the various groups.

"Even the Hawaiians," she continued. "I don't understand our young people today. They want, but they do not work for what they want. So they become angry. They blow things up. They burn things up. They have temper tantrums and demand respect, yet they do nothing to earn that respect. Respect, they argue, must come from one's existence. It no longer need be earned.

"My grandson and his wife are worried about James," said Tutu Mae, watching my face. "They have raised over a dozen children in their lives. Their children are very important to them. My great-grandson is not someone who has been taken lightly, or ignored, or who has been abused in any way. Kimo and Neolani are strict, but they are loving. They have rules, and they welcome conversation. On any subject. The children learn the art of critical thought, which is something that I have insisted that they learn in the home since they are not taught it at school."

She sipped her tea and cleared her throat. "But not all of the children are the students that we would wish them to be, nor do they become the people that we would have liked them to be. James, I'm afraid, is heading for trouble, if he hasn't already arrived at that destination.

"Was he on the tape?" she asked Kimo, surprising me with her knowledge of the afternoon's events.

He nodded. "It was him," he said.

"Mr. Caine," Tutu Mae said to me, reaching out and grasping my arm. "This is more than a group of young men thinking they're going to change the world. This is not revolution. I see more than that, depending upon your view. I see it as less, not more. As seen by Jefferson, a revolution can be a positive thing.

"James has joined a group that pretends to be something it is not. James is getting deeper and deeper into trouble, following a leader who does not have the goal he says he does. Silversword pretends that it stands for Hawaiian autonomy. They are tired of asking the American government for justice. They now claim the moral authority to take matters into their own hands. Things are seldom as they appear. I have learned something that I must share with someone equally knowledgeable in the history of my islands, but from the viewpoint of another culture."

"How can I help?"

"You are a warrior. Your actions, your thoughts, the way you live your life, you are the embodiment of a warrior. I know that you have been severely tried lately. I'm sure that there are even more challenges ahead, both physical and mental. But before you go to the mainland for your criminal trial I wish that you and Kimo could find James before the officials and the FBI. You will not harm him. I know that about you. He knows you. If he does not present a threat you will not hurt him. If he is a threat, then you will protect my grandson."

I nodded.

"Kimo knows where Silversword hides. He will tell you on the way. I trust you in this as I would trust no other man." She reached across the table and grasped my hands in hers. Her fingers were cold. "Please. Whatever you do. Bring my grandson and his son from there. Rescue them from themselves. We'll let the authorities deal with the rest of them. But this is family."

She nodded to Kimo, who reached down and pulled out a little revolver. I recognized it as Kimo's off-duty weapon, a Chief's Special five-shot .38. It wasn't good for much. I wouldn't want to use it even if I had to. I had little faith in handguns under .40 caliber. But we weren't considering a firefight. Whatever we did would be close combat. If there was combat.

Kimo placed the revolver on the table in front of me.

"Please, Caine. You and me. The two of us. We need to go in there and bring out Donna before the others find the location."

Kimo had put his life and career in my hands. And the life of his son. He needed unofficial backup.

I nodded.

There was nothing else I could have done.

41

I slipped the revolver in the hip pocket of my shorts and stood up. The room seemed filled with sadness. "We'll be back for you," said Kimo, kissing his grandmother.

"Be careful," she said, closing the screen door.

Kimo's cell phone rang again. He looked down at his belt, but made no move to answer it. "Gotta be the chief. I'm going to be in big trouble keeping you around, but this time I figure it's your deal as well as ours."

We climbed into the Mustang. "How do we do this?"

"That bar? That's just their hangout. But Bumpy's got a commune not far from there, out by the old airport. I figure we just drive on in and take the girl away from them."

"Come in with guns blazing?"

"Nope. Just take her back."

"Front door approach."

"I'll talk her out of them. I'm good at it."

"You're serious."

"You've got the gun."

"Yeah."

"If I can't talk them out of giving her over to us and coming along peacefully, then you can shoot them."

We rode along in silence between deep green hills and a pale blue gray ocean. The air smelled faintly of salt. We stopped once so Kimo could consult his map. I watched a pair of bright red cardinals perched on a tree limb. They cocked their heads at us and then flew away in a flurry of crimson.

"It's over there," he said, parking the Mustang in a grove of coconut palms. Beyond was a dense tangle of shrubs and vines. Beyond that was the beach.

"We can get up there through the cane field." Kimo pointed across the road. "Good cover."

"You lead," I said. "I'll follow."

Kimo gave me an appraising look. "You sure you're up for it?"

"I'm fine." I wished I were fine. But I told him I was. I would be fine, anyway. At least until this thing was done.

"You know you're going to have to go back to California after this is over."

"Yeah."

"And I might not have a badge."

"Yeah."

"And I can't think of anything else to do."

"I know."

Kimo gazed up the hill, across the cane fields, toward the commune. "I hope she's up there."

He went across the road and I followed. We entered the cane field, walking single file through the narrow rows. The stalks were lush and green, not yet ready for harvesting. The air was thick with the sweet smell of the young plants. We made little noise, and we couldn't be seen except from the air. Even then, I doubted we would be anything but a couple of ripples roiling the leaves as we moved through the cane, two predators, a couple of sharks hunting a lagoon.

We saw the first two members of the commune as we emerged from the cane. Two women working a taro patch looked up as we walked by. They called out to us, but we ignored them.

A group of children played in a sandlot, watched over by an older woman. She gave us a sharp look, but said nothing. She had a more disapproving look when my eyes met hers than when she saw Kimo. He was local. He was Hawaiian. But I was the outsider, the haole.

"Stop!"

As we reached the main building, two men with lever-action deer rifles carried in the crook of their arm approached us. "You are trespassing," said the leader. Neither man threatened us with their rifles, but the threat was there.

"Police," said Kimo.

"You have to have a warrant. Unless you have a warrant, you'll have to leave."

"I have reason to believe that a felony is being committed on the premises. The law gives me the right to search the place."

"Not our law, Lieutenant," said Bumpy Kealoha, coming around the corner of the building. "You two are trespassing. Get out." I noticed that Bumpy carried a .45 in a holster on his belt.

"Can't do that, Bumpy," said Kimo.

"Why are you here?"

"I want the girl back," said Kimo. "Give me the girl and we'll go without causing you any trouble."

"What girl?"

"Donna Wong."

Bumpy shrugged. "Ain't got no Pake here, Lieutenant. Aside from your haole sidekick, we're all pure Hawaiians here. This is our land. Here we're sovereign."

"If we leave without her, the FBI will come in and burn this place to the ground."

Bumpy smiled. "Turn this into another Waco? I don't think so. I think those guys have been tamed a little bit, you know what I mean?"

"Don't count on it, Bumpy. They'll come in here and level this place. The only thing that'll be left standing is your headstone."

"I'm through talking to you, Lieutenant. Leave now or my boys will have to make you go."

Kimo turned and looked at the men behind us. "You up to

shooting a Honolulu police officer in the line of duty?" he asked. "They'll hang you out to dry in one of the mainland prisons for the rest of your lives. You'll never see this island again. You up for that?"

I kept my eyes on the riflemen. They started to show disinterest in the game after Kimo's speech. All the same, I was happy to have Kimo's little pistol in my pocket.

"Why don't you just send her out," said Kimo. "Whatever happened can't be changed now. But we can make things go easier for you, Bumpy. All we're looking for right now is the two lolos who took Donna. And we want her back safe and sound. You turn them over to us you'll probably skip any charges. You can say you didn't know she had been kidnapped. Whatever, you'll probably be all right.

"But if you don't, then this whole place, every man, woman and child, will be targets. The feebees don't care who they kill, you know what I mean? This is a nice place. It's peaceful. You want them to burn it to the ground?"

Bumpy looked at the ground. Kimo had given him few options. Fight us, fight the State of Hawaii. Kick us out and the FBI comes in. Kimo had caged his argument exactly right, feeding the fears of a separatist like Bumpy. If he feared anything, he feared those who had participated in the Waco disaster. And Ruby Ridge. In both places, children had been killed.

Bumpy looked up. We were still there, on his property, in his face. We would not go away. I saw his face when he reached the decision. All the iron drained out of him.

"I'll take you," he said softly, "but you've got to promise me no bloodshed."

Kimo said, "That's why we're here. Caine and I don't want bloodshed. We just want Donna."

Bumpy sighed. "Follow me. And remember your promise."

"I'd feel better if you hung up your pistol and sent your boys with the deer rifles back to wherever they came from," said Kimo.

Bumpy took off his gunbelt and handed it to one of the riflemen. "I'll be back," he said. He turned and walked toward a small house on the far edge of the clearing. Kimo followed. I took one look back toward the riflemen and went after them.

Taro patches surrounded the little frame house. Two women worked the muddy patches, wading up to their knees in black water. Bumpy ordered them back to the main house. They left without a word.

It bothered me that no one questioned his authority.

"You there on the porch," said Kimo. "Come down here."

A man moved in shadows. As he passed the window, sunlight glinted off of the barrel of a long gun.

"Put the gun down," said Bumpy. "Things are under control."

The man on the porch stood in shadow watching us. He didn't threaten us with his weapon, but he didn't move either.

"Put the gun down," said Kimo, his voice carrying the weight of authority. It also carried something else, something I did not recognize until the man stepped forward into the sunlight and I recognized the face of his son.

James came off the porch and leaned the shotgun against the wall. "It's okay," he said. "I cannot shoot my father."

"You are coming with me," said Kimo.

"Yes sir."

"Stand over there until this is done."

"Yes sir." James walked slowly to where his father had pointed and waited. I was surprised at his docile attitude.

"Who's in there?"

"Ricky and Donna. Fred and Barney, too."

"Who?"

"Fred and Barney. That's their real names, and they look like the Flintstones. One's big, the other short. They're brothers."

"They dangerous?"

James shrugged. He knew his father. Dangerous was a relative thing.

"You there when they took her?"

"Yes sir."

Kimo nodded. "You're in big trouble. You know that?"

"Yes sir."

"You're going to be all right, son. We'll take care of you."

"I know."

"Ricky's armed?"

"Might have a pistol. I doubt it, though. He doesn't like firearms. He says he's better without them."

"What about the Flintstones?"

"Shotguns," said James. "They also have a M-16 and a lot of ammo."

Kimo glanced at me. The little pistol hadn't seemed very effective in the first place. If they wanted to make it into an OK Corral I'd be heavily outgunned. "I'll take the shotgun," I said.

"Okay, James. Where in that house is Donna? Exactly?"

"He locked her in the bathroom. It's in the back of the house. Near the back door."

"Which window?"

"That one." James pointed to a small window that a mouse might have trouble getting through.

"Caine, you want to take the back door?"

"Sure."

"James, you and Bumpy go back with the children and stay with them."

"Dad? What are you going to do?"

"I'm going to talk to Ricky. If he talks nice and hands Donna over to us, he'll be okay. Now go where I told you, and Bumpy, call the police station and tell them we've got three felony suspects in here and we're getting them to surrender right now."

Bumpy blinked.

"Go," said Kimo.

They went. He watched them for a moment, then turned to me. "You feel okay?"

"Never better."

Kimo trudged to the front door and pounded on it while I slipped around to the back and waited for the door to open.

"Open up, Ricky Lee!" shouted Kimo on the other end of the small structure. "I know you're in there. Open up!"

The lock snapped with an audible click and the knob twisted. I backed away from the hinge side, waiting, the shotgun held low, pointed toward the grass.

The door opened a crack.

A young Polynesian man put his head out.

I held the shotgun like they taught me, one hand on the fore-grip, one hand near the trigger. I could use it for shooting or for clobbering, either way would work. It made no difference to me now, as long as we got Donna safely out of here.

The door opened wider.

"Hey!" I whispered.

I kicked the door with all of my strength, catching the kid as he turned to look in my direction. The door bounced off his skull and rebounded back at me. I dodged the door, reached around, and pulled him by the hair out into the sunshine.

He lay silent, his hands at his sides. I rolled him over and checked him for weapons. He was clean.

"Hey you!"

A huge man charged from the back door. "You killed my brother!" It was like facing the charge of an Indian elephant.

I stepped aside and butt stroked him in the kidney. He roared and turned on me, swinging one huge fist as he turned. Fred Flintstone was light on his feet for a big man.

I ducked the swing and hit him again with the butt of the shotgun, striking him behind the ear.

He went down.

I reversed the shotgun again and put the barrel in his face, pressing the cold steel against the bridge of his nose.

"Don't. Move."

He rolled his eyes, bright with pain, but he didn't move.

"I'm going to back away," I said. "You stay like that you'll live. Hear me?"

Fred Flintstone said nothing, but his eyes communicated his acceptance. He had no wish to die here on this beautiful day.

Ricky Lee flew out of the back door just as Kimo broke down the front.

"Stay," I said.

Ricky ran around me and headed toward the trees, running like O. J. Simpson on one of his good days.

Kimo came lumbering over.

"Cuff these two!" I shouted, handed him the shotgun, and took off after Ricky Lee.

He had the advantage of youth, conditioning, and a head start. And he had not been banged around as often lately. But he was a city boy, not used to the ways of the jungle, and he tripped over a root about twenty yards in and sprawled into a muddy pit along a stream beneath an ohia tree.

"Easy, Ricky," I said. "I want to see your hands." I pointed the little revolver at him.

"You gonna shoot me? I'm unarmed."

"You're an asshole, Ricky. It would be easy to shoot you."

He sighed. And raised his hands.

"Get up," I said, backing away. "Carefully."

He did as he was told, keeping his hands away from his body. I had him walk ahead of me until we reached the clearing and I could turn him over.

Kimo put handcuffs on Ricky Lee and left him facedown on the lawn, next to the Flintstones. I stood over him while he went in and brought Donna from the bathroom. She seemed dazed but unhurt. She smiled when she saw me.

"I knew it would be you two. Thank you. How's David?" she asked.

"Fine," said Kimo. "We'll take you to him. We're going to have you checked at the hospital anyway. You two can share a room overnight."

"This creep locked me in the bathroom because I kept asking to go. I do that when I'm scared."

"You're okay now."

She looked around. "Where are we?"

"North shore."

Sirens wailed in the distance. Kimo turned and listened to them getting louder. "That would be the cavalry," he said.

"You have another set of handcuffs?"

Kimo looked stricken. "James."

"No, me. I'll bet you that Detective Henderson will be here, along with the troops. Kind of embarrassing if you've got an armed prisoner, and without cuffs." I handed over the little revolver.

"Consider yourself under arrest, Caine. And thank you. Thank you very much."

"Glad I could help."

"The main thing," he said, "is that nobody got hurt."

"Except for Ricky Lee."

"He don't count," said Kimo. "And he's oh for three with us."

"So far," I said, remembering the little man's temper.

Shirley Henderson did ride along with the troops. So did a couple of FBI agents who looked disappointed when we handed over four prisoners. All four were charged with a variety of crimes. The US Attorney would add still more when their cases were reviewed.

Henderson saw me standing apart from the group, walked right up to me, spun me around and threw the cuffs on my wrists.

"You are under arrest," she said, her voice angry. "I am adding the charges of flight to avoid arrest, resisting arrest, and evidence tampering to go on top of the murder charge."

I didn't expect to be treated like a hero, but I didn't expect the wrath with which she greeted me. I stood among the FBI field guys, with their dark blue jackets and baseball caps and their stubby little submachine guns, my hands cuffed behind me, and hoped they wouldn't think I was any kind of threat.

"And you," she said to Kimo. "I am lodging an official protest about the way you treat felony suspects."

"He needs medical attention," said Kimo.

"He'll be checked out before we go and afterward. There's just enough time so we won't miss our flight tonight."

"He saved me," said Donna Wong.

"I'm sure he's charming, but he's going back with me. Can we have a ride to the hospital here? I've seen Oahu and I can go home now. As soon as possible.

"Come on, Mr. Caine," she went on, tugging on my hand-cuffs. "They've got to out-process you and I don't know how long that'll take." She stared at Kimo, who remained silent, but she spoke to me. "Maybe you should take a good look around. I think it's going to be a long time before you get back to Honolulu."

I didn't think about other people's worries over the course of the next three weeks. I forgot about Kimo's problems. I forgot about Donna Wong. I damn near forgot about my wounds. I didn't think about my boat. I didn't think of Hawaiian history, nor did I concern myself with the fallout resulting from angry young men filled with enthusiastic venom and the vigor of youth. Even though I spent the majority of my time lounging in a holding cell with three other once-and-future felons, and even though I seemed to have a lot of time on my hands, my mind didn't roam. I focused on the issues. I knew that my future lay in the tasks set before me. What happened now determined the rest of my life. I could only concentrate on what they'd laid out for me. Whoever "they" were. Whatever "it" was.

And besides, thinking of home was too painful. I didn't think I was tough enough to go there. I didn't need to be that tough. Not just yet.

Even though Chawlie provided an excellent attorney in California, I wished that Tala was at my side. I trusted her, and I knew how she approached the trial. But Tala was busy defending James Kahanamoku in Honolulu. I didn't know anything about Clifford Smith or his partner Andrew White, except that they were white-bread, white-shirt and Gucci-tie attorneys, who seemed to have been stamped from a mold at some Ivy League law school. They appeared competent. And smart. And very organized. I wondered how they would stand up in front of a local jury whose majority would most likely be from the same minority as the woman whose death I stood accused of causing.

I should have known better. Smith and White were the front men, the fine-edged lawyers who talked to judges, who filed motions, who papered the case with endless pleas and prayers. In military terms they were the artillery. Their job was to soften up the opposition to make certain that the other side kept its head down before we engaged them in battle.

It wasn't until I'd been a guest of the City and County of San Francisco for more than a week that I met the litigator.

He was a small, wizened man of no particular age. He wore a bright red tartan tie and a threadbare suit in gray glen plaid. His shoes were old, but polished to a high sheen, and they did not have lifts. He stood flat-footed, and walked with certain steps. His eyes were small and dark and he wore thick, gold-rimmed glasses that shone like his shoes so that he sparkled top and bottom. His hair was thin and plastered against his freckled skull almost as an afterthought.

"How do you do, Mr. Caine?" he asked, extending his hand over the interview table. We were in one of the tiny rooms set aside for counsel and client. Everything was gray. The floor was gray painted concrete. The walls were cast concrete, finished and unpainted. The door and frame were painted gray. In this world the color of fog his bright red tie stood out like a rose in an ash heap.

"I am Albert Chen."

"Mr. Chen," I said, standing to shake his hand.

"Please sit, Mr. Caine." When I sat he adjusted his glasses and opened his notebook and read a paragraph of notes. He nodded to himself, closed the notebook, and looked up at me, his eyes made enormous by the correction of his lenses.

"It says here that you wish us to file a motion for a speedy trial. Would you please explain?"

"I'm tired of sitting around here."

He nodded. "Yes. So you would like to travel up the Sacramento River to a place where they will keep you for the rest of your life. Where will you go if you then tire of the state prison?"

He didn't expect an answer. He merely smiled. "You are not a criminal, Mr. Caine, despite what the prosecution says. You saved two people's lives that day at considerable risk to your own. They do not have much of a case, and I have spent a great deal of time trying to convince the District Attorney that this will not be one of those cases that he will point to with pride when he next comes up for reelection."

He smiled to himself, as if relishing the thought. "The district attorney is an old friend and adversary. We view a lot of things the same way. I am pleased to inform you that he has familiarized himself with your case and he made me an offer that I am obligated to put in front of you."

I nodded.

"The prosecution has agreed that they will not press first-degree murder charges if you plead to a lesser offense. They stipulated that you must agree to serve six months in the San Francisco County jail in return for a guilty plea to the lesser offense. You will be given credit for time served, both here and in Honolulu, and you will most likely be granted an early release. All considered, you would only serve three months, and you will have paid your debt to society. It will, however, still be a felony, with all that implies. I told them that I would report their most generous offer to you and ask for your opinion in the matter."

"They want to drop the murder charge?"

"Yes. In return for a guilty plea of involuntary manslaughter."

"That's a felony."

"That is correct, Mr. Caine. You would be a convicted felon. You would lose your private investigator's license. You would lose your firearms and your license to carry them. Your retirement status as a United States naval officer would be jeopardized. You would not be allowed to enjoy many of the freedoms you previously enjoyed with equanimity."

"I didn't kill anyone."

"Nobody is saying that you did."

I nodded. "You see the problem?"

He smiled and I saw a lot of gold fillings. "Of course. Do I take this as a negative response?"

"It's a 'no.' "

"And you are aware that by turning down this most generous offer from the District Attorney you are placing yourself in dire jeopardy? Wait, don't answer yet! Are you aware that the district attorney still can try you for first-degree murder? And that your life may be forfeited if I am not up to my usual standard?"

"Is your usual standard very good?"

"My usual standard is excellent. If I say so myself."

"I didn't kill that woman."

"That is so."

"It wasn't even an accident. I had nothing to do with it. The murderer was on a roof across the street. He was one of those idiots who start shooting innocent people in a public place."

Chen looked at me from behind his thick lenses and said nothing. He knew the truth, apparently judging it to be impolitic to refute my version.

"I will not voluntarily put myself in prison for a crime I did not commit. These people are crazy."

"The district attorney knows this. The facts of the case are very clear."

"Then please tell the district attorney that I regretfully decline his offer."

"You regretfully decline. Very well, I shall tell the district attorney that you cannot accept his kind and generous offer. And shall I tell him that we are ready for trial immediately on the murder charge?"

"You're ready?"

"I didn't say that. I merely asked if I should tell the government that we are ready for trial. There's a difference between reality and what you tell the government. Which is as it should be, as they have no compunction in lying to us."

In spite of myself I smiled. I liked the man and felt comfortable in his presence. This old gunslinger could outthink a platoon of government lawyers. I was sure he could even teach Tala Sufai a thing or two.

"There is already an attorney in Honolulu who knows this case."

"Miss Sufai. Yes, I've spoken with her. She is an extremely bright strategist, and she seems to know her way around the courtroom, too. I read the transcripts of your hearings. I must tell you that I was impressed."

"I know she isn't licensed to practice in California, but could she help you. She already knows the case."

"You said that, Mr. Caine. And I would like to have her to sit by my side for the trial. She would be most helpful. We have ways to make it legal for her to become a temporary member of the California Bar, but it would take too much time to process the applications."

"It's just the paperwork," I said.

"Exactly. With the stroke of a pen Miss Sufai could become an honored member of the California Bar. But the time required is more than we have if you wish to proceed immediately."

"And with the stroke of a pen a man can be charged with murder when all he did was defend himself."

"Well said, Mr. Caine. I trust that you wouldn't mind if I use that analogy if and when I may find myself before a jury."

I shook my head. "So you think we can win?"

He smiled. "I think we can win. Even without the formidable Miss Sufai. But it is never certain. There are twelve strangers walking around somewhere in this city who at this moment have never heard of you. Twelve men and women who will be hauled into court against their wishes and forced to sit and hear all kinds of tales told about you. And they will not be a happy lot. Nor will they be a particularly intelligent lot. Most of the really bright folk seemed to feel that they have a duty to find a way around jury duty. More's the pity, Mr. Caine, more's the pity. And yet, despite what I just said, those twelve people will somehow manage to figure it out and they will get it right. Time after time the juries I encounter continue to get it right, even when you know that their entire collective intelligence is most likely approaching that of lemon yogurt. It is amazing, a freak of nature. It shouldn't work, but it does. The jury system, as flawed as it is, is the best system in the history of the world. You are in good hands, Mr. Caine."

"I feel better already."

He laughed, barking a long stream of *haws* around the room. His laugh was infectious, and I found myself joining in.

"Very good, Mr. Caine. A man with a sense of humor will not be easily cowed. I am depending upon you not to be cowed. Is that understood?"

"Yes."

"I thought it would be. You don't seem to be the kind of person who is frightened of anyone or anything. I've read about you, and your benefactor told me stories that would make exciting reading. It is too bad that you do not have a biographer. How is your health, by the way?"

"It's fine. They're taking good care of me here."

"That is as it should be," he said, smiling. "Now, I must go. I've got a message to deliver to the district attorney. I am going to have a little fun and deliver it personally."

"Do you expect them to drop the charges?"

"Sadly, no. This is now a test of wills. The prosecution has ego involved. While it is necessary for trial lawyers to have a strong ego, it sometimes gets in the way of sound judgment. I think that is the case here. That detective, that Miss Henderson, bullied them into taking the case, based, I believe, solely upon your extremely violent history. They will have a very difficult time getting that into the record, however. And one word out of court and we shall change venue faster than the prosecution can blink."

"So we'll go to trial. When?"

"We have a hearing tomorrow. I'll expect you to shave and look presentable. Not the pirate I see in front of me now. Shave the beard. Shave it all off. You have a nice face and I believe that you should not hide it behind such a bushy monstrosity. And wear your best suit."

"I'll shave."

"Had it long?"

"Since . . . I was in mourning."

"The ancient Romans used to do that, grow a beard to demonstrate their mourning. Are you over it?"

"Over what?"

"Over what caused you to mourn?"

"Yes. Part of it."

"Then shave it off and leave it off. At least during the trial. Afterward, when you're a free man again, you can grow hair down to your ankles for all I care."

He looked expectant so I laughed politely.

"So be prepared for your hearing. Dress well, look smart, keep silent. You won't have to say anything. I'll do all the talking. You just have to sit there and not cause a disturbance. Can you do that?"

"I can do that."

He smiled again. "Then I am blessed with the best kind of client." He got up to leave and then he stopped. "*Second* best kind of client. Someone once said that the best kind of client is a scared millionaire."

"I'm scared. And a millionaire is paying the bills."

He nodded.

"Good enough."

43

Her Honor Judge Sylvia Santo looked up from her desk and peered over the top of silver half-glasses at Mr. Chen. She glanced down again at the paper in front of her as if she did not believe what she had read there the first time. Then she looked at my attorney again.

"This is something new to my experience, Mr. Chen," she said in a low, cigarette-roughened voice. "Usually the defendant wishes to delay the case as long as possible."

"We are ready to proceed, Your Honor. The defendant not only stands accused of a crime that he did not commit, but he is accused of capital murder in a case where his only actions resulted in saving the lives of at least two people. And if I may be so bold, may I remind the Court that justice delayed is justice denied."

The judge nearly smiled. "I haven't heard that old saw since law school, Albert. Motion granted. I've never seen someone so eager to drag his own client into court."

"Thank you, Your Honor."

"Excuse me." Christopher Turley, the young attorney prosecuting the case for the county, spoke without rising. He had risen once and had been chastised for it by the judge. He had tried to interrupt once, and had been chastised for that, too. His senior was not present at this hearing and he was not having a good day. If I read the situation correctly, the judge was continuing the young man's education. The experience was a kind of on-the-job training. It could not have been amusing for the young man, edifying as it was.

"Yes, Mr. Turley?"

"The prosecution needs more time."

Mr. Chen grinned and winked at me, his face shielded from the front of the courtroom by a copy of the motion he had just filed.

"Are you saying, Mr. Turley, that the City and County of San Francisco is not ready to proceed? Is that what you're saying?"

"I believe that we're going to need a little time, Your Honor. I—"

"The defendant is ready to proceed. He has filed papers to that effect. It's a fish-or-cut-bait thing at this juncture. Either you are or you aren't. You're aware, aren't you, that your office brought the charges? Are you not ready to proceed?" Judge Santo's voice was a low and menacing growl, reminiscent of a large jungle cat regarding its prey.

Young Mr. Turley may have been *young* Mr. Turley, but he was not young and *stupid* Mr. Turley, because he instantly understood where she was going with her questions and began backpedaling.

"The prosecution will be ready, Your Honor," he said quickly, blushing furiously from his hairline to the spot where his neck disappeared into his tight white collar.

"Is? Or will be?"

"Is, Your Honor. The prosecution *is* ready to proceed."

"So you have no objection to allowing the defendant his Constitutional right to a speedy trial?"

"No, Your Honor."

"And the People will be ready, no matter when I set the trial date?"

"Yes, Your Honor."

"Very well." She shuffled some papers and leaned over to speak with one of her clerks.

"Are we ready?" I whispered to Mr. Chen.

He nodded and put his finger to his mouth.

"We seem to have an opening, gentlemen," said the judge. "We can begin jury selection Monday, Mr. Chen. How does that fit into your schedule?"

"That would fit perfectly. Thank you, Your Honor."

She looked at the deputy district attorney, who merely nodded. He almost looked afraid to speak.

"You sound very sure of yourself, Mr. Chen."

"It is the case, Your Honor. This is a travesty. The charges should never have been filed against my client. This one will be a pleasure to try."

"Tell me that when it's over," she said. "You know all about the cup and the lip, don't you?"

Chen gave her a perfunctory bow of acknowledgment. "Your Honor, we have one more piece of business."

She nodded. "Your office provided me with some very interesting reading. Are you prepared to post bond for Mr. Caine?"

"Of course."

Turley seemed to have found his voice, but he spoke without rising all the same. "Your Honor, the People oppose bail in any form. May I remind the Court that this is a capital case. We are not after the death penalty, but we are citing special circumstances."

"Thank you, Mr. Turley. The court appreciates the reminder. Have you read the motion prepared by the defendant?"

"I have, Your Honor. It reads like a novel."

"Then you are aware of the sworn statements of a Honolulu police detective detailing Mr. Caine's activities of the night he was to fly here to California?"

"Yes, Your Honor."

"Mr. Caine apparently apprehended a kidnapping suspect while on his way to jail. And then he voluntarily waited while the arresting officer got to the scene. Don't you think that warrants some trust from the People of California?"

"Mr. Caine did not make the arrest alone. He was in the company of a Honolulu police detective."

"Who apparently trusted him."

"The People believe that he represents a flight risk."

She gave me an imperious look over the rims of her reading glasses. "Mr. Caine, are you going to run away?"

"No, Your Honor."

"And you are not going to get into trouble again here in San Francisco, are you?"

"No, ma'am."

She looked at Turley. "Have you read the other supporting documentation?"

Turley nodded.

"And you still oppose?"

"The People do."

"The People's opposition is noted." She looked over at our table. "Bail is set at one hundred thousand dollars, Mr. Chen. Bail will remain in effect until the verdict, or until your client does something stupid. I do not expect your client to do anything stupid, and you will instruct him not to play with firearms, knives, or any other weapons, nor should he become involved with any troublesome characters while he is in our fair city. Any other motions?"

"No, Your Honor. Thank you, Your Honor."

She looked to Turley, who shook his head. "No."

"Then we'll meet back here at nine o'clock on Monday. Have a nice weekend, everyone."

"Sylvia Santo is a tough judge, but I think she likes you," said Albert Chen to Christopher Turley after the judge had left the bench and the attorneys were picking up their law books and papers.

"Likes me? I feel like I've been beaten like a rented mule."

"She likes to keep the momentum going. And she likes to mentor young attorneys she feels have promise. She mentored you today, nothing more. That, to me, told me she liked you."

"I guess I'm flattered," said Turley, closing his briefcase. "Funny, but I used to think it was a pleasant thing to be flattered."

He shrugged. "We'll see you on Monday. Steven will be here, too. I'm not going to endure this flattery alone."

"He is learning. He will be an excellent litigator when he has some experience under his belt," Chen said to me after Turley left. "His senior is not so shy. Steven Brancato can be a passionate man in the courtroom. It is his weakness. When he gets going he puts on his blinders and rushes straight ahead. He looks neither left nor right."

Chen grinned at me, showing me all of his gold. "We will use that passion against him. It is the basic principle of aikido. It works in aikido. It will work here, too."

"Yeah, well, I'm sure they're great people, but I'd like them a whole lot better if they weren't so intent on putting me in prison."

"Young Mr. Turley is not inept, he is inexperienced; Mr. Brancato is experienced, but very inept. We could not have been given a better team to fight in court. This could not be anything but a gift from my good friend, the district attorney."

"Why didn't your friend just drop the charges?"

"That is not the way of a politician. He is embarrassed that his office brought the charges against you in the first place. After I forced him to see the true issues, he made the offer that you rejected. Both actions were foreseeable. You would not take the offer. He could not back down. It would not look good, even though it would have been best for the community."

"And for me."

"And for you. But he could not do that because of the way it would look." Mr. Chen looked at me sadly. "So he gave us these two, Mr. Turley and Mr. Brancato, so that if he lost the case he could blame it on his inferiors."

"*If* he lost?"

"There is nothing certain in the courtroom. There is always the chance that the prosecution will win. Mr. Brancato has certain negative qualities, but he does win a case from time to time. And if he wins, then my friend the District Attorney will have won as well. His actions may be lacking in principle, but they are predictable. It is the way of the politician to cover himself in layers of immunity."

"I don't like this."

"As indeed you should not."

"No wonder I hate politicians."

"Yes." Chen smiled, but his heart wasn't in it. "They are a breed apart."

Andrew White finished gathering the papers and notes that he had spread out on the top of the table. He nodded, but didn't smile. I wondered if they taught that in those Ivy League universities.

"When do you post my bond?"

"Mr. Smith is posting it as we speak. We are waiting here for word so you may be processed out. Andrew will accompany you and take you to your hotel. Mr. Choy instructed me to put you up at the Mark."

"Of course he did," I said.

"Everyone is there. We have a floor. It makes it easier."

"And Daniel is here?"

"He is here, as is your bodyguard. The one from here. His name is Chen, too."

"Any relation?"

"There are many Chens in San Francisco."

"And in China, too, I'd imagine."

Chen showed me his gold collection again. "China has only fifty-two surnames for a billion and a half people. There are therefore many, many Chens, regardless of where you may find them."

"So how long will this take?"

"Do not worry, Mr. Caine. We will get you out of here. But you must be patient. I guarantee you that you shall sleep between clean sheets tonight, and that you may lock the door from your side if you wish."

He reached over and patted my hand.

"Or you may leave it wide open. That is entirely up to you."

44

As trials went, it wasn't much. From jury selection through the final argument, the whole thing took less than a week.

As trials went, it may not have been long. But for me it was long enough.

The experience taught me many things, not the least of which was that justice had nothing to do with the truth. Everyone swore to it. The system was supposed to be based on it. But if it ever started to peek out from behind the layers of theory, rules and opinion that obscured it, the system immediately reacted and removed it. Truth was not the goal.

I wondered how they knew it when they saw it.

I liked it that the prosecution went first. I liked it that we could present our own witnesses, and then drag theirs back to testify again if we wanted to. I didn't mind that the system was skewed toward the defendant. In this case, the defendant was me.

The State offered its medical examiner to lay their foundation. A woman had been killed by a gunshot. The coroner's deputy testified as to how and where and when the victim had been struck, what the damages were, and what, if any, other injuries she might have suffered. My attorneys emphasized that the woman had been killed instantly. They treated the deputy coroner as if he were an old friend. They asked very few questions and sat down.

They disputed nothing. Everyone knew that Jackie Chang had been killed in the gunfight.

Then came the forensic experts who testified in excruciating detail about shell casings and slugs removed from the wooden structure where the gunman had hidden. Mr. Chen had them enumerate the number of 9mm shell casings found as opposed to the number of .45 ACP casings, their locations, the total number of firearms extrapolated by the laboratory based upon the shell case markings and the striations on the bullets. He asked if they had matched any bullets to any particular firearm. They had. To only one, the gun found several days later hanging from the corpse of the young man who had been murdered by persons unknown. Shell casings found on the roof of the building across the street, and bullets removed from bodies, both living and dead, matched that firearm. Mr. Chen also asked if there had been any fingerprints found on the .45 shell casings, and if so, if they had been matched to any particular individual.

"No," said the technician. "There were no fingerprints."

"So you cannot tie that firearm to any particular individual, is that correct?"

"That is correct."

By the time the forensics people stepped down from the stand I wasn't certain that I knew what had occurred and I had been there. The lasting impression from their testimony was that they had identified the dead shooter's weapon using two inalienable methods. Of a .45, Mr. Chen had reduced the memory of their earlier testimony to a distant murmur. Yes, there had been a .45. No, nobody had been shot by a .45. But several people had been shot by the other gun, the gun somehow connected to a corpse.

Oddly enough, the State did not present my bloody holster. That particular piece of evidence was a double-edged sword, as Chen explained it. If they presented it, it could support their case against me—that I had come prepared and possibly planning violence, and that I had come with a large-caliber automatic firearm, and, by implication, had used it. The other edge of that sword was the blood on the holster, how it got there, whose it was, and the circumstances surrounding the mixture of blood soaked into the old leather.

Eyes twinkling, gold teeth flashing, Mr. Chen said that they had probably weighed the risks and rewards and decided that the jury should never view the holster. He said that this must have been the subject of lively debates in the prosecutor's office. Their conundrum, he said, was that without it, and without an eyewitness testifying to the fact of my using a firearm at the scene, the state had nothing to connect me to the shooting.

"You might as well have been passing by," he said, smiling. "They have little to work with and they know it."

The prosecution called its last witness, the police officer who had sworn that he had seen me indiscriminately fire a pistol during the gun battle. Turley took the man through the sequence of events on that bright spring day. When asked if the gunman was present in the courtroom, the cop pointed in my direction. I felt the jury turn and examine me, as if expecting horns.

And the prosecution rested.

Judge Santo looked at our table, raising her eyebrows. "Your witness, Mr. Chen."

"We have a few questions, Your Honor," said Albert.

"I'll bet you do," said Judge Santo. "Mr. Kelly, you will remember that you're still under oath."

Mr. Chen led Kelly through his previous testimony. The man had been insistent that I was shooting. He saw me, he said, firing blindly. His testimony was damning and specific. I was there, I was armed, and I was using a pistol in what the prosecution tried to characterize as a gang war.

Mr. Chen allowed all of this damning testimony to be repeated. He emphasized the police officer's main points. He made me look like evil incarnate.

And then he paused and lowered his chin onto his chest, as if examining something on the yellow pad in front of him.

I looked. It was empty.

"We have heard your testimony as to your actions on that day, Mr. Kelly," said Mr. Chen in his soothing and gentle voice. "Do you recall filing a report?"

"A report?"

"A situation report. A sort of after-action report. Department policy requires it."

The man nodded.

"Excuse me, please, but could you answer verbally? This young lady," he indicated the court reporter, "has no symbols for a nod."

"Yes."

Mr. Chen went to the defense table and Andrew White handed him a piece of paper. "Is this your report, sir?" Chen handed it to the judge, who entered it and marked it as evidence. When she returned it to Chen he placed it before the man.

"Yes."

"This is your handwriting?"

"Yes. It's mine."

"In this report you state that you did not fire your revolver."

"We have to account for every bullet. I would have had to account for the reason I fired my service pistol."

"Rightly so, Mr. Kelly. And so you did not fire your service revolver at any time during the events of that afternoon in May. Is that correct?"

"I could not—"

"Please, sir. That was a yes or no question. Did you fire your revolver?"

"It's a pistol."

"Is there a difference?"

"The department issues us an automatic pistol. We don't carry revolvers. An automatic pistol is self-loading. In a revolver the chamber is the cylinder, which turns."

"You are an expert on firearms, Mr. Kelly?"

"Sort of. I shoot a lot."

"So you carry a *pistol*, is that right?"

"Yeah. A pistol is the correct term. Not a revolver."

"So, did you fire your service pistol at any time during the events of that afternoon in May? Did I get my terms correct this time?"

"Yes."

"Is that a 'yes' you fired your pistol or a 'yes' I got my terms correct?"

"You were correct."

"Thank you. Now did you fire your pistol?"

He hesitated. "No."

"Was your pistol loaded?"

"Yeah."

"Did you chamber a round?"

"Huh?"

"Did you chamber a round? As you've stated, the San Francisco Police Department issues automatic pistols to its officers. An automatic pistol does not fire unless you chamber a round, pulling back the slide to bring a round into the firing chamber. Did you chamber a round to make it ready to fire, sir?"

"I . . . don't remember."

"Did you remove your pistol from its holster?"

"I don't really remember."

"That is understandable. Have you ever been under fire? Has anyone ever shot at you before?"

"No. This was the first time."

"Have you ever had to pull the trigger of your pistol while it was aimed at a man or a woman while you were on duty?"

"No."

"Were you in the military?"

"No."

"So this was your first time ever under fire?"

"Yes."

"Difficult circumstances, weren't they? Did you feel that your life was in danger?"

"Yes."

"Did you feel that others' lives were in danger?"

"Of course."

"Are you a good shot, Mr. Kelly?"

"Pardon?"

"Are you adequate with the pistol that you carry when you are on duty with the San Francisco police department?"

"I'd say so."

Chen consulted his notes. "And your records do indicate that you, in fact, are rated expert on the shooting range. You have won departmental trophies. Isn't that so?"

"I won a few rounds in the combat pistol range. Hogan's Alley."

"You won?"

"I won some competitions."

"Hogan's Alley. What is that?"

"It's like a street. Different targets jump out at you. You have to make a determination whether it is a civilian or a criminal. If it is a criminal, and if it represents an armed threat, you draw your weapon and you shoot."

"Your weapon?"

"My pistol."

Chen nodded. "And you won such a competition?"

"Once or twice."

"I see here you won it four times. You are too modest, Mr. Kelly."

"I'm pretty good. I guess I forgot how many times I won it."

"You're pretty good. So it would be accurate to state for the record that you are an excellent shot. Under simulated combat conditions, you are expert enough to see the target, determine instantly if it is good or bad, determine whether or not it presents a threat, then draw your weapon, fire, and hit the target. And all in the course of a split second. You are pretty good with your pistol, good enough to win competitions against other professional police officers. Isn't that correct, sir?"

"Yes."

"Proud of that?"

"Yes."

"So last May, people were being shot right in front of you. For real this time, not on a range. Granted, it was the first time you had ever experienced something terrible like that. Granted, you were not prepared for such a circumstance. You were only supposed to direct traffic for a funeral that day. Isn't that correct?"

"Yeah . . . Yes sir."

"What is the policeman's primary duty?"

"To keep the peace."

"Well . . . I was thinking of why you are out there on the street. Keeping the peace is part of it, of course. But what is the primary duty? Why do you carry a firearm?"

"To protect the public."

"To protect the public," repeated Chen, his hand on his chin, his posture that of a supplicant. "So if people were being shot down in front of you, and if you were an armed and trained policeman, on duty, proficient, no, *expert* on the use of your weapon, wasn't it your job to remove the pistol from your holster and chamber a round and use the training and the expertise you so obviously possess to protect those innocent people?"

Kelly sat riveted to his chair, shaking his head.

"We are waiting for your answer, sir."

"No. Yes. I was going to . . ."

"You didn't look, did you?"

"What?"

"It's nothing to be ashamed of. Survival is an important instinct. We all have it, in one form or another. You heard the gunshots and you dove into the gutter and you kept your head down until the shooting stopped. Isn't that correct, sir?"

"No!"

"You did not fire your pistol. You did not chamber a round into your pistol so you could return fire at the man who was shooting the innocents. You did nothing to save others. You saved yourself. Admit it, man, you'll feel much better."

"I'm going to object, Your Honor," said Brancato from the prosecution table. "This police officer is not on trial."

"My client *is* on trial because he is accused of doing what this officer should have done and failed to do."

"Gentlemen," drawled Judge Santo. "Please. In light of the fact that the defendant is contesting for his life and freedom, Mr. Chen is pursuing a line of questioning that has merit. I shall therefore overrule the objection. Please continue."

"Mr. Kelly," said Mr. Chen in a soft and gentle voice. "We have a number of witnesses who will swear that they saw you with your face pressed against the curb, hiding under cover. It is no shame to be frightened. I would have done the same had I been there."

"Yes."

"Yes, you saw nothing because you had your face turned away from the scene and you could not see anything?"

"Yes."

"So you could not have seen my client holding a gun."

"No. I must have been mistaken."

"An easy mistake. Completely understandable. I'm sure no one will fault you for making that kind of an error. Anyone could have done that."

"Thank you," Kelly said, as if Chen had given him absolution.

"So, once again for the record, you did not see my client, Mr. John Caine, over there, with a firearm in his possession. You did not see him fire a pistol. You did not even see him hold a pistol in his hand. The next time you saw him was when he had already been shot in the back and had his hands inside the neck of another man, effectively saving his life. Isn't that correct, sir?"

"Yes."

Mr. Chen stepped back. "No more questions, Your Honor."

The judge looked to the prosecution table. "Redirect."

Turley stood up. He looked shaken, as if this trial meant something to him. Brancato wrote something on his yellow pad and shoved it across the table. Turley glanced at it and nodded to himself. "Your Honor," he said, "we have a few questions."

"Proceed."

"Mr. Kelly, you testified before the grand jury and in earlier proceedings that you saw the defendant with a gun in his hand.

And now you tell the Court that you didn't see it. Which version is correct?"

Mr. Chen patted my arm.

"I just said," answered Kelly.

"Did you, or did you not, see the defendant, John Caine, fire a handgun during the gang shooting—"

"Please," said Mr. Chen to the judge, his voice soft, yet allowing the courtroom to hear the steel beneath the velvet. "We have been over this before. I am forced to object to Mr. Turley's characterization of the events of that day as a gang shooting. The prosecution presented no evidence of gang involvement or violence. The gunman has not been identified. *That* crime remains unsolved. The State has not shown any connection between the actual perpetrator of the crime and my client, which, if I read the law correctly, is crucial to the charge."

"Your Honor, this is clearly a gang war shooting!"

"Try to remain calm, Mr. Turley," said the judge. "Counsel is correct. You presented no evidence of gang involvement. Objection sustained."

Turley took a moment to compose himself. "Mr. Kelly," he said after a long pregnant pause, "did you see the defendant fire a gun?"

"No."

"Did you see him hold a gun?"

"Well . . . not really."

"Not really?"

"No. Probably not."

"Which is it?"

"When I reached the coffee shop I found him on the floor all covered in blood. He lay next to an Asian male. He was holding his throat. I thought he was choking him. I saw his suit coat was up in the back, and he had a large leather holster on his belt, right over the kidney, the way the FBI wears them. So I thought I saw a gun."

"Thank you."

"I wasn't sure. I couldn't see his hands."

"That will be enough," said Turley.

"The holster was one of those leather ones that is form-fitted to a mold of the firearm. This one could only have been for a .45 Colt automatic. I recognized the outline—"

"Your Honor!"

"He could have had a gun."

"You may step down," said the judge. "A copy of this transcript will be forwarded to your superior officer. And I shall take it under consideration, as well. If you hadn't gotten creative with the facts we most likely would not be wasting our time here today."

"I object!"

"Please approach the bench. All the attorneys. Not just Mr. Turley."

When they assembled in front of her, the judge smiled her catlike smile. Her voice carried. Even though she spoke in a low voice, I could hear her clearly. "You object to what the Court is saying, Mr. Turley?"

"It's prejudicial. And in front of the jury."

She nodded. "I am about to excuse the jury. If you don't mind, Counselor."

"No, Your Honor." Turley's face was hot.

"Thank you." She spoke up, addressing the jury. "The jury will be excused momentarily. I apologize for this inconvenience. We shall try not to take too long. Make yourselves comfortable, ladies and gentlemen." She turned her attention back to the attorneys in front of her. "I think I'd be more comfortable in my chambers. Would you please join me there? And bring the defendant."

The bailiff closed the door to the judge's chambers and we were alone with her and the prosecution. It was a plush office, with teak paneling and a desk the size of a small state. It smelled vaguely of lemon and lilac, but it felt like a lion's den.

"Sit down," said Judge Santo, regally taking a seat in her over-sized leather chair behind the desk. She indicated a collection of chairs and tables placed like petitioners before her. There were two groups of furniture, theirs and ours, separated by a round marble-topped table. The arrangement had been carefully thought out. This judge had done this a time or two before.

"Was that the best you've got?" She regarded the prosecution team with a baleful glare.

"Officer Kelly was our last witness."

"That was your case?"

"Yes, Your Honor."

"Your case just got shredded," she said to Brancato. "You didn't have much before. Now you've got nothing."

Brancato sat silent in his chair. He looked through a file in a Manila envelope as if he could find salvation inside.

"Mr. Brancato?"

"I'm sorry, Your Honor, but we have other evidence."

"Then you had a duty to present it. Now it's too late."

"I understand, Your Honor."

"Do you? The People are not well represented in this case, Mr. Brancato."

"There were . . . other considerations."

The judge raised her eyebrows. "I don't think I want to hear about 'other considerations,' Mr. Brancato. And will you stop pawing through that file?"

"Yes, Your Honor."

" 'Other considerations' aside, we are going back out there in a few minutes and you are going to motion to the court that, considering your witness's unexpected turnaround on his testimony, you have no other option but to move to dismiss the charges against the defendant."

"But—"

"You had your chance, you blew it. And now you are going to move to dismiss the charges against Mr. Caine so we can all get on with our lives. Your office wasted the Court's time and wasted your time, not to mention the defendant's time. There are other matters more important to be dealt with in this city. We will not waste one more second, or, seeing that time is money, waste one more dollar on this process. If you fail to motion to dismiss the charges against Mr. Caine, then the Court will direct a verdict of not guilty. Is that clear?"

"Yes, Your Honor."

She looked at me. I could not read the expression on her face. "Mr. Caine, the court will dismiss the charges against you. I don't for a moment believe that you were not armed, or that you did not fire a pistol on that day in May, but I also do not believe that you did anything other than commit some minor infractions and save some lives. I've read your history. I don't expect that I shall see you again in this courtroom. At least I hope not."

"Thank you."

"The section of the Penal Code under which the defendant is charged was not drawn to cover actions taken by Mr. Caine. I researched it, and I believe that the law was severely misapplied in this case.

"But the law grants extreme latitude to the People in the crafting of their cases. It must. And the system works very well most of the time. In this case, this section of the Penal Code was created to arm the People with the power to charge every member of a criminal partnership with murder if, in the commission of a felony such as an armed robbery, someone is killed. Even the death of a member of the criminal partnership would trigger the statute.

"I thought this case a stretch in the beginning, but the People have the right to be heard. I smelled a whiff of zealotry behind the charges, and I still suspect it. But for whatever reason, you failed to present the evidence. And now your witness self-destructed in front of the jury.

"What I am saying here, gentlemen, is that Mr. Caine did nothing wrong in the eyes of this Court. The People did not prove anything other than malfeasance and dereliction of duty on the part of the police.

"So I'm going to dismiss the charges."

"Excuse me, Sylvia," said Chen. "I would prefer that you did not dismiss the charges against Mr. Caine. That—"

"Leaves him open to the district attorney refiling the case. Yes, I know, Albert. But I'm not going to do that. Your client will have to take his chances."

"I understand," I said.

"Do you?"

Mr. Chen nudged me gently. "I shall explain it to him. On our own time."

Judge Santo nodded. "Thank you." She looked at Turley and Brancato. Both men had sat silently through her speech and now stared at the judge. "Anything else?"

"No," said Brancato.

"Mr. Turley? You're always eager and ready to instruct the Court."

"No, ma'am."

"Then I'm going to take a short break and we shall meet back in the courtroom in, let's say, fifteen minutes."

The jury filed back in, Mr. Brancato stood and made the motion, Judge Santo dismissed the charges, discharged the jury, and I was a free man. Chen patted me on the back and flashed his golden smile.

"This was a good day," he said.

I nodded. I could not find my voice to argue the point.

"Excuse me," said a familiar voice behind me.

Shirley Henderson stood at the defense table, her body stiff and defiant.

"Looks like you won," she said.

"I don't think anybody won."

She nodded. "Just watch yourself the next time you come to San Francisco."

"I watched myself that time."

"You should have gone to jail." She gave me a flat, harsh stare. "I know about you and your criminal friends."

"I don't have criminal friends. I just have friends. And the judge didn't agree with you. That makes me innocent."

"You're not innocent. You're not even not guilty. The charges were dismissed."

"Miss Henderson," said Mr. Chen quietly, "this is uncalled for."

"Really?"

"Your actions border on harassment."

She nodded.

"Did you ever solve that other killing? The young man someone hung from a building?" I asked.

"That is none of your business."

"Can't we just shake hands and go our separate ways?"

"You're leaving for Honolulu?"

"Tomorrow, the next day." I hadn't thought of going home yet. I had not dared to think that I could win this easily. Her question made me think of green mountains, cool breezes, bright sunny beaches, the smell of flowers, and warm brown skin.

"You ever come back to San Francisco, I'll be watching you. You do one thing wrong and you'll be back in jail. Depend on it." She walked away, ignoring my outstretched hand.

Chen patted me on the back. "You can't win them all."

"We won the one that counted, didn't we?"

He gave me another flash of gold. "Andrew and I would like to show you something, Mr. Caine. Can you spare a few hours this afternoon?"

"I had no other plans."

"Just so. We are going to take a ride to a very special place. We thought that you might like to accompany us."

"This have something to do with me?"

"It does."

"Then of course."

"I think you will find it instructive."

Leaving the courtroom I noticed that Felix wasn't there.

Looking around, I also noted that Daniel was missing from his customary chair in the row behind me. He had not come to congratulate me.

Neither man had been in the courtroom.

46

I was hungry. An evening stroll through Chinatown can do that for you, proof that life exists after a murder trial. Especially when you win.

Every other shop on the street was a restaurant, with chickens or ducks or a collection of unidentifiable animal parts roasting on spits in the storefront windows. The commingled aromas of exotic food permeated Chinatown like no other section of San Francisco. With the stress of my prosecution, recent meals had not been memorable. We were on our way to meet Daniel for dinner. I hoped this one would be different.

Felix was still missing, but I didn't care. I didn't miss him, I didn't need him, and I hoped that Daniel would release him now that he was back home and I was a free man.

Albert Chen met Angelica and me in the lobby of the Mark. It being a pleasant night we decided to walk. To be honest, *I* had decided to walk. After incarceration in a variety of gray bar hotels, enforced attendance in a dank courtroom without windows, and dodging the bullet of San Quentin and all that implied, John Caine was ready to stretch his legs and exercise his freedom.

Physically, I felt good for the first time since I had been shot. Truly good. I could feel my body healing. There was a spring in my step. I almost felt young. Angel had helped me celebrate my freedom in a way I might never have again had things gone the other way. It made me grin. I had to catch myself. Several times I caught myself wearing a foolish-looking grin on my freshly shaved mug, certain that a casual observer might think I'd gone daft.

The neighborhood was typical Chinatown, part city, part suburb, and all shops. Besides the aroma of food, both cooked and raw, the city air smelled of fog and exhaust, fresh flowers and aged garbage. Tomorrow, I gathered, would be trash day. The sidewalks were lined with old galvanized trashcans, filled to overflowing. Some of the cans had lids, most did not. Some were so pungent you had to hold your breath and walk a little faster when you passed by.

Not good for the appetite, but excellent for conditioning.

When we decided to walk, Mr. Chen went to his car and returned with a stout black cane topped with a heavy silver knob. "I have had it for years," he explained. "Purchased it on a whim from an antique store in London. And when I walk the streets of San Francisco I always feel better when I have it than when I do not."

"You have a sword in there, Albert?"

"Nothing of the sort. It's ebony and silver. Solid silver. They told me it once belonged to a British gentleman who had it made for himself in India some time in the last century. Or was it the century before last?"

"Does it matter?"

"Not really. It is just a concept to which one must now become accustomed. We are in a new millennium. I understand that it is only numbers, and therefore artificial, and that the experience of our living in these times is a mere accident of birth. But by turning over into the two thousands, we are further cut off from the past. Not only into a new century, but into the next millennium. We now live, it seems, in the future."

"We live in the now," I said.

"Indeed, Mr. Caine. That's your Zen talking. But I read a great deal of history, and I often delve into the past. To them, we live in the future."

"Not that they care."

"My, you are definitely into the Zen this evening. But you're correct. When our time is over, it is over, and it doesn't matter if we have been gone for one second or two millennia. The children you saw this afternoon are the future of Jackie Chang. Her grandchildren will live on."

White and Chen had driven me to the exclusive private school where the Chang grandchildren were boarded and educated, their scholarship provided by an anonymous benefactor. He didn't have to tell me that Chawlie paid the bills. I already knew that. I think he wanted me to see that they were well off and protected, their lives enriched instead of impoverished. Chawlie could not make up for the loss of their grandmother. She could never be replaced. But their lot could have been worse. Given the circumstances, I wondered if it could have been better. Their future seemed assured.

As much as anybody's future is assured. Money and prestige cannot guarantee security. Ask Diana. Ask John-John.

Hell, ask any of the Kennedys.

"So you feel safer with the cane?"

"It is now a habit when I walk. The streets here are gentle nowadays. It wasn't always that way. The cane is not a necessity, but I still like having it."

I smiled. I knew all about having a friend. The Buck knife was back on my belt, hidden in its snug little sheath beneath my coat. I had carried the Buck for decades. I'd had it so long it was now an extension of my person. I did not feel whole without it. Much better than having a firearm, the Buck had been my constant companion in many parts of the world. Sometimes my only friend.

"Where are we going?" asked Angelica. She had been silent during our conversation, although I knew she had much to say. The woman was a gentle goddess, wise and intelligent, playful and dignified. I still had not sorted out my feelings for her. All I knew was that I enjoyed her company. She had made me realize that I still lived. And she was easy on my eyes.

"Daniel will meet us at The Jade Palace. A friend of Mr. Choy owns it. They are preparing a celebration."

"I hope there will be a lot of food," she said, squeezing my hand. For a tiny woman, Angelica had huge appetites.

"You need not worry."

I heard quick footsteps and realized, too late, that the street was deserted. I released Angelica's hand and spun around just in time to deflect the blow that had been aimed at the back of my head.

A blunt force smashed into my forearm, numbing me from wrist to elbow.

The second attacker ran headlong into me, taking me down to the concrete. He pinned my arms to my side while he sat on my chest.

He struck me twice in the face with his fists.

I wiggled out from under him and rose to a half crouch, only to be struck in the back by an unseen assailant.

Pain exploded in my kidney, a bright red blossom of agony.

I staggered, blocked another strike with my forearm, elbowed the man behind me and felt him go down.

I sensed that Albert was occupying one of the attackers with his cane.

Out of the corner of my eye I saw Angelica lying in the gutter, her silver party dress hiked above her knees.

One of my attackers carried a pair of sai, the Chinese fighting irons that could inflict a huge amount of damage.

I reached for my knife.

Before I could get it open, the sai fighter attacked with an overhead strike.

I leaped out of the way, diving between two parked cars, and rolled into the street.

He followed, flowing over the ground like a ballet dancer, effortlessly pacing me.

His companion circled somewhere behind me, an unseen threat.

I felt as if I had been attacked by a pride of lions. They didn't go for the immediate kill. At once aggressive and then shy, their on-again, off-again style of combat a function of time and teamwork. Functioning together, they seemed to have all the time they needed.

The small dark man with the sai was in superb condition and he seemed to be enjoying himself. He had drawn first blood. Sensing that he was one of those who would wish to draw out this combat, I began looking for my response.

There weren't many.

There was one. He would toy with me first. He'd had his chance. He could have finished me quickly.

But he didn't.

His hand came up to warn off his partner behind me. He wanted to take me on his own.

That told me all I needed to know about the flashy asshole.

My kidney felt as if it burned with a white-hot flame. Pain grew and became a living entity all its own. It consumed me from the inside. The fire grew hotter every moment, and as it grew hotter, I grew weaker.

I flicked the blade of my knife open.

He advanced, holding the fighting iron level with my chest in a feint thrust. When I parried with the Buck, he swept the trailing sai past my head, whipping the air like a bullwhip.

I ducked, and he kicked where I would have been had I not reversed course and leaped the other way.

Off balance, he whirled and circle-kicked me high in the shoulder. I went down on one knee, then rolled, continuing in the same direction. When I rolled, his leg went over the top of my head, his foot so close the hard end of his shoelace snapped against my cheek.

I kept rolling and came up again on my knees and blocked another kick with the brass pommel of the knife, striking his ankle, sweeping his legs out from under him.

He fell, then jumped to his feet before I could catch him, apparently unhurt.

Black spots appeared in front of my eyes; my body vibrated with pain. Something had gone terribly wrong with my kidney. I didn't know how long I could continue this fight, let alone stand.

It would be easier to let him kill me.

Not yet.

Not tonight.

Glancing to my right, I saw Mr. Chen giving as well as he was getting, the heavy cane inflicting some notable injuries to his opponent. The third man retreated into the alley across the street. He stood in the shadows watching the fight. For a brief instant the street light illuminated the side of his face, and I thought I recognized him as the face from my nightmares, the long-dead soldier who had come to kill me on that distant hill so many years before.

The sai fighter attacked again, striking me in the right side with his iron.

I fell to the concrete, nearly spent, but my mind refused to let me give up. We had work to do, places to go, people to see. Somewhere out there people needed us. Needed me.

I wanted to see my Islands again.

I rose to my feet and he attacked again. I ran and crashed into an empty trash can, rolled over the top of it, sprawled across the sidewalk, came up with the metal lid and thrust it into his face. He backpedaled and I came at him, the metal lid my shield, my knife at the ready.

It was ancient combat. With my shield and my knife, he could not gain access to my body with those deadly sai without getting the lid shoved in his face or suffering cuts on his arms from the razor-sharp blade of the Buck.

He tried for my head, and I blocked the strike with the lid.

He thrust hard with his left and I met it again. The thrust strike pushed me back, nearly knocking me over, jarring my teeth.

He tried a low strike, but I protected my body with the lid and attacked with the knife, slicing his bicep, drawing blood.

We were at a standoff, but time was on his side. With every thrust and parry I got weaker. Every beat of my heart throbbed with pain. Every pore of my skin screamed for relief.

He wore me down with a frantic rush, banging on the garbage can lid with both sai like a mad drummer. He forced me back until I tripped over the curb and sprawled into the street.

I lost the lid, rose to my feet and stabbed blindly at him, knowing it was a fatal mistake.

He parried my thrust, slapped me easily on the side of the head with the tang of the sai, and sent me crashing to the ground again.

I lay there stunned, unable to move.

Putting everything I had left in me I tried to rise.

He brought the sai down onto my left arm and I felt something break, crushed between the concrete and the steel. More agony exploded through my body. My world grew smaller. I could only see through a dark narrow tunnel. If I focused I could barely make out the man who would be my executioner.

He kicked me and I rolled away. He followed, giving me the opening I wanted.

I lay on my side, blinking from the pain.

He stood over me, panting.

"Good-bye, John Caine," he hissed, a whisper of hatred only the two of us could hear.

I jackknifed off the ground and thrust the Buck into his groin with all my remaining strength, slicing muscle and grinding bone, burying the blade to the hilt, twisting as I stabbed him at the fork of his legs.

He screamed, doubled over, then righted himself and fled across the street, wrenching the knife from my hand.

Albert struck his assailant when the man turned his head toward his partner's scream. The man fell, then got up and scampered toward the alley, where the third man stood in the shadows. When the two men disappeared, the third man backed away, still facing us, until he, too, vanished. It was as if he had faded into nothingness. If I believed in ghosts or vampires I would have believed him one of those creatures of the night.

He was scary enough just being flesh and blood.

He looked familiar, but if it were the Vietnamese soldier, he would have been a ghost. I had killed him on that muddy hill, killed him as certainly as he had killed me.

The dream flooded into my consciousness. The end of the dream, the memory from so many years before, winked at me as it floated past on my synapses. The end of the fight that I had forgotten, that had haunted me, had come and then vanished. I remembered. And then I did not.

"Albert," I said, my voice a hoarse rasp.

"Yes," Chen had started after the two men, then thought better about entering the alley alone, armed only with his Indian cane. He was panting heavily, his breath coming in whoops and cackles.

"Angel," I said, pointing. I was in no better shape.

He knelt next to her, felt for a pulse in her wrist, shook his head impatiently, and tried the artery in her throat. He must have felt something because he smiled quickly, replaced by a grim determination.

"She's not dead," he said, "but we have to get her to a hospital."

"She's not dead," I said stupidly.

He crawled over to me. "Can you walk?"

"I don't know."

He looked around. The street was deserted. No cars, no pedestrians. Nothing came our way. Except for the veil of fog bestowing a halo to the neon lights, the street was dark and deserted.

"I think we'd better call the police," he said, reaching for his cellular telephone.

"Yeah," I said. The black spots were growing. When I looked at his face he had a strange complexion that reminded me of a leopard. I almost expected his ears and teeth to grow into points. "Get an ambulance, too. Angelica needs one."

"You're hurt," he said.

"Yeah," I said, trying to sit up and not making it. I lay down in the street, my back against the cold, rough surface, and closed my eyes. I saw the ending of the dream, just the way it was. I concentrated, trying to hold the memory, and then it floated away again.

"They hurt Angel. Can you believe that? Just because she was with me."

I rolled over and tried to look at the sky, obscured by a thick blanket of fog. "I don't think I like this town."

47

I lay on a cot in the emergency room for two hours before I saw a doctor. While I waited I gave my version of the events to both a uniformed officer and a detective. Each time I gave a statement my attorney was present. He was present because he was lying on the cot next to mine. He had taken a nasty bump on the head and the powers that be decided that it would be better for all concerned if a medical professional took a look at it. So we waited among the ill and the injured, the accident victims and gunshot casualties, for the next available physician.

They took Angel into surgery as soon as they looked at her. Something to do with a cervical and cranial injury that the doctors feared might paralyze her if they didn't get to it immediately.

Daniel waited with us, having come upon us while the police were still at the scene. After we had not appeared at The Jade Palace, he called the hotel. Learning that we had walked, he came looking for us.

Using his California Bar Association membership card he got inside the ring of police and yellow tape. It was Daniel who had taken charge, reminding the officers just who Chen's friends were, and how seriously injured we were. It was Daniel who had secured us our ride to the hospital, instead of the jail. It was Daniel who had found a physician for Angel. It was Daniel who had convinced the police that we were victims and not perpetra-

tors. And it was Daniel who had finally called in a private physician to look after Mr. Chen's head and another one to look after
my injuries.

Fortunately Chen's head was just bruised. My arm was broken. The stent they had put in the kidney had also become dislodged during the fight and had slipped down the tube between
the kidney and the bladder, blocking it. Some blood was pooling
beneath the organ, which caused them even more concern, and
they wheeled me out of the emergency room directly into surgery.
I waved at Daniel and Chen just as the anesthesiologist injected
me with a wonder drug that took me up and away in the space of
a heartbeat. One moment I was waving, my hand in the air. The
next instant the world turned black and John Caine was gone.

An angel hovered above me. Standing next to my bed, she looked
exactly like Angelica, and I decided that the beautiful vision in
front of my eyes must be she. Somewhere, deep down in the
crevices of my cerebellum I knew that it could not be Angelica
unless this time she was a real angel and we both were dead. But
in my fuzzy state I decided that the bad dream I'd had had been
just another one of *those*, and she was there to comfort me once
again. My arm snaked out of the covers of its own volition and
cupped one firm buttock beneath white nylon and spandex, just
the way Angelica liked it. It was one of her favorite places. And
one of mine.

"Stop!" She slapped my hand down.

"Looks like he's getting better," said a familiar voice.

"He's a pig," a familiar female voice said.

Dim as I was, I concluded that Angelica and I were not alone.

"That's assault, buster." The female voice sounded angry. My
heart sunk. I recognized its owner.

"Come on," said the male voice. "He's just coming out of the
anesthetic."

"It's a natural reflex," said the angry voice of Shirley Henderson. "The anesthetic is just an excuse for him to act like a pig."

"Hello, Detective Henderson," I said with a mouth that felt like dry brush. "How nice to see you again."

"Caine, the police person is here to see you." That voice I recognized.

I opened my eyes. Chen had a puffy face, and he would have some souvenirs of the fight, but he looked none the worse for wear. Behind him, the police detective who had put me in jail the last time I'd come to San Francisco stood waiting, her arms crossed, an impatient look on her face.

"He's right," I said, my brain beginning to emerge from the fuzz. "I apologize, Nurse, and to you, too, Detective. It's just the drugs."

The nurse patted my hand.

I noted that she stood several feet away from the bed and leaned over to pat me before she left the room.

"The good news," said Chen, "is that they took out your stent. You no longer have it."

"Then there's got to be a bunch of bad news."

"Not so much. Your arm is broken, you've had more surgery on your kidney, so they sliced you up again. But your injuries are not as great as they feared when you first came in. You're going to feel terrible for a few weeks, and," he indicated Detective Henderson, "this lady still wants to put you in prison."

"Now wait a minute," she said, indignant.

"How is Angel?"

Chen smiled sadly. "They say she will be fine. She had a fractured skull, but her neck was not broken. It will take some time, but they say she will fully recover."

"That's good news." I focused on the San Francisco detective. "What did I do wrong this time, Detective? Mr. Chen here is a highly regarded member of the Bar, not an assassin, not a gang member. I almost lost a good friend tonight, and my friend here was hurt, and I was hurt. What are you going to charge me with this time? Is it the practice of the San Francisco Police Department to let the felon go free while they jail the victim? Or is it just your idea?"

"John," Chen said. "You are tired, and you have just come out surgery. I'm going to go get the doctor to chase this young lady out of the recovery room." He stared at Henderson. "Do not ask him any questions while I'm gone."

She nodded, and Chen went out the door.

"I'll go," she said to me. "It's not my case, anyway. Every time you're out there on my streets someone gets killed. Tonight we found two bodies near where you had your fight. I don't like it, and I don't like having you here. Please. For the sake of peace in my town, please just leave. As soon as you can."

Two bodies?

I wanted to ask, but didn't dare.

She looked at me, as if expecting me to confess all. True to her word she did not ask a question, although I knew she must have wanted to ask dozens. When I did nothing but stare back at her she turned and left the room, almost running into a woman who looked like a doctor on the way out.

"I'm leaving," Shirley said to the woman.

"Are you okay?" The physician smiled down at me. She had a kind face.

"Hurt like hell. Otherwise . . . okay."

"You need anything?"

"More drugs."

She shook her head and smiled. "Not so fast. You're not totally down from your pink cloud yet."

Chen looked embarrassed. "Oh, this is Dr. Nancy McDevitt. Dr. McDevitt is your surgeon."

"Am I going to live?"

"Well, that's up to you. I read your chart. You seem to like it here in our hospital. But, yes, you're going to be fine. We had to go in and open you up again and make some minor repairs, and you'll have another scar to add to your collection, but everything should be fine in about six weeks."

"Six weeks."

"I know, we always say that. But it's true."

"I got shot six weeks ago. I just started feeling well for the first time tonight."

"It was last night, but you'll be fine." She scribbled something in my chart and patted Chen's shoulder and left us alone. He stood at the foot of the bed and looked sadly at me.

"Two bodies?"

"They found the bodies of two young Asian males lying in an alley about a block from where we were attacked. One was shot. They found a knife embedded in the other's pelvic bone. It had sliced through a major artery in his leg. They're assuming right now that he bled to death. The blood trail went all the way back to our location."

"He knew my name."

"What?"

"One of the killers, the one with the sai. He knew my name. How did he know my name?"

"I don't know."

"This was personal. This wasn't random."

Chen nodded.

"They going to arrest me for this?"

Chen tried on a ghastly smile, held up the empty knife sheath that had been on my belt and shook his head. Then he put it away in his pocket.

"Then I want to go home, Albert." I lay back and closed my eyes. "I just want to go home."

"You have a visitor," said Felix, my bodyguard, much chastened, and back in his old location just outside my door. He stuck his head in, made the announcement, and backed out, still too embarrassed to confront the evidence of his failure. His absence had not been adequately explained, and from what Daniel had told me, he had felt terrible when he had heard the news. Some bodyguard, my Felix. The only time I really needed him he was missing in action. His assignment outside my door was his obvious penance. I wondered what else Chawlie had in mind for him, but I didn't want to dwell.

Barbara came in wearing a tight white top and some kind of calf-length pants that I think used to be called Capri pants the last time they were in vogue. She was tanned and she looked healthy, the way people do when they've spent a lot of time outdoors. And under the tan, and under the healthy exterior, she glowed, and I suddenly realized that Barbara Klein was in love.

She leaned over and kissed me on the forehead. "Between you and David I have spent way too much time in hospitals," she said.

"How's David?"

"He's fine. He's got two of those," she indicated my cast, "but he figured out how to use his laptop, so he doesn't mind all that much, and he's really, really happy. That young lady he met over there, the archeologist, she seems to be a wonderful girl. I don't like it when he is hurt, but I understand that you helped catch the ones responsible for it that night, and so I thank you again."

That was a lot of words for her to say in a short amount of time, and she seemed to rush to get them all out of her at once.

"How's Colorado?"

"Telluride's wonderful. I'm there full-time now, when I'm not flying off to Honolulu to see my son in the hospital, or stopping off in San Francisco to see an old friend in the hospital. They're still having problems making the schedule, but they're really trying now that I'm there watching them every day. We're about to open the first phase, and I've got to run. Bill's downstairs with the car. I just wanted to see how you were."

"I'm fine." *Bill?*

"Did you shave off your beard?"

"For the trial."

She nodded. "You should think about keeping it off. It makes you look a little less fierce." She gazed at me and I wished I could read her thoughts. Probably wondering how a woman like her could have ever found herself involved with a man like me.

"Well . . ."

"I know. You gotta go. I'm glad you stopped by."

"I would have come to your trial, but I didn't think . . . it was appropriate. I was afraid that they were going to put you away forever."

"There was that possibility."

"I stayed away because I didn't want to be linked to you. I cannot afford to be tied to you, or to your activities."

"I know. I'm a pirate. Is Bill respectable?"

She blushed. "He's . . . very respectable. We met in Telluride. He has one of his homes up there."

"And you're in love."

"He's asked me to marry him and I said yes."

"Then I wish you both much happiness."

"Really?"

"Oh yes, Barbara."

She leaned over and kissed me again. On the forehead. Again. I caught the scent of her perfume and it made me remember.

"You take care, you old pirate. I'll never forget you."

"I'm unforgettable."

She nodded.

"David's still in Hawaii. He went back to the site, wherever it is. It's all so hush-hush. There's a lot of excitement between those two. Do you know what they're doing?"

"Yes."

"It's all some big secret, isn't it?"

"It is, but I'm sure David will tell you about it."

"He said he would. But not yet. Why does that bother me?"

"Because he is an adult now, and he has obligations other than to his mother."

"You're so flip with your answers, buster, but this time I think you're right." She looked out my window and I followed her gaze. The fog had moved in over the tops of the hills again. "I've got to get going. Bill's holding the plane, but I wanted to stop by and see you."

"An old friend. Does he know about us?"

"No."

"He won't hear it from me."

She smiled, nodded, and left the room and my life.

Smart woman.

48

I sneaked out of the hospital without telling anyone but Angel. I kissed her good-bye, squeezed her hand and promised to come back for her when she was ready to travel, slipped past my bodyguard, and flew a commercial jet to Honolulu. I'd had enough of California, and I'd had enough of that beautiful, but cold and clammy, city by the Bay. I'd had enough loss and enough hurt. I'd had enough of the state's problems and its weird laws, and the cold burning anger that seemed to permeate my experience there.

Finally, I'd had enough of hospitals. Assured that I was out of danger, Dr. McDevitt wasn't quite certain she wanted to let me go.

"We'd like to keep you here for a few more weeks just to make certain that you will not relapse," she said.

Relapse, hell, I'd had enough of their advice and their treatments. They would keep me there until I died of old age before they would be absolutely certain that I wouldn't relapse. Chawlie's mandate, I believed, had been very strong, indeed. So, free from consultation or prescription, I took myself out of the hospital, signed waiver after waiver, releasing them from all liability, including one that I particularly liked, a smart piece of legalese that indemnified the hospital "until the end of time." I kept that one, wondering at the mind that could have produced it, and tossed the rest.

I wasn't suing anyone.

That wasn't the way I settled my disputes.

I flew first class, the only grade that was tolerable in my condition, and slept for most of the six-and-a-half-hour interval of suspended animation, waking only at the last minute to fill out and sign the little paper that reminded me I was a returning resident.

A returning resident. I liked what it said. I was a resident. Returning. I liked the word. I had been gone. And now I was home.

But back in Honolulu I found I had nowhere to go. Without *Olympia* I could not do as I normally did when recovering from trauma. For some reason I didn't want to seek Chawlie's help. Not yet. I was sick of depending on others and I needed time to heal and lick my wounds without the benefit of well-meaning friends. And I didn't want or need another nurse. Angelica was still in the hospital. I didn't want a replacement.

Feeling physically ill, weak and exhausted, I checked myself into one of the anonymous tourist hotels along the Waikiki shoreline and hid among the tall buildings and the sandy playgrounds. In a week I began to feel better. Solitude gave me time to reflect, and to heal some of the emotional wounds as well as the physical ones. I still had my nightmare. The young soldier came to visit nearly every other night and I would wake with the memory of a scream and the taste of copper in my mouth. I had no one to rub my back and comfort me in my terror, and no one to chase the adrenaline shakes away with her warmth and her tenderness. I was forced to confront my fear, exactly as I had confronted that soldier on that hill so many years before.

Someone had harmed my Angel, and someone would pay.

Someone had wanted me dead and had harmed an innocent, just as they had wanted Chawlie dead and had killed an innocent.

I was glad to quit their town and come home.

The question, it seemed, was home to what?

49

F ew secrets remain so for very long, and in Honolulu, where everyone works at least two jobs and has an interconnecting web of contacts and alliances, my secret remained so for only a week. A week was enough. I had started once more to venture out for sunset excursions along the shore, once again beginning the all-too-familiar process of recovering my health.

The timing was eerie, the knock coming when it did. I'd been given a week. The only conclusion I could reach was that Chawlie had known of my whereabouts as soon as I had checked into the hotel, and had granted me the illusion of independence out of mere compassion.

I peered through the peephole, saw Daniel's impassive face, and opened the door.

"Caine." Daniel's voice was a roughened gargle.

"Daniel."

He stood at my doorway, his shoulders filling the frame. He made no move to enter and I had no inclination to invite him in. Despite my gratitude to the family for allowing me my self-imposed isolation, I instantly resented the imposition.

"Chawlie wants to see me?" I asked.

"You worry him. He wants to know that you're all right."

"I owe you both an apology."

"You owe nothing, Caine. You got a right to go where you want to go. Where's your bodyguard?"

"California. I didn't tell him I was going, either. I just left."

"He still had a duty to tell me."

"Felix was getting bored with the assignment."

"Doesn't matter. He still had it."

"You'll have to talk to him."

Daniel nodded, and I knew that he'd planned on it. "Your boat's still off Kona. You know that?"

"I saw it on television." A local station had run a story on Hualalai's sedulous progression toward the sea. They showed the lava flow blocking the road. They made it look like the end of the world. One of the long shots showed *Olympia*'s black hull riding at anchor, a little closer to the volcanic flow than I would have wished.

"Tomorrow at six. Be at our hangar. We'll fly you to Kona. You'll feel better once you're back on your boat."

"You'll fly me over?"

Daniel nodded.

"I'm grateful."

Daniel almost smiled. My secret exposed, I ate alone at the Hilton Hawaiian Village, in the elegant restaurant fronting the sea. I was the only single in the room and I ate sparingly. Since the last injury, my taste for wine and coffee had vanished. Food was little more than fuel. My time and money wasted, I dropped some bills on the table and started to rise when a familiar figure sat down across the table from me.

"Kimo," I said. "How are things? Or should I ask?"

"Ask. They're better than they should be."

I waited. He had come to talk story, most likely about James. I had an investment in the kid and wanted to know how he fared. Kimo glanced at the ocean, just across the white sand, but said nothing.

"Should I ask about the family?"

"James pleaded guilty to reduced felonies for his cooperation and testimony. The judge gave him five years, then released him on probation. He's a cop's kid. Prison could be fatal, you know?"

"It would have been harsh."

"It's bad enough. He's home now. Electronically monitored. He hasn't realized yet how good he's got it."

"Still want to throw us haoles off the island?"

"That's part of it. He won't admit that it was wrong. He did it. He admitted that he did it. But he insists it was the right thing to do. He's proud, that's all."

"He'll grow up someday."

Kimo looked sad. "I hope so."

Suddenly I was grateful that I had no children. It couldn't be easy dealing with the little ones. It must be impossible trying to deal with proto-adults, full of wants and wishes, desires and fears, topped by a lack of knowledge and judgment.

Children, it seemed to me, were as much a curse as they were a blessing.

"How is Tutu Mae?"

"She sends her love. She and Chawlie spend a lot of time together. They seem to have joint interests."

"Romance?"

"Geez, Caine, you're lolo sometimes. No. The Islands!"

The thought rattled around my skull for a few brief moments. Then I thought, why the hell not?

"Someone told you I was back?"

"Got an anonymous e-mail. Said you were going to the Big Island tomorrow morning to join Donna. Just wanted to stop by to thank you."

"For a moment I thought you'd come to arrest me again."

"You know that wasn't my idea."

"Want some coffee?"

"Thought you were leaving."

"Not if you have something to say."

He looked at me, his huge black eyes regarding me with sadness and suspicion, mulling his options. "You remember Ricky

Lee? He's making noise about James. Says he's going to kill him if he testifies against the group."

"Saying this out loud?"

"Couple of informants reported it this week. He's hot. Blames James. Blames you."

"He blames me?"

"You were with him. Come to give you this." He shoved over my passport and gun license, the documents that had been surrendered to the judge so many weeks before. "Could have given them to Tala, but I thought you might want them tonight."

I picked up my license. "This permit only covers my .45 Colt."

"So?"

"I don't have it."

"Give Chawlie a call. I'm sure he could find it if you asked him."

"You think I'm in trouble? What about James?"

"James is safe. It's you I worry about."

"Ricky Lee is here in Waikiki?"

Kimo shook his head. "Not sure where he is. Since the informant report he's vanished. We're looking for him, and he knows it. We can bring him in on terroristic threats, another felony, and void out his bail. Just wanted to let you know. Wanted to make sure you watched your back."

"Ricky Lee did Professor Hayes."

"We don't have evidence to support that one, but it's likely, it fits. There are others. We're waiting. He'll slip up. We'll find him. You can do something for me."

"Name it."

"You're flying over to Kona tomorrow morning. Can you take James and Tutu Mae with you?"

"We're leaving at six."

"I know. Tutu Mae wants to see the site before it's too late. And she can bless the volcano. It would be important to her and important to me."

"What about James?"

"Be good for him to see that all haoles aren't so bad."

"And he could see something that he'll never forget. What about his probation?"

"I'll handle it. He's working with his great grandmother as a community service project."

"Does James know what's supposed to be in the tomb?"

"We haven't told him. We did talk about the treasure. But nobody talks about the bones except the group."

"And Tutu Mae wants to dive the site."

"And she's ninety-two now."

"She wants to dive the site at ninety-two. Have them meet me at Chawlie's hangar in the morning."

"They'll be there."

"You going, too?"

"Can't. I'm hunting."

He got up. "And Caine?"

"Yes?"

"Watch yourself tonight."

50

Watch yourself tonight," said Kimo, leaving the restaurant and stalking off toward the koi ponds and the lushly landscaped gardens of the Village. I watched his brightly colored shirt disappear into the darkness and sank down into an overstuffed chair in the lounge, choosing a vacant spot next to one of the white Chinese temple dogs.

Watch myself. That had many meanings. It could be a warning and it could be a threat. In this case it was both. Kimo provided the warning. Little Ricky posed the threat.

The dog snarled its own silent marble threat. What would you do? I asked the beast, ugly enough to take care of itself regardless of the circumstances. I knew what it would do. It was the only thing I could do, too. Watching my back was not something I enjoyed or wanted to adapt to as normal behavior. And in this case the cause was just.

It might even have been right.

I just wished I wasn't so tired.

I sat in the brightly lit lounge, listening to the music, trying to find reasons why I shouldn't just go back to my hotel, crawl into bed and pull the covers over my head.

But I kept seeing Kimo's son in handcuffs, and I kept seeing the misery on the father's face, and I kept picturing the snarling face of Ricky Lee, the enforcer. And I knew that the little punk was more than capable of killing anyone. He was a prime suspect in the murder of Professor Hayes. Just because Donna had not seen him that morning Hayes pulled her into his living room didn't mean he wasn't there. He would have had the other man visible, a front man. Ricky would have been the one unseen—the silent figure in the kitchen, almost a ghost. Like the specter I saw in the alley.

Ricky Lee would know how to get away with it. He was an experienced criminal. He would have an alibi for his deeds, including killing James, including killing me.

Word I got from Kimo was that the killing of people was Ricky's business. Off guard, James would receive a call from Lee, and he would sneak out to meet him. James would not tell his family, and he would find some way of getting around the electronic collar, or whatever the hell they had on him, and nobody would know where he went, or even when. Lee would specify the middle of the night, or early in the morning. Some time when the boy's brain was foggy. They would meet in a secluded place, and only one of them would walk away from the rendezvous.

The more I thought about it the greater the expectation I had that Ricky Lee was more than just a loudmouthed little punk. He was as mean as they came. And he was not afraid of putting people to death, not particularly picky about who he killed, or why.

In this case he had his excuse. He perceived that Kimo's son, in going over to the prosecution in his plea bargain, was going to sell him down the river. He was right. And he would kill the young Kahanamoku as soon as he could corner him.

Then he would come after the private eye, the one who had come with the boy's father. He could not come after a cop directly. That would be suicide. But if you already were a sociopath, and if you had put enough people away that one or two more or less wouldn't create a problem for you, killing the PI would be just tidying up. Nothing to think about. Just a minor problem.

Ricky Lee was going to kill me unless I stopped him.

There was but one solution.

I heaved myself out of the chair and wandered through the

koi ponds and landscaped pathways until I came to the public street where I found a taxi, which took me to River Street on the edge of Chinatown. There was a man there I had to see. And a pistol there I had to retrieve.

And a score left that I had to settle.

Gilbert met me at the door, congratulated me on my freedom, and escorted me into Chawlie's presence. Usually a cold fish, the young man was unusually warm. Strange behavior. I hadn't been gone that long, and I knew he didn't like me all that much.

Chawlie waited until I had lowered myself to a seated position across from him in his private quarters. Instead of the two girls who normally kept him company, he was caring for another tiny bonsai tree, this one a perfect miniature of a Japanese elm. Even the leaves were diminutive.

"That's a beauty," I said.

He nodded. "This you can control," he said. "If you care for tree it will outlive you, perhaps outlive your children. And it will grow the way you have intended it to grow."

Chawlie was feeling introspective.

"You did not come see Chawlie when you returned to the Islands. I know, John Caine, that you needed your time alone. Every man needs his private thoughts. But the world cannot wait for you to feel sorry for yourself, so I sent Daniel before your thoughts became too menacing."

"You sent for me."

"I am worried. Your policeman friend is worried. You have had a bad time. Now it is over. No murder charge hangs over your head. And your wound, is it finally healing?"

"That last operation slowed me down some," I said, "but I'm on my feet."

"It takes a great deal to slow you down. And this is a time of great upheaval." He took a midget clipper and pruned a tiny piece of one miniature branch. Then he sat back and admired his creation. "We have a common enemy," he said.

"Ricky Lee."

"Your policeman friend spoke with you, I see. Ricky Lee is a mad dog."

"He told me that Ricky is out on bail, and that he made threats against me and Kimo's son."

"That is true. He also wants to unseat me, to take over Chawlie's poor business interests. It would be remarkable if he could achieve that, but Chawlie knows more than Ricky Lee knows, and Ricky Lee has someone in Chawlie's family who helps him."

"Someone in your organization?"

"Someone in my *family*." His fingers caressed the mossy base of the bonsai where tiny tree roots sprung from the trunk. "Everything is related to the shooting in San Francisco."

"How?"

"Someone wants to take my business. Who would do that? Who *could* do that?"

"I have no idea," I said. "Did someone want to kill you?"

"Not me. I was not the target. It was Daniel."

"Ricky Lee was behind the shooting in San Francisco?"

"And others. I have not yet learned everything that I am going to learn, but you must be aware that this is not about you. It is not even just about me."

"It is a power grab."

"Power shift. Nobody can grab for power. It must be shifted delicately from one shoulder to another. When someone grabs for it the balance is lost, and nobody has it."

"You're starting to talk like a fortune cookie, Chawlie."

"Alvin Toffler does not write fortune cookies," said Chawlie, looking pained. "You are a good friend, John Caine. I can trust you with what I know. But I do not know everything yet. You must learn for yourself, if you can. Then come and talk to Chawlie again. And be careful of Ricky Lee."

"If Ricky Lee were to have an accident, would that upset your plans?"

Chawlie grinned. "I am counting on his having an accident."

He reached behind his seat and took a cloth-wrapped object and pushed it across the table toward me. "You lost this," he said.

I took the package and found my Colt .45. It had been recently cleaned and loaded. It had the sweet smell of Hoppes No. 9 and glistened with gun oil.

"Thank you," I said, "for everything."

"Just in case you run across a mad dog. Mad dogs must be shot down where you find them."

"Just in case a mad dog doesn't have an accident."

"The mad dog you speak of will never die an old man. Or in bed. He threatens everybody. The justice system took him to jail and then let him out. It makes no sense."

"They let me out, too."

"That made no sense, either. But in your case I was grateful." He put the potted tree aside. "Be aware that things are not what they seem," he said. "And be aware of those who walk behind you."

"As in San Francisco."

He nodded.

I sat in the front seat of my old Jeep and watched the parking lot of the old worker's bar in Waialua. The night was warm enough, even with the onshore breezes skipping across the dirt surface of the lot, and I was comfortable in my dark sweatshirt and black sweatpants, recent acquisitions from the K-Mart in Iwilei, around the corner from Chinatown.

It was late, nearly three. The crowd was breaking up and heading for whatever passed as home. Nobody saw me sitting across the parking lot, my primer gray Jeep just another worker's truck. I didn't see my man, and I didn't expect that I would until well after the bar closed. This was when Silversword did business. This was when Ricky Lee would inform his associates of his plan to kill the haole PI and the young boy who had once been their constituent.

Ricky's car was there, the red Corvette snugged up tight against the building, surrounded by plastic trash cans. I wondered if he brought the cans with him, or made them a requirement of his presence.

The lot emptied, the crowd dwindling to only three or four pick-up trucks and an Isuzu Trooper that had seen better days. When the lot was deserted, I slipped out of the driver's seat and padded quickly across it, not running, just a hurrying trot, my body still fragile. But even when you're injured there are things that must be done.

Taking the new Buck Strider I had purchased earlier, I went to work on the front tires, carving into the sidewalls, careful to leave the thinnest margin of rubber and steel, so that they would hold the pressurized air until he hit a bump at speed. Then one or both tires would blow, leaving him running along on his expensive rims. The roads near the bar were not in the best repair. Cane roads, surrounded on both sides by vegetation, they were largely deserted at this time of night. Lee would not get far once he left the lot and then I would have him. I did not want to confront him while I was carving his Corvette, so I finished my chore and scuttled back to my Jeep and waited.

Three o'clock in the morning, the constellations ranged across the sky. I was tired and would have felt sleepy but for the urgency of my self-assigned mission. I drank no coffee. I took no painkillers either, the discomfort from my injuries all that I required to stay alert. I glanced at my watch at regular intervals. Time was running out. If Ricky Lee did not come out of the tavern soon I would have to resort to other means.

While I waited, I eased the blade of the Buck Strider back and forth, wearing in the new metal. Buck's new folder was bigger than my old Folding Hunter, and I liked it as soon as I saw it. The Strider had a different mechanism to open the blade, and I would have to spend hours practicing with it to master the technique, but the blade was thicker and longer than my old Hunter, and had a sharp tanto point.

But it was stiff, as all new knives are stiff, and I spent the waiting time moving the blade back and forth, letting the parts and pieces of the knife get to know one another.

I sat for over an hour, working the blade, watching the bar empty, waiting for Ricky Lee to leave. I was about to try something else when a dark-colored SUV entered the parking lot and parked directly in front of the bar. The doors opened and four men got out, quickly climbed the stairs, and hurried inside. Each man held something long and wicked in his right hand, holding it down by his leg as he filed through the door.

Almost immediately a staccato sound like firecrackers rolled across the parking lot and disappeared into the night.

The four men were inside for less than a minute before they sauntered empty-handed from the building, casually climbed back into the SUV, did a slow circle of the dirt lot, and disappeared down the lonely cane road.

A dull flickering light appeared through the painted windows of the bar. As the flickering light became brighter my cellular telephone buzzed.

"Caine."

"Get out of there." Daniel's voice rasped briefly in my ear and the carrier went dead.

Despite his warning, I waited in the lot until fire speared through the old rotten roof. I glanced through the entry door and saw only solid conflagration.

No one had come out after the men from the SUV. Whoever was in there when they went inside remained inside.

As I drove away I watched in my rearview mirror as a blazing section of roof fell away and covered the Corvette with flame.

51

Two hours later I boarded Chawlie's Gulfstream. Tutu Mae and James Kahanamoku were already at the gate. Daniel met me, eyed the other passengers, but said nothing. Felix stood behind him, silent and moody. He began to loosen up when Tutu Mae welcomed him home with a hug and a pat, but like a lot of young people, he took pains to share his displeasure.

Regardless of Felix's mood, the flight was uneventful and in less than an hour we were offloading equipment and supplies at the Kona airport.

David met us there, driving an ancient muddy flatbed. Even with both arms in casts, he seemed to have survived his confrontation with equanimity. If anything, I think it suited him to have gone to war for his Lady Love. His fiberglass casts were stained with grease. It appeared that he had forgotten them.

There was an uneasy moment when David saw James. He knew he was Kimo's son, but he remembered the day when Donna had been kidnapped and his arms had been broken, and he recognized James as one of the men who had tried to ruin his summer vacation. He stared at him for a moment, looked at me, then shrugged. He recognized James, but he knew Kimo, and he knew that James was Charles's brother, too. That apparently counted for something. And this young man was in love. Revenge, for David, was way down on the happiness scale.

Daniel took me aside before he left, walking me away from the group at the truck.

"Felix did not want to return. I want you to watch him."

I watched Felix while Daniel spoke. He stood apart from the group staring at us, as if he knew he was the subject of our conversation.

"It is important that you keep Felix here for a few days. If you can." A fresh breeze blew across the tarmac, blowing down from the north. It carried the faint scent of rotten eggs. "If you can," he repeated. "I need some time in Honolulu without him."

"Why did you bring him back?"

"I want him out of San Francisco, too. This was the best place for him. And you're the excuse."

"I baby-sit."

He nodded.

"Does this have anything to do with this morning?"

He stared at me and said nothing. Chawlie would have been proud.

"Okay," I said. "I'll baby-sit."

Daniel patted my arm, then climbed back into his airplane. He would eventually tell me what this was about. Or he wouldn't. Regardless, I would keep Felix on ice. For what reasons I could not imagine.

Sometimes it's better if you don't know.

I sat in the front seat of the flatbed with Tutu Mae and David. Felix and James rode in the back with the equipment.

"California's too tough for you," David said, watching the careful tenderness with which I climbed into the truck, right behind Tutu Mae. Compared to her spry activity, I was a fragile old man.

"I'm staying away if they'll let me."

"We're almost a matched pair," he grinned, knocking one of his casts on mine.

"Ouch," I said.

"Mom's getting married," he said, looking over the top of Tutu Mae's iron gray head.

"She told me."

"The guy's rich."

"Good."

"He's a nice fellow."

"That's even better."

"Runs investments, or something. Spends most of the year in New York."

"Wonderful."

"You don't want to talk about it, do you?"

"I'm happy for her."

"I'm sorry to hear about what happened to you in San Francisco. Did they catch the ones responsible for it?"

"Most of them."

He shook his head. "It's just not right."

"Yep."

He looked at me out of the corner of his eye, stealing only a glance from the road ahead. "You're not very talkative this morning."

"Nope." I turned away, looking out the window. "We're here. You're going to do some diving. Tutu Mae, you're going to have to hurry."

The wind carried the eye-watering stench of sulfur. Hualalai had buried the road and marched across the old flows to the sea. By land we could not proceed any farther north from this point. Yellow barricades and island police guarded the road to make certain no fool continued to drive on, oblivious to the peril. A giant parking lot had been cleared almost overnight from the desert landscape, and a tent city populated by news media and scientists had sprung up since my last visit. Generators, temporary power poles, media tents and portable toilets decorated the landscape.

And just outside the zone, bobbing like a toy boat in a bathtub, was my lovely sloop. Something stirred inside of me when I saw her. I was home.

"Aren't you guys done?" *Olympia* lay anchored directly in the path of the lava flow. Steam and smoke rose from the place where the lava poured into the Pacific. Up on the flank of Moana Loa the lava had already burned the forests in its path, leaving a black smoking scar on the hillside. Along the rocky coast very few things existed that could burn. Hualalai, without eruption for nearly two hundred years, had still proved its active state. "It's getting a little close, isn't it?"

"We keep finding more stuff in niches. We're almost finished."

It took longer to ferry the equipment out to *Olympia* than it took us to fly to Kona. By the time I arrived on the boat the girls were on their second dive of the day and Charles was working as divemaster, worrying like a big brother. When he saw James, however, he forgot his worries and raced to hug him.

"You're here!"

"Yeah."

"How long have they been down?" David asked, taking the boy's position.

"Twenty-two minutes," said Charles. "They have another twenty before things get critical. The lava keeps moving. I don't like it."

I doubted that they liked it either, given that the lava had begun piling against the shallow side of their lava tube, as David had told me.

Knowing Donna, she would force her work into every waking moment in an attempt to document everything. There was no second chance. Once the lava reached the point of no return, the find would be gone forever.

Donna surfaced beside the boarding ladder, took off her mask and tossed it onto the deck. She did not look happy.

Charles and James assisted her up the ladder. She did a double take when she saw James.

The last time they had met he had been one of those who had kidnapped her.

"Miss Wong," said James.

"James," she said, her voice subdued, unsure what was happening until she saw Tutu Mae. "Oh, wonderful!" She flashed a huge smile at Kimo's grandmother. "You're actually here!"

Tutu Mae grinned.

"We don't have much time," she said to Charles. "I have to change regulators, and you need to clean this one. Something's fouled it. It's both of them, so it's the J-valve, not the regulator. And the lava is getting close." She saw me. "Hi, Mr. Caine."

"Good morning."

"We're pushing the envelope." She glanced toward the billowing tower of steam rising from the ocean. "I don't know how much longer we can do this." Donna Wong had lost weight since I had last seen her. Blue smudges encircled her eyes to the point where she looked bruised. Her cheekbones, prominent before, now protruded like ridges from her gaunt face. She was exhausted, ill-fed, ill-used, and happy, the state people achieve when they're living their dream.

"Is it him, The Lonely One?" I asked. Below the boat, a cloud of bright yellow reef fish darted in and out of *Olympia*'s shadow.

"We may never know. Personally, I think it's him, but I can't say for sure. Tutu Mae is going to bless the bones before we seal up the entrance."

Tutu Mae smiled. "That's why I am here."

"We discussed taking a small sample of the bones so we could DNA test it. Tutu Mae and other kupunas debated removing a single knucklebone from his left hand. In the end, the decision was to leave the bones alone."

"Scattering the bones is the worst thing you can do," said Tutu Mae.

"I thought DNA wouldn't work in an island population."

"There is a man who claims direct descendence from Kamehameha. They would have used his blood."

"You think you can finish today?" I watched the shoreline. The white-orange lava continued pouring into the sea. The land looked as if it had pushed out to sea since I had arrived this morning.

"One more day."

"Do you have that much time?"

"We *have* to have that much time. One more day, then we'll relax."

"Doesn't look like you'll have to use explosives."

She grinned, her eyes sparkling, although rimmed with exhaustion. "Madam Pele takes care of her own. But we don't have much time left."

"We have to allow Tutu Mae time to dive. It's still safe, but for how much longer I don't know. We've done almost everything we can do here on the site. The real work will be when we get back to the university."

"No more interference."

She nodded. "Tutu Mae went to the president of the university while you were . . . while you were in California. She told him the whole story. He is personally watching this dig, and he says he has told no one about it."

"You haven't said anything about the bones?"

"No. Not until the cave is closed forever."

"They're not all like Hayes."

"Sure," was all she said.

52

All day long the mountain growled and rumbled, a pale, hot orange stream pumping a continuous river of molten magma into the sea. The volume seemed to fall off occasionally, and then increased, the rhythm of the flow unpredictable.

Everyone but David and I suited up. No one wanted to miss the ceremony. Even Felix, who had been aloof since he had been drafted, was going. Nearly every piece of gear aboard was in use. David and I were the only ones remaining topside. We would watch the proceedings on the closed-circuit television. It was a poor second to being there, but under the circumstances I was happy just to be along.

Someone had to keep an eye on the volcano.

Tutu Mae had taken the short course back in Honolulu and was now certified for SCUBA. This would be her first ocean dive. Both James and Donna would be beside her every moment, assisted by Charles. Donna's sisters would wield the cameras and the lights. Felix was tagged to be the lookout at the entrance. The lava was not so close to the entrance that they thought they might be trapped, but anything might happen, and if something occurred high up on the mountain they wouldn't know about it until it was too late unless we relayed the message. They should have enough time to get out if it all worked as planned. David was topside lookout. My job was to man a radio linking Donna,

Felix and *Olympia*. I kept an eye on the clock as well as the volcano, making sure the party was safe. Felix would position himself outside the lava tube to relay my messages. The radio waves were line-of-sight and wouldn't penetrate the rock.

"Smile for the camera, Tutu Mae!" One of Donna's sisters snapped her photo when she was ready. The tank was a little heavy for Tutu Mae, and made her unsteady on her feet. Charles and James stood close, making sure she wouldn't fall over backwards. The photograph would show the three of them close together, the grandsons and the great grandmother on her first dive, to replace and bless the gravesite of the first Hawaiian king. This was an occasion to memorialize.

Tutu Mae had trouble with the ladder. She couldn't do it wearing the tank; it was just too heavy. It was decided that she would climb down without it and get into the water while James and Charles assisted her there. That proved impossible and finally she had to dive from the Avon dinghy, sliding backward into the sea.

The other divers jumped into the water from the side of *Olympia* and paddled around her stern.

"Testing. Are you awake?" The voice screeched out of the radio Donna that had given me. I picked it up.

"I read you five by five."

"What?"

"Loud and clear. And yes, I'm awake."

"Don't go to sleep up there in the sun. We can hear the volcano down here. It's roaring." Donna's voice was nearly covered by background noise. Over the carrier came a low menacing rumble.

"Thanks," I said to the radio, picked up the field glasses, and lensed the shoreline. Lava continued to pour into the sea, lending its incandescent Halloween colors to the brown and blue and green of its surroundings. The flow seemed to have increased since we arrived.

I was back on my boat for the first time in months. I had not liked my life in recent times, but I had lived through it. It had not been easy, and for the first time in recent memory I had been faced with an opponent I could not fight, whose rules I found inconsistent with strategy or logic, and who required that I had champions of my own. Tala Sufai and Albert Chen were my legal warriors, the doctors and nurses my medical saviors. Without them I wouldn't be sitting on the deck of my own yacht again. Without them I honestly did not know where I would have been.

The sun beat down on my face and I thought of Angel. She had loved the sensation of the sunshine on her warm brown skin. She loved most the simple sensations of being alive. She had brought me back into my body after my wounds, and she had, in her own way, saved me. Her injuries were far more serious than they had first thought. Her skull fracture had caused some brain damage; when I last heard, she had undergone more surgery and remained in California, trapped in a hospital bed in a city far away from her home in paradise. It would be months before she could be moved, before she could return. Chawlie had promised to bring her home when she was ready.

I hoped he had dispatched some young men, skilled in all the arts, to keep her company while she recuperated.

Whoever hurt her would be punished. Two had died that night. One still lived. It had been a long, long time since I had felt such a towering rage; it had been so long that it surprised me with its vehemence. An Angel had been grounded, her wings clipped. And some devil would pay. That the Angel had been grounded only because of her proximity to one John Caine didn't make it any easier. Another innocent bystander had been destroyed. Add her to the list. It was dangerous just being in my vicinity.

Like David, she could not countenance revenge. A caregiver, that was not her way. But some things have to be done. There was no reason to allow those responsible to continue to walk the earth when she no longer could walk again.

"Radio check," crackled the radio next to me.

"I read you, Felix?" His voice was muffled, barely recognizable.

The background noise was louder.

"Yeah. I'm lookout. Anything on the surface?"

"It hasn't changed. What's down there?"

"Dante Alighieri would have felt right at home. The lava is pillowing off to the side. It's not the runny kind. This stuff just turns into big rock pillows, and then they explode. You should see it."

"Sounds charming."

"I'll be here."

"Give me a check in five minutes, unless you need me."

"What could you do?"

That angered me until I understood that he was right. I could do nothing. Not in the face of the volcano. I couldn't even enter the water with my cast and open wounds.

"Ten four," I said.

"Out."

It appeared that there were many things that I could no longer fight alone. This had been a humbling experience. All my life I had been the lone wolf. Now it seemed that the predators ran in packs and a single wolf was incapable of doing anything alone.

Somewhere there had been a reason for it all.

If only I could see it.

The mountain gave a great belch and a column of thick black smoke rose above the caldera high up on the flank of Moana Loa. I remembered what Donna had said, that white smoke was good, that gray smoke was bad. What the hell did black smoke mean?

"David?"

"Shit, I don't know."

I picked up the radio.

"Felix."

The mountain rumbled and shook. I could feel the vibration of the island through the deck of my boat.

"Felix."

He did not answer.

"Felix! Anybody!"

A huge orange wall of lava spilled over the top of the caldera, slowly tumbling down the mountainside. Finding a different path, the flow set new fires in the jungle as it made its way toward the sea.

Another stream spilled over the lip of Hualalai and started down the other side of the lava flow.

"Anybody!"

The radio sat silent in my hand.

"John," said David. "We've got to get them out of there."

I looked around for spare diving gear and found nothing. They had taken everything I had. There wasn't even a spare regulator.

"Well, crap," I said. Then I remembered and ran down to my stateroom. In my personal diving gear I had a five-minute emergency bottle. I couldn't remember the last time I'd had it charged, but I turned the nozzle and air hissed, so I was satisfied. It would be better than trying to hold my breath, and I could snorkel along the surface until I came to the cave and only dive then, when I saw the entrance.

I tried the radio one more time and got no response.

"You stay on the radio," I told David. "I'm going down."

"It's better if I go."

"It's better if you stay here. Get the engine going, raise the anchors and motor us as close as you can to the entrance. I'll go down and bring them up."

He nodded, glanced up at the mountain, and went to work.

The mountain rumbled and bellowed, sounding like one of those Japanese movie monsters in pain.

I was not supposed to get my wounds wet, the doctors told me. Severe infection would result, they said, along with other dire consequences. And that was if I just took a shower in soapy clean water. But those big pharmaceutical companies still made Keflex and other wonder antibiotics, didn't they? We'd just have to see how well they worked, now wouldn't we?

David brought *Olympia* as close as he dared to the coral reef. He shifted into reverse and kept her stable in the currents.

People on the shore were shouting at us and waving their arms.

I took one more look toward the mountain. A curtain of orange flame was descending, rolling down the hillside, forging an inexorable path directly toward us.

Madam Pele was on the move.

Grabbing my fins and mask, I carefully shed my shirt, kicked off my sandals, and jumped into the ocean.

53

The resonance of the volcano overwhelmed my senses as soon as the water closed over my head. It thundered like a freight train. It rumbled. It sounded like a living creature, mumbling incoherent incantations one moment, roaring curses and imprecations the next. Much louder than on the surface, it felt as if I had dived into the caldera instead of the sea. I was as immersed in the sound as I was in the Pacific.

The water grew warmer as I swam closer to the shore, and the sea turned sterile. Even the fish had deserted the area. I felt a fool, swimming toward the lava flow. There was no sane reason to be here, other than the lives of Tutu Mae, Donna Wong, James, Charles and the others.

I wondered what had happened to Felix.

It couldn't have been good.

I snorkeled along on the choppy surface, the cool ocean water percolated by the cavitating disruption of Hualalai's lava. The water was so disturbed that the normal visibility had dropped and I could barely make out the bottom. Following the heavy black electrical cables that ran from *Olympia* was difficult from the surface. Twice I had to dive to see which direction they ran from the point where I lost them in the tangle of rocks and coral, but I managed to swim to the place where they disappeared into the rock face.

It looked about thirty feet down, just as Donna had reported. The entrance to the ancient lava tube lay in a pocket below an overhanging wall. The noise of the lava reached a crescendo this close to its entry to the sea. It was so loud I could hardly think, and I could see flashes of orange light just to the north of the cave entrance as the lava pillows exploded. Black rocky shrapnel from detonations littered the coral bottom in front of the cave opening. It would be tricky getting in. I hoped that would be the trickiest part.

Felix had vanished. Remembering his demeanor the first time I met him in San Francisco, I didn't worry about him, knowing that he valued his own hide far more than anything else. The heat and the danger might have been too much for him, and he would have simply fled. There are things you can fight, and there are things you can't. That kind of thinking was forgivable in certain circumstances. What was not was his abandonment of the others.

Certain I had the right place, I put the emergency air supply into my mouth, cleared the mini-regulator, exhaled sharply, kicked my legs straight up into the air, and sank like a stone toward the bottom.

Clearing my sinuses twice before I reached the depth, I hovered only briefly outside the cave, cursing my stupidity at not bringing a flashlight. I must have pictured the entire cave lit up like a mining tunnel, not thinking that the lights would only be used at the location of the dig.

The cables were there, and I could follow them into the cave. That was now my only recourse.

Lava exploded nearby, stinging me with red-hot pellets. It was much closer than it should have been. I rocketed into the cave, hoping the entrance would be there when we wanted to swim out.

I groped blindly through the cave for what seemed like an eternity, keeping toward the top of the tube after I banged my head painfully against a boulder on the bottom. The tunnel was constricted at this end, jumbled with rocks and boulders of jagged lava, and there is no dark on the planet like the darkness of an underwater cave. I pushed myself into the black hole by sheer will alone, forcing my body to do things my mind absolutely forbid me to do. It may have been only a dozen meters or so, but it felt as though I had crawled like a worm through the darkness all my life. I was one of those pale cave creatures, born to exist in the void, until I came to a bend in the maze and saw the pale glimmer of electric light.

I followed the yellow rays until I swam up into a larger chamber. Off to the side was an obviously carved opening, square cut and chiseled. Inside, the light was brighter.

I swam a little faster and came to a tableau.

Tutu Mae was hovering above a large skeleton. The ancient bones were surrounded by gold and silver artifacts, jeweled candelabras, swords with golden guards and silver inlay, golden crosses, silver chalices, boxes of treasure. I had imagined what it might look like, but seeing it in the reflected glare of camera lights and electrical illumination it was the personification of a childhood dream of pirate treasure. And if that wasn't the skeleton of old King Kamehameha, I had no idea who it could have been.

The others did not see me swim into the chamber.

I grabbed Charles, pointed at Tutu Mae, and signaled for him to take her up. He nodded and gently touched his great grandmother. She turned, startled; her eyes found mine and I pointed toward the roof of the cave and then crossed my throat with the same finger. Charles tugged at her and she did not resist.

Donna and her sisters kept the lights on and the cameras rolling and followed Tutu Mae, as if documenting her presence was somehow important to the experience. James, his arms filled with equipment, brought up the rear. I took one more look around, took in the bones of the giant skeleton, the treasure, the carvings on the tomb wall. It was a find, all right. And Donna had left it all in place. I had to admire her lack of greed. Had I found it first I might have stripped the cave of every valuable before I said anything about it, if I said anything about it at all.

I looked, and didn't touch, and swam out the narrow tunnel toward the open sea.

Outside, the lava was now piling up near the entrance, exploding at regular intervals. The others had made it out. Only James and I remained inside the tube. And both the frequency of the explosions and the volume of molten rock had increased.

I shoved him, and he balked.

My emergency air supply whistled and stopped flowing.

Rapidly cooling lava dripped over the edge of the entrance and piled on the rocky ocean floor in front of us.

James backed away, deeper into the tube.

I shoved him forward. He shoved back, refusing to move.

I willed him to move. He stayed at the mouth of the tunnel, his knuckles white, gripping the rock walls.

Another puddle of lava spilled across the entrance. This time the lava was hotter. The water churned from the catalytic heat. Bubbles streamed from the steaming rocks. I had never seen fire underwater, did not know it was possible, but dull orange flames licked the bottom of the newly minted rocks, and smoke swirled out into the ocean. Water boiled around the rocks. The water at the entrance to the tube grew so heated that it hurt. If we didn't move now, and if we weren't sealed into the cave by the lava, we would be boiled alive.

We had no more time and I had no more air in my lungs. I grabbed James's harness and swam as hard as I could from the tunnel and into the open ocean, dragging him along beside. He was so surprised by my sudden assault he didn't fight me until we were outside of the area of the nearby lava flow, in the relative safety of the sea. And he stopped fighting once we reached open water. He grew eerily calm, and I let him go and we swam to the fractured silver mirror of the ocean's surface above us.

I drew in a deep breath, and immediately regretted it, inhaling a lungful of the thick sulfur fumes that hovered on top of the surface of the water. James surfaced beside me, saw me coughing, handed me his emergency regulator, and together we submerged again, kicking along the bottom until we came to *Olympia*'s shadow. We rose slowly together and hung floating in the water, hanging onto the boarding ladder, panting and gagging.

"Hey, you going to get up here before you boil?" Charles peered down at us. "Can I take your equipment?"

We tossed up masks and fins, and James climbed up first, painfully, carefully. Something was wrong, and I didn't see it until he was halfway up the ladder and then I saw the raw, charred flesh of his calf.

"Help him! He's burned!"

Charles appeared from out of nowhere and helped drag his brother on board. I followed him up the ladder.

Donna appeared. "Get the first aid kit!" I told her. "Get us the hell out of here," I ordered. David cut the cables and goosed the engine. *Olympia* spurted ahead, clearing a coral head, and turned, heading out to sea.

"You going into shock?" I asked James.

"No."

"You sure?"

"It hurts like hell, but I'll be okay."

"You'll have a hell of a story to tell. How you spent your summer vacation."

He closed his eyes.

"Hey!"

"Hey, yourself, Mr. Caine. I'm just resting." He put his hand on my arm. "I'm sorry. I just panicked. That lava, the heat . . . it terrified me."

"Me too."

"But we got out of there."

"We did."

"You got us out of there."

"Don't worry. I'm not telling anybody anything."

He looked at me with Kimo's eyes, nodded once, and closed them.

Donna came with the first aid kit and knelt beside him, her face a mixture of fear and concern.

"Get the antiseptic and the burn ointment. Then get on the radio and see if we can rendezvous with a police launch or Coast Guard. They'll have to get him to a hospital burn unit chop-chop."

Despite what he told me, he looked like he was going into shock.

"I'll finish here, Donna. Get on that radio."

She handed me the antiseptic and ran to the cabin.

Charles appeared at my elbow.

"Anything I can do?"

"Stay with him," I said, standing up. "Elevate his feet. I think he's in shock."

Charles propped his brother's feet on the railing and sat beside him.

"Cover him," I ordered. The boy had nothing on but his shirt, and he took it off and covered James's torso. He sat next to his injured brother, alert to any change in his condition.

"Let me know if he gets worse."

"Sure."

"Anyone see Felix?"

Charles shook his head. "I was just wondering. He was on lookout outside the cave. Is that why you came?"

"He didn't answer the radio. I thought he was hurt. Or something." I didn't tell him my real fears.

"He didn't like what we were doing. I didn't think he'd stay."

I wondered where he'd gone. He couldn't have made it to shore except by swimming all the way around the reef and finding a beach on either the north or south side. And then what would he do? There weren't any beaches along this coast, and damned few of them on the island. Hawaii was too young to produce many beaches, and this side was one of the youngest.

The youngest now, Hualalai competing with Kilauea to create new land for Pele.

It was, I decided, not my problem. Felix had never been my problem. He was Chawlie's problem. I just never understood why my old friend had insisted on hanging him around my neck on this trip. It made no sense.

"You're bleeding."

"I know." I'd lost my bandages in the salt water and my wounds had opened again. No telling what kind of bugs had entered my body. These tropical waters had sea maggots and other worm larvae, and I wouldn't be surprised if a host of microscopic creatures had taken up residence in my flesh. The doctors would be apoplectic when they learned what I had done. It was a sure bet that I would be back in the hospital. I might even have company, but at least I wouldn't be alone in the world. Hualalai's lava and Madam Pele would have buried my friends in old King Kamehameha's tomb. I could not have lived with that.

I sank down on a stern cushion and let the others carry out my orders.

"You want to raise the sails?" David asked from behind the wheel.

I shook my head, too tired to consider the process. "Keep her under power. Make a course for Kailua Harbor. And see what Donna's raised on the radio."

I felt exhausted and exhilarated, the adrenaline rush peaking as I sat there, giving me a tingling from the small of my back all the way up my spine to the nape of my neck. It was a familiar feeling. It meant that I had won. We had beaten the odds. We hadn't lost anyone to the volcano. Aside from the missing Felix Chen, we were all aboard and headed toward safe harbor.

Madam Pele, the goddess of fire, the mistress of the underworld, had been good to old John Caine.

It helps to have friends in low places.

54

The Coast Guard plucked James from the deck of the *Olympia* and flew him to the trauma hospital in Hilo, on the far side of the island. Tutu Mae and Charles went with him for moral support and to relay information to the family back home until Kimo and Neolani could get there.

With James on his way for treatment, and Felix among the missing, what remained of the crew motored back and forth off shore, watching the lava pile onto the reef over the cave. We watched the lava advance until it covered the reef completely, pouring molten rock down into the crevices and crannies that had once supported abundant life forms. By the time the sun went down it was obvious to everyone of us that the cave had been sealed. Whatever and whomever was down there would remain. Treasure hunters would have to spend more than it was worth to uncover the rocky tomb, even if they knew the location. If those giant bones were the remains of old King Kamehameha, he would continue to be the Lonely One, secure deep inside the rock of the island that had been his birthplace.

Of Felix there was no sign. It was inconceivable that he had been killed or injured. At the time he disappeared his station was relatively safe. Had something hit him I would have found him. No, he had cut and run. I used the field glasses to search the shore all afternoon, but I saw no sign of him, and I spotted few places where a swimmer could easily come ashore. But I knew he had made it. I knew he was gone. When, and to where, I did not know. Felix had not wanted to be with us in the first place. He had been drafted by Daniel, forced to come along, told to dive near the volcano without his consent. A free spirit, and an intelligent one at that, he must have resented all of it.

Felix had wanted to work for Chawlie. He must not have thought it all the way through before he found out, too late, that working for Chawlie meant doing things Chawlie's way for as long as it was agreeable to him. The simplest way to disengage from Chawlie's service was to disappear.

That's just what he did.

I didn't understand the kid, but I wished him well. All the same I would have to tell Daniel that I had not been able to hold onto the lad.

I went below for my cell phone.

We sailed into Kailua Harbor at sunset, just one more boat riding at anchorage off the little seaside village. We crowded into the Avon for a quick trip to shore, showering and changing clothes, and finding an agreeable Italian restaurant built like a houseboat directly on top of a seafood restaurant, which was, in turn, constructed atop a dock at the edge of the sea. The outside deck overlooked the harbor. We ate angel hair and Caesar salad, drank four bottles of a light pinot grigio, and topped it all off with one of each from the dessert tray, the meal accompanied by the sound of the gentle surf washing the pebbles on the shore below. We had a quiet celebration, somewhat muted by our concern for James and the disappearance of Felix, but satisfied that what Donna had set out to do had been accomplished. Of the skeleton's identity, we would never be sure. Refusing to take a sample because of her respect for the Hawaiian people's feelings, Donna had sacrificed what could have been the most important find. She disagreed with me when I asked her about it.

"The fact that I have proven that the Spanish reached Hawaii more than a hundred years before any other Europeans is good enough," she said. "We will have to live with the mystery."

Legends would grow. She did bring back video and photographs. She had measured and analyzed the bones. There would be speculation enough to last her for the rest of her career.

We agreed to sail *Olympia* back to Honolulu on the morning tide. It would be an easy sail, one that we would remember. Donna called the university, told them that she was coming and what she was bringing back, arranging for a truck to meet the boat and pick up our equipment and supplies. They asked about artifacts.

"Artifacts?" she said into her little cell phone. "Artifacts are nonexistent. We left everything in place."

Whoever she had called gave her a long speech that made her close her eyes and pinch the skin of her forehead together. "No," she said after a long pause, "we can't go back and retrieve the artifacts. You'll have to get along with the photographic evidence."

The treasure would remain hidden where it had been deposited.

And would remain hidden forever.

It was a peaceful sail home. My last view of Moana Loa was of a long, humped peak jutting through the clouds, barely recognizable in the marine mist. Another giant lay off my starboard. Haleakala, Maui's own massive shield volcano, brooded silently, brown and barren from the sea.

I took us into Pearl Harbor and sailed right into the slip, a neat job, one that can only be accomplished when the winds are perfect. And they were. It was the perfect ending of the perfect day. Donna's university contact met her as promised, and soon her gear was unloaded and the entire crew trudged up the dock and vanished into the evening air. And suddenly I was alone.

It felt good. It was the first time in months that I had been alone on my own boat, with nothing hanging over my head, and no obligations to fulfill. I had done what I'd had to do. I retained my freedom and some of my sanity. *Olympia* needed a lot of work. As I began to feel better I would tackle the small chores, then the larger jobs, and then the big ones, until she was like new again. A classic wooden-hulled sailing vessel of the thirties, *Olympia* demanded constant attention. The tropics demanded even more. She had been neglected. But I was back now. Injured and hurting, but back, and in one piece. Maintenance would be my therapy. It would be good for *Olympia* and it would be good for me.

Nothing lasts forever. Peace, whenever I find it, is always one of those fleeting destinations, a mirage that vanishes even as I approach it. So when I find it I celebrate. I opened a bottle of La Crema Pinot Noir and drank half of it, savoring the taste, sitting in my lounge listening to some favorite old CDs and becoming reacquainted with my home. Other people's mana had invaded the place. Their scents and leavings surrounded me. It would take some time, and the investment of my own Mana, to recapture the place. But I was comfortable. And I was home.

I went below, dug into my private stash and came up with a Ramon Allones. Taking it topside, I lit it and accompanied the remains of the La Crema. Evening breezes found me on my aft deck, brightening the end of my first cigar in months.

I was safe.

Until I closed my eyes.

My old bedtime partner, that Vietnamese warrior, returned for his regular visit.

"They're in the wire!" I heard the call again from that panicked, disembodied voice, the terror and the realization of the man's own mortality manifest in his cry. It might have been the last sentence he ever uttered. I'll never know. It was instantly followed by the chaos of M-16s and AK-47 fire, explosions, the sound of men screaming, the sound of their dying. And in my sector, men started dying in front of me, killed by my hand, dead because of political implications that none of us cared about or fully understood.

I shot the man in the trench, firing from the hip, blowing

away most of his head. The figure crumbled, collapsing into the mud at my feet.

Above me, Felix Chen lunged toward me, armed with a long-bladed bayonet at the tip of an old rifle.

I aimed my carbine at his center mass.

It clicked empty.

The bayonet slid into my chest.

I started awake, sweat pouring off my body, opened my eyes and looked directly into the face of Felix Chen.

He stood over me, armed with a long Bowie knife. The blade hovered near my throat.

"Don't move!"

I lay absolutely still, watching him, watching the knife.

"Caine?"

"I hear you."

"I'm going to turn on the light. Don't do anything that might annoy me, okay?"

"That's reasonable," I said. I felt a trickle of sweat run down my neck from my hairline to dampen the pillow.

Felix took the knife away, but kept it in his hand while he closed the curtains and turned on the cabin light. He wore shorts and a new sweatshirt and carried a small backpack. And that long knife.

"Hello, Felix."

"Hello, John."

"You could have knocked."

He put his finger to his mouth. "I don't think anybody saw me come aboard. You never know who's watching."

"You could have called."

"I could not. Your line's tapped."

"Not my cellular."

"I forgot your number."

"Okay, fine. What do you want?"

"I need your help. I have to get to San Francisco. Can this thing make it?"

He saw me glance at my headboard bookcase where I stored the Colt .45. Felix smiled, and wagged his finger at me.

"You never know who your friends are," I said.

"Just stay away from it." Felix motioned with the knife. "Come into the lounge."

I rolled out of my bunk, careful not to get too close to the huge pig sticker he held in his hand. The blade looked to be at least a foot long. "Mind if I put on my shorts?"

"Sure, old man."

He stepped away as I reached down and picked up my old khaki shorts. The comfortable weight of my new knife told me he hadn't checked them. I watched him as I slipped them on.

"You first," he said, and followed me into the lounge.

I touched a bench seat and sat down, conscious of the Colt .22 automatic that I kept behind the paperbacks near my right hand. I'd put it there last night, right after I'd cleaned it and reloaded it. Safety on, clocked and locked.

Felix sat across from me, within striking distance of that deadly knife. "Can you take me to California?"

"Why would I do that?"

"I was your bodyguard. I looked after you."

"Why don't you get on an airplane? You need money?"

"I can always use money, but money won't get me to California. Daniel is after me. He and Chawlie want me dead."

"Why?"

"You don't want to know, Caine. Just take me to California. I'll be fine then."

"Chawlie is my friend. Why does he want you dead?"

Felix shook his head.

"You'd better leave," I said. "I won't take you to California. And if Daniel wants you dead it must have something to do with the attempt on Chawlie's life. Is that it?"

Felix smiled. He looked exhausted, the strain evident in the way his smile sagged. "You are stupid, Caine," he said. "I heard stories about how tough and smart you were, but you must have lost it. You sure missed it this time. Nobody wanted to kill Chawlie. He was never the target."

"What do you mean?" Chawlie had told me the same thing, but I must have forgotten it. Now I remembered.

"Can I trust you?"

"If Daniel knows about you already, you're a dead man. You can't run far enough. Nothing I have to say will save you. Who was the target?"

"Daniel was the main target."

"Daniel?"

"You know the story of Cain and Abel?"

"Which brother wanted him dead?"

"You can guess."

"Gilbert?"

"Maybe you aren't so stupid. But it's been all around you for the last six months and you didn't see it."

And then I did see it, all of it, the vision that I'd had just before the volcano erupted in its one final spasm. I remembered Chawlie's mentioning that the family had been in revolt. And I knew now who he was talking about. "Gilbert wanted Daniel out of the way."

"Chawlie is making noises like he wants to retire, all those bonsai trees and the meditation garden, and his work with the old Hawaiian woman. He has other interests besides the business. Gilbert is his oldest son. He naturally assumed that Chawlie would leave everything to him."

"But Chawlie chose Daniel."

"Right. He's the natural successor, not Gilbert."

"So Gilbert . . ."

"So Gilbert decided that if something happened to Daniel, Chawlie would have nobody to turn to. Except him."

"Back in May. You had something to do with that?"

Felix nodded. "Tit for tat," he said. "Simultaneous revolutions. Gilbert had an idea. My lover and I wanted to take over the

San Francisco Triads. The old men were running them into the ground. No energy. Other interests. Gilbert wanted to take over Honolulu. He set it up over a year ago, just after Chawlie had been so damaged by the woman with the emeralds. Gilbert thought the old man was growing weak and stupid; letting a woman steal that much from him damaged his credibility. When Daniel suddenly rose as the heir apparent, Gilbert contacted my brother, who lived here."

"Your brother," I said. "He *lived* here."

"Yes. Daniel killed him."

I remembered what Tutu Mae had said before my trial. She must have repeated the same thing to Chawlie, who started thinking. And I remembered the Cadillac SUV in the Waialua parking lot. "Ricky Lee was your brother."

Felix nodded. "They executed my lover and they murdered my brother and now they're going to kill me. I'm trapped in the Islands and I have to get out."

"I can't help you."

"I was hoping you would, but I am prepared to take this thing out myself."

"Or get rid of me as soon as we were close to California."

He nodded. "Gilbert brokered the bodyguard job for me. The thinking was that I could get Daniel and Chawlie together at one time. Do them both. Daniel must have smelled something, because he never let it happen."

"You almost got close."

"Once, but I would have died. Staying alive is always my first priority."

"So what are you going to do now? Kill me? Take *Olympia* out and head for San Francisco? They'll find you. They'll track you down easily. As soon as you key the satellite phone or use the GPS they'll zero in on the signal and send the Coast Guard after you. Or the Navy. That's a big flat ocean out there with nowhere to hide."

"You'll take me out of Pearl Harbor. I can head for Canada or Mexico or South America."

I nodded. "And then what?"

"I've got money."

"No, Felix," I said patiently. "And then what about me?"

"Your choice. Either join me or die."

"I don't think so."

"I thought you'd say that," he said. He reached into the back-pack and drew out a sawed-off shotgun. I saw it coming out of the bag, tossed paperbacks off the bookcase with the tips of my fingers, grabbed the .22, aimed quickly at center mass and fired twice.

Felix fell over.

He lay on the deck, the bag and both arms underneath his body, the knife on the bench seat. His breath came in quick pants. But he still breathed.

"Felix," I said quickly, "let me see your hands."

He pulled his right hand from beneath his chest and wiggled bloody fingers.

"That's one hand. Now the other."

He lay still, as if thinking it over. Blood was pooling under him and running along the grooves of the teak decking.

"Come on, man, I don't want to shoot you again."

He rolled over and brought the shotgun with him. I kicked his arm with the ball of my foot and the shotgun sailed across the lounge, skidded over the lounge table and wedged between two cushions on the bench seat.

He grabbed my leg and I went down, my gun under me. He scrambled for traction on the deck, punching and kicking me, gouging my eyes, trying to reach my pistol.

I fought him off but his strength was enormous, and he almost ended up on top of me before I recovered and slammed him under the chin with my cast.

It didn't phase him. Blood weeping from two tiny bullet holes in his chest, he fought as if nothing mattered. In the confines of the small space I had the advantage of leverage and reach, but he was younger and stronger, and he fought like a cornered animal.

I fought off another attack. I could tell he was getting weaker. Time was on my side.

He attacked again, knocking me down. As I fell I dropped the gun. He reached for the pistol and I kicked it away, sending it scooting down the lounge toward the bow.

He followed and I tackled him, smashing his face against the deck. He wiggled out from under me. We both struggled to our feet and I hit him with two elbow kites that staggered him. He struck back and I blocked the last attack, using his momentum to crash his body into the teak bulkhead.

He reeled back, then faded away.

And raced for the shotgun.

I looked for the pistol, saw it lying under the table, thought about it only long enough for the synapses to come back with the calculation, my cerebrum screaming, "NOT ENOUGH TIME! WRONG DIRECTION! GET THE OTHER GUN!"

I raced for my stateroom, leaped onto the bed, reached into the bookcase for my .45, stretching until I got clumsy fingers around the checkered rubber grips.

Felix got to the shotgun first, cocked it while he turned, and ran into my stateroom with single barrel aimed directly at my head.

I brought the .45 around and aimed it at him.

Too late.

We fired simultaneously.

I took four BBs in the right shoulder and three or four more in the neck. The rest of the load passed over my head, punching into the bookcase and the teak paneling.

Felix slumped against the bulkhead, his shotgun on the deck beside him. I kept the .45 trained on him until I could get down from the bunk and hobble over to pick up the shotgun. I broke it open. It was a rusty single-barrel, single-shot affair that had been crudely cut down. Harmless now, I tossed it behind me onto the bunk.

I had hit Felix three times, all of the rounds so close together I could have covered them with my hand.

He opened his eyes. "You shot me again," he said. He seemed surprised.

"Of course I shot you. What did you think I was going to do?"

"Should have known better," he said, his breath coming in quick pants, like a dog run hard on a hot day.

"Why?"

"Why did I do any of it?"

I nodded. He reached out and I held his hand. Anything now to give him some small comfort.

"We wanted to rule, Caine. Jesse and me, we wanted to be on top. It's just that simple."

"Were you Silversword?"

He laughed. I wasn't sure it was a laugh because it was so soft, but I leaned closer and found that it was. "Ricky's contribution. It was just a front to hide our true motives. Ricky had these dreamers and college students in the palm of his hand. He taught them lua, he told them stories, and suddenly they were an activist group. Down with the government. Establish the new monarchy. They really didn't mean any harm."

"Kidnapping? Bombing? Murder?"

"Not a threat, not them. Honest. Ricky did most of it to give them standing."

"You wanted Daniel dead, and me dead?"

"Uh-huh. When you were charged with murder it changed the plans, but then we thought how convenient, you would be out of touch. Then the court let you go and I had those two ninjas take you out. Or try to."

"That was *you* in the alley?" I'd decided that it had been Ricky Lee.

"Yeah. I went along. They were supposed to be very good. You were injured. I didn't think you'd live to recognize me."

"All you guys look alike to me. Who killed the professor?"

"Don't really know, Caine. Probably Ricky. Why would you care?"

"And you cooperated with Gilbert. You were allies."

"Yeah. We would rule the Pacific Triads. He didn't want to harm Chawlie. Only Daniel. He would wait until Chawlie retired or died. Then Gilbert would be the undisputed leader in Hawaii."

"Jesse was your lover?"

"Yeah." He closed his eyes. "Gonna be with him soon, wherever he is. I'm going to die."

"Probably."

"That's cold, Caine. You killed me."

"You didn't have to come here. You didn't have to pull a gun on me. I'm sorry, though."

He smiled a ragged smile. "That's something, getting an apology from you. It had to be this way, Caine. I didn't have anywhere else to go. Chawlie or Daniel would have got me one way or the other. They would have killed me for three days. Just the way they did with my beautiful Jesse. This way is better."

He closed his eyes, his breathing rapid and small. "I'm afraid, Caine," he said, his voice small and quiet. "I don't want to lose this . . . life. I like it here."

"We're all afraid, Felix."

He opened his eyes and looked directly at me, but he wasn't seeing me. He saw something beyond me and behind me, and I thought he might have smiled. "It's okay, Caine," he said. "It's okay."

He closed his eyes again and lay still and I held his hand until he stopped breathing and I felt the life drain out of him. He had been a complicated little guy, witty and articulate. More sly than smart. He had not been one to trust. He had sought my death and the death of my friends. But I had liked him all the same. And I was sorry to have killed him.

I laid him down on the deck, the hardwood awash with his blood and some of mine. The pain from my wounds had not yet come but I knew it would. I felt a little woozy, and debated whether to call Chawlie first or to call the cops. The decision was made for me. Two squad cars pulled up at the end of the dock, their bubble machine lights revolving, flashing a circumference of blue light over the marina restaurant and the yachts.

I knew they would be nervous, and they would have their survival at the top of their agendas, so I left the .22 where it was, unloaded my .45, locked back the slide, and placed the pistol on the teak tabletop. I switched on the spreader lights, opened the hatch and stood on the deck, my hands in the air, my bleeding wounds all too visible, and waited in the cool evening breeze for the officers to make their way down the length of the dock to my slip.

I wondered if I could reach Tala Sufai this evening.

I wondered if I should bother Kimo with my problems.

And I wondered why peace, when it comes to me, only comes in infinitesimal chunks.

56

In the weeks that followed, the official agencies issued their findings, blaming the murder of Professor Hayes on Ricky Lee and Felix Chen. Both men were dead, themselves casualties of what the *Advertiser* labeled as tragic gangland executions. I was not mentioned in the newspapers this time, much to the credit of Chawlie and Daniel Choy, who exerted an undefined amount of unofficial pressure on the members of the fourth estate to keep my name out of print. The hunt for the murderers continued, according to the local media, who issued broad hints that the second worst crime spree in the state's recent history was the result of a difference of opinion on the distribution of profits derived from the sale and distribution of unauthorized pharmaceuticals.

The official also gave me a free pass on the killing of Felix Chen. This time self-defense was ruled as a permissible offense. In Hawaii, at least.

James came home from the hospital after a month of skin grafts and operations on the leg that had been kissed by Pele. He would always bear the scar. Tutu Mae called it an honor and a sacred burden.

Using James's newfound wisdom, Tutu Mae took over the name of the former group, calling it the Silversword Alliance. The group's new function was educational and spiritual, dedicated to preserving the culture and history of the Hawaiian people. That they took a more genteel path from the previous group did not change the fact that they espoused the same goal. Hawaii, they affirmed, should in fact belong to the Hawaiian people. Somehow I felt better hearing Tutu Mae saying that than someone like Ricky Lee.

David eventually went back to California. Already late for classes, he was intent on petitioning his professors for late admission, something he assured me would be feasible, especially when his role in the summer's activities eventually came out in the press.

All in all he seemed to have come through his adventure with his sense of humor intact. He and Donna came to visit me before he flew home. I noted that they were still holding hands.

"Mother sends her regards," he said, "and her gratitude."

"Then you didn't tell her what you really did."

"Not all of it," he said, his mouth in a wry twist. "Thank you for showing me some great diving in Hawaii. This was supposed to be a summer of leisure. This lady," he indicated Donna, "made me work like a slave."

"Come back anytime."

He stared at Donna when he answered me. "Oh, I will. I'll come back often."

"Stay out of caves and volcanoes."

He nodded.

"And sunken ships."

"You can depend on that."

Donna later kissed him good-bye and returned to her cloistered office provided by the university. *They* knew what she had. She had shared it with them, in all its glorious detail. Her doctorate assured, as well as her future, the university president who had been shepherding her project in the absence of Professor Hayes provided her with everything a graduate student could have wanted.

She had an office. Well, sort of an office, she told me. They gave her a table in a corner of a room in a basement, the room largely dedicated to the storage of film and video and image retrieval equipment. She had to edit and catalog thousands of images of the tomb and the site. A doctoral candidate, she had no assistants other than her sisters. That suited the university. The Wong sisters had worked together at the site and now they labored in another underground chamber to prepare Donna's initial report.

It would be initial because what she had discovered was not just a find, it was the foundation of an international career. I wondered about her decision not to take the bone sample. That way it would have been a sure thing. The way she explained it, DNA testing would have assured the identity of the skeleton. Now it would always be conjecture. Now the world would never be certain just who had been buried with all that treasure. But I understood the reason for her decision. Scattering the bones would have demonstrated extreme disrespect, and might have caused outrage in these peaceful islands. That would have gone against every precept that she held. She was right. Some things are not meant to be done. Because we *can* does not mean that we *should*.

Even without a positive identity the find was earth shaking. The university president persuaded the magazine to quash Hayes's pending article, managing to do so by a combination of threats and promises. Donna would announce her initial findings in the same publication when she was ready, and under her own name. She would share the credit with only one other person. And Tutu Mae didn't even know it yet. That was Donna's surprise, recognition for Tutu Mae's contributions. Donna told me, but swore me to secrecy.

Hualalai, the little volcano that erupted just enough to blanket a mysterious tomb with thirty feet of solid rock, quieted down after Madam Pele had achieved her goal. If the bones were those of her darling, The Lonely One would never be disturbed again. Not after she had displayed such obvious displeasure. Donna's photographs, drawings and video would be the only record of his final resting place.

I did a lot of reading as the summer turned to fall. Not that there's much of a difference here. In October, the golden plovers begin returning from Alaska, and Hawaii is only two hours behind the West Coast instead of three when their daylight saving time expires for another year. The hurricane season has one more month, but aside from that there is very little change. Tourists still crowd the hotels and the sandy beaches. The sun still plays its light upon the pale blue water. Trade Winds tease the palm trees on any given afternoon. And rainbows still grace the Waianaes every morning and the Ko'olaus every afternoon.

As I said, I did a lot of reading. The doctors had been right. Diving with open incisions had not been a good idea. After they had treated me for minor gunshot wounds, I came down with a vicious systemic infection. I spent three weeks in Tripler, the great pink army hospital that attended wounded American soldiers and veterans for more than just a few wars and "police actions." I'd been there before, and it was where I went when I realized I was very sick. I parked my Jeep in the long-term lot, shuffled to the front counter, showed the nice admissions lady my identification and reported that I was probably suffering from a variety of infections and parasites, that I had been a sailor, and that they should not treat me for that malady alone.

The doctors didn't give me much of a chance, as weakened as I was with my injuries and surgeries, and at one point a well-meaning chaplain leaned over my bed and asked in concerned but plummy tones what my religious affiliation was. The man gave a visible start when I said, "Epicurean."

Finally it became apparent to everyone, including the disappointed chaplain, that I was not going to die.

Shortly after David returned to California I checked out of Tripler, walked over to my Jeep and tried to start the engine only to find that the battery had died. I shrugged, appreciating the ability to enjoy the view of a magnificent double rainbow. Better the battery than me. I called a taxi to take me home. The Jeep would be there when I needed it.

Daniel met me at my dock. *Olympia* floated at her slip, forlorn and lonely, reminding me of her terrible neglect. I sighed, gazed longingly at my home, remembered that duty to friends was a man's highest duty, nodded, and climbed into the back of the Cadillac SUV double-parked in the lot above the Marina Restaurant.

"It would have been easier if you'd just called and asked me to come directly to Chinatown," I told him as the driver goosed the Caddie up the Nimitz Viaduct.

"I just follow orders," he said without inflection. His voice would always have that raspy quality. He would always sound as menacing and as dangerous as he really was.

"You shouldn't use a company car when you fill your special orders," I said.

He looked at me sideways. "I don't know what you're talking about."

"You called me and told me to get out of there. Right after the place was shot up and burned."

"Yeah, I called you. But that was just to tell you that your hotel room was a hole, man. I wanted you to come back to the suite at the Royal."

"Sure it was, Daniel."

He stared at me impassively. Chawlie would have been proud. Of all of Chawlie's sons, Daniel was most like his father. When I looked at Daniel I sometimes wondered if Chawlie had been as tough and as silent as this young man when he was his age.

"Okay." I leaned back into the leather seat and closed my eyes. "You know what this is about?"

He shrugged.

Sometimes it's best just to let things flow the way they are going to flow. Sometimes talking to Daniel is like talking to a granite boulder. Except you might get more information from the boulder.

The Cadillac stopped in front of Chawlie's restaurant and I climbed out and tottered across the sidewalk.

Daniel ushered me into Chawlie's den and backed out, leaving the two of us alone in his father's private quarters.

I found Chawlie elaborately fussing with another elm bonsai, a perfect living miniature the same shape as one of its larger cousins. Fascinated, I watched him prune and prick it, carefully grooming the plant the way one would groom an expensive pet.

"We are alone," he said, not looking up from his task. "Sit down."

I found a pillow and gingerly planted myself. Nothing worked exactly right just yet.

"You have had a hard year, John Caine," said Chawlie, when he had finished his task.

"I've had better."

"And worse, I would imagine."

The fever almost killed me when the gunshots did not. The State of California did their best to put me away. As did a couple of malcontents who saw me as a roadblock to their success. And then there was the volcano. But all in all, things could have gone much worse. "Yes, Chawlie," I said. "I've had worse."

"I am concerned about you. I know what you do when you are hurt. You go into hiding until you are better. I knew that if I did not not see you before you became a hermit I would not see you for months. Maybe more. You must rest."

"Now I try to get my strength back."

"It will not be easy," he said, and I heard echoes of another conversation I had had before, unsure of where, or with whom.

"It's not easy being me, old friend."

He smiled. "Nor is it easy being Chawlie."

"How is Gilbert doing?"

Chawlie's eyes twinkled. "They report that he is doing well, given the circumstances."

When Chawlie had learned that his son had planned to assassinate his brother for succession to the throne, he had not done what I had expected of him. In the past he would have killed the young man, but Chawlie was evolving, or attaining enlightenment or wisdom, and he did something so out of character that I had to have Daniel repeat Gilbert's sentence twice before I understood what he had done.

Gilbert was a thoroughly Americanized young man, typical of second-generation immigrants. Princeton and Yale educated, Cornell hotel school, Wharton School of Business, Chawlie had invested a fortune in the young man's training. But the old Chawlie would have had him killed for far less, I knew. I had been there when he had dispatched another son to his fate when he had become an embarrassment to the family.

But not now. Chawlie had invested heavily in casinos and hotels in Saipan, down near Guam, and he needed an assistant night manager, one of the more menial jobs available. He sent Gilbert down there to take the position. "For a few years," he said. "He will not get a vacation, he will not come home, he will work sixteen hours a day, seven days a week until he learns the business of the family. The business of the family is not killing one's brother. That is no way to succeed."

Deep down I was glad that Chawlie had begun to mellow. I also had a random thought that Daniel would have dispatched his brother without a second thought, and that, perhaps, was the main reason he was the natural heir to the family fortune. Gilbert would not get his hands dirty. Hiring others, even talented others, was not the same. Chawlie's interests sometimes required hands-on problem solving, like the night Ricky Lee and his associates died in the bar fire in Waialua.

"Are you still going to China?" I asked.

"Not yet. I will. Someday. But not just yet. Will you retire?"

"I wouldn't know what to do with myself."

His eyes crinkled and he opened his mouth in silent laughter. "That is a big joke, John Caine. All this trouble. Because I said I wanted to live in China. I send architects to build me a house in Hong Kong. So oldest son thinks that I am going to name another as head of the family. And now that I am faced with going to China, now that I have my new home, I do not want to go. Like you, John Caine, I wouldn't know what to do with myself."

Chawlie laughed until tears rolled down his cheeks.

"You see the joke?" he asked.

"People died, Chawlie."

"Gilbert is paying for it. He will be in exile for many years."

"And that's enough?"

Chawlie looked at me with his little obsidian eyes, his face expressionless. "It will have to be. Better *I* punish him than anyone else. The world is in balance. I will not lose another son."

57

The awful dream, my companion for nearly three decades, had come to me again while I was in the hospital. At Tripler, where they had seen their share of battlefield trauma, the night nurse recognized it for what it was and mentioned my experience to the local physician serving with the National Center for Post-Traumatic Stress Disorder. The Center is a network of research sites based at Veterans Administration hospitals around the country, where our nation has deposited many of those who cannot manage to rid themselves of the horrors they experienced. People who are regularly tortured by a sudden reliving of that single, defining moment that changed their lives forever.

People like me.

Dr. Goldman, the PTSD psychiatrist, spent some time with me before I left the hospital and asked me to come back afterward. I had enough to do on the outside making repairs to *Olympia* and getting physically healthy, and was reluctant to return. I wanted to end this thing, but I didn't want to attend a group. I couldn't see myself sitting around a circle of folding chairs sipping coffee from a paper cup and sharing my story with a group of strangers. I also had the vague feeling that my story would be written up somewhere and published in some obscure medical journal. I didn't want to be under a microscope. I didn't want to share my innermost thoughts and feelings with people I hardly knew. I wanted to lose this nightmare, but there had to be other ways to do it.

Finally, after the dream had come two nights in a row, I called Dr. Goldman and made a private appointment. He agreed to have me come in alone for a private consultation.

"Just to talk," I said.

He chuckled. "That's mainly what we do here."

His office was a tiny cubicle at the end of the fifth floor. He had no couch, he said, because he had no room. Metal bookshelves lined two walls, crammed with books. They weren't just stacked, they were stuffed in in all directions, vertically and horizontally, and in no particular order. A small, bright carpet covered the vinyl asbestos tile floor. Dr. Goldman sat at his desk, a battered government-issue model for GS-6 assistants. He offered me a chair next to the desk.

"Be it ever so humble," he said, smiling.

"You go to ground here," I said.

His eyes brightened. "You are perceptive, Commander Caine."

"John. I haven't been Commander in a long time. And it was only Lieutenant Commander, at that."

"Have it your way. I'm a captain, and I like being a captain. Got the white eagle on my windshield and a good parking spot at the driving range. What more could I want?"

"And in Hawaii, too."

He nodded. "Would you like some coffee?"

"No thanks."

"You're still having the dream?"

"More often lately, I didn't have it for years at a time. It was a nuisance, nothing more. Lately it's gotten out of hand."

"Tell me," he said, and I did, explaining my life, giving him the short version. He nodded encouragement when I hit the rough spots—when I spoke of Jayne and Kate and Angel—and his eyes widened in disbelief when I explained how I had made my living. I highlighted the shootings, the fights, and the pitched battles in Mexico and Kauai. Coming face to face with monsters had been the way I had lived. I had sought out the violence. If trouble didn't come looking for me I had gone looking for it. And I had found it, time after time after time.

"You've just described to me one of the classic responses to PTSD. Let's discuss that for a moment. Aside from your violent history, you seem to be an intelligent man, and there's no need to be evasive with you. We know the cause of PTSD. It is learned fearfulness. It is the most intense kind of learned fearfulness. Its source can be personal tragedy, a mugging, or a rape, or it can have its genesis in a natural disaster, such as an earthquake or a fire. In your case it was the imminent loss of your life. Let me ask you, you felt helpless at that moment? That precise instant when you awake from your dream?"

"My gun ran dry."

"And you felt helpless?"

"Impotent was the word."

"To us psychiatrists, impotent has many meanings, but let's just say unable to respond appropriately. The bayonet was about to enter your flesh and there was nothing you could do about it."

"Yes."

"And did—in the actual event— It *was* a real event?" He nodded, matching my bobbing head, "did—the man stab you with the bayonet?"

"Yes."

"You survived."

"Of course."

He smiled. "How?"

"I pulled my knife, a Randall, and killed him. Then I pulled out his blade, reloaded, went back to the business of killing people."

He thought a moment. "How did that battle end?"

"We had a break in the weather. Fast movers napalmed the perimeter for six hours. At first light we had reinforcements. It was a very close thing."

He nodded, deep in thought.

"Was that your first time?"

"Yes."

"And there have been many times after that?"

"Yes."

He scribbled on his notepad and then looked at me with a kind of compassion I had not seen in a long time. "Sherman said that war is hell. After more than thirty years in this business, I've found that war is pain. Some pain can last a long, long time. You understand, don't you?"

"I do."

"We have found that PTSD can be accounted for by chemical and physical changes in the limbic circuitry in the brain, the amygdala, the locus ceruleus, the hippocampus and the hypothalamus, extending into the cortex of the brain. After a stress such as the one you described, the limbic system physically changes the way it works. The locus ceruleus is a structure that regulates the brain's secretion of catecholamines, adrenaline and noradrenaline, our fight-or-flight chemicals. One can actually mobilize the body for bursts of super strength, such as you have described in your own life. In PTSD, the limbic system becomes hyperactive. A superabundance of catecholamines is secreted to what would to other people be an ordinary stimulus. A backfire of a car, the popping of a balloon, the smell of rain. Anything that is associated with the experience tends to release this superabundance of chemicals.

"In one study of Vietnam veterans with PTSD, we found that they had forty percent fewer catecholomine-stopping receptors than men without the PTSD symptoms. This suggested to us that their brains had undergone a lasting chemical change. Are you still with me?"

"So far. You're saying that the fright that I had that night on that hill so many years ago changed the structure of my brain?"

"You would make a good student. That is exactly what I am saying."

"So how does that help me?"

"There are many ways people cope with PTSD. Some become withdrawn from society. There are groups of Vietnam vets living in the jungles of the Big Island convinced that that is the only way they can live. I see them come in here, when they're ill and need medical attention, dressed in fatigues and tiger stripes. They are unable to get over the war. So they cope by withdrawing from society. There are others who make the leap into chemical salvation: heroin, crack, cocaine, methamphetamines, and alcohol. And then there are those who appear to lead what a politician would describe as normal lives. They just suffer through it. They have their dreams, as you have had your dream, and they flinch and they wail at night, and they divorce and they remarry, always seeking something that they don't understand. But they are not a burden on society in general. To their families, certainly, but they suffer in silence. They were maimed by the war, but some of them didn't even receive a medal."

"I have met some like that."

"We all have, whether we know it or not. And sometimes we read about them in the newspapers. And then there are others, men like you, who spent their lives going after the adrenaline rush. We saw it after World War II and we didn't know what we were seeing. We were not prepared for the Vietnam veterans in the seventies. They had a double burden to overcome. Their father's generation, at least, had won that war. Their war, they perceived, was something to be ashamed of. But that's another issue."

I could see the flare of anger in his cheeks. "So you're saying that I've got this PTSD. Sounds like a gasoline additive."

"You may joke, but it's serious. It's not just in your head, it's in the wiring in your head. It's a physical ailment, not just a mental processing one."

"Someone recently told me that we're just chemicals."

"That someone was correct. We're learning that more and more. Your body physically craves the adrenaline rush."

"I used to describe myself as an adrenaline junkie."

"You were right and didn't know it."

"Knowing something does not necessarily tell you how to get over it."

"Your experience on that hill determined the remainder of your life, John. You became addicted to the seeking of those chemicals. Your adaptation to PTSD has been your continued campaigning against what you see as evil in the world. In your narrative to me you described yourself as bad, but not evil. I don't see you as bad. I see you as a good man who deals with his personal demons by attacking—and I mean that quite literally—the evil that he sees in the world. And if you can't find it, you go looking for it. That's how you have dealt with the problem. And that's why you continue to suffer from this dream."

I stared at the clock in the bookshelf, jammed haphazardly between two volumes of *Gray's Anatomy*. I had come seeking answers, but had found answers that I did not expect. If what the good Dr. Goldman was saying was correct, I had not been the master of my fate or the captain of my soul. I had been the mere response to a chemical addiction. John Caine, PTSD, limbic-disordered veteran, attacker of evil; if I can't find it, I'll go looking for it. I could put that on a business card.

"So what do I do?"

"Fortunately, medicine has come a long way since the seventies and we now understand that if the brain can be trained to react to certain stimuli, then it can be retrained *not* to react. The body is an amazing organism. It heals itself most of the time. Sometimes it cannot, for whatever reason, and it needs help. People like me are here to help." He smiled, and I could see the warmth and the tiredness in his eyes. "In PTSD, spontaneous relearning does not occur. We don't know why it doesn't, but it doesn't. You can get over it. But it is going to require your active involvement in the learning process."

"What do you want me to do?"

"We've got a group . . . what?"

"I don't like groups."

He smiled. "You just said, 'What can I do?' and the first thing I suggest you tell me you don't like. What is it to be?"

"I'm sorry."

"We have a group that meets Thursday evenings here in the

hospital. Could you fit that into your schedule? It would help if you heard the others' stories. Just once, at least. You need to know that you're not alone."

"Yes."

"The strong emotional memories that trigger the patterns of thought caused by PTSD can change. It is cortical. You're got to learn how to actively suppress the amygdala's command to react with fear. There are ways we do that, and it is easier if we work with a group of people, rather than one at a time. It has to do with funding." His smile was weary.

"I'll be there."

"Fine. Your hour's up. Was up a long time ago, but I thought it was worth the investment of the taxpayers' money. And I had no other patients scheduled, so it worked out. You're a hard man, John Caine, but I think you're worth rescuing."

"Rescuing for what?"

"We'll get into that. You ever have a lasting and meaningful relationship?"

"No."

"Well, there's a goal."

I smiled. "You?"

"Mrs. Goldman and I celebrated our thirtieth wedding anniversary two weeks ago. We are, as Paul Harvey would say, on our way to forever together."

"Congratulations."

"Thank you. It's at seven o'clock. Be in the lobby. Someone from mental health will meet you and take you up there."

"Mental health?"

"What did you expect, OB-GYN?"

I smiled, liking the man. "Thank you."

"Thank you. If you hadn't been on that particular hill on that particular night, there would be some other fellow sitting here. Or not. I will not debate the evils of that time, or the fact that America sent its young men and women to a faraway land mainly because the President of the United States, a being who picked up dogs by the ears, feared that he would be seen as a man with small cojones. Seems like a trivial reason to order young men to death and maiming. But that may just be me. I'm a lowly captain of the United States Navy, and I never get to see the Big Picture, you know?"

He patted me on the shoulder.

"I'll look forward to seeing you Thursday evening. We will begin with what Freud described as the Primary Process."

"Oh?"

"We'll talk about it Thursday."

I strolled out of the hospital and looked to the hills and was rewarded by another rainbow. I had much to contemplate, and much to learn. If I was a man at war with myself I never knew it. Maybe it was something I had merely suspected. The cause had even been hinted at by my small joke about being an adrenaline junkie. That had been closer to the truth than I had ever known.

I got into my old Jeep and started the motor and took one more look at the rainbow. The colors seemed to brighten and change as I stared at it. Elusive and beautiful, they filled my sensations. I could never get enough of rainbows. They had always fascinated me. They were a bonus for living here, an added attraction.

If I were honest, the real reason I had come to this rock to live in the middle of the largest body of water in the world had been simply to hide. Like those men in the hills, I hid out from the rest of the world. I ventured forth only reluctantly. Here my soul felt as if it belonged to the rocks and the trees and the crystal aquamarine waters. It was peaceful here, and it was just small enough to be manageable.

To compensate for my affliction that I didn't even know I had, I had scaled down my life, confining myself to this one rock, the rest of the world be damned.

I wondered what the world would be like if I changed. I wondered what I would be like.

I wondered if I wanted to change.

As damaged as I was, I was still John Caine. I wondered if I had the courage to challenge myself as I had challenged the volcano and the sea, as I had challenged those whom I had labeled as "evil," as I had challenged life itself.

I wondered if I would have the fortitude to challenge the deeper darkness within me, to oppose it, and to eject it.

I put the Jeep into gear and slowly drove from the parking lot, reluctant to leave the rainbow.

But there would be other rainbows on other hills on other afternoons. And there would be sunsets and sunrises to be savored, the occasional pelagic fish to be slain, beaches to be walked, and waterfalls deep in the jungles to surprise me. And there was the hunt for The One. I wondered where she had gone while I had lusted only for the continuing adrenaline rush. I wondered where she was now, and if she would ever come into my life.

Of if I would continue to savor my rainbows alone.